DEFIANCE

C.J. CHERRYH & JANE S. FANCHER

DEFIANCE

A *Foreigner* Novel

DAW BOOKS
New York

Jacket art by Todd Lockwood

Jacket design by Katie Anderson

Book design by Stanley S. Drate/Folio Graphics Co., Inc.

Edited by Betsy Wollheim

DAW Book Collectors No. 1947

DAW Books
An imprint of Astra Publishing House
dawbooks.com
DAW Books and its logo are registered trademarks of Astra Publishing House

Printed in the United States of America

ISBN 978-0-7564-1590-7 (hardcover)
ISBN 978-0-7564-1592-1 (ebook)

First edition: October 2023
10 9 8 7 6 5 4 3 2 1

To my readers:

Jane is no stranger to this series. She's bounced ideas back and forth with me on no few of Bren's stories. And since she has been co-author with me on the Alliance books, it seems only just that she share credit in this series as well, in which she has definitely had a hand and written many scenes. This is a book from 2020, that year of trial, several health crises, and five surgeries amid a quarantine, and we both survived it and both worked on this book—not only have we survived, but we have come out of it with books and renewed energy, and we are very glad to present this one, after a two-year gap in Bren's account. Credit also to the most patient of publishers: Betsy Wollheim, who waited and waited, and kept waiting for us. And very much to our readers, the most excellent readers on Earth, we cannot thank you enough. To you, our readers, to our excellent surgeons and doctors, and to our very patient publisher and editor, we respectfully dedicate this book; and a very special dedication to Jane's brother, Allen "Chip" Fancher, pilot extraordinaire, our technical advisor— clear skies forever, Chip!

—C.J. Cherryh

Table of Contents

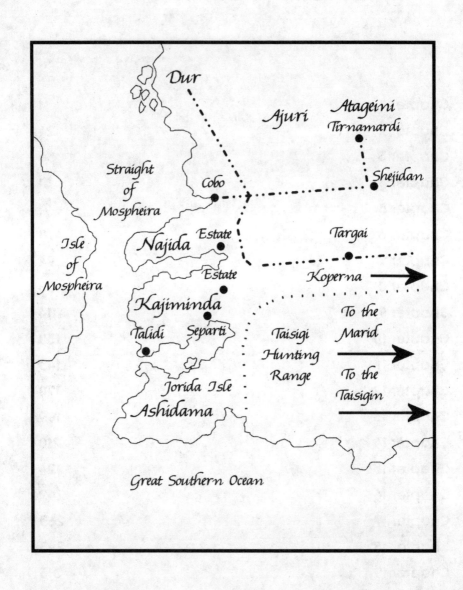

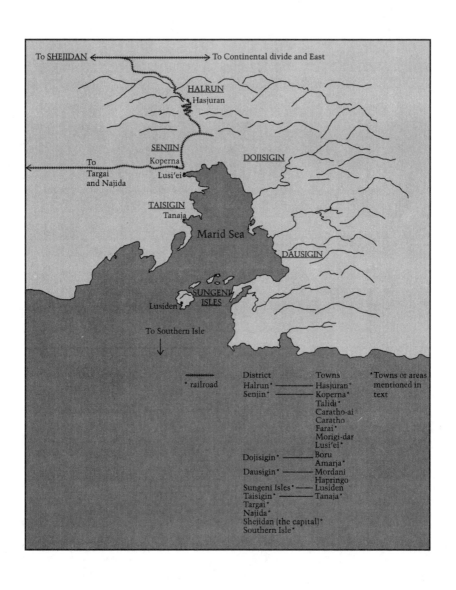

To SHEJIDAN ←--------------------→ To Continental divide and East

HALRUN
Hasjuran

SENJIN
Koperna
Lusi'ei

DOJISIGIN

To
Targai
and Najida

TAISIGIN
Tanaja

Marid Sea

DAUSIGIN

SUNGENI
ISLES

Lusiden

To Southern Isle

↓

	District	Towns	
·············· railroad	Halrun* ———	Hasjuran*	*Towns or areas mentioned in text
	Senjin* ———	Koperna*	
		Talidi*	
		Caratho-ai	
		Caratho	
		Farai*	
		Morigi-dar	
		Lusi'ei*	
	Dojisigin* ———	Boru	
		Amarja*	
	Dausigin* ———	Mordani	
		Hapringo	
	Sungeni Isles* ———	Lusiden	
	Taisigin* ———	Tanaja*	
	Targai*		
	Najida*		
	Shejidan (the capital)*		
	Southern Isle*		

1

Rock and sway, rock and sway as the Red Train raced along the track in a ceaseless envelope of sound. It wearied the body, day upon day of it—at least—one assumed day and night, since the Red Train had no windows . . . just a little port atop the evacuation panel through which one could see a thin double handspan of sky.

One recalled too easily a handful of recent encounters with the world beyond that portal. Tall wooden buildings looming beyond a thick veil of falling snow; a star-studded night sky, turned to day by the roaring exhaust of a lander's engines; a terrifying bus ride between the Koperna rail station and the home of Bregani, Lord of Senjin.

A final glimpse of that same war-torn capital as the Red Train once again swallowed them up . . .

Bren—Bren Cameron, paidhi-aiji, which was to say human translator to Tabini-aiji, the head of the atevi aishidi'tat—had, with his aishid, his bodyguard, been assisting Tabini's grandmother Ilisidi, the aiji-dowager, on . . . a *little train trip.*

That was how the aiji-dowager had described it, in prospect.

Thump-thump. Thump-thump. Constantly. Eternally.

Bren lifted his head, swiped back strands of blond hair that escaped his ribboned queue. He sat then, elbows on the too-high table, head in hands, with a cold cup of tea in imminent danger of vibrating itself off the edge. A book lay open before him, his recent pillow.

"Nandi." Narani set a fresh pot of tea on the let-down table, and silently provided a clean teacup, rescuing the cold one.

Supper had been his most recent meal. Which meant it was, more than likely, dark outside. Narani kept track of these things.

The light inside the car reflected them both off what appeared to be a velvet-curtained window, a window designed to hide armor plate, an illusion maintained on both sides of the wall—a smoky reflection, image of a travel-frayed pale human and an elegant and tall black ateva.

The motif throughout the original cars of the Red Train was dark wood carved in vines, or mythic figures, red velvet cushions, well-polished brass wherever metal was involved. The Red Car itself, usually rearmost on the train, was centuries old, even predating the arrival of humans on the planet; and Ilisidi's car and this one might be of the same vintage as that ancient elegance. Lighting was, in all the historic cars, live flame. And where the lighting was, in mercy, not as old as the motifs, it mimicked fire with exquisite, hand-blown bulbs.

That antique lamplight glistened gold across Narani's aquiline profile, lending a gold tint to honorably-gained silver hair, most properly queued and ribboned.

Bren, less elegant, had gotten a tea stain on his lace cuff, needed a shave, wanted a bath, and wished there were some chair, any sort of chair, that would let his feet rest comfortably on the floor. A tallish human, he was of boyish size to an ateva. His feet, in any seating designed for atevi, never touched the floor, and his person was, to say the least, unique on the mainland.

Narani was head and shoulders taller. Atevi had universally black skin, black hair. Gold eyes that, in the centuries-old lighting of the Red Train, often caught an eerie shimmer. Keen nightsight came with that trait. Human eyes struggled with the print of the book Bren had been reading, on a table somewhat inconveniently high, with the lovely antique lamps.

It was eyestrain and exhaustion that had brought him to go head-down. Sleep came erratically on this trip, in two-hour patches, with all the clues of day and night suspended: it might be blazing noon for what it even mattered by now.

And the motion and the jolting never ceased.

The domestic staff—Jeladi and Narani—waked and slept as

Bren did. His aishid, his bodyguard, Banichi and Jago, Tano and Algini, Assassins' Guild, followed their own schedule, at the moment resting on velvet benches in the unlighted end of the car—not oblivious. They maintained electronics alert to any message from elsewhere on the train. But there had been no message. Not for days. They, with him, existed in suspension. They were in scale with the train and the benches, but even they were finding discomfort in the antique, stiffly stuffed furniture.

He could only imagine what it must be like for those in the cars further back in the train, cars with less luxurious appointment, packed with regular Guild and their equipment, awaiting orders that could send them against an enemy, or home to the ease of Shejidan.

In the next car forward was Nomari, who might become the next lord of Ajuri—if he gained approval. Bren had visited him, but there was painfully little to say between them. Small talk had died early in that atmosphere of uncertainties, and if Nomari knew things, relevant things, *significant* things regarding his old associations with significant people back in the Marid, which was behind them . . . he hid those details or, charitably put, failed to volunteer them; while Bren, who had some influence on people who had to decide on Nomari's future appointment—was unwilling to talk about that, either. Oh, Nomari was very accommodating, habitually taking on whatever character one wanted, reshaping himself continually. That was how Nomari had lived his life before this. Nomari knew the darkest side of the Dojisigin and the Senjin regions of the Marid all too intimately, having been a target for their Shadow Guild assassins from his childhood on, and having spied for more than one lord in the region they had just left.

And with his future depending now on his acceptance in the north, within the aishidi'tat, in which Bren had influence, Nomari was understandably anxious in the paidhi-aiji's presence. At least—that was the impression he gave.

There *was* the car shared by Homura and Momichi and the guard assigned to them. But both in social rank and in terms of casual conversation—a visit would not be comfortable for either side there. They had *been* Shadow Guild, part of that splinter group devoted to the overthrow of the aishidi'tat. They claimed that that association was not by their choice. They claimed to have changed loyalties—were sworn to Bren, and to the aiji-dowager. But their loyalty had yet to be proven beyond any reasonable doubt, there was *plenty* of reasonable doubt in Bren's view, and casual conversation had no chance in that car.

Ilisidi's car, *behind* his, was the source of all current information on the situation they had just left and on where they were going, taking a train full of armament and Assassins' Guild with them. But no information had been flowing to this car. Banichi, and even Tano, who was particularly good at ferreting information out of other units, got nothing from her bodyguard. The dowager's chief bodyguard, Cenedi, technically in command of all the Guild aboard the train, had not visited them or the car devoted to Guild ops since Koperna.

There had been a major revision of the train at Koperna, in Senjin province, several boxcars of Guild equipment being attached behind the Red Car and a sizeable number of Guild units being added with them. That addition *could* be a simple relocation of units and equipment back to the capital at Shejidan—the operation in Senjin was finished and Red Train could not haul all that number of cars up the way they had come, the infamous Hasjuran switchbacks: they had to go the lowland route, across the entire width of the south, over to Najida, north past the mountain ridge, then back half across the distance they had just covered *below* the mountains—finally to reach the capital in Shejidan.

The units they had with them might be returning to the capital. But the capital was *not* where *Bren* wanted those units set down. Their turning point, Najida, on the west coast, was his own lordship, and while the war in the Marid was trying to take down the Shadow Guild establishment in the Dojisigin, word was—the last word they had had, in fact—that the leadership had fled the Dojisigin, escaped the Marid Sea, entered the Southern Ocean, and were sailing along the southern coast parallel to their route, headed somewhere with something in mind. There were no ports along that unpopulated coast, and no port would want them, but maybe one: the Dojisigin's longtime trading partner, Jorida Isle, in Ashidama Bay, that let out onto the Mospheiran Strait.

Ashidama Bay was only a day or so south of Najida—Bren's own estate. Najida was where the rail took a northward turn, and where they all hoped for an overnight stop on this interminable train ride.

Bren's own estate. Not because he was born to the honor. Because it was a trouble spot already, and Tabini-aiji had appointed *him* to take over a province that hated the Ragi, which was to say, the dominant ethnic group of most of the continent. Najida was home to the Edi people, who were *not* native to the mainland, and who had been continually at odds with the rest of the mainland *and* south.

Had it been better for them, that he was human? Humans had dropped out of the heavens and moved in on the west coast—thus starting a war that had ended when the Ragi atevi forcibly cleared the large island of Mospheira—a haze on the horizon of Najida, and now the place on Earth where humans were permitted to live and atevi were forbidden.

The Edi and the Gan peoples had been removed to create that atevi-free enclave.

The Edi had been granted Najida peninsula as their own—it had not been Ragi land to dispose of, but Maschi clan, who did hold it, had been too disorganized to protest. So in went the Edi, who were not happy about it. Humans, excepting only the appointed translator, were confined to Mospheira, and that had ended the War of the Landing, centuries ago.

The Edi might not have been happy about having a human lord, either—Bren had been apprehensive about it; but they had treated him extremely well. He had come to have feelings about them. *Love*, even, that emotion he tried to be very careful with among atevi, who were differently wired, and who felt different, instinct-driven things. He had that kind of tie to them—and to his aishid and his staff—he had tried not to, but it was a hopeless effort. He *was* human and much as he tried not to develop such expectations, for his own sake and theirs, he did. But they forgave him. Warmly so. In their way. It was all complicated, his feelings all tangled up with theirs. It was not as intimate with the Edi as with his aishid, his bodyguard—and his staff. But it was still a connection he had to think about, and not abuse. He let himself love the place. His occasional home. He did not want it harmed because of him.

And damn it, that stray ship, headed out of the Marid, and almost certainly bound for Jorida, was not small-scale trouble. The atevi style of conflict was rarely massive movement of forces and pitched battles. It was much more intimate, much more personal—small units of extremely skilled professionals, who did not observe battle lines or conventions of war, were very good at slipping in and out and dealing death very precisely so as to satisfy a grudge, or, in the case of war, cause maximum damage to the other side. When the Assassins' Guild moved legitimately, they preserved the law, went after a legally defined target, and damage was minimal: the Shadow Guild was a splinter off the legitimate Guild that applied the same skills to gain power for themselves, completely reckless of collateral damage. Power was their game. Getting it, and keeping it.

And their style of conflict was coming, to a people who were governed differently, who had no desire to be ruled by the Ragi—or by acts of terror and retaliation from Ashidama, who had been their enemies for two hundred years without the Shadow Guild getting into it.

He wanted the train to stop at Najida. He wanted the Assassins' Guild they had with them to deploy at the train station—set up there, and stay there. There was no immediate employment for that force in the midlands and the north. Here, they could keep the war in the Marid from spilling over into the Mospheiran Strait and entangling itself in Ashidama, which was, first, not a part of the aishidi'tat; and second, a major grain supplier to the aishidi'tat. Having a cell of that damnable organization recruiting and training down in Ashidama, involving the tangled history of the three peninsulas in their plans, and being right on the Mospheiran Strait, which divided humans from atevi—

That was a situation with just too many flashpoints.

The aiji-dowager could order the train on to the capital . . . he could debark here with just his own aishid and try to explain to the Edi what was moving in to the south of them . . . he could ask Tabini-aiji to send the force *back* to Najida to do what the dowager had declined to do—all of these were options.

But the first was the most logical option. And the best for her. If he could get past Cenedi to talk to her.

He worried for *her*, these last days. Worried about her uncharacteristic silence. A polite written message, his latest effort, returned unopened.

It probably was night by now. It had rather the feeling of night, in the quiet that had settled over everyone. He ought to give up, have staff fold up the table and let down the bed, but if there was a torment beyond sleeping on a table surface, intermittent with something informational to read, it was lying abed staring at the ceiling and counting the thumps and bumps as they rattled through his frame.

For a time, now, though, the last few minutes, it seemed they had hit a smoother stretch of track. It rocked. It soothed. One hoped . . .

A bump, soon followed by another, and another: the respite was always brief. The train just could not make speed. There was no hope of it . . . probably none until Najida. Tensions in the Marid had reduced the number of trains on this run for years. Maintenance had suffered immensely.

Had she known that? Surely she had.

But to deal with Koperna—if that had been her real objective—this was the route.

He sighed, had a sip of tea, leaned his head on one hand, and turned a page in the book he had brought from the capital, trying to bring his tired mind to concentrate and sift currently relevant information out of accounts of early clan warfare in the north—interesting, but fairly irrelevant, as it turned out, involving no clan that had survived to the current day.

He had a pocket watch. It was spring-driven, encased in elegantly etched gold, an atevi creation. It kept excellent time . . . but in the press of things he had forgotten to wind it.

Turning on his computer could tell him.

Asking Narani could tell him. Narani kept up with everything.

But if he were honest with himself, he had been avoiding counting the hours—unable to affect events inside or outside the train. The whole south of the aishidi'tat was in jeopardy, with damn-all he could do about what was behind him or what lay ahead, involving people he cared about, until someone, *anyone* gave him some options.

Or until Cenedi let him have one of the special com units.

Only hours before their arrival in Koperna, they had gotten those. Lord Geigi, up on the space station, had diverted himself from his own pressing problems to set down the last of his somewhat mobile lander-relays on the border between the Senjin and the Dojisigin Marid. This relay tower, one of several devised years ago and scattered throughout the continent, had joined with its fellows and created their new and, better yet, *uncompromised* communications network, which the Shadow Guild absolutely could not penetrate.

He and his aishid had had two of those new communications units during their short time in Koperna, in Senjin province, and they had been beyond useful. But Cenedi, without explanation, had confiscated the units before they got back on the train—so one assumed they were dear indeed, possibly urgently required for the Koperna forces to coordinate with Tabini's, who were operating in the neighboring Dojisigin. *He* had no idea.

Given access to that unit for ten minutes . . . *five* . . . he could consult with Tabini-aiji in Shejidan. He could have all his answers. Could establish his priorities and options. He could arrange protection for Najida . . . even over the aiji-dowager's objections . . .

And get some sleep despite the condition of the track.

But Cenedi was not leaving the dowager's car. And requests for brief use of one of the units went unanswered. *That* was the returned message.

It was not just the fate of Najida that hung in the balance. Given one of those units, he could also reach the space station where Geigi's crisis—five thousand humans too many on the space station—had reached criticality, even *before* the dowager had coopted him for her "little train trip." He *personally* was supposed to be in the north right now, on the other side of the mountains, preparing to meet the first shuttle load of Reunioner humans coming down: an unprecedented landing of humans on the atevi mainland, politically sensitive as hell.

And he did not want to go on to that crisis before he did something about Najida. The Edi people were not supposed to have weapons. They did, which was beside the point—they could not be taking on their own defense and shooting random intruders. The aishidi'tat was, by treaty, obliged to keep the peace—*their* peace, as well as everybody else's; and defending them from their ancient feud with the legitimate power of Jorida Isle as well as the illegitimate threat of the Shadow Guild, who truly wanted to work harm on their lord—namely Bren Cameron—was a fairly ceremonial obligation turned suddenly very real.

The Shadow Guild, fleeing the Marid, had gathered up their sole claim of legitimacy, Lord Tiajo, their nominal employer— and run for the boats, leaving the rank and file to stand against the legitimate Assassins' Guild. One need not feel sorry for them. They had made their choice. But their own leadership had certainly served them the way they had served the aishidi'tat— underhandedly and with no thought of their honor. That ship had run for it while the Red Train was still up in Hasjuran—and that ship had several days' head start on them.

Possibly the dowager was actively planning how to deal with that—granted the silence back there was her choice. But it did not *feel* right. She had been perfectly communicative when they left Koperna, even cheerful and outgoing—Ilisidi at her most approachable. And then—this.

Was she angry? He doubted it. Was she *unable* to respond? She was old, fragile, it had been a hellish trip just getting to Koperna, and the head of her aishid, Cenedi, in command of the whole operation, would go to whatever length it took to protect her—personally, and figuratively; and to protect her power and the public perception of her. But if there was a division of opinion—if that communicator that Cenedi had and Bren Cameron, paidhi-aiji, advisor to Tabini, did not—produced orders from Tabini with which Ilisidi would not comply—

That was one possibility.

The other was—

If she were seriously ill, then Cenedi might want to get her back to Shejidan. Her physician was always with her; rode in her car, with her aishid and her staff. But there could be a need of resources only available in Shejidan.

Meanwhile a sensible order could halt the train and order that Guild force detached at Najida, along with the extra cars. The train, whittled down to just two or three cars, on good track, would make far better time getting her back to the capital.

There was that, in the worry about her health.

And there was the matter of the documents *behind* the war in the Marid, documents they had left up in Hasjuran, signed by her, by Bregani of Koperna, Lord of Senjin, *and* by Bregani's erstwhile enemy and southern neighbor Machigi, the young lord of the Taisigin Marid. The documents said first, that Bregani would join the aishidi'tat, the Western Association. Secondly that Bregani would extend Machigi a railroad connection to Koperna. And other things, pulling strings that would gather the entire Marid into a favorable relationship with the north, define the Marid's internal relationships, and *end* the several hundred years of war and near-war with the north.

All that *had* to be filed, formally filed in Shejidan *while all signers were living* for it to be legally binding. Which—Ilisidi's state of health put in question.

It was not just the documents. Not just the Marid. Not just the escaping ship and the question of where they were going to detach the Guild force.

She had no appointed heir. Well, she had Tabini, of course, for interests in the aishidi'tat. But the entire East, a province of very few people but great wealth of metals and timber—half the entire continent—had no appointed heir.

God.

He truly should rest. He could *order* night whenever he pleased. He could turn out the lights in the car. He had a bed, if he let it down. He had every luxury the Red Train could provide—and given what the Red Train was, a luxury far beyond ordinary— except the damned overstuffed benches; but for days now, sleep had been a great deal of lying flat with his eyes closed, and a mind that jolted awake with each bump, to questions that had no answers.

She had told him at Koperna that she and Tabini had settled their differences.

They had discussed the Dojisigi lord, Tiajo, agreed it was past time to settle the south as a whole—which statement on Ilisidi's part *might* have been rhetorical, except one troubling sentence.

I do not build for my grandson. I build for his son. And my time to accomplish these things is somewhat less than I want.

She had seemed well enough in that last meeting. Certainly in good appetite.

God, he could not think about that last sentence. He found his place in his book and tried to keep his mind there . . . without much luck.

I have obligations, he had protested, to the idea of accompanying the dowager to Hasjuran. Five thousand refugees, strangers to the entire world, had to be gotten off the space station, a necessity shortages and their own riots had made urgent. None of these humans spoke Ragi, they were terrified of atevi, they were hostile to other humans, they had never been on a planet, and they were needing to come down to this one to live. The Mospheiran shuttle was in for repairs. Atevi had a shuttle fleet that could handle the job, but for various reasons, the aishidi'tat was not keen to land and service a shuttle at Port Jackson airport: they wanted to land at Cobo-nai, the atevi spaceport north of Cobo—but atevi law, dating to the War of the Landing, had pronounced all sorts of ceremonial and religious infelicity to any region that permitted an unsanctioned human to set foot on atevi soil.

Well, thank the basic sense of religious atevi who always left a loophole in grand prohibitions and permissions. A priest could religiously sanction the lot of them and get them down—not without some furor about it all; but legally—solved. So they were getting humans. The paidhi-aiji, the aiji's interpreter, needed to be there to interpret, escort, reassure, and deal with it.

The dowager had needed him for a short trip to Hasjuran.

They would be back in time.

Hasjuran led to Koperna and Koperna to days on the worst track in existence—with a war in the Marid and a crisis developing at Najida.

Things had gone so well in Hasjuran.

Until Homura had shown up.

Then a bomb had blown up the local transformer, a clear indication the Dojisigi both knew and were upset about the situation.

One still worried who had planted the device.

They still had Homura. And his partner Momichi. Former Shadow Guild agents—they *swore* "former." Homura and Momichi, who had a Guild detachment of their own, polite, but a guard, not an aishid. They were only two cars ahead, just the other side of Nomari. They were half of a former Shadow Guild unit, their two partners, so they claimed, being held hostage by the Shadow Guild to force *them* to assassinate Lord Tatiseigi, in a very critical northern association.

Their try at Tatiseigi had not gone off—but they had gotten terrifyingly close. And when, rather than being shot on the spot, they had found themselves offered protection and help, they had sworn man'chi to the dowager *and* to Bren.

Trustable, to this day?

Was *that* not the unknowable question? They were tracking the same ship that was carrying Tiajo and the Shadow Guild leadership. And they were three cars removed from the dowager. He was not happy about that. He was very sure her security was not.

But Ilisidi, for reasons she had yet to disclose, had allowed them aboard.

They *had* been sources of information.

Maybe she was just doing them a final favor. Maybe she had asked them for one.

Meanwhile the thing Ilisidi had set in motion had *not* delivered the paidhi-aiji up to Cobo-nai to deal with the shuttle—and Lord Geigi himself had diverted his attention from the ills of the space station long enough to launch the last of his mobile landers as a relay for the communicators Ilisidi's force already had aboard the Red Train—which said *something* about the degree of preparation that had gone on for Ilisidi's train trip, and anyone who believed that that trip was extended to the Marid coast on the spur of the moment was not paying attention.

There was a damned lot that had not been communicated to the paidhi-aiji in that invitation to snowy Hasjuran.

Ilisidi, before ever starting the trip, had diverted two of the three naval vessels on eternal watch in the Mospheiran Strait—to sail for the Southern Ocean and the Marid Sea, to meet her at Koperna harbor.

As one of Geigi's landers descended onto the border between Senjin and the Dojisigin.

Of *course* it was all unexpected.

Like hell.

Citizenry throughout the northern Marid had taken shelter and let Guild fight Guild, as Tabini then diverted one of Ilisidi's—actually *his own*—naval vessels to move against the Dojisigin capital of Amarja—striking at the headquarters of the Shadow Guild, anxious to preserve records. He wanted to lay hands on the Dojisigin lord, Tiajo, as vicious a young woman as one could imagine, and most particularly—to take down Suratho, a woman they now knew fairly reliably as head of the Shadow Guild.

Both of whom were headed now for Marid Strait having sailed right *past* the inbound naval vessels at some point—not even Lord Geigi had spotted them, not as if Lord Geigi did not have other things to distract him on the station. Dojisigin ships were hardly an anomaly in the Marid.

Now they knew, however. So onto the train the dowager went, not even staying for courtesy with Bregani. She had snatched up several boxcars of Guild equipment, a number of Guild units not immediately needed in Koperna, and taken Homura and Momichi—Nomari was, well, an afterthought.

And on they went, on this catastrophe of a rail. *Thump-thump. Thump-thump.* At times a man walking afoot could keep pace with it.

They had dropped off *one* uneasy companion in their hasty departure from Koperna. Machigi had left the Red Train to return to his capital, Tanaja, in the Taisigin, in case any of the mess in the north spilled in his direction.

Bren was just as happy not to have Lord Machigi involving himself on the west coast, and happy to have him back in his capital and out of trouble.

So they were confident nothing would be storming down the track behind them to cause them trouble.

They had stopped for refueling halfway, at Targai, the Maschi clan capital, but there had been no visit to the Maschi lord at his estate, though Targai was an important, an essential ally. It had been in that silence at Targai, when she had chosen to forgo the sort of gossip-filled dinner that ordinarily was her delight—that Bren had truly begun to fear something serious was going on with the dowager.

How many years had he lived elbow to elbow with atevi—held his aishid and his staff as his nearest and dearest—and right now he was, he admitted it, in emotional isolation, having his own personal reaction to the situation with Ilisidi, and not being able to figure it.

Worst—not being wired to figure it. The closest persons in the world to him, his aishid—right at the end of the car: they had no answers, even for their own relationship. He could never use that word *friend* with them.

They would throw themselves between him and trouble because they *were* attached that way and it was a deeply, profoundly satisfying arrangement to them, especially as he was attached to a power they were attached to—namely Tabini—and the whole world spun on that axis. At times he looked at them and thought he could cross that barrier, there was such a feeling he had about them . . . but that was dangerous territory, to try to go there: a human just was not quite wired for it; and they were, and they were happy.

As he was. Absolutely happy, never to leave them, absolutely never to do what his predecessor had done, and leave the mainland for good. His predecessor had formed no such relationships. But he—had. He was involved way past all intention, as attached as *he* could be, in his way. He understood extremes and anomalies. He trusted them. And he felt his way through situations. He understood how terrible was the situation that Homura and Momichi claimed to be in: loss of connections, loss that would never heal while there was a chance their partners were alive, to make them kill . . . in violation of their code.

The machimi, the historic dramas, several times invoked that nameless condition. The Ragi language had words for all sorts of mental states, but not for that one . . . though God knew it was a staple of the dramas. A retainer bereaved . . . gone anchorless, mentally. That was his own word for it.

Why in hell was he thinking down this dark alley, here in the dark, with the rail for an ominous heartbeat . . . what was his brain trying to resolve?

Cenedi? Greyer than Ilisidi was, with narrow gold eyes that never ceased their suspicion except when *she* was his focus. What state was he in, if she *was* sick?

And what if *his* man'chi went suddenly anchorless? Cenedi, who had the ability, perhaps even the mandate, to wield Ilisidi's power on her posthumous objectives . . . ?

That was about worth a shiver, thinking that if Ilisidi had no appointed heir, Cenedi would continue to wield that power. And he could not, somehow, bring himself to discuss that with his own aishid, not on this trip, not with Banichi necessarily serving as Cenedi's second-in-command, handling the things that had to be handled.

But *not* in charge of the decision to camp at Najida. That had to come from Cenedi.

Or Tabini.

The protocols grew muddy when it came to whose province,

whose authority relative to Tabini's, and who was directing this entire force, with the dowager not seeming to be in charge at the moment. The paidhi-aiji had no military power. His aishid did, Banichi being high-ranking in the Guild; while Cenedi's authority was complicated—being Eastern born, Eastern-trained, never even coming through Guild Headquarters, holding what he had by reason of Ilisidi's authority . . . it grew very complicated, were Ilisidi to—God help them—die. The paidhi-aiji, not even atevi, could end up the highest official on the train.

His own bodyguard, his aishid, his four companions, with whom he shared things he would say to no one else—he did not feel like asking them that question. Not here. Not in this dark place. When they were in the field with Ilisidi's aishid, Banichi deferred to Cenedi. It was not always a comfortable dynamic, as Ilisidi's orders were not always compatible with Tabini's, but overall it had worked.

God, he did *not* want to be thinking these thoughts.

No. Until he had absolute proof to the contrary, he would trust Ilisidi *was* there, awake, and planning. She had something in mind. *She*, through Cenedi, could be in current consultation with anyone who had one of the new units—Geigi. Tabini. Probably the Guild commander in the Marid. Likely the Guild commander who was on this train.

He wished his brain would quit, give up, go to sleep. He was tired, sore, and short of sleep, having found a point of discomfort in every seat in the car. And he had napped earlier and now only he and Narani were awake, Jeladi drowsing peacefully in the chair by the door, his aishid having curled up in a knot of black uniforms and shadow at the other end of the car. He was on his own. Frustrated.

It did not help that even his wardrobe had turned out misinformed, wool and warmth, while now they were in the more temperate south—it was too warm, with atevi body heat in the car. And in discomfort and distress, he played solitaire on the computer that he had brought for far more serious business, none of which he could do without information.

He was tired of solitaire. The only books he had brought on

this trip were references on Hasjuran, the mountaintop province that *should* have been their destination. He got up, gathered it up, opened it, looked at the text disconsolately, shut it, put it back on the shelf, and sat down again, despairing of sleep or diversion.

Narani, dutifully, bravely awake, refreshed the tea.

"Go to sleep, Rani-ji. You absolutely should not stay awake to tend my insomnia. Get some rest."

"Is there anything I can bring you, nandi?"

"An entertainment. A solution to the Reunioners. A message from the dowager. A timetable for our arrival. Any of those. My books are worthless. But the tea is welcome. One of the little cakes." Bindanda had brought some in, earlier—Bindanda was Bren's staff, a chef, who had chosen not to be simply a passenger: he lent a hand in the galley, and provided far better than field rations to the Guild traveling with them.

Narani brought the dessert on a little saucer, with a napkin. And laid beside it two little books, one a worn leather volume entitled *The Dual Regencies of Ilisidi of Malguri, Her Acts and Proposals on the Southern Coasts*. Bren lifted it. The second appeared to be a companion volume, *Alliance and Betrayal: The Dual Regencies of Ilisidi of Malguri, Her Acts and Proposals in the Midlands*.

God, how had he missed those in his library?

"I cannot provide a letter from the dowager," Narani said, "but I have these—a little overdue at the library, I fear. I did not know I would be taking them into a Guild action."

The Bujavid library, on the first floor. An amazing collection. He had never come across these two.

"I think they will forgive us if we ask them nicely," Bren said. Narani had been marking places with thinnest tissue, neatly cut little strips. "I shall not lose your markers, Rani-ji. I shall be very careful."

"You are very welcome, nandi. I shall leave the pot." Narani bowed, obviously pleased, and moved back into the shadows as Bren randomly sampled the first of the books. In scholarly detail, in scholarly fashion, indexed, its bulk increased with a great number of tissue strips, it zigged and zagged into what-ifs and personalities of the era, in an elaborate typeface that would not be hurried. It would have daunted him, earlier in his career. He read the old type like a veteran now.

Ashidama Bay is the largest natural harbor of the Great Continent. Jorida, the substantial island in the middle of the bay, has held power over it, both political and financial, from primitive times . . .

A second bookmark: *The Masters of Jorida, who claim to have records predating the Great Wave, aver that Ashidama Bay was once a trading center for the Great Southern Isle, and say that it alone, of all the major Southern Isle settlements, survived the cataclysm intact.*

Well, indeed, the Great Wave was as far back as any coherent atevi records tended to go.

He settled with the first book and followed the bookmarks.

The Ojiri clan . . . had ties to the northern Marid. So the trade that flowed from the Dojisigin to Jorida was not just a recent relationship.

There were three cities in Ashidama: Jorida itself. Separti, which backed up on the shore of Lord Geigi's land, on Kajiminda Peninsula—Geigi's estate traded with Separti, a convenient drive through the woods. And there was Talidi, also on that shore, down near the tip of Kajiminda. In fact, though Separti and Talidi both sat on Kajiminda land, they acknowledged the Master of Jorida as their lord—so to speak. Master was the title he held.

Bren knew that much. Geigi had gotten along with minimal trouble with Separti—in the days when Geigi had lived on the estate.

But once and long ago the Ojiri had pretty well dominated the whole west coast. The aishidi'tat, largely a Ragi association north of the mountains in those days, concerned itself mostly with the north. Then humans entered the world and the War of the Landing happened.

The human landing site was on Mospheira, not originally in numbers or that fearsome. Then more arrived. And began to deal with the mainland. War resulted. The Ragi atevi established lordships and provinces in the south as part of their defense, bolstering Maschi clan, a powerful south central clan, as a power on the middle peninsula, Kajidama—the Ojiri at that time traded only with the Marid and were not involved.

The humans, better armed, but fighting among themselves, lost the war.

Mospheira was cleared of atevi, and humans would be left in peace so long as they stayed to their island, an arrangement which required that a place on the mainland be found for the atevi inhabitants of Mospheira: the Tribal Peoples, two clans who had been at war with each other and with the Ragi atevi throughout the conflict. So one people, the Gan, were settled near Dur, in the north, the other, the Edi, were settled in the south, on the rocky shore of Najidama. To appease the Maschi for the loss of Najidama, a new lordship was created and a Farai lord, kin to the Maschi lord, built Najida estate to watch over the Edi, who had had a long-term quarrel with the Ojiri, who used to raid Mospheira in the long ago.

The Farai fell out of favor in Tabini's time, and, far from fearing a human invasion these days, Tabini-aiji appointed one Bren Cameron as lord of Najida.

Even in his role as Lord of Najida, Bren had scarcely heard Jorida mentioned, except as a market that Kajiminda used but Najida did not, and as the offended party whose trading ships, on their way to the northern port of Cobo, had mysteriously gone aground off Edi shores.

These days, with Geigi no longer in residence at Kajiminda, Najida tried to keep the market road open to Ashidama, with precious little reciprocal help from the Townships of the Ashidama coast. Goods did come and go, so it had been moderately profitable to keep the route open, at least seasonally. It had been a principle, with Geigi, so long as he lived at Kajiminda, to maintain it year-round clear down to Ashidama. *Bren*, in charge of the road work and employing Edi, did not want Edi workmen operating that close to Jorida—given the history.

The Taisigin had utilized Jorida's shipping services.

The book was . . . he checked the date . . . twenty-three years old. *Before* Machigi took over the Taisigin. *Before* Machigi's father was killed by the Shadow Guild.

Machigi had broken Taisigin ties to Jorida and sent his own ships to Cobo to trade with the aishidi'tat.

Little wonder Machigi wanted that rail link.

Machigi had warned them, at Koperna, about the Shadow Guild's links to Jorida, using terms like black market and artifacts, and with allusions to the near-sacred and forbidden Southern Continent. Machigi had placed the blame for funding of the Shadow Guild directly onto the too-rich collectors in the aishidi'tat itself, with Jorida as the even richer enabler.

God . . . what a tangled mess.

Thump-thump. Thump—Bump!

Bren, steadying his cup, thought suddenly about the state of the rail they had been passing over for days now in terms other than aching joints. It was passable . . . freight moved on it, between the Marid and the aishidi'tat, but one wondered, with one's newly increased understanding of Jorida, just how much freight in recent years. The Dojisigin had let its own connecting spur fall into utter ruin.

Now Machigi wanted a rail line to connect to this one—and this one was due for repair. A lot of repair.

Better rail, more trains.

Jorida was *not* going to welcome the news of the collapse of the Dojisigin, and would not welcome a conference of Bregani, Machigi, and the dowager, even if that Dojisigin ship had left too early to know all of it.

And the Farai . . . *Oh,* yes. Farai clan would be right there, with Bregani.

He had had no good opinion of that clan, personally, and his path kept crossing them. Before his time, they had promoted themselves right up to the third floor of the Bujavid, had used to own the apartment that now was his, right next to Tabini's, and had enjoyed all manner of privilege—in the reign of Valasi II. And, indeed, the Farai had been the first lords of Najida—in fact almost everything he owned and touched on the mainland had been a Farai property, before the Farai had pushed Tabini too far and one Bren Cameron, human though he was, had ended up a titled lord of the aishidi'tat with a great many unasked-for side benefits . . . and one wished one could be entirely sure Tabini had done that for better reasons than to outrage the Farai, insulting them with a human presence.

Certainly the Edi people and Lord Geigi had never had a good word to say about the Farai—Lord Geigi being the sort of fellow who could find some virtue in just about everybody.

Though he knew one Farai he found pleasant—Lord Bregani's wife, a brave lady; and their half-Farai daughter, Husai, who in a certain naivete, combined with Farai brashness, seemed to have set her sails for that other passenger on this train: young Nomari, ex-railway worker, potentially the new lord of Ajuri—whose appointment awaited Tabini's approval, largely dependent on this trip. Nomari had been hauled into this often chilly, sometimes life-threatening mission apparently because Ilisidi, with a short time before Nomari's appointment became a public issue, wanted to see what sort of lad he was.

Nomari traveled in isolation in his car, with four bodyguards and a single servant—all the dowager's appointees—all of whom doubtless carried reports to Cenedi, though nothing contained in those reports had come in Bren's direction. Nomari had politely declined all attempts to dine with him. Perhaps it was shyness, but it could as easily be uneasiness about questions from him that might turn up differences from his answers to Ilisidi. Or it could just be that having grown up in the Marid, an intimate supper with a human was just, well, too much for him. He was reportedly eating with the four of the dowager's young men assigned to guard him, quite an informal arrangement, indicative of much greater familiarity than a Guild unit on guard duty ordinarily permitted, but quite typical of an aishid . . . which they could become.

Not a bad thing, in Bren's mind, considering the damage Nomari's disappearance in Koperna had had on his relationship with those four.

If they were sorting things out, *if* Nomari's assigned bodyguard was sending good reports to Ilisidi, it might well affect her endorsement of him, which would, yes, be a good thing in his opinion.

"*You favor him.*"

Her comment on Nomari that last morning, following his brief explanation of the previous night's events.

"*He has not lost my good opinion.*"

"*You approve what he did.*"

"*He saved her.*"

Ilisidi had responded with her enigmatic smile and an equally enigmatic: "*He shows us obfuscation. Illusion. Modesty, when it serves. The innocence of a child. He charms us all. Even you, paidhi.*"

Had Nomari charmed *her?* Only if she allowed it.

Nomari's life was still at issue—at least the sort of life he might lead. His becoming lord of Ajuri was far from a given. Failing that, he might insert himself in Lord Bregani's household tomorrow, given the looks Bregani's daughter cast him, but, God—Nomari and Husai? Another Farai romance, another Farai marrying her way into potent associations?

That was not going to happen.

Back to Machigi's court? Possibly. He appeared more comfortable with Machigi than any northerner ought to be.

But if Tabini approved him, what Nomari was destined to do was to take over one of the most rotten and corrupt clans extant and bring them back to respectability. Ajuri had been the seedbed of the Shadow Guild, and its lords did not tend to die peacefully abed.

Possibly more importantly, Nomari apparently had his own clan's backing. Ajuri refugees had gathered around him and appealed en masse to his neighbor, Lord Tatiseigi of Atageini clan, to support him: he was what they wanted, and, ultimately, Tatiseigi had decided to back him, as strong an endorsement as he could get, Ajuri being the immediate neighbor to that most powerful lord in the Midlands.

Redeem the clan in Tabini's eyes? Maybe. Eventually.

Bring the Farai back into northern politics?

A cold day in hell. *He* opposed that. Husai was charming; he did not know her relatives.

He drained his cup, poured a new one, and returned to his book:

—*This grant of a lordship on Kajidama both strengthened the Maschi clan, with now two seats of power—and incidentally deprived Talidi Township of the source of their timber, vital to their ship maintenance, a source which they had taken as naturally theirs, as close at hand.*

This of course greatly vexed the Master of Jorida—who now had to negotiate with three lords of the aishidi'tat for trade in timber, grain, and fish. It is commonly held that only the fact that both Kajidama and Najidama harbors are rocky and problematic for ships of large draft kept the Ojiri from launching war against the Edi from the sea.

Well, that was an interesting observation. And at least partially true. His own yacht had no trouble, but it did get rather shallow under her keel as she came into dock, and there were places one had to stand well off the shore.

But would the Ojiri, who had based their entire trade reputation on lucrative neutrality, truly have risked setting off the Maschi of Targai just for a bit of timber? Somehow, he doubted it.

The tea was cold. He got up, drew more hot water from the samovar, spooned more tea into the strainer . . . Narani, blessed man, had fallen quite asleep in the chair by the wardrobe, and Jeladi had done the same on the other side of the doorway. He added sugar, a practice that lifted brows among atevi. Added two spoonfuls. He was not sleeping, but bodily energy was at an ebb.

And he was just getting to the part he really wanted to know.

He sipped the new cup. And reopened the book.

2

The Unexpected Rise of Ilisidi of Malguri
In his seventh year as aiji in Shejidan, Valasi I sought a contract marriage, but reports brought him word of a more strategic match that could gain him access to the wealth of iron and timber beyond the Continental Divide . . .

Namely Ilisidi. The railroad again. Always the railroad, which had begun to shape the aishidi'tat shortly before humans had appeared in the atevi heavens. There were no highways on the continent, just market roads, few of them even paved. It was all railways that united regions—it was the first railroad that had created the aishidi'tat.

Railroads, trains and rails alike, were resource-hungry, in particular, for iron and timber, which were indeed abundant in the East, and increasingly hard come by in the west. Big timber had been disappearing, except in the land of the Taibeni clan, which would not surrender their trees to the axe. Two small wars and an assassination proved that.

Which had led, indirectly, to Tabini. Ilisidi's son, Valasi II, had taken a Taibeni wife to mend those tensions. But that was far ahead of the text.

Ilisidi, Lord of Malguri, received the proposal from Valasi I, but insisted on marriage by her custom, namely a permanent, not a contract marriage. This reduced the influence and the conflict of the larger clans, and reduced the likelihood of conflict among potential heirs. She had no desire, she was reported to have said, to spend her life breeding heirs for others, and indeed,

Valasi's heir, Valasi II, was her only offspring, leaving the future control of her own region of Malguri in question.

Control of Malguri, in the East, after Ilisidi, was still a concern. Ilisidi, being no fool, had to have considered the problem, but if she had declared an heir, he certainly had never heard about it.

As for Malguri, lying far across the Continental Divide, it had been little involved with the Ragi atevi of the aishidi'tat, and thus brought no troublesome ties into a permanent marriage. Regarding her own reason for accepting the marriage, she is said to have used the martial strength of Shejidan to reinforce her rule over the East, which, by the terms of the marriage contract, she holds to this day as independent of the aishidi'tat, including the rights to declare war, choose her own succession, and install an heir without the approval of the aishidi'tat.

Without approval? Curious. He had never heard that. Was the writer correct? He made a note to delve into the question: best *not* to wait for it to become an emergency.

Thus through correspondence and emissaries, the marriage was arranged.

Another bookmark . . .

There is a story that Ilisidi so hated the journey across the Continental Divide that she insisted on extending the rail across the Divide to her province. This may be legend. What is true is that the eastern rail project carried on during her marriage to Valasi I and into her regency for her son, Valasi II.

Conquering the divide had been truly epic, but personally, he doubted that Ilisidi's comfort had been a major reason for the cross-continental rail. If she was going to leave Malguri but still rule there in absentia, she would need the means to get back and forth quickly. If she was using the western Assassins' Guild to stabilize the East, fast response and culturally aware response would be mandatory. Even before the marriage, she had established her own branch of the Assassins and of the Transportation Guild in Malguri, some of whom she had brought with her to Shejidan. To this day, there was Cenedi, who attained high rank inside the original Guild once she became regent. There were others, all trained in Malguri, all acknowledged by the aishidi'tat's Guild, who maintained the peace there now. But while she was unifying the East, the rail link would have allowed the newly formed Eastern Guild to reinforce Ilisidi's guard with her own people.

And if raw materials for the western railroad were Valasi I's reason for the marriage, getting those massive loads across the divide rapidly and economically would be a necessity, not a whim. The railroad had had to cross the divide.

For her. For the one who controlled the source of it all.

God. *Did* she not?

Valasi I had died before the rail was completed. Assassinated, rumor said. It was never proved.

Following the completion of the transcontinental line, Ilisidi, now aiji-regent to her infant son, Valasi II, was instrumental in driving the rail to Cobo, which made the flow of goods much faster between that shipping center and Shejidan. She also extended it up into Taiben, a gesture toward the powerful lord of Atageini.

Tatiseigi? Possibly it actually *had* been Tatiseigi who held Atageini in those days. He was no older . . . but not much younger, either. But a gesture? Of what kind? Once again, the author failed to expand. Tatiseigi was notoriously conservative where it came to modern technology. He would never have agreed to a station on Atageini land. So the northern line went to the edge of Taibeni land . . . and stopped, still within relatively easy reach of Tirnamardi, giving Tatiseigi the convenience of the rail to Shejidan.

It might also have served Atageini in less obvious ways. The Taibeni had been very contentious neighbors in the years before Ilisidi's marriage—primarily because of the timber question. It was possible that line, giving the Guild rapid response to trouble in the area, had been meant as a deterrent, but one had to wonder just how effective it had been, in that sense, considering the contract with Valasi II—which had resulted in Tabini—also had been made to placate the Taibeni.

It would make for an interesting conversation . . . likely a lively one, considering the principals involved.

He turned back to the book.

There was a considerable section without markers, and when they started again, they were of a different shade of paper, newer, in a section titled **The Southern Extension.**

As aiji-consort Ilisidi had made a very generous approach to the Master of Jorida as well as to the councils of Separti and Talidi, renewing the offer for Ashidama Bay to join the aishi-di'tat, provided they would agree to the mutual defense provisions of the charter, and offering a rail line from the planned Cobo terminal down to the Townships of Ashidama Bay, to facilitate the flow of goods between the Marid and the North.

Jorida Isle refused outright and restrained the others.

Surprise, surprise.

Ilisidi then formed an alternate plan for obtaining Marid trade without the assistance of Jorida, proposing an eastward extension of the rail from Cobo east to the Marid, but could gain no approval for it from the legislature—and no support from Valasi.

This would have been her husband, Valasi I.

When, however, Valasi I died, her son Valasi II being still an infant, she assumed the regency, and among her first acts, following the completion of the Cobo line, she ordered an extension of the railroad down from Cobo to a refueling stop and small station at Najida.

With the link to Najida completed, she again approached the powers of Ashidama, but when the Master again refused, and dominated the others, she sent a rail line east from Najida to the Maschi seat in Targai, and in the next three years, pushed it all the way to Koperna in Senjin, thus setting up to import goods directly from the Marid, without reference to Jorida Isle. Trade between the regions flourished.

And now that track, once welcomed, was neglected. Still trafficked, but nothing compared to what must have been at the time this account was written. Transportation Guild records of rail usage during Tabini's administration—and the rise of the Shadow Guild—would likely be highly illuminating.

Maschi clan, sitting midway on the Cobo–Koperna rail line, was delighted to have a physical connection with the aishidi'tat. Najidama Bay, site of the southernmost rail station at Najida, was already a territory of the aishidi'tat, as a protectorate for the Edi, under their Farai lord, who had Maschi connections. Thus the connections became firmer.

There was no mention of tension between the Edi and the Farai lord, at this point in time, but it was a Ragi account of events, and Farai clan had been important in Shejidan at the time this was written. Marriages, both contract and permanent, had insinuated the Farai influence into no less than five lordships in the heart of the aishidi'tat. Lord Geigi himself had had a Farai wife at one point, while the Farai lord of Najida had had a Maschi spouse. Marriageable offspring were the Farai's mode of conquest.

And then, a decade and more ago, as the Shadow Guild would have been gaining dangerous momentum, the Farai lord had turned greedy, and Geigi himself had been forced into a very messy divorce, with no heir therefrom. Kajiminda had slipped their grasp, and soon after Najida had followed, as Tabini expelled the Farai holding that lordship.

Perhaps it had taken Shadow Guild influence to turn the Farai into utter fools. Perhaps, if Tabini succeeded in eliminating the Shadow Guild cancer in this round, sanity might reassert itself in that clan.

One could only hope.

Among other political moves, and to soothe Jorida, lately vexed by conflict with the Edi people, Ilisidi offered unconditional favorable trading status to the two Townships of the Ashidama coast, Separti and Talidi, and actually secured their agreement, Jorida not objecting, since they were suffering from the diversion of Marid trade.

So that was how the Townships had linked into trade with Geigi, during his time resident at Kajiminda.

The Townships were thereafter called provincial states, for legislative neatness in Shejidan . . .

A few pages on . . .

In the twenty-third year of Ilisidi's first regency, the Master of

Jorida died quite suddenly. There were accusations, unproven, that it was Guild action.

That was interesting. One might ask, given the opportunity. Ilisidi might even answer frankly, if she were in a good mood.

But not as a conversation opener on this trip, no.

. . . the new Master of Jorida, Hurshina, eleventh of the name, came to power, a new administration, which might have posed an opportunity for Shejidan to make diplomatic gains on the Southwest Coast, but a serious issue arose with Mospheira which took three years to settle.

That situation ended with the Ancillary Agreement of Cobo, appointing a port wherein ships from Port Jackson could dock for repair in bad weather . . .

All this was Mospheiran history as well. Next bookmark.

Meanwhile, troubles were brewing again in Najida. The Edi fisherfolk, differing from both Ragi and Ojiri in language, customs, tradition, and ancestry, neither writing nor growing crops, and generally with a different idea of property, ownership, and warfare, did not obey decrees of the aishidi'tat, and expanded from Najidama into summer camps on Kajidama, thus intruding, ultimately, into the Townships' territory, which brought armed force from Jorida to dislodge them. This happened while the aishidi'tat was distracted by Mospheira.

Then two Joridi ships went aground off the outer shores of Najida and survivors who made their way back to Kajidama claimed a light commonly seen on Najida shore had moved. There followed claims and counterclaims and attacks on Edi villages, as the Ojiri moved to curtail a resurgence of what they declared piracy.

Ilisidi of Malguri now called in favors from the Maschi lord she had appointed to Kajiminda. She instructed this Maschi lord, right at the back door of Separti Township, to discourage the Edi from wrecking along the Najida rocks, but to do so by gifts rather than by arms.

This unexpected gesture succeeded. Jorida Isle, who had lost the ships, was furious at the settlement and more so at the independent treaty the Townships signed with the aishidi'tat. The

Maschi lord of Kajiminda did succeed in persuading the Edi to do no more wrecking there, which removed the official cause of outbursts from Jorida. But Kajiminda was ill-placed to restrain the Edi from wrecking off Najidama Peninsula, so Ilisidi sternly approached the lord of Najida with instructions to develop relations with the Edi.

She herself offered certain benefits to the Edi, namely that if the Edi would refrain from attacking the fuel and water stores at the depot (a recurring problem to the lord of Najida) she would assure that both Najidama and Kajidama Peninsula were safe and secure from intrusion by Ashidama. So Najida would be Kajiminda's neighbor and natural ally, with full membership in the aishidi'tat, enabling them to stand off any threat from Ashidama, while moderating problems with the Edi. The Farai connection in both lordships was persuasive: the Farai being a large clan also in the Senjin Marid, the primary source of Ashidama's trade, the Master of Jorida did not wish to offend them.

Thus relative peace ruled the coast for a time.

Ilisidi had brokered that peace. And *he* had been worried about how she would deal with the Edi if he left her here . . .

In the thirtieth year of her first regency, with Valasi II campaigning to establish his majority, Ilisidi again proposed to extend the rail from Cobo to Ashidama Bay by way of Najida, an offer which Separti Township now supported, but Jorida still vehemently refused—stringing negotiations along until in his thirty-second year Valasi II successfully asserted his majority, effectively putting an end to Ilisidi's regency, to Ilisidi's great displeasure.

Bren poured another cup of tea and added sugar.

Valasi II peacefully assumed the aijinate, after which Ilisidi retired to Malguri in the distant East—indeed she had returned there periodically since the rail had gone through, affairs in the East having proven as troublesome as the southlands.

He truly needed to educate himself on the history of Malguri. Not trusting his currently overtaxed memory, he took another note.

While she was engaged with those matters in the East, her son fell under the influence of the new paidhi-aiji, Wilson, and began the unimpeded (and in this historian's view, ill-advised) import of television, electrification, aviation, and manufacturing techniques, which created unprecedented stresses in the economy and unbalanced the relative power of the Guilds, forcing Ilisidi back to Shejidan to attempt to salvage what remained of the aishidi'tat.

Wilson. A very strange and bitter man. The word was, Wilson had *changed* during Wilson's tenure on the mainland. In Bren's estimation, the old man's hold on sanity was tenuous at best, as fragile as his insistence on hundred-year-old rules and his challenges and nastiness over the dictionary, which had more than doubled in size since Bren had replaced him. But Wilson retained a special, fond relationship with the Committee . . . partly because the Committee on Linguistics was minimally fond of Bren Cameron, who had dared to bypass the rules and actually *speak* with the aiji . . . at Tabini's explicit request.

Hence the massive expansion of the official dictionary.

That defiance of the rules was ancient history now, and his ability to actively engage with the atevi had become essential in recent history—but the Committee, which consequently had lost control over the paidhi's office, still hated him for it.

Ilisidi's relationship with her son Valasi II became increasingly troubled in the matter of her grandson Tabini. When Valasi II dismissed his Taibeni wife and surrendered the care of his son and heir to a tutor of whom Ilisidi disapproved, Ilisidi took the boy, then felicitous seven, to her own estate at Malguri, where she proceeded to train him according to her own standards. Valasi II made moves to disinherit his son, but the legislature refused his motion by a sizeable majority, to Valasi's great displeasure.

And within four years, overcome with excess, and with human technology woven through the aishidi'tat, Valasi-aiji died, unmourned by the frustrated legislature, and by means still unexamined.

Ilisidi returned to Shejidan without her grandson—and declared herself again aiji-regent, this time for her grandson Tabini, and with the full support of the Assassins' Guild . . .

Full support? Well. Well. Well . . .

Long sip of tea.

Cenedi, though Eastern-trained, had never come under serious question by the Guild. The Messengers, always troublesome, had raised the issue once, so he had heard, but they quickly pretended not to have objected, as no one, by that time, questioned Ilisidi's rights. Recognizing Cenedi—and all her Eastern Guild—had been part of the marriage contract, and this history seemed to imply that when Valasi II died, the Guild itself had shifted man'chi to Ilisidi as smoothly as if she had been the designated heir.

If Valasi II had ever truly had it. Ilisidi was a force of nature. Peacefully surrendering the aijinate did not necessarily affect the biology of dominance—and Ilisidi's influence had continued from behind the curtains, so to speak, not quite in harmony with her son.

In the first year of her second regency, determined to stabilize the spiraling economy, Ilisidi expanded the power of the Assassins to exercise their own discretion in cases of public emergency.

A promise of increased autonomy might also explain the Guild's stepping carefully around the issue of Cenedi's Eastern origins.

She limited the expansion of technology, and vetoed her late son's proposal to consolidate all imported technology under a separate guild. Some suggested this last proposal was Valasi's undoing, that he had expended the last of his influence to force it through the legislature, he was now dead, and she refused to put her seal to it.

The Guild would never accept their security devices being controlled by another Guild. Yet one more reason for backing Ilisidi . . .

Instead, Ilisidi proposed the regulation of imported technology be distributed under the traditional guilds, each guild to determine its own governing principles by the ancient rule of kabiu—which pleased the Guilds and the traditionalists considerably, re-established familiar principles, and greatly expanded her support within the legislature.

And confused the hell out of Wilson, who was caught in a whirlwind of policy changes, in a system he had never truly understood.

She also renewed her offer of a railroad connection to Separti, but to no one's surprise, the Master of Jorida declined the offer . . .

The account reached its end still within Ilisidi's second regency, a book contemporary with that.

A few years later, Tabini had returned from Malguri on his own, and assumed the aijinate in what some had feared would be a bloodletting and a massive upheaval among the Guilds. That part was vivid in his own memory, Ilisidi's relationship with Wilson-paidhi being notoriously fraught, and Tabini being, at the time, a total mystery to everyone on Mospheira.

In fact, what he knew now about politics and the Assassins' Guild cast Tabini's seizure of power into a different light. Mospheira had never questioned Ilisidi's absolute control of the Assassins' Guild while she was regent. They assumed that since Ilisidi's influence had been that strong, the transition could have gone badly had Ilisidi moved the Guild to take exception to Tabini's assumption of power.

So . . . credit to Ilisidi's own restraint.

But with perspective . . . yes, she was regent, but she was not Ragi. She was not even *of* the aishidi'tat at that time . . . except by marriage. The miracle was—that all the western Guilds *had* followed her, perhaps because she was to a degree impartial and might be open to persuasion. And always at her side, there was, perpetual enigma, Cenedi, the outsider, with his unit, and her personal guard of what Ilisidi called her *young men* . . . all male, indeed, all Eastern, and all adept at servants' skills, and demolitions, and overcoming locks, and dealing with intruders. It was still a wonder the Assassins' Guild—*the* Guild, first organized of all Guilds, and entitled to the distinction—had not only respected Cenedi through all of it, but supported both her and Cenedi through both her regencies.

Well.

Bren gently closed Narani's book and rested his hands on the leather cover.

One thing was undeniable: through two regencies and clear to the present, Ilisidi had fought to connect the four great regions of the continent by rail . . . specifically, in the south, to break the shipping monopoly of the Ojiri and bring Ashidama into the aishidi'tat.

What the book did not mention—or the bookmarks had not led him to it—was the rise of anti-human sentiment, particularly in the Marid, which had always stood apart, geographically, culturally, and politically, from dealing with humans. Anti-human sentiment had been a prime mover in the rise of the Shadow Guild. And the Farai's marrying their way into Ajuri, in the Padi Valley, the heart of the aishidi'tat—had seeded that movement into vital places . . . until Tabini defiantly moved one Bren Cameron, the only human on the continent, into every place and every honor the Farai had ever had.

It all fit.

A Farai connection, and an Ajuri one, a movement that gave rise to the Shadow Guild . . . with Jorida's stubborn neutrality funding it, not deliberately—perhaps—but providing it an economic lifeline, all the same.

And now, with her time foreseeably running out, Ilisidi finally had secured the necessary agreements for a rail extension south of Koperna—not on the west side of the southern plateau—but on the *east*, in the Marid. Machigi's district and the several districts of the Marid would benefit greatly from it, and in addition to the rail, there was the lure of an eastern sea route, hitherto impossible, to reach Malguri. Steel ships. Space-guided weather forecasts. Pie in the sky promises. All of it . . .

But trains . . . first.

Not air travel. Mospheira had steered the world away from that until they went to space, ironically enough. Air linked Mospheira and the mainland by one thin thread; but where atevi tended to settle had no good flat spaces for airports.

At least, that was the official reason handed out when asked. The truth, Bren suspected, was far more complex, and grounded in the very nature of the atevi. The fact was *trains* were an atevi invention, before humans, penetrating multiple clan territories by agreements atevi worked out. Trains were still how the aishidi'tat functioned. Shejidan had an airport. Malguri had one. And there was the spaceport north of Cobo. Anything else was simply superfluous. If one wanted to go to Shejidan, or even to some other district, one could always use the train.

Right now, at this moment, Ilisidi was reading the winds—and implied she was running out of time. Time to do one thing . . . settle the peace? Stop the Shadow Guild?

Or was all that just leverage . . . leverage to get Ashidama into the aishidi'tat at last?

Damn, damn, and . . . damn. Surely, *surely* she would enlighten him, once they reached Najida. Najida was rural, it was sane and quiet, it had, despite being a century and more old, modern plumbing, and soft beds, and heat and cooling as one pleased. She enjoyed the place. She had gifted him the beautiful stained glass for the dining room. It was a *good* place for her to rest and heal.

And himself being her host—she could not entirely ignore him there.

His eyes were blurring and he rubbed them. In shadows beyond his area of light, Narani slept. So did Jeladi. At the far end, in deeper shadow, his aishid slept. Rare that Guild took that luxury all at the same time, on a mission, but there was, in a moving train, very little to be done about the world's problems.

Or his. And their decision to sleep said that now was a safe time, an appropriate time to rest. The world outside was perilous. But here . . . there was nothing to be done.

He laid the book aside and rested his arms on the table, head on arms, just for a moment. He wanted to think. But all the lights were dimmed. The racket of the train persisted, steady as a heartbeat. They seemed to have hit, God save them, a prolonged smooth patch of rail.

He wanted to think. His body wanted to sleep. The brain struggled to keep going.

Sleep won.

3

Boji wanted another egg. Cajeiri took a second from the bowl and slipped it into the ancient filigree cage. This egg was boiled, but Boji was not to be fooled. He turned his prize this way and that in black skinny fingers, testing its balance—hunched little black-furred body, quick gold eyes, thin toes clutching the branch as he reached his conclusion. Then, holding the egg in both hands, he expertly sank an impressive fang into it.

From that beginning, Boji set about to peel the leathery shell with atevi-like purpose and dexterity, casting the pieces—in very *un*atevi-like behavior—in every direction. Nothing ever amended his untidy ways. He had used to play with his prize, hide it, find it and chitter to it, but now he was larger, wiser, less inclined to play, and more set on his privileges . . . more inclined to rattle the cage and shriek if his supper were in any way delayed. Cajeiri had taken on the feeding himself since Eisi and Liedi had acquired a more elevated status: there were new servants, now, under them, and the new staff were a little afraid of Boji, who, indeed, was strong, fast, and very clever.

All manner of circumstances in the apartment had changed in recent days. Boji would be leaving soon, going to a new home with large spaces and trees and others of his kind. One wondered if he would just be a bully . . . or if he would care for them. One wondered if Boji had man'chi to anyone. Boji had warned them, once, of intruders, but Cajeiri suspected that was his complaining of strangers intruding into his territory. He rather suspected that if Boji were ateva, he would be aiji. Either way, he would be happier not spending his days in a small cage.

Boji's future seemed clear and his outlook happier. But changes in Cajeiri's own future—seemed less productive of personal happiness. His patient personal staff, Eisi and Liedi, had become his senior staff in the apartment. Two new domestics, Dimaji and Tariko, a husband and wife, had moved into the new annex. Their fear of Boji was risky, apt to provoke bad behavior, and there was no point in making his care an issue—it was not fair to either side, Boji's departure now being set, certainly unmourned by those two. Eisi and Liedi confessed they would miss the little rascal, and he knew that he would in some senses, but not all.

Changes had poured down on Cajeiri's little domain. His apartment, really part of his parents' apartment, had always had its own living room and dining, had a study, an accommodation, a servants' quarters near the front door, and a bedroom suite at the back, which comprised his room and two rooms for his four bodyguards.

But in an amazingly short number of days, the number of his bodyguards had doubled, and the backstairs of his parents' apartment had surrendered a set of storerooms, available in the mazy convolutions of the Bujavid with the mere insertion of a doorway at the back of his bedroom, giving him a stub of a hall and space—with a great deal of pounding and dust—for a laundry, a bath, a room for the two married domestics, with potential space for more to come—given another wall taken. So he was informed. Right now the end of the hall was full of construction supplies and a spare sink. In the mostly finished section, too, across from his servants' apartment, were two sleeping rooms and a separate lounge for the new bodyguards, making his aishid not four, which was ordinary for a lord, but a full eight, the same as Father had.

All because Father had declared him the official heir to the aijinate.

They had all gotten along so well, just the seven of them . . . and Boji. So trusted. . . . And now there were six more people in his household and all of them, well, *adult*.

Boji wanted yet another egg. The last.

"Behave," Cajeiri said, this time opening the larger door in the cage to pass it in as far as the perch. Boji wanted to snatch it—fairly trembled with the idea—but restrained himself, furry arms about furry knees, mannerly so long as the egg was in sight.

Cajeiri held it still. Boji reached out and took the egg so delicately, so nicely that one could think that maybe the plan to send him off to the animal park was entirely unnecessary, and a parid'ja could after all be civilized.

Numerous scars about the apartment denied that. One antique and precious spoon, one of a set of nine, remained missing to this day. There were scratches on the walls and on the antique chest, a relic carved with hunting figures, damage that one day would have to be explained to the Department of Antiquities, which managed the household furnishings of the Bujavid. One doubted the scratches would be called *history* of the piece unless he retained it in his apartment until he was older than Uncle Tatiseigi.

No, Boji clearly had to go to the zoo, for reasons beyond the furniture. The little rascal, who was not quite so light or little as he had been, and was developing a bit of a belly from far too much confinement, *bit*. And his adult teeth were formidable. He might be a treasure and an entertainment, but he could truly hurt someone.

The zoo would be a big change for Boji. He would have to work for his eggs from now on, digging them out of the sand where his handlers would bury them. Alas for Boji, having the layers of the eggs in reach of those fangs would not be a long-term proposition. The eggs would be brought in from farms, as many as were good for Boji.

He hoped they would boil at least some of them: Boji liked peeling things.

But there would be no more cages and no more leash. Boji would have real trees to climb instead of the china cabinet. Someday soon he would have other parid'ji to chase. Female parid'ji. A family. And no predators. It would not be a bad life at all. Children could come and watch him and he could show off to his heart's content.

Boji liked being the center of attention. And perhaps, if he became a celebrity, if the name *Boji* became known throughout the aishidi'tat . . . formerly a valued pet in the Bujavid . . . at least some of those scars on the dining table might be forgiven.

The spot against the wall where the cage had stood for all this time might need some repair. Staff would see to that, the way staff had obligingly seen to all the inconveniences of one notion and the other that had entertained his childhood. He knew he ought to feel remorse for that. But like Boji, he was still a little selfish.

His childhood, though he did not feel he had had enough of it, was indeed coming to an end, and might already be there, for what he could tell. He was pressing hard on his tenth year—the chancy tenth, composed of a dangerous two of risk-fraught fives, comprised of fortunate and unfortunate numbers, no matter which way one figured it. He was old enough to know that, being a child, he had been beyond unreasonable, and wild, and he had done various things dangerous to his family and the aishidi'tat. He had been kidnapped. He had been shot at. And, a fact which disturbed him the more as he grew older, though at the time he had seen it more matter-of-factly, he had, yes, killed a man. It had been necessary, even commendable that he had done it.

But there it was. He had ended someone's life. He never liked to remember it when he was lying abed at night, but he had to. It was part of him. It was part of what he knew he *could* do, in necessity . . . what he might one day have to do again, in defense of the aishidi'tat.

He had, with mani and nand' Bren, traveled on the starship farther than even humans could imagine. He had talked with the kyo, who were much stranger than humans, and he had understood them, well, as much as anyone did. He knew them by name, and they knew his.

He had done all those things. Though he had not thought it remarkable at the time, most importantly, he had gained human associates, only recently landed safely on Earth—near him, though as good as on the moon. He wanted them to visit; and he wanted to visit them, but while meeting on the starship and on the space station had been easy, meeting here was not: by law, humans, with one exception, had to remain on the island of Mospheira.

Rules were different on the space station, where humans and atevi worked together all the time. But down here—well, the world had reasons. So he plotted, and he looked for ways that would not shock the aishidi'tat, or break laws.

He and his human associates might meet on a boat . . . that had been a hope. It still was. There had just been no chance for it yet. They had to get used to their new home and living on a planet instead of inside a ship, and he . . . he had to finish remodeling his household, catch up on his studies . . . and get Boji established safely in his new and lifelong home.

But they would find a way, a way which would not break rules or cause unnecessary worry to his parents . . . or his household. He had to consider such things now more than ever. Father had recently declared him officially heir, and that meant he was more a target of people with bad intentions than he had been before. It was because of that increased danger that Father had doubled the size of his aishid—which had meant more rooms, more staff, more people to think of. . . .

And Father had trusted him to make those arrangements, for all he was only fortunate nine. But it had come to him while making those arrangements, that the increased guard Father had felt he needed were not just Guild, but senior Guild *instructors*, meant to keep them all safe—and safe, among other things, from his less fortunate ideas.

They were all four good men. Rieni and Haniri, cousins, of the ancient Suradi clan. They had taught tactics in the Guild academy, and had impeccable court polish; Janachi was another aristocrat, but he was, of all things, Kadagidi. Kadagidi clan was outlawed for having tried to assassinate Uncle Tatiseigi, and for being linked to the Shadow Guild, but it was not Janachi's doing, any of it, and Father said not to mention it.

Janachi had taught hand-to-hand combat at Guild Headquarters.

And the fourth instructor in the unit, Onami, who really was his favorite, had no remote idea what his birth-clan even was. Onami understood explosives and traps and deviosity.

Together, the four, grey-haired and usually frowning, were beyond a sobering presence in the household, which made things less fun—but he also appreciated that they were a special gift, and protective of him *and* his younger aishid—who had spent so much time protecting him that they had had no time in the Guild to learn how best to do it. Now, after decades spent teaching the highest-level Guild how to stay alive, his four grey-haired bodyguards were teaching him and his young aishid and even the domestics how to defeat all sorts of trouble.

They had brought a certain sobriety to the household, which made for a little less laughter. But only a fool would challenge them in doing the things they *could* do. And they would keep his younger aishid alive until they could keep themselves alive. That function, above all others, convinced him.

Father, of course, had assigned them here. Personally. Being Father's son, he had been in danger of one sort or another all his life: that was just who he was. But he had done some truly foolish, reckless things in his life, trusting that he knew more than he did. Mani had said once, on the starship, that *that* was who he was as well, which had confused him, but when he had asked her what she meant, she had said to ask his father . . . the implication of which he had not thought of until now.

But adventures were all in the past. The older he grew, and especially now, being officially Father's heir, the worse the consequences to the aishidi'tat from the mistakes he could make. He knew that, too, and he would try, *really* try not to do foolish things anymore.

Father would not be at all pleased if his heir got himself assassinated.

Not so long ago, maternal Grandfather had gotten himself assassinated—not Father's doing, he was sure, though he hesitated to ask, for his mother's sake. But he truly believed it was the Shadow Guild's doing. Grandfather had betrayed Father and Mother, and mani, and him and all of Ajuri clan, and entirely deserved what had happened, on principle. He had changed sides one too many times, that was what, and *might* have been killed by finally doing something right, so he might deserve some respect for that. . . .

But whatever the cause, Grandfather was dead and Father and Mother and Uncle . . . and even mani . . . were all searching up the answers for what had gone on in Ajuri and how to fix things—in which cause, mani had kidnapped new-found cousin Nomari to go on this train ride with her, a train ride which had turned out to be about far more than just Grandfather's doings.

He knew *he* had done reckless, foolish things, but mani was running all sorts of risks going on this trip, and scariest of all, she was doing it without him, which meant she would take even *more* risks because when he was along, she thought of *his* safety, if not her own. He was very glad to hear the Red Train had crossed into safe territory, that Great-grandmother and nand' Bren were well out of Senjin province and nearly out of Maschi territory: halfway home. They were still with cousin Nomari, a good thing; and without Lord Machigi, which was also a good thing so far as he was concerned. . . .

If only he was certain they were leaving all their danger behind.

Father was extremely worried about Great-grandmother. The Red Train had left Koperna even before the fighting was done, headed west, but for days now, she had not wanted to communicate. Cenedi had said only, She is resting. She is resting. She is resting. No, she has given orders. I cannot wake her.

Cajeiri had heard all this himself, just this last hour. He had been in Father's office hoping to speak to Great-grandmother, too. But Cenedi had refused, after which Father had used language he did not ordinarily use, but not to Cenedi. Just to mani in her absence, after Father had closed the connection and put down the phone.

"Is she ill, do you think?" Cajeiri had ventured to ask, not because he could not guess for himself that she had exerted herself too much and made herself ill, but because he wanted Father to say something sensible and wise and tell him it was all better than that.

"I think she is too *old* to be doing this sort of thing," Father had said. "She has been a pillar of the sky for so long she makes no plan that involves *me*, let alone another generation. She will never *retire* from this life, never facilitate a smooth transition of power. She will drop out of the sky like a thunderbolt, damn the wreckage it generates!"

"She cannot die!" The words came out unplanned, unguarded, unwise, the worst of all his fears. And the unluckiest.

"She will give *us* no fair notice of it, if she is wobbling on the brink," Father had said, and then reached out and laid a hard hand on his shoulder. "Do not say any of this to staff, do you understand, son of mine? We cannot afford uncertainty, least of all about the situation in the south. It is not just the problems there. The space station is in absolute crisis. Lord Geigi cannot stave panic off much longer. Five thousand humans *must* be gotten down from the station as soon as that can be managed, or systems up there *will* begin to collapse, thanks to the disorder among that population. They have to come down *now*, they have to come down in some orderly fashion, and they have to be made orderly *here*, because the peace cannot bear a governmental crisis on Mospheira. War in the Marid? That was coming—that has *been* coming for the last hundred years, though gods less fortunate! your great-grandmother *could* have waited 'til spring for this."

"Father,—"

"Listen to me. We have the unknown dimensions of your great-grandmother's new-made agreements with Hasjuran, Senjin, *and* the Taisigin, not to mention her promised railroad to Machigi's capital, and all *he* will try to wring out of it. These agreements have been signed, but not yet filed. We have not even *seen* them. The official archive documents will be sent down from Hasjuran, as soon as we can get a train up there and back— when they *ought* to have been brought down in the Red Train, *directly* after they were signed. All these will have to be managed, with *or without* your great-grandmother. *Listen* to me and stop objecting. This you do not know. The lord of the Dojisigin, Lord Tiajo, has deserted her people. She has escaped, with the chief officers of the Shadow Guild, has gotten out of the Marid.

Days ago—by ship, along a route Dojisigin traders ordinarily take. Her destination is beyond a doubt where that route ends, Jorida Isle, in Ashidama Bay."

Cajeiri knew about Jorida. Jorida Isle dominated Ashidama Bay. Jorida Isle had two main trade connections: one to the Marid in general, and the other with Cobo, the main port of the northern aishidi'tat.

It was one of those dull old geography lessons turned significant, no longer a matter of memorizing answers like what products Ashidama Bay produced or imported. This situation was real, imminent and serious. The Marid's most profitable shipping all ran to Jorida, and Ashidama Bay, on which the aishidi'tat relied for grain and game and fiber and a long list of commodities very boring to memorize—

But it was suddenly a very critical problem, if the Shadow Guild began operating on Jorida Isle and took over that supply line.

It was a problem only hours away from Najida . . . where the Red Train was now headed.

"Then Najida is in danger, honored Father. So is Kajiminda. And if the train is going through Najida—if they know Great-grandmother is aboard, and nand' Bren—"

"And what if the Shadow Guild gets there first?" Rather than stop his thoughts, Father added to them. "What if they try to succeed at Najida where the assassin they sent to Hasjuran *failed?*"

"They will not!" Cajeiri protested, and his father's expression became somewhat less grim.

"We trust not. But not too much trust." Father had allowed him to see the concern they shared; then Father continued: "We may rest somewhat more comfortably knowing your great-grandmother has ample Guild to protect herself and those with her. She took, if we are to understand the reports, a third or more of the force she had had stationed in Koperna. Gods less fortunate, she has *field artillery*, if it comes to that, and we earnestly trust it will not."

"But—"

"And *if* she stops at Najida, she will deploy defenses. Or Cenedi will. Get accustomed to it, son of mine. She takes chances. Gods less fortunate, she takes chances like this whenever she wishes. But she is no fool."

"But does she know—?"

"Assuredly she knows. However, son of mine, I have long since had to reconcile myself to the belief that ultimately we shall lose her on one of these flights of ambition. It may be this time. We cannot say. But trust with me that your great-grandmother, *if she is in charge*, does know what we know, and has something definite in mind. Unfortunately, exactly *what* that 'something definite' is, *we* do not know, so we do not know whether to commit yet another regiment of Guild, while we are already stretched thin in the north—or to keep that regiment where it needs to be. She is coming to Najida, and so let her rest—let her take a rural holiday, if only nand' Bren can keep her from opening a second front while we are elsewhere occupied. What she has can defend her."

"Surely, surely, Father, the Shadow Guild will not come with an army. They never do."

"Rely on her if they do, son of mine. She will do as she pleases now, gods less fortunate! Our displacing that creature Tiajo from the Dojisigin to Ashidama is a misfortune to the whole continent, but it has also placed them at *Machigi's* back door, at the very moment of his achieving his ambitions in the Marid. If I had your great-grandmother to hand at this moment, I would point that out to her, with the admonition to leave Machigi *some* ambition yet unachieved, to keep him busy until he becomes *your* problem, son of mine. Never trust that young man. Ever. And never forget that your cousin Nomari took service in that court."

Machigi . . . when he had been worried about Tiajo and Shadow Guild. He was set off balance. Machigi was just scary. Cousin Nomari was another issue entirely. He knew Father had never been entirely happy with Nomari, and he now knew how Nomari had spied for Machigi—Father had told him that part, which Father had found out from nand' Bren.

"So you will not approve him to be lord of Ajuri?" he asked.

Mother would be unhappy if that was the outcome. Uncle Tatiseigi would be. Uncle approved of him, and Uncle, who was Ajuri's neighbor, was hard to please, usually much harder than Father. Worse, the Ajuri fugitives would be upset. They wanted Nomari as their lord. He had been there, had seen how they acted around Nomari.

"We are still thinking," Father said, frowning.

"Cousin Nomari is aboard with mani and nand' Bren," Cajeiri said. "And Lord Machigi has signed with mani and Senjin has signed with Lord Machigi for the railroad. So Lord Machigi already has a lot to keep him busy."

Except—he suddenly realized—mani's proposed new rail link from Machigi's province up to Senjin and Cobo would mean a *lot* of things would no longer go by ship. They could go from Cobo to Senjin and right down to Machigi's port, and then all over the southern Marid, which would be new markets, with *their* products coming up to the aishidi'tat by the same route.

But it would all be done using the rail and *Machigi's* ships. Jorida, which made much of its money by shipping *other* people's product, was going to be *upset* about the new deal with Machigi. *Very* upset. Had mani thought of that?

Of course she would have. *Certainly* she would have. It was impossible to think she would *not* have. Still:

"The new rail is a problem," he said. "Father."

Father gave him an analytical look. A mildly surprised look.

"I do understand, honored Father. I see it."

"Well," Father said with a nod. "So you see why. And what. Good. We have heard railroad, railroad, railroad too often. So, well, she is about to get her dearest wish, and meanwhile we have Jorida poised to become quite annoyed with Machigi, even *without* the added problem of the Shadow Guild moving in."

"Do you suppose that is what Great-grandmother *wants?* Machigi is her ally."

There was a little silence.

"I know that you should not bet heavily on chess with your great-grandmother."

"Am I right?"

"You very possibly are. You and I, son of mine, have had the same teacher."

Mani. Great-grandmother. That was true.

"Meanwhile," Father said, "while she is at Najida, with an ample contingent of Guild, we have Najida secure . . . if she just refrains from adventures that can engage that force, or risk her life. Once rested, we must convince her to return to the capital . . . and *retire*. Most soberly, son of mine, far too much depends upon her. If we lose her in some folly, we have her new agreements with Hasjuran, with Senjin, *and* with Machigi and the entire southern Marid apt to evaporate, that fast. I *trust* she is sensible enough *not* to waste all her prior effort, before we have even mopped up the situation in the Marid. Tiajo and the Shadow Guild elite will be bottled up on Jorida Isle. There is nowhere for them to go. We can watch them. We can keep them there until we have sufficient force free to go in and clean them out, once and for all. *Meanwhile*, son of mine, we have an equally pressing problem here in the north."

The station, he meant. And just like that, they had left mani, Machigi, and the Shadow Guild behind, to move to an entirely different topic. It was enough to make one dizzy. It was, he had suddenly realized, how his father's mind had to work, day in and day out.

"Nand' Bren," Father said, "who did not intend in the least to become involved in the Marid, has his attention divided between the situation in the south and the situation involving the station above our heads, which Lord Geigi is holding together with binding twine and promises. Five thousand humans, three times what the treaty permits, twice what the station can support. Shortages. Hunger, if we delay them. They are overwhelming the water and air."

It was a terrifying situation. He understood. He had been there and knew the conditions in the refugee area.

"Clearly," Father said, "the excess humans must come down in a safe and orderly fashion, and clearly nand' Bren cannot be in two places at once. *Someone* must deal with the landing of these unfortunate humans. Someone who speaks both Ragi and

Mosphei' must deal with them on this side of the Strait, someone who can reassure them, who understands all the problems space folk have, and move them over to Mospheiran hands *without* violating treaties or setting precedents that will trouble us for the rest of time."

Someone who speaks both Ragi and Mosphei'. Suddenly, the shift in topic, his very presence here, began to make absolute sense.

Cajeiri's heart began to beat faster.

"I can, honored Father."

"We are aware."

"Except—not Mosphei'. Mosphei' is different than ship-speak. And the refugee humans use ship-speak. Like my associates on Mospheira. Like their families. *They* could help, too."

"Just so," Father had said. "When we move them across the Strait, your young associates can indeed help. As can their parents. But on this side of the Strait, there must be someone to command both civil authorities and Guild. Someone who represents the aishidi'tat. Someone who knows the law. Someone who can translate in both directions and do so with authority."

"Authority?" That had held a strange weight, beyond simple translation between ship-folk and atevi.

"You have had the privilege to be a child, son of mine. So you might be for years. But once I set you into the public eye, as this will do, you are no longer sheltered and you *will* meet criticism if there is any misstep. Such criticism can last many, many years, and resurface at the most damnable moments. That lesson also you will learn. Are you afraid?"

It was scary. It was scary, because all the business of the clans and the Guilds was involved, and his authority would likely be small. But it sounded as if it would be real. Father talked about consequences and gossip. *That* was scary.

"One would be foolish *not* to be worried, honored Father." He had answered as formally and honestly as he felt his father expected, and Father had nodded.

"Indeed," Father had said. "I hold the aijinate. You know what that means."

"Yes, honored Father."

"Let me explain something to you from where I sit. The day your great-grandmother's hand falls from the staff, you will no longer be heir-apparent. You will be heir-designate. Your mother can never have the power your great-grandmother has, because, unlike your great-grandmother, *she* has a clan, *and* she is guardian-designate for Atageini, when your sister inherits Atageini. So there can be no regency after me, such as your great-grandmother claimed. Your mother knows this . . . knew it when she offered Seimei as heir to your great-uncle. *Atageini* is where her man'chi lies, far more than to the aishidi'tat. She will support you, but she cannot and will not stand *for* you. Should anything happen to me, *you* will be accounted as of age whether you are— or not."

Father was talking about *two* deaths, now, mani's, and his own. And a day that would never, once it was invoked, let him be a child again.

I am only fortunate nine, he wanted to say. As if anyone had forgotten.

As if Father could have.

But if he had to . . . if he ever had to . . . on his own . . . if anything should happen to mani. And Father.

He could reappoint nand' Bren. He would have nand' Bren. And he would have nand' Bren's aishid as well as his own. And Father's and Great-grandmother's, and Lord Geigi would support him—if Lord Geigi were still there—

And within the Guild units behind those three was power enough to hold the treaty with Mospheira; and Great-grandmother's East; and the north—he had Great-uncle, and probably Ajuri.

He *would* appoint cousin Nomari to Ajuri, if it were his decision to make. He had been in Tirnamardi in the recent trouble; his father had not. Mani had not. He had seen Nomari with Great-uncle and with the other Ajuri, and he felt strongly that Nomari had earned a chance to help his people. And if it were Nomari in that lordship, he was confident he *would* have Ajuri, in any crisis.

And Najida, and Kajiminda. And Dur. He could always call on

Dur. And Taiben, because half of his younger bodyguard was Taibeni, and the other half was Maschi. He had made his map, from
earliest days. He had marked his allies with pins in the board. He
had not been a fool in that. Mani had warned him and he had
listened, all that time between the stars, in the great ship. Gathering man'chi was life and death.

And if necessary, he could become mani's heir, claim the
man'chiin mani had held, and help Father to see the Marid settled
as she meant to do. He would see that rail spur completed for her.
He could, *would*, find a way . . .

And he would make certain Machigi was so busy with his new
rail and trade with the East, that he would have no time to be a
problem to the aishidi'tat.

"Yes," he had said into all that silence. His heart beat so hard
he could almost hear it. "But I shall ask advice if anything happens. I will not follow all of it. But I shall ask people like nand'
Bren. And Banichi and Cenedi."

Father's hand rested gently on his shoulder. Father's eyes, paler
gold than anybody's, even Great-grandmother's, seemed to look
into him and dispel all the shadows he owned.

"Good," Father had said. "Well said in that, son of mine. I
shall draw up a paper to formalize the succession and to give you
the necessary authority. You will have a copy. One will be filed
with the Guild. One with the Court Records. But do *not* wait for
the need to utilize that authority to arise. Gather your resources
before it comes—being my son. Hours count in that sort of
change. Remember that. And for now, study the laws regarding
humans, what they may do and see on the mainland, and be ready
to take nand' Bren's place with these refugees."

4

"Less than an hour, nandi," Narani said, handing Bren a cup of tea, and added. "We are now told, *all* the baggage."

"All?" Bren stood out of the way as his staff quickly and efficiently prepared for offloading.

"All," Narani said.

Orders direct from Cenedi, at last? It was unusual enough to be possible. *All* the baggage was hardly necessary: the third wardrobe case held the court clothes they had deemed necessary for Hasjuran . . . one hardly needed that degree of dress for Najida.

Which was blessedly close. The train had found smooth track last night, and used it, making excellent time. He sat down smoothly, no longer fearing a jolt.

"Have we been told, then, how long we are staying?"

"Two days, nandi, is the latest report."

Infelicitous two? That was unusual. With all the wardrobe cases? And strangely ominous—two. The dowager despised 'counters, but *two days*, especially for public notice, was not in any sense usual.

"Have we called Ramaso?" It was far from a given that they would have called his Najida major domo, Najida's communications being far from secure, and their operation being obsessed with security all during this trip. But if they were to have the bus for transport, they should have done that. Someone should have done that.

"Not that we have been told," Narani said. "We do know it is still raining. The front has stalled at the coast, and we are headed into the heart of it."

Which did nothing to allay the greatest of the post-dream fears that had greeted his waking mind. If Ramaso was able to report and send the bus, it would prove some Shadow Guild operation had *not* taken over Najida in anticipation of their arrival. They *should* call if they were not to use the limited transport they had with them—the market truck was not suitable for the dowager. The fact that Najida had no secure coms was irrelevant. If the passage of the Red Train with an uncommon number of passenger and freight cars was not enough to advise the world at large that some personage was arriving at Najida station, the world was not paying attention.

And those of most concern, the Shadow Guild, would know *exactly* who was on this train.

He was *worried*, damn it. The Edi were *his* people and *his* responsibility. They had, he hoped, come to trust him, and now he arrived without warning and with the worst possible element on his tail.

With what they had taken on at Koperna, they now had an entire Guild force aboard, extra cars, tents, communications . . . artillery . . . and he could think of no better disposition of them than to set it all down at Najida on an extended deployment. There was a flat area suitable for a camp . . . at least he thought so—a protection against whatever might be brewing on Jorida Isle. The Guild just had to sit here keeping things from happening until Tabini's forces could join them, and together and on their own schedule, they could deal with whatever had happened down in Ashidama.

Just keep the trouble bottled up. That was all they needed to do.

That was *his* expectation, and, dammit, if *she* had thoughts on the matter, she could damned well talk to him. Or Cenedi could to talk to Banichi, who was technically Cenedi's second-in-command in this operation.

But the only word thus far out of Cenedi was to offload all the damned wardrobes.

Oh . . . and it was raining. Had *been* raining. Of *course* it was raining.

His neck ached from last night, he was still tired, still muddled, and still unhappy with himself, that he had brought this trouble home with him.

Issues unresolved, that was the problem. Were they staying or were they going?

His staff at Najida had a right to hear from him, but *they* were still under communications silence. The Transportation Guild would call—

No they would not. *Could* not. Damn the communications blackout. It was possible, Najida station being generally unmanned, that Ramaso had *no* idea the train was even coming.

How were they to get transport?

Someone had to call Najida on regular com. It was a damned long hike, even for him. The dowager certainly could not travel in one of the runabouts.

Was she even in charge? Was it possible Cenedi was giving *all* the orders?

It was even possible the Red Train was dumping every car *but* hers to take her on to the medical facilities in Cobo as quickly as possible.

God. But why offload the wardrobe cases, which could as easily sit on the train? He had clothes in his own closet in Najida estate.

He should make that call, security be damned. They were within his province. It was his area, and his Edi major d', Ramaso, was very apt to forget his fluency in Ragi if unreasonably pushed by Ragi authority.

"Banichi-ji, we will need the bus and the truck. Is there *any* relaxation of the order for silence?"

Thunder boomed, over the racket of the train.

Banichi said, "Cenedi said he would call."

That was a relief. And not. It *was*, damn it, still his province, his staff, *his* train station, and *his* aishid that was being ordered about with no grace of an answer to previous questions, as if *their* loyalty or competence could be an issue.

Anger. Yes.

But there was also a leaden concern. One sort of thing might rate this kind of silence, that thought that had begun to gnaw at him last night—if Ilisidi *had* died. That news would have to be kept absolutely quiet until they could get to the capital. It might even warrant letting the lord of Najida . . . and a large number of Guild . . . off at Najida, while the Red Train made a different sort of run north.

If Cenedi was acting on Tabini's orders—

No. That was absolutely excessive. Tabini would never keep him ignorant. And Cenedi *could* be a damned pain—especially under her orders. *She* had to be in charge . . . which was *why* they were getting nothing from Cenedi.

Which brought him right back to *why?* Was she just generally set on her way and consulting no one, avoiding any and all interference with her intentions? Or was he being shut out because he had failed in—whatever she thought he should have done?

In Koperna, he had had his orders from her. She had sent *him* to Bregani's home to represent those orders, allowing her to stay in the relative safety of the train—with all her aishid. And under his administration of the situation, Bregani's daughter Husai had been kidnapped, Nomari had eluded his guard and disappeared— to turn up later—and they had made a deal with a scoundrel. It had all worked out eventually, but the cap on it all, none of his fault, had been Tiajo's escape from Amarja, capital of the Dojisigin, accomplished before they had even left Hasjuran . . . so she could not blame him for *that*. But *might* she have sent one of her two naval ships after that fugitive ship . . . had her grandson not stolen one of the warships she had stolen from him and moved it out of Koperna harbor to block the Dojisigin port? Both ships were thus engaged: neither was available to pursue Tiajo, Tabini having decided to take on the Dojisigin while she dealt with Senjin.

But did she remotely think the paidhi-aiji had had any part in Tabini's move?

Did she believe he had known from the start that Tabini would send a train full of Guild speeding past them in Hasjuran, or that

Geigi would send down that lander, complete with a new, secure communication system—which allowed Tabini to order things from the convenience of his office in Shejidan, and take over *her* operation?

He had not expected any of it. Nobody had warned him of any of these things. None of them were *his* doing. And it was not his fault that Tabini's force was currently pummeling the hell of out whatever supporters of the Shadow Guild could still be found in the northern Marid—while the core of the problem spread to the west coast.

Tabini was finishing Ilisidi's war for her, outright taking over *her* operation as well as one of her ships . . . and *she* had pulled out of Koperna before the gunfire had even died away.

Not running from the fight, never Ilisidi.

Going after that escaped ship, he had no question, the train being what she had for pursuit.

And shutting out the paidhi-aiji ever since. Not receiving him. Not listening to him. Not trusting him with her plans, even knowing, *knowing*, damn it, how much those plans would affect *his* responsibilities at Najida—

And that might be the point, might it not? He was not atevi, might not have the overwhelming, gut-deep drive to protect his own. She did.

More of that gut-deep emotion, that primal drive, than she admitted to.

As he—gut-deep—came at the same conclusion by a different route, with different wiring, different imperatives. Did she think he would fail to—

Care in its diverse senses did not even translate well into Ragi. Trying to equate what she felt with what he felt stepped right off the logic of it all into that vast gulf between what was atevi and what was human.

She was going to do something. Days of dogged movement across a long, badly maintained rail said that if she was still in command, she was either mad at Tabini or set on pursuit—or both.

She just did not want *him* making calls to Tabini. That had been clear. Could she—thunderbolt of a convoluted thought—possibly think that *he* had had one of those new communication units all along and was still using it?

It was possible, as she might see it, that Tabini had handed him one of those units before he left Shejidan. He had understood *Cenedi* had gotten them from Tabini's force, when the train stopped to watch the landing . . . but that did not preclude Tabini having given him one earlier, before he ever boarded in Shejidan.

Certainly the operational shift onto the new network all had been pre-planned, somewhere, dependent on Geigi getting a lander down to do that job. But *he* had not been in on that planning, not in the least. He had been one of the *least* knowledgeable individuals in the whole operation, with the possible exception of Nomari and Bregani. . . .

But in her reckoning, it could be. He *could* have such a unit. Cenedi had not gone so far as to order a search of his premises. She had stopped short of that.

And if he *had* such a unit, he could have known things about Tabini's operation, being in Tabini's confidence, that even Cenedi might not know.

God. It was ridiculous. If she truly believed that he would deceive her, after all this time . . .

But no. If she believed he and his aishid had crossed her, he would not be standing here a free man.

Perhaps she was supposed to have stayed up in Hasjuran. Perhaps she was *not* supposed to have taken the Red Train, with all its equipment, down that horrendous grade. Tabini had certainly not been ignorant that two-thirds of his naval force supposed to be in the Strait, official barrier between human Mospheira and the atevi mainland, was headed instead for the Marid.

Perhaps she was not supposed to have made the move on Bregani, turning him from adversary to ally.

If one removed Bregani and Koperna from the operation, the lander could have come down, the new communications system could have gone into operation, leaving her informed, but safe, in Hasjuran . . . to simply reverse the Red Train and go tamely, safely back to Shejidan, her part in the operation done.

But before they had ever left Shejidan, she—he was fairly sure it was she—had sent a well-equipped force to Koperna, ready to attack or aid Bregani, in the guise of a train needing service.

She had directed the two warships south. Tabini had *let* that happen, possibly because Tabini had decided he was going to use them. Tabini could not have missed that move.

He took a deep breath. He was letting his imagination run wild. It could drive one just a little crazy trying to track the chess game those two played every day of their lives.

They were coming in at Najida, that was all. The whole mad operation at Koperna was over. The train was going to stop. Things were going to sort out. She would give orders—there was no chance anyone else was going to. They could get ahead of—whatever was going on down in Ashidama Bay. Ilisidi and Tabini were both wrought. That had happened before. There would be time to work it all out.

Another deep breath . . . a deliberate sip of the sugared tea.

He had dressed as far as his shirt and trousers and an older pair of boots. The coat could wait until they were ready to leave the train—he was reasonably confident they *would* leave the train, though there might be—he hoped there would be—a simultaneous offloading of equipment for the entire Guild force. Tents. Field pieces. Ammunition. It all might be setting up by the time Cenedi used some roundabout means to contact Ramaso, perhaps asking Tabini's office to make the call, if they wanted to maintain themselves opaque to observers—and settle them comfortably at his own estate. Thick, wonderful mattresses. Floors that did not shake.

No, it was going to go as it had to go, things would finally make sense, and he was relatively sure he would not escape the bulletproof vest on this short trip: indeed, yes, there it was, hanging with the coat. Considering the general situation, and all the other pieces milling about in confusion, he did not plan to complain about it.

Hopefully he could talk Ilisidi into more than an infelicity of two days' stay and allow everyone to get some *real* rest. Take time to brief Ramaso about the potential trouble south of them, and possibly, if they could gain a few extra days, set up a situation that let *him* be free to answer Geigi's needs. Granted Geigi would be needing him to be up at the spaceport; it was a straight run up to Cobo and a shorter one to the spaceport, actually closer from Najida than from Shejidan. There was that in favor of his being here.

Hopefully, too, Ilisidi would be content just to keep Tiajo contained in Ashidama until the mess to the east was mopped up and the saner heads who accompanied Tiajo had time clearly to contemplate their future, and their best options. He had far rather negotiate the Shadow Guild out of Jorida than try to remove them by force. Deals could be made—amnesties, untidy as that would be, granted the damage they had done—mercy not for the Shadow Guild's sake, but for the sake of innocents in the way of future action. It was very much the Shadow Guild technique—hostage-taking. Living shields. And moves that generated terror and disruption.

Mercy put the legitimate Assassins' Guild at a disadvantage in dealing with them. But given the situation—the Shadow Guild might rather live than be hunted down.

He could put it to them that way. He would *enjoy* putting it to them that way.

"The bus is coming," Algini said, drawing everyone's attention. Algini's earpiece had evidently found some confirmation on the ops feed. They had been getting nothing from Cenedi. "The market truck is also coming."

Bren paused with teacup in hand, so long that Narani began to hover by, anxious to take it before he outright spilled it. He surrendered the cup and stood up.

"Well," he said, about to say that he was relieved.

Thunder boomed right overhead. Nerves assaulted by the explosion up in Hasjuran—twitched.

"Personnel will board the bus," Algini continued, unperturbed. "The truck will be a little late. It was on the far south side of the peninsula."

On Kajiminda Bay, that was to say, ferrying supply, perfectly ordinary activity. The Edi were building on the end of Kajidama, and moving material over from Najida: Lord Geigi had granted the Edi more land on Kajiminda, and the market truck, as well as the earthmover and Bren's yacht, were frequently in service to their needs. The ordinary reality of Najida asserted itself, a balm to frayed nerves.

A second thunderclap.

"Dare one guess it is raining?" Bren asked, in dour levity.

Jago cast a glance up at their tiny patch of sky, midway across the car. "Pouring," she said, and more cheerfully: "But not snowing."

It never did, on the Southwest Coast. It might be chill, but it would never be snowing. In Hasjuran they had been up to their knees in it.

"*Will* the dowager disembark?" he asked. "Do we have word on that?"

"She will," Banichi said. "We shall go in the first lot, with Cenedi's unit. We will move all principals in the first run, some staff in a second."

So, not a wholesale dumping of rail cars to speed the dowager north. His gut untwisted another notch.

Seven seats for him and his household, not counting Bindanda; nine for the dowager and her aishid, eleven counting her physician, Siegi, and her attendant, Asimi. Nomari, without his assigned guard, though they would likely accompany him to the bus door. That left seats . . . and only two other potential "principals."

"Homura and Momichi," he said. "Are *they* coming?"

"That is the question," Tano said dryly.

"That will be Cenedi's call," Banichi said.

"Better they be with us," Bren muttered. Their guard was, to be precise, under Cenedi's command. And best that pair be under watch while bodies were shifting about.

As for comforts, all the regular staff would be there to greet them, preparing rooms and meals. It was possible Ramaso was only now summoning staff from Najida village to come to duty— there was no knowing how much warning he had had. One *hoped* the new network had taken care of that mundane matter some time ago, ending in a perfectly ordinary phone call from the Bujavid, advising Ramaso to bring in staff and turn on the lights.

With the possibility that could be intercepted, the sort of risk they always had, but with heightened security on this trip, Ramaso and staff might have gotten very short notice. That was no matter. Najida was secure. Kajiminda, likewise under Edi management, would be. And their enemies aboard those Dojisigi ships might have reached Jorida, but they would not yet be well set up—one hoped.

All the same, an abundance of caution, reckoning that there might have been operatives on Jorida long since, was decidedly in order.

There was that hill near the station, part of the foothills of the Southern Mountains, to the north, and another to the east, a perfect spot for spies . . . or snipers with a death wish. That had not been as high a consideration when Ilisidi's engineers had sited the train station.

Guild would cover what the wooden barriers did not. It was just a matter of crossing the platform to the steps with fair dispatch. It was always a worry—more or less so—depending on current politics, but it gave his mind something to worry about.

He could deal with the dowager's displeasure. Given the configuration of the train it had been impossible to gain access. In Najida estate, it was nearly impossible to avoid contact, in one sense or another.

And the jolting and racket would have ceased. That, above all else. Everybody would benefit.

He consulted his watch out of habit—discovered it set and wound: *not* by his hand.

Late afternoon. Was that right?

Supper? He could not remember when or whether he had had breakfast.

In the real world, dinner would be far along in preparation. A Najida dinner. He was not sure he had the capacity for it. But it was the first chance at sociality they had had since Koperna, and could go far toward setting the tone for the rest of their stay, however brief.

A dinner. Brandy. An update from Ramaso, perhaps more from him to Ramaso, but not necessarily so.

A sane conversation with the dowager . . . would be a welcome relief.

Information. She would tell him things Cenedi would not.

Another brandy. Stiff one, if you please.

Then sleep . . . on a bed that did not shake.

The rail approaching Najida from the north, he knew down to every bump and jolt; he knew all the routine of arrival—but the route they now used, coming from the west, was, frustratingly, a cipher to him.

At least it was well-maintained track as they neared the station—a brief flirtation with proper speed before they slowed. And by the thunder and the persistent wash of water over that little patch of visible sky, one could forecast an extremely soggy arrival. The station had a new concrete strip to afford dry footing for the bus this year, and a loading ramp for the market truck so no one had to haul freight up the old incline. He had not seen the new arrangement yet, but it should have been done. The estate had been planning to pour concrete. Weather permitting, it should be done, and with luck, they would not have to wade in mud to get to the bus. They could just descend from the train level into a forest of wooden pillars and step from clean new concrete onto the bus.

With very little exposure on the platform. That was a good thing.

Preparation belonged to his staff and his bodyguard, all the coordination with Cenedi's staff, all the matter of the bus and the reception at the house. There was nothing for him to do but be sure of the location of his briefcase, his computer, and Narani's book, then settle on the bench seat at the dining table and wait while his staff released the massive wardrobe cases that, bolted to the wall and decking, had served as closets. Those would go into the passageway to be loaded with the baggage. Tano and Algini had a set of cases to go with them. Jeladi had a valise.

Jago ventured a look out into the corridor, then came back to stand beside Bren's table, her mere presence helping to set his roiling thoughts to one side. They were lovers, so to speak, except in public view—the Ragi word was *biseti*—which otherwise meant *unofficial*: everyone on his staff knew it, and there was no formality, not even so much as Banichi observed. But they had not been together on the train, or between-times: it was just not what they did in such a lack of privacy.

"The bus will be there when we arrive," she said, in her calm, matter-of-fact tone. The train lurched a little. "There is that hill overlooking the station, always a small worry—today a larger one. The decision is to have the bus between us and that vantage. A precaution. We will be exposed briefly on the platform."

"So we will need to move." He would not have been surprised had the Guild delayed them to take possession of that hill, close, steep, and wooded.

"Cenedi's orders," she said with a shrug. "There will be live bodies around her. There will be ours, around *you*, Bren-ji."

"I protest. I have no desire to have any of my aishid intercept a bullet. You know, we might wait until the hill is cleared."

"Cenedi is determined, as it seems." Jago shrugged, not happily. "Possibly Cenedi has consulted at length with Lord Geigi. He can see things despite the weather. As to what size and type of things—we are not sure. But we are moving."

It had the flavor of Ilisidi's own orders. Her breakneck approach to situations. God, they were here. There was no need to push.

"And we," Jago said in measured tones, "will have you as our priority. We have made that clear."

God. Had Cenedi dared to suggest otherwise? It went beyond everything he understood about aishid. Still . . .

"One believes the aiji would rather have his grandmother back than me, Jago-ji."

"We," Jago said, "have only *one* priority. And we shall hope Cenedi is right. That that ship has not had time enough to get its own situation in order, granted Jorida does not welcome them all with flowers and ribbons. If anyone is out there in this downpour, they are likely Ashidama's own spies."

Jorida did keep an eye on comings and goings at Kajiminda and

Najida, never obtrusive, mostly limited to the old market road, mostly interested in the trains that went to Senjin and back. The Taisigi took a dim view of intrusions south of here, in their hunting range. But intrusions happened, and sometimes, poaching there being too risky, hunters ventured up into the foothills to the north of Najida station. It was technically Maschi hunting range up there. Operationally, it was a region of rock and scrub set aside for wildlife.

"One hopes," he said. "Sit, Jago. We have time, yet."

"What you will be glad to know," Jago said, settling onto the facing bench, "the Guild force will be offloading."

"She has ordered deployment?"

"*He* has ordered deployment. Artillery. The mobile units. Everything."

He. Cenedi. Significant distinction. Meaning *only* Cenedi's name appeared on the orders.

He sensed increasing distrust between Cenedi and his aishid. Understandable, but he wondered if he should address it.

"That *is* a relief," he said cautiously.

Jago's face gave nothing away. "How long the force will stay, *he* may know, but we do not. It will certainly not go back aboard tonight. We are deploying to the south of the station, beside the road. And—" She paused, pressed her earpiece. "We now have a team moving, taking possession of that hill."

A wave of relief passed through him. It bothered him, that hill. Had he chosen the place for Najida station, it would have been a little further south—if he had anticipated times like this one. But he had not had that choice. It was what it was.

And the fast-moving mobile units being offloaded—there were five of those—would mean flexibility in their stance, with heavier equipment, and the ability to get a team up on that hill. It was, overall, excellent news.

"I shall do what I can to see the Guild stays here," he said. "I had rather see her back in Shejidan; and I have to be in Cobo in short order, but Najida's safety will be a consideration."

"That is *our* assumption," Jago said. "Command is lifting the silence in the deployment as of a quarter hour from now. Com will be restored to routine operations and ordinary chatter. For our enemies' benefit."

Normal noise was being restored. Under strict discipline. Let the Shadow Guild hear what they would expect to hear . . . a camp being set up. All of it.

High command would have a different information stream. All of that was well and good. Reality was another matter. Reality was what they were going to sort out when they got off the constant rattle and shake of the train, had stable ground under their feet, and, one hoped, a restoration of face-to-face communication.

With just one chill, rainy, too-exposed spot to get through first.

"I assume Headquarters knows this. I assume Tabini-aiji does." A breath. "This is insane, Jago-ji. Have we *any* sense what is going on next door?"

Jago gave a slight shrug. "We have no idea. If things have come to a crisis with her, he will follow her orders above those of the Guild *or* Tabini-aiji—have no doubt. And why Banichi should be shut out of communication we do not know."

"*I* might be the reason." He voiced his concern for the first time.

"Bren-ji, she can have no complaint of you."

"I could have stepped left in Koperna, where she would have stepped right. One has no idea."

"She has never been resentful of you, Bren-ji. You were set in charge in Koperna. Decisions were made. They worked. There is no reason at all to think this silence is against you."

He looked at the empty teacup before him, and recalled another cup, in the drafty, medieval fastness of Malguri, in a hall unblessed by electricity or fan-driven heat. "Still, things in the Marid have not gone all to her liking, and I am not sure what I could have done to anticipate . . ."

"With information withheld, even from us," Jago said, "*even from us*, Bren-ji, only Cenedi knew what she intended. She can have no complaint. *You* certainly did not enable Tiajo's escape. It happened before we descended from Hasjuran."

"The leaders having escaped the net," he said, "one wonders what they brought with them to Jorida. Not the nicest of their followers, one is certain."

"We may have numbers from Lord Geigi. And from our force in the Dojisigin—more information. The Master of Jorida will know useful things if we can make contact with him, which is what we would attempt, were we in Cenedi's place. We do *not* expect a major move on Najida at this time. A tactical force to try and take out the dowager . . . or you . . . is our deepest concern at the moment. The Shadow Guild moves by individuals. By stealth. One does not catch them in the field. We anticipate a period of offers—negotiation between the Master and Suratho: the Guild might well prefer to enlist him and dispense with Lord Tiajo and her whims of the hour—but not yet, is our opinion. The Master is no fool, by reputation, and Tiajo certainly is. They know her, they know how to control her, but a fool is a fool and of limited use. *If* he is still alive, the Master will, we think, negotiate and cooperate—at least for a time. He is reputed to be intelligent. He *may* be smarter than they are."

"And being here, this is our window in which we can do something about them. They will need time to rebuild, if that is their aim, to plan their revenge, if they decide all hope is lost. Granted we have an opportunity, but the timing, Jago-ji. The *timing*. With every Guild resource concentrated in the Marid, Ajuri with a lord yet to confirm, Kadagidi vacant and scattered, the Padi Valley down to one reliable, experienced lord, and *he* as old as the dowager, not to mention the difficulties of five thousand refugees with a history of riot and disorder literally hanging over our heads . . . At times I feel I am standing on quicksand. We do not have infinite time to deal with any of these things."

"We have the Shadow Guild uprooted, stripped of resources and as yet unplanted. Jorida, if they take it, has the *economic* power it has wielded for a thousand years—but has no Guild, no force, no weapons to speak of. Without the Master to manage Jorida, the Shadow Guild has no trade to produce funds for their bribes. Ammunition and food, they can steal, but they need backing. The Master *could* win them away from Tiajo. He might try.

But what would he gain? The question is whether the Master's goals are in any wise compatible with theirs."

"Machigi's rail line," Bren said, out of a sudden realization.

Jago looked at him.

"The commonality, Jago-ji," Bren said. "Jorida has made its fortune monopolizing the sea trade, but with Bregani allied with Machigi and rail connecting their two capitals, that monopoly's days are numbered. The Dojisigin is in major disruption. With Tiajo . . . and more importantly, Suratho . . . out of the way, it would take very little for some disgruntled leader to rise up in the Dojisigin and *back* the aishidi'tat forces, rallying a significant number of the citizenry to join him in a new regime—even joining the aishidi'tat. Resurrect that old rail line into Dojisigin, repair relations with Senjin, trade by rail, and Jorida's cash flow is entirely gone. That is leverage."

"But not for years," Jago said. "While that rail is being built, while the lines from Dojisigin to Najida are repaired, Jorida's near monopoly remains. —Possibly through the Master's lifetime. It is possible that is all that matters to him."

"The Marid can begin to ship direct to Cobo. That is a stroke of the aiji's pen. We can dry up their funds. And benefit new trading partners in the Marid."

"There is one more trade," Jago said, "in corrupting man'chi. Illicit trade. They have been brokering artifacts from the Southern Continent for years. High value, small bulk. Drugs. We saw a sample of that in Koperna. If that ship is carrying more than Shadow Guild stowed in it, if they have been collecting those objects for years, doling them out at need . . . Suratho could win her way quietly, without openly challenging the aishidi'tat, and rebuild. If it funds the Master of Jorida—both sides of that transaction can be happy, before the railroads begin to dominate. Continue that trade as a cover for his second set of books. Unrest among his people? The Shadow Guild can take care of that. It would not be a good neighbor to Kajiminda and Najida."

"It is only scarcely so now. The commerce in fruit sustains Kajiminda. Najida ships its own fish by rail."

"Poverty," Jago said, "makes Shadow Guild recruitment easier.

And Ashidama could become a new Marid for them, with much greater access to the provinces of the aishidi'tat. All they need is a few years. And the threat of the railroad and the pressure of changes in the Marid would only hasten the conditions that send them recruits."

It was a bleak outlook on the situation, one in which time was not an asset. He knew all the pieces of the things Jago said. And three more, that Jago had not mentioned: the absence of Lord Geigi from Kajiminda, the old, old resentments of the Edi at having been removed from Mospheira and settled on this coast to enable humans to live there, and the issue of the Edi having supported themselves in poor years by wrecking Ashidama ships on their rocks.

"There is certainly plenty of resentment to feed the situation," he said, "with the Edi."

"And the Shadow Guild excels at sowing chaos. Staging attacks on the Townships to appear Edi in origin might make their presence more welcome. Present themselves as protection."

"Machigi's hunting range extends clear to Ashidama," he said. "Ample opportunity for mischief there. If Ashidama goes a bad direction, Machigi *would* act—but I would not depend on him to take care of Jorida, if the Master cooperates. One cannot see a future for Tiajo taking power in Ashidama, except as a figurehead."

"She may already be food for fishes. One cannot imagine she has been pleasant on the voyage, and what use has she, outside the Dojisigin?"

"Suratho might need her to gain entry in Jorida, but nothing beyond that unless she can rapidly make herself key to the Master's approval. Even if Tiajo survives as a figurehead, Suratho will do the negotiating. But there is no way Suratho can make herself a lord."

"Of a kind, she is," Jago said. "*She* owns the man'chi of the Shadow Guild, not Tiajo. But she has no way to attract the man'chi of merchants, honest or otherwise. And I have never heard that the Master is other than a merchant, not lordly, but not ill-served, either. He has real power. And he knows with whom he trades. This is not the man Suratho would hope to deal with, but he is the man she will *have* to deal with, and persuade. Trinkets will not win him. This was never the situation with Tiajo, who is asi-man'chi, and nothing would ever improve that."

Asi-man'chi. A dimension of that emotion humans did not and *could* not grasp in atevi terms. Self-absorbed did not remotely describe it. Psychopath came closer. With, in this case, a taste for whatever glittered.

One began to grasp the significance in that—that Tiajo had a position, hereditary, over the Dojisigi, which gave her the power she had wielded, and the Shadow Guild had enabled her to maintain it. But Tiajo was not going to impress anyone in a region where that hereditary office was meaningless. A proper leader, capable of inspiring man'chi, might emotionally influence others. Tiajo lacked that dimension. That *thing* that drew others. Be it pheromones or something less substantial—Tiajo lacked it. Critically. Outside of her hereditary domain—or coldly legal authority—she *had* no power.

"So it is all Suratho," Bren said. "In Jorida, it has to be Suratho."

"If I truly understand Tiajo, that is what it was even in the Dojisigin. Tiajo had the title that legitimized it. Suratho had the power to rule."

Interesting, that. Disturbing. Tiajo was a monster in human terms. He had never dealt with one in atevi terms. Never conceptualized one that simply would evaporate in foreign territory. Why had they kept her? Perhaps to legitimize, coldly, what inherited authority could do, but unless Suratho chose to humor her whims, Tiajo was incapable.

"Suratho," Jago said, "does have what Tiajo lacks. And the economic choice she will offer is potent—considering how Machigi's railroad and the shift of power in the northern Marid will threaten the Master's future income."

"The future." Concern for Ilisidi's health had him thinking in new ways. "One wonders just how far into the future matters to the Master. He has held Ilisidi off for a lifetime. Now he has to deal with someone like himself—with the power, perhaps, but not the paper."

"Power enough to procure paper. One would not wish to trade Suratho for the Master—who has been a relatively modest threat."

He drew in a breath. "One does begin to understand why Ilisidi has pushed so hard to get here. Just as well the Master is looking behind him as well, before accepting Suratho's offer. But that ship will have made it in. Negotiations between the Master and Suratho will have begun—unless he has gone to ground. We cannot precisely sail down in my yacht and ask for a meeting."

"We believe no more than twenty Guild units arrived on that ship. We have forty-two aboard, with what we picked up at Koperna."

"That many?"

"Cars were transferred to the Red Train at Koperna." She gave him a level gaze. "The day we arrived."

"You think she was *planning* to leave Koperna early."

"I think there was no ship of ours in position to counter the one now at Jorida."

"Deliberately so?"

"Possibly. The aiji was the one to move a ship toward Amarja, and by then it was too late: Suratho had already folded resistance in the Dojisigin, removed Tiajo from *her* base of power."

He took a distracted sip of icy tea, the prospect of convincing Ilisidi to retreat to Shejidan getting dimmer by the moment.

"All in all," Jago said, "it was well-done, Bren-ji, what we *have* done. Do not think otherwise. The situation has arrived on the west coast, and the Master is not ignorant who Tiajo is, even if he might not know Suratho. Both leaving the Dojisigin means at the very least the aiji's forces will prevail, and that Bregani will come out well to his advantage in signing as he did. He has every motive to keep his agreements."

"I hope so."

"I am certain." She touched her ear. "We are to stay, the word still is, two days."

"Two days," Bren said, puzzled. It was clearly an infelicity unless something else was implied, and it did not seem so.

"I have no idea." Jago answered the unspoken question.

"She is not going on to Shejidan," Bren said. "I am strongly suspicious it is not two days."

Jago received something over com, and pressed her earpiece closer to her ear. "The bus is here. We are to board as quickly as possible. The truck will follow, under escort."

"Nomari?"

"Will come with us."

"Homura and Momichi?"

Banichi said, from near the door to the passageway: "They are coming, Bren-ji. Cenedi's word."

Homura and his partner Momichi, who had *asked* to go with them out of Koperna. Two former Shadow Guild who were not in the Dojisigin, the most logical place for them to be, if they were truly looking for their two missing partners. Two former Shadow Guild who might believe there was little chance now that their missing partners were still alive. They had wanted to come west, but whether it was to find their partners and rescue them, or to avenge them—was a question.

And Cenedi had said bring them. Into *his* house.

Damn.

The train blew a long blast that, the wind being right, might be heard clear to Najida estate. That, indeed, was a sound he had heard more than once from a different vantage, and he was doubly glad to hear it now.

5

Rain pelted down as the Red Train opened its doors onto the platform and cold, wet air wafted back into the train corridor, along with the sound of the still active engine. The dowager's party was first to exit, and she had emerged from her cabin cloaked and looking, from what Bren could see beyond broad, black-clad atevi shoulders, very much herself.

The line moved—Cenedi and Nawari on either side of her, Casimi and Seimaji in front, and the four others of her guard behind, with Asimi, her maid and dresser; and her physician, Siegi. Banichi and Jago were after that; and Bren was sandwiched behind them, viewless, with Tano and Algini behind.

Behind them, Nomari and his party, then Momichi and Homura and their guards, who were not, properly, an aishid. The line moved out, reached the steps, and the rain, which a brisk wind carried into the train.

A large black umbrella went up, above the dowager. Bren noted it with envy before he made the calculated step—more a jump—down to the boards of the platform, with Banichi and Jago waiting to assure his safe landing.

Fresh air. A faceful of hard rain, wind-borne. Not a concrete and roofed platform such as city stations offered, but an open boardwalk and the guttered eaves of an office and storage.

While the occupants of the Red Train, under ordinary circumstances, might have sat here an hour or more waiting for the rain to stop, as the train refueled and took on water, security concerns indicated no delay.

An umbrella, Bren thought, would have been a grand idea, had any of them except the dowager known to pack for other than snowy Hasjuran. Now with a driving rain beating down and soaking the shoulders of his coat, he necessarily kept to the dowager's pace across the platform, as needs must everyone behind him.

It was indeed evening, a murky grey evening, and the train let off gusts of steam that rose up in clouds from below the platform. Cold rain puddled on the weathered boards faster than the gaps between them could drain it.

Keep moving, was the rule. There was the untrustworthy hill, though the windbreak wall screened them somewhat. The station occupied an otherwise (if one could see it) barren flat beside the turning wye and the water and sand towers. Stairs pierced the broad wooden platform, a descent down to ground level, where they had shelter from above, but no longer had the windbreak, and Nawari, holder of the dowager's umbrella, struggled to maintain it. Bren was stalled for several moments on the top steps of the wind-whipped descent, before they were clear to follow the dowager's company down and enable the ones following them to get under cover.

The modern, sleek estate bus sat below amid clouds of steam, its door open for them. Less visible than the gleaming red bus, the market truck had made it after all. It hulked behind, serviceable old creature, a dim brown presence obscured by its own headlights, upper structure faintly lit by the taillights of the bus.

Rain reached them sideways, intermittent with the warm breath of the steam engine, but there was no hurrying for those stranded on the stairs, neither up nor down. The dowager took a step, paused, then took another, with Cenedi on her right, who supported her now with an arm about her—distressing sight. The intermittent progress stopped altogether, and nand' Siegi, the doctor, pressed forward through her escort.

For several heart-stopping moments, they were utterly blocked. Rain-soaked. Exposed. But that was not the concern for anyone in that dripping line. Every thought was focused on the completely inaudible discussion taking place around the dowager.

They waited. There was no way to see what was happening.

The umbrella completely blocked the view of the center of that black-uniformed huddle.

When they finally began to move again, her black-uniformed bodyguard moved both ahead of and behind her, keeping her slow pace. Bren immediately lost the vantage of the steps, unable to see the dowager or Cenedi past a sea of black-coated shoulders. A low-voiced word from Jago informed him that her personal physician remained beside her, likewise sheltered by the umbrella. Had there been an incident? Was she in difficulty?

He very much feared the answer to that.

God. Was it just the long train ride? Certainly the constant jolting had him aching and short of sleep . . .

Or was it something far more worrisome?

. . . my time to accomplish these things is somewhat less than I would want. . . .

He felt suddenly quite ill himself. Aside from his personal and human affection for her, which she was not remotely equipped to understand—on those thin shoulders rested all the concerns he carried and a thousand more. The agreements she had made with Machigi and Bregani were all new, contrary to precedent, and worse—the ink scarcely dry, so to speak, were hopefully on their way to filing in Shejidan by now. But the future of those agreements was problematic, if anything happened to her. If she should fall, with all her recent and carefully constructed agreements untested, in the Taisigin Marid and all across the transmontane East, and even on the space station over their heads—all those agreements would come into question in a succession, and lords now newly united in those documents would quickly be entertaining any second thoughts they had ever had.

Not just the recent agreements, either. If she were lost, God forbid, all sorts of things would rattle loose. She had no heir but Tabini himself, whose position precluded him holding her title as lord of Malguri—not to mention the fealty of the Eastern lords was bound up in Malguri itself. The stability she had gained there with the aid of the aishidi'tat . . . would go.

And that was only the beginning of what could come unstuck. Years ago, Tabini had taken over the aijinate, but he had, for all practical intents, shared that honor . . . and that power . . . with his grandmother, twice regent and strongly supported by the traditionalists. Atevi politics balanced on a knife's edge of man'chi. How many agreements she had personally had a hand in for three generations would destabilize, if half that partnership in the aijinate suddenly disappeared?

All these things flashed through his mind, cold as the rain coming down on them, as the dowager, who had *just* gotten those assurances and those signatures for another expansion of influence, stopped on the rain-soaked sub-platform, supported by two strong men and attended by her physician. Was she on her feet?

Bodies shifted and he saw her, fully supported on either side, with Nawari's arm having joined Cenedi's about her waist, and Casimi having taken over the umbrella.

Her head came up. She pushed at them, and attempted a faltering step.

God, just pick her up and get her onto the bus.

She would die first.

No. She would *not* die. She could not. He was a heartbeat away from pressing forward past his own aishid, not that he would ever get past Ilisidi's guard. Not that there was *anything* he could do if he did get past. No. He could only watch, along with the rest of the line—including Nomari; including Homura and Momichi. All of them witnessing what was happening, none of them, including himself, knowing what it meant.

She moved then, arranged her own hands, one in Cenedi's, one in Nawari's, and began to walk again. Not rapidly. Not surely. But toward the bus. Casimi passed the umbrella to Seimaji, climbed onto the steps of the bus, and provided her assistance as she climbed up. She disappeared through the door . . . and Bren started breathing again.

Others followed, but slowly, elderly Siegi himself having to be helped aboard.

Bren's heart still raced. He reached the steps himself, behind Jago, gripped the assist bar and with a little push from Banichi, reached the deck of the bus, in time to see Cenedi settle Ilisidi in her usual second row, in the window seat, which was not usual, then remain standing to shelter her from view as well as from the bustle of boarding. Bren followed Jago to his normal seat, opposite Ilisidi, as Tano and Algini moved past to the seats behind him. He settled in the aisle seat, Jago always insisting on the window in chancy situations, and she did this time, while Ilisidi had her aishid around her, front and back, Easterners all, shielding her from the eyes of other, western, Guild.

It was not the way they normally did things. It was not ordinary at all.

When he first had known Ilisidi, Tabini-aiji had told him she was in frail health, threatening to die at any moment. He had long ago decided that that had surely been the line the aishidi'tat *chose* to give to outsiders. The dowager had shown *him* nothing of frailty, from the first cup of tea she had served him.

The woman had ridden to the hunt, for God's sake, down mountainsides. She had nearly killed him on that slope.

But that had been years ago. He tended to forget that. She plotted and moved and generally won, had traveled in space and twice dealt with a species foreign to humans and atevi alike. She had set outright fear into more than one warlord, had set her grandson back in power after a brief overthrow. Just days ago, she had won the allegiance of the provinces of the Marid basin and driven the Shadow Guild into flight by pure strongarm politics.

On the train since, however—the isolation—the silence—

The refusal to answer queries . . .

Days of jolting and racket, a brutal trip even for him.

Granted it was an absolute downpour, and cold, and Najida's isolate, wooden station had no protection, but still . . .

Thunder cracked. The heavens seemed, for the instant, ominous. Terrifying.

Others were boarding the bus now, moving with dispatch. Nomari passed him, alone, his Guild-appointed bodyguard having to wait for the return of the bus. Nomari glanced from the dowager's side of the aisle to him, with worry and a questioning look on his face. Everything in Nomari's life was in suspension. He had been useful to them in the Marid, but he knew nothing yet about the dowager's intentions regarding him; and certainly there was nothing suggesting cheerfulness in his look at the moment. He had surely seen the dowager falter.

The look asked questions.

Bren had no idea. *He* could not reassure the young man of anything. He simply nodded . . . and Nomari moved on to his seat.

After him were Homura and Momichi, who did not look at him, but that might be because they were surreptitiously looking toward the dowager, and getting a dour look from Cenedi. Was it their usual uncommunicative expression, or that they simply wanted to sit down and be invisible for the next while? It was uncertain which.

Their guards were with them, one before, one between, and two behind.

They were the last. The door shut, greatly diminishing the noise of the storm, and Cenedi sat down, giving Bren a brief glimpse of the dowager's diminished, slumped form next the window, head bowed. It never was. But now—

God, give us those few days here, Bren thought, wishing to be moving, wishing to be in the warmth and comfort of the house. There was no grand formality in Najida, just a warm bath, soft beds, excellent, basic food. She could sleep without clan heads or causes or threat of enemies. Two days, she had indicated. Two.

Infelicitous two. The whole request had been ominous—perfectly possible that the infelicity was her wicked humor, designed to get a question from him, the human.

Or a message to the balance of the universe—a damn you to fate or her own weakness. Ilisidi scoffed at the 'counters, firm traditionalist that she was, and wielded others' superstitions with an extremely deft hand. Whatever she meant, it was surely not a surrender—though the cold rain had been, perhaps, just too much for a body at its limit. Whatever comfort Najida could manage for her, he was more than willing. She could rest secure. They had an entire Guild force about to make camp in this deluge, to assure her safety *and* Najida's. For two days.

Three, damn it. A proper three. Superstition had its place in the universe. He would get her to stay. Rest. Recuperate.

If he could not . . . if she, God help them, needed more than nand' Siegi could manage here, then they could leave the bulk of the cars and the Guild force here at Najida, detach the massive weight of the train and simply take the Red Car and the venerable but powerful engine on toward the northern line, on much better track and at far greater speed than they had used reaching Najida. Najida would be protected, with the camp here—besides that they would have removed the principle reason for attack. He need not worry about that.

Above all other concerns now had to be Ilisidi's health.

And somehow, some *way*, he needed to get word of the situation to Tabini. Cenedi might have done it, with the new com system, but God knew what orders Cenedi was under.

As paidhi-aiji, as a civil official, his own ability to command the Guild forces or the Red Train was limited—nothing compared to Cenedi's, in Ilisidi's chain of command. Even Tabini's authority . . . reaching out from Shejidan . . . might not overcome Ilisidi's standing orders, or Cenedi's interpretation of them, because Cenedi, an Easterner, *her* man, was the highest ranking officer present and *he* controlled communication and commanded the force aboard the train.

They could have a serious problem, in that. Banichi might be second in rank here. But pitting one against the other, if he had to. . . .

The door opened. A last Guildsman came aboard, Casimi, one of Ilisidi's. The door shut, as Casimi went down the aisle. The driver, herself an Edi out of the further peninsula, her neat and complicated queue pierced with a carved stick and jaunty strings of beads, her jacket embroidered with ancient patterns, at strong contrast with grim Guild black, put the bus in gear and smoothly set them underway. They turned away from the platform with the rain flooding the window and distorting the familiar landscape. Thunder still muttered, but distant now, as the bus turned past the truck, toward the common road.

Bren glanced to the side. Cenedi was looking at Ilisidi. In the grey light of the breath-fogged window, Ilisidi had her head bowed, perhaps studying something in her lap, perhaps not aware at all.

6

Najida had a fine, broad portico, affording ample room for the bus to deliver its passengers to a dry cobbled surface. The driver pulled up opposite the carved double doors, which were already swinging open to welcome them and pouring out excited staff.

Ramaso, Najida's major d', led the gathering, and Bren saw more familiar faces through the rain-dotted window, past Jago's profile. He reached for the rail of the seat in front, prepared to rise, then pulled back. Ordinarily he would be first to debark, it being his house, his estate, his man who stood waiting below, but he waited; Ilisidi, Cenedi, Casimi, and her people had to take precedence. Nawari and Seimaji blocked any traffic from behind. Bren stood, as Banichi did in front of him, holding his place as the driver opened the door. Casimi and nand' Siegi passed down the aisle and went down the steps first. Ilisidi followed with Cenedi's assistance and Nawari's, a slow progress, with her maid Asimi and others of her party following. She walked. Her gaze did not seem to focus, even yet, and on the steps it was Cenedi's care that got her down safely to Casimi's support, nand' Siegi hovering over them from the steps.

It was not encouraging, not in the least. Bren eased out into the aisle as Jago stood up to follow him, while below the rain-spattered window, Ilisidi and her guards met Ramaso, who respectfully gestured a welcome to the open doors of Najida.

Then for one heart-stopping moment, in view from the

window, Ilisidi seemed again to falter, even to lose consciousness. Cenedi supported her as Bren held his breath.

It was only a moment. Cenedi's arm encircled her. Her head came up. Her hand found Cenedi's, and Casimi passed the collapsed umbrella—there was no need of it under the portico—to Nawari. With Ilisidi between them, Cenedi and Casimi moved toward the doors. Nand' Siegi and the maid, Asimi, came hurrying after them with the rest of her aishid, while Ramaso stood by in dismay. House staff around the doors, usually a happy crowd, instantly gave way and stared after them in silent consternation.

God, what an entry, and in front of all the staff. One wanted to get down there. Quickly. There was no hope of pretending it was other than it was.

But they were an Edi staff. They reported to no one but him, and Ramaso—to the whole rest of the Edi population on Najida, yes, but that was not the news services in Shejidan. The incident would not be gossiped, not on the streets of Shejidan. He would have a word with those aboard the bus on that score. Just not right now.

Banichi waited in the aisle. Tano and Algini had blocked those with Nomari, Homura, and Momichi by taking the aisle. Bren left his seat with Jago close behind, and descended the steps to the cobbles.

Ramaso met him there, the dowager having entered the house. There were no words to explain—there just were not. There were no answers to be offered. House staff, gathered to welcome them in a festive mood, were all standing about, struck silent. Some hesitated at the closed door, uncertain whether to go in and attend the dowager and her guard, or to stay back and hope for orders.

Ramaso stood in the midst of it all, clearly dismayed, likewise uninstructed.

"This has just happened," Bren said, which was the sanest thing he could think to say. "We hope it is simply exhaustion. A long trip. Far too little rest. Her physician is with her. You remember nand' Siegi."

It was not the dowager's first visit to Najida, no. They knew her. They all did.

"They said not to attend, nandi." Ramaso was thoroughly at a loss. "Her room . . . is ready."

"Supply whatever her staff wishes," was all he could say.

The staff stood by, in stunned silence, as the bus began to disgorge strangers.

God, what to say about them? Homura and Momichi were not quite in the category of honored guests. Indistinguishable in uniforms matching those of their guards, they might be mistaken for part of Ilisidi's contingent; not to mention the other problem, well-dressed, with a bodyguard yet to arrive, that was not properly his . . . Nomari, a lord and not a lord, who should not hold any authority beyond ordering his own supper.

It was all far from the usual arrangement.

"Take care of everyone, Rama-ji. This has been a brutal trip. Please offer the dowager whatever we can—assist her physician. Supply his needs first of all. Answer requests from everyone, but with the ones you do not know—the Guild with them is in charge: they themselves, not so."

"I will see to it, nandi." Ramaso waved signals to staff. "We are ready with every preparation. There is cold food, there are fresh linens, there is quiet. A small quick supper now or a large hot one in an hour, whatever you wish."

"One regrets the lack of communication beforehand," Bren said, "but we have been under tightest security, because of the dowager—I could not, Rama-ji."

"We understand. We certainly understand. When we knew you were coming and the size of the party, we simply called everyone to duty. Beds are ready. Tea of every sort. Wine. Brandy. Communications, should you need, nandi. Or whatever the dowager's staff may need. And your staff . . ." Narani, Jeladi, and now Bindanda were in the hall. Those individuals, Ramaso well knew. "We can deal with everything, so your Shejidani staff can all rest and be cared for, if you will. We have the second and third baths heating. And the dowager's guard—one assumes they *are* her guard . . ."

"They are," Bren said. "And that young man a moment ago, that I cautioned about, with his bodyguard yet to arrive, is the presumptive lord of Ajuri. Give him all due courtesy, but his bodyguard and a servant will be arriving in the next busload and they are under Cenedi's command, not his. You can trust them. Please assign two staff to assist him until they arrive. He is to stay in his room until then. In fact, while he is here, if you see him out of his rooms without his guard, observe courtesy with him, but locate them immediately and advise them. And advise my aishid. He is new to his position and sometimes forgets to be cautious." It was the only explanation he could give, but Ramaso seemed to accept it. "The group of six Guild—the first two are under close guard of the last four. If you see *them* out unescorted, notify me and the closest Guild immediately—do not attempt to deal with them."

"Prisoners?"

"Allies, professed," Bren said quietly—atevi hearing was extreme. "They *were* Shadow Guild. Courtesy but extreme caution with them, Rama-ji. Whatever they need in food and clothing: no implements, no weapons. By no means engage them in argument. Report anything untoward with them, even silence. They are Guild. Let Guild handle them. Gently. Gently with them, and courteous. They may try to leave us. Make it inconvenient, but do not risk argument.—I have brought you a collection of difficulties, Rama-ji. I am sorry."

"Nandi. We are concerned. Is there trouble following?"

"There is trouble entering Ashidama, nadi. The Shadow Guild has come there—with what force or what success we do not know—at least one ship. The trouble in the Marid is well toward settling, but it has spilled a very unpleasant mess to the south of us. I am extremely concerned. As the dowager is. These are enemies of the aishidi'tat. The Edi do not deserve this unpleasant gift. The dowager has come here. A large number of Guild are making camp near the station, and they will not permit any harm to come here. Be assured of that. They will come no closer unless we need them, and I hope they will remain, Rama-ji, until this threat is dealt with. I shall try to see to that." It was a great deal to promise. But it had to be. He had to make it so. "Tell the people not to worry about them."

"I will say so," Ramaso said. "We had no idea you were coming until the call for the bus—but we can manage for the house. The people camped—"

"The people camped are not your responsibility, Rama-ji. They will feed themselves from their own supplies. But those of us in the house—we will greatly appreciate a sandwich, a bowl of soup, anything you can manage for people who arrive unannounced. A large supper—the Guild with us may appreciate. I fear I am too tired. Likewise the dowager."

"Nandi."

"You are much appreciated, Rama-ji. I can hardly express how deeply appreciated. We have been traveling for days, and drenched as we are, we are glad to be here. I shall want a pot of tea—the samovar filled—the little sandwiches. Those I favor. You know."

"We can do those, indeed, nandi."

"The Grandmother of the Edi needs to know as much as we know. Advise her that I will send information as I get it—I do not know how the dowager is faring and I may not be able to come down to the village under these circumstances, but I shall try to visit her. Tell her there is a problem in Ashidama Bay. The dowager herself would send salutations to her if she were able. Please say we are determined to protect Najida. Say that the aiji-dowager is here and that the possibility of immediate trouble is very high because of it. The other—I shall try to deal with." Weariness overwhelmed him, astonishingly urgent. It was coming on full dark and suppertime, and the energy he had summoned was beyond running down—it was heading toward a crash. All things being safe, he would go to bed and be done with the day, given two spoonfuls of soup and a brandy.

But he was not a guest here: he had a responsibility to warn the residents of the peninsula, besides a responsibility for their defense—and the dowager's. They might all, even himself, be under Cenedi's command, but he was resolved to protect his own staff, his own province, and get information to Tabini-aiji, damn Cenedi's priorities: if anything was happening to Ilisidi, Cenedi's man'chi was without an anchor, and if she were incapacitated, where was his focus *or* his man'chi? Not to Tabini, one feared. Even the silence that had surrounded her for days might not have been of her ordering.

And what could a human do to get around Cenedi's emotional state and set Najida as a Guild priority—at least within primary consideration—not alone because it was *his* concern, but because it had strategic importance, the man'chi of its inhabitants being perhaps indeterminate and less important to Cenedi, but certainly not to him. He desperately wanted to get a word with Ilisidi herself on that score. He wanted to have *her* set priorities for the Guild force sitting back there at the station with its weapons and gear, and have them dig in and form a formidable and immediate barrier to anything the Shadow Guild could possible send up here, not only for Najida, but likewise for neighboring Kajiminda, Geigi's estate—vacant, but not vacant. Its defense was a duty the aishidi'tat owed to Geigi *and* to Najida. Edi were resident there, as well, and shared a shoreline with the Townships on Ashidama Bay. Ashidama had seasonal commerce with Kajiminda—still maintained it, though the history of Edi involvement with Ashidama was not a peaceful one, and not that many years ago. Trouble was set up and waiting like a tight-wound spring, if it were Cenedi's concern to know that right now. It likely was not.

He had to give Cenedi that information, at least. He had to have it clear with the Guild force spreading out near the train station that Edi were a recognized, entitled member of the aishidi'tat. The force out there came from all over the aishidi'tat. They were not likely to be aware of the situation of Kajiminda and the Edi. Banichi could explain it to them—Banichi could, better than any Easterner; but Banichi had no authority to order that force, because the paidhi-aiji's own power was civil, and the Guild deployment was under the aiji-dowager's orders, meaning, again—Cenedi.

Call Tabini? There was no guarantee the phone lines out of Najida were not compromised already: the Messengers' Guild, who managed them, was notoriously problematic and the old coms were certainly compromised. Cenedi, who had the only safe means of communication, would not surrender it to him.

There was, however—

—what the paidhi-aiji did have, an ability very rare among atevi on Earth.

"I shall need a phone," Bren said. "I shall be calling Lord Geigi."

Their neighbor, lord of Kajiminda . . . who was not at home, but who had a vantage point like no other.

He *would* have called Geigi long since, had he had the new communicator that Cenedi had taken back.

But with the near certainty that the Shadow Guild was at Jorida—if Cenedi was operating on some order from Ilisidi, who was not doing well, and if Tabini was *not* getting reports. . . .

Yes, he needed a phone.

"I would like to make a call," he explained to Ramaso. "I would like that first. See to the other things, Rama-ji. There are so many things to tell you. But the phone, first."

"Yes. Yes, nandi. And this new young gentleman . . ."

God. Nomari.

"Nomari. Presumptive heir of Ajuri," Bren said, "pending the aiji's approval. You and I shall have a brandy at leisure, once I am rested. Then I will tell you everything."

"Of course. Of course, nandi. Refreshment is laid out. The baths are heating. Dry clothes are in the closet."

A steaming bath. A glass of something. Anything. Dry clothes . . . he kept mostly comfortable ones here, and what he was standing in was dripping on the polished floor.

All these things—but first:

"The Grandmother needs to know as soon as possible."

"I shall see to it all, nandi. I shall send the phone. Please rest. Leave everything to us."

Us. The Najida staff. The Edi folk. One and the same. If Ragi atevi were a mystery, the Edi and the Gan atevi, the Tribal Peoples, were an enigma to the Ragi, let alone to a human. But he cared for them in ways that would confuse their atevi hearts— they protected him for what he was sure were their own reasons, too, neither wholly understanding the other, but expecting good behavior. He permitted himself an emotional attachment, risky as that was with atevi—trust, and a sense of being home, whenever he was here.

He went through the door to his own suite, Banichi and Jago preceding him, Tano and Algini following, into the comfortable familiarity of the rooms. Banichi and Jago immediately began to check the sitting room, while Tano and Algini disappeared on an inspection of the other rooms where, presumably, Narani and Jeladi were already at work laying things out. Familiar pattern, familiar surroundings. Sounds were muffled here. The light was old-fashioned lamplight. Smells were spice, and the fragrance of new evergreens from an arrangement on the mantel, the furnishings simple but polished. Two servants were in the room adding finishing touches, and by the time he had crossed the floor to the buffet laid out on the other side of the sitting room, they had quietly escaped out the door.

"Serve yourselves, nadiin-ji," Bren said, as Tano and Algini reappeared. It tempted. But, not yet. "We are home. Rest."

The room was warm. The fire in the fireplace and the metal stove in the next room were doing their job, but he was still shedding water onto, fortunately, a wooden floor. His bodyguard, somewhat more waterproof, had hung up coats and Jeladi was busy toweling off boots. Narani moved in to claim his coat. Even the vest was wet about the shoulders, his lace cuffs were sadly dripping, and the shirt had to go, right there in the sitting-room, before he dripped his way further. Bindanda held up a bathrobe and he gratefully shrugged it on, warm and dry, though his hair was dripping onto it and the white ribbon that tied his queue, badge of office, was undoubtedly beyond saving.

An Edi servant came through the doors with a phone.

"There," he said, indicating the desk in the corner, which had a socket for the phone, and after the servant left, he sat down and plugged it in.

Phone was at once one of the lowest and least secure communications to be had, and theoretically included in the communications silence, but Cenedi had released general com, had he not?

And the Red Train sitting at the station and a camp being set up rather well indicated to the whole west coast that at least he was here. He initiated the requests and gave the authorizations to the operators up at Cobo to reach the boards of the Bujavid itself. Codes given there bounced the call back to Cobo operators and finally into the upper echelons of that least trustable guild, the Messengers, who clung to their control of the big dish, the first earth station at Mogari-nai.

Fine. The fact the paidhi-aiji had phoned Geigi could be spread across the continent and broadcast on the daily news, for what he cared.

The Messengers' Guild operator at Mogari-nai requested numbers and names. He repeated the codes and gave another. The opposition wilted.

Interest at Mogari-nai certainly would become acute: the call once launched blazed up to automated station operations, direct to the atevi side of the station, and finally, with a series of beeps and blips, to wherever Lord Geigi was, personally, and interrupted whatever he was doing.

"*Bren-nandi,*" came the familiar voice. "*One is delighted. Felicitations. Are you well?*"

"Nandi," he said in Ragi, and then switched to ship-speak, a step beyond Mosphei'. Ship-speak was the language of the starship *Phoenix*, even distinct from the dialect of the Reunioners, and atevi not in the space program had no foothold in that.

But Lord Geigi did.

"I'll be quick," Bren said. "I'm not using names. You know where I'm calling from. We're here. The lady—you know who I mean—is not doing well. She fainted once at the station. We're in the house, she's safe and resting. Her doctor is with her. We hope it's just exhaustion—tired from the trip. The track was a mess, we were very slow. We know about trouble to the south. My house where I am I've informed and they'll be watching. I don't want them to get involved in it. I know you'll keep an eye on that situation. Warn us if it travels. We've had a driving rain, heavy cloud. Can you see the lowermost peninsula?"

"*Yes,*" the answer came back a few seconds later. "*Dojisigin ships in port. We have sight through cloud. We advise of any movement. We monitor transmissions up here, down there."*

Ships? What did he mean, ships? Was there more than one? Possibly just locals as well as the Shadow Guild ship. But . . . *down there.* Kajiminda, did he mean? Dared he take time to ask?

"We should be safe where we are. We have a force at the station. She is our greatest worry. She'll rest here, tonight, maybe tomorrow—she is not talking to us. Not able to talk to us. You-know-who is standing in the way. Call the city, call *him*, let him know the situation. Do you copy that? Tell him order her guard. He won't regard my orders."

Thunder cracked. The phone could go out.

It stayed. *"I copy. Got it. You safe?"*

"Yes."

"Why phone? Com not working?"

"They're working fine. I don't have one. He does. He might call you."

"You suppose to have one unit."

"We had two, but he took them back—possibly greater need with the force that protects us. Call her grandson. He needs to know where we are. He urgently needs to have my report. But I can't give it on the phone."

"Understood clear. I am distress about the com."

"I know. So am I. But we're secure here. And it's possible she's just exhausted. Bad track most of the way. Bumps and racket for days. I hope sleep will help. And a floor that doesn't vibrate. We're safe here. I trust our people. But I'm afraid—I'm afraid I could have trouble getting north in time to help your problem. Let her grandson know that, too. Tell him call my brother. He doesn't have ship-speak, but—"

"Yes. Yes. I hear. But you should have com! My order."

"I don't know. They didn't expect to have to equip the camp, maybe. I don't know. It could be the dowager not wanting reports. Tell her grandson that, too. All right? We can't stretch this call too long. Call us and call her grandson if you see trouble. We're safe, we're protected, and I'll get up north as soon as I can, straight from here, if I have to."

"Got it," Geigi said. *"Got it. You stay safe."*

"Absolutely agree. You too. Ending now."

Geigi closed the connection from his side. Bren hung up the phone, staring into space and seeing for a moment, in memory, Lord Geigi and *his* steel-and-plastics environment, and his capabilities—those panels blinking awareness of everything that moved under the station's view. Godlike power—threatened by a mass of panicked human refugees tearing their own environment apart.

And atevi power struggles doing much the same down here.

It was going to take time to solve. He was supposed to be part of that. He was *supposed* to handle translation for the refugees they were going to bring down. Reassure them of their safety.

Welcome to the planet. Pardon us. We're having a war at the moment. Your translator is delayed.

Skittish humans—who had survived hell already. And were terrified of other species.

Geigi had multiple reasons to call Tabini, with questions to ask as well as to answer. Bad news to deliver, if Ilisidi herself was failing—disaster affecting not only herself and the power structure of the aishidi'tat, but all that they had done.

The documents. The agreements left in the hands of Lord Topari, the lord of Hasjuran, to get down the mountain to Shejidan. Topari—a decent man. But erratic. With his capital suffering a total power outage. And no train to send until one reached him, there on the roof of the world.

God help them. There was a technicality: the documents had to be filed *while all the signers were living.*

He had to talk to Cenedi. If he could get to Cenedi in a calmer frame of mind.

"Bren-ji." Tano put a cup of hot tea into his hands, anchoring him to this room, this place, the current situation.

Geigi would act. No question. Geigi would get the message to Tabini. Presumably, charitably thinking, *Cenedi* would be doing the same thing, with his own view of events. One had to assume that, professional that he was—everything that Lord Topari of Hasjuran was not—Cenedi was taking logical actions.

Within the sphere of his last orders.

Whenever those had been.

God.

He took a sip of tea, set down the cup and opened the desk to extract one of his several message cylinders, then decided on a more direct route.

"Banichi," he said, and when Banichi came near: "The documents. Have we heard anything on them? Have they gotten out of Hasjuran yet?"

"We will ask," Banichi said. Which meant that Banichi himself went to the door and out to face Cenedi, while Bren took a shaky sip of tea. And another. Trying not to think until Banichi returned.

"Nawari believes Cenedi has indeed messaged Tabini-aiji about the documents needing to be picked up," Banichi said. "There *is* the train bringing in a transformer."

God. The replacement transformer.

"They will go back on that, then," he said with relief. "*Topari* will see the documents aboard. He will not fail that."

Banichi gave him a look that said—it was Topari.

But if Topari knew one thing, it was surely that Hasjuran's future depended on those documents. Topari himself might be on that train with the documents, sleeping with them, headed to Shejidan . . .

With the highest security little Hasjuran could muster, in fur-edged hunting leathers and with personal rifles . . . because the order for that transformer might have launched that train with no one at operational level even imagining how precious its return cargo might be, and not realizing its urgency. Topari would assuredly explain that, however. Passionately.

God.

"We know the man is unstoppable," Bren said. "In this case— an excellent quality. Sit, Banichi. Rest. We have done what we can for now."

Banichi settled his large frame into an accommodating chair. There was space to breathe. A good chance the documents had moved or would move soon. Down the hall, in that suite Najida maintained for her, the dowager was resting in, one hoped, far greater comfort than she had known in days. The only sound in hearing for the moment was the crackling of the fire. The tiny squeaks of certain boards in the floor. The distant closing of a door somewhere in the house.

Rain, on the roof.

He hoped the Shadow Guild was equally soaked and water-logged tonight, wherever they were.

But likely they had moved onto Jorida Isle—not even troubling to look like a merchant operation in doing so. The Master might not favor such a force arriving in his hall. But there they would be, not necessarily with armament evident. The approach might even be soft, appealing to the Master's vanity.

The force would come when they had seen everything they needed to see. Should he just phone Jorida, warning the man?

If they had been a few days earlier, it might have helped.

By now, there was no knowing whether the Master was still alive. Probably he was. Probably he was regretting by now not having made a phone call himself, while he had time. The number of Guild on that ship, if it was the only ship, was entirely sufficient to take the town unless there was a very good plan of defense. It would not stand long. Tiajo, if they had not dropped her overboard, was likely sorting through whatever glittered.

Possibly by now the Master was hearing offers from the Shadow Guild, propositions before the threats.

After which there was the reality of a Shadow Guild operation setting up a day's drive south of Kajiminda.

Dislodging it was going to be a problem. Najida had no influence in Ashidama. The nature of the aishidi'tat was cooperative unity. Participation, not compulsion. But that was precisely the Shadow Guild's own way of operating—in reverse. They would find the weak points very quickly. Take hostages. Apply force. Appall the populace with their acts. Instill terror—but not quite enough desperation. Promise rewards. Pay off a few. Promise better things soon.

And once they had the populace well under their heel, without an organized underground resistance, it was very, very difficult to dislodge them.

The Assassins' Guild was committed to the hilt over in the Marid—in terms of moveable units. They had another sizeable contingent here at Najida. The rest were committed to the security of critical households and enterprises all over the continent. Those units could not be sent to the south without disruption and moves of opportunity across the continent, not necessarily immediately violent, but setting it up. Feud might be an increasingly outmoded convention . . . but it was culturally there.

Feud was capable, for one thing, of being exploited *by* the Shadow Guild, and the Shadow Guild threat was as diverse, as personal, as defiant of codes of conduct as the Guild itself was particular in such. Highly necessary codes. Without them to embody and civilize the historic system of conflict resolution, there was damage. Institutional damage. And erosion of the peace.

The large Guild force setting up under canvas out there was physically protecting Najida because the Guild force he had, his personal aishid, four in number—committed wherever *he* was—was potentially under assault from enemies not of him personally, but of the aishidi'tat. But that force would not remain at Najida beyond a season or two, if that. The Guild forces were, first and last, Tabini's, which was to say the aishidi'tat's, and pressing problems at more important places would, piecemeal, call them away. The Southwest Coast was a largely unpopulated land, excepting certain key holdings. It could not be taken in the military sense, just maneuvered upon, sat upon, temporarily moved across and fought over. Beyond it, up toward Cobo, just past the Southern Mountains, were truly fragile places, populous and vulnerable, the heartland of the aishidi'tat. That was where the defense line against the Shadow Guild would truly be drawn, if it became necessary. The south, the vast district called, collectively, Sarini was generally left to its own devices. It was largely rangeland, hunting range, with only one recognized but minor resident clan, the Maschi of Targai . . . until one reached the Marid.

As for who would be technically in charge of the force that would, he hoped, remain a while, that would be Banichi, eventually, because *he* was lord of Najida. But Ilisidi outranked him, an issue which Cenedi and Banichi had managed to pave over all during the trip from Koperna, despite Cenedi's loud silence. They both had emergency codes they could send even over the compromised network, to reach Headquarters and Tabini's office and, if authorized, issue orders to the units traveling with them, but if *Banichi* used the codes to reach those authorities or issue orders before Cenedi had resigned command here, that set Banichi to operating outside Cenedi's clearance and raised the issue of Cenedi's legitimacy in command, itself with uncomfortable consequences, old prejudices, and a plethora of old regional attitudes inside the Guild itself.

Headquarters and Cenedi had gone head to head multiple times, in Shejidan, Cenedi being Eastern Guild, not trained by or ordered by the Guild in Shejidan. Outside Shejidan, however, Cenedi's authority came from the aiji-dowager, whose power in the field potentially equaled that of Tabini.

And should the paidhi-aiji—the agent of peace, for God's sake—stir that pot under these circumstances? His loyalty—because biology did not give him atevi senses—his decisions, and his invoking Tabini's authority in that call to Geigi, had the potential to rouse what could become a serious divergence of opinion between himself and Cenedi, if *he* undertook to argue with Cenedi. He could not move the officers of the Guild force that was set up at the station to protect them . . . when it was not *his* Guild senior who commanded that guard. But he commanded his own Guild senior. And the Edi of Najida.

Politics, politics, and more politics. What they were getting over the compromised com system had at least to puzzle, then frustrate the Shadow Guild. There was no way the Shadow Guild could even know about the new coms, but they had to know they were noticed, and Najida had to be high on their list of problems.

So that had left the paidhi-aiji to call his neighbor Lord Geigi— his neighbor happening to be lord of half the space station *and* of Kajiminda, which shared a shore with Ashidama—and take a route that did not put Banichi in a position and that *did not use* that compromised network.

He had done it. He worried about *what* he had done and how Cenedi might take it. But if Ilisidi took offense, he would happily take the whole onus on himself. He would be happy to have the dowager *toweringly* angry at him—if it meant she was recovering.

The problem foreseeably arose—if she was recovering, but not as aware as she needed to be. Tabini alone could override her orders. Tabini *could* order help down here, and also order the Red Train to take her car back to the capital at all the speed the engine could manage, when not hauling a Guild force with its equipment.

He, however, would have to get her aboard that train.

He kept seeing that scene below the platform, that small, black figure under the umbrella in the steam and downpour, and that sudden collapse on the driveway.

But she *was* resilient. She had her spells of exhaustion and impatience, brought on by her astonishing flurries of activity. But she recovered quickly, and if all went to pattern, she might well be on her feet and giving orders in the morning. If not—

Thinking *stopped* there.

She had never outright collapsed. Ever.

At least that he had witnessed.

He became aware of the teacup in his hands, the tea cooling. He took a perfunctory sip of it, and scarcely tasted it. Movement in the room, his aishid's voices . . . all seemed in distant fog. Eyes were blurring.

Nothing—however—was helped by stupid decisions, and he was too tired to be rational. He had done what he could from Najida. He had gotten a message to Tabini. Geigi was watching the scene. The documents were on their way to Tabini.

There was one remaining choice for him to make, the only decision he felt qualified to make at present.

Food. Or bath.

Grimy and exhausted as he felt, foul from the one decision he'd had to make—bath won.

7

Cajeiri waited.
And waited.

His older aishid (it never felt right to call them his *senior* unit: Antaro and Jegari, and Veijico and Lucasi were senior in *his* service despite their years; but his *older* and mostly grey-haired and conservative aishid, Rieni and Haniri, Janachi and Onami) unquestionably had the best lines of communication from all sources, and wielded far more authority in Father's household. He never felt fully in control of the elders, rather more like a subject under surveillance, careful and polite as they were of protocols. To tell the truth, he was a little scared of them, in the sense that adults were scary, and occasionally delivered unpleasant surprises.

One thing his older aishid could definitely do that his younger aishid could not: they could gather information through channels right up to his father, and from the upper levels of the Guild. He had to be careful about using that resource, because information definitely went both ways when he called on them, but there were times he did want to ask.

Unfortunately, and to his frustration, those times he most had questions like that generally seemed to coincide with their absence on Guild business. He might not hear from them for a day or more.

But this evening, right as he was arranging supper with his younger aishid—they sent a note with one of Father's servants, to the effect that, yes, officially and surely, mani and nand' Bren had gotten to Najida safely, and the Guild units with the Red Train were setting up to maintain a watch on Najida, which was good news.

But the note went on: there was concern about mani's health. She had taken to her bed. She had held that information secret until now. She was suffering *spells*.

Spells. What sort of medical answer was that? Mani took medicines. She surely had enough on the trip, or Father would move quickly to assure she had them.

What was wrong with her?

And what could his older aishid find out from Lord Geigi or nand' Bren? He sent that query back as a note to them, hand carried: Liedi took it.

Which left him out of sorts entirely. Nand' Siegi was a good physician, and surely knew everything about mani's health. He had no other patient, except now and again when one of her staff had some problem. His whole care was her.

But what did nand' Siegi mean, that mani was having spells?

In frustration, he wrote to Father: *Is mani sick? They could leave all but the Red Car and the train could go faster and get here tomorrow, could it not? The Red Car has all sorts of medical things, better than Najida does, surely.*

He sent that note off, this time with Eisi. Liedi came back with only a messaged statement from Guild-senior Rieni that they were as yet uninformed, but they would report when they had any answer.

That left him only the request to Father, less likely a source of information. But Eisi stayed gone a very considerable time, and brought an unexpectedly long reply in Father's own hand, not his secretary's, and in haste and full of abbreviated forms, which were never part of ordinary communication from him.

Your questions have merit, and are among options under consideration.

Nand' Siegi has indicated that further travel will be inadvisable for the next several days. It is his opinion it is in your great-grandmother's best interest to break her journey at Najida.

Son of mine, I strongly opposed her journey in all its aspects because of the risk, though I am grateful for her success in Senjin, and I will back her negotiations there to the full.

But we have received confirmation that Lord Tiajo and heads of the Shadow Guild, Suratho and others, who escaped the Marid some days ago at the mere rumor of her arrival, have now reached Jorida Isle in Ashidama Bay, where Lord Tiajo has trade connections. It is likely that the Shadow Guild has already had a presence on Jorida to monitor those trade connections at the very least. Thanks to our operation in the Dojisigin capital, the Shadow Guild may now be cut off from information about events in the Marid, except as they have been reported in the news, but they knew that your great-grandmother would not stay long in Koperna, that the Red Train returning up the grade to Hasjuran was unlikely, and that she would most logically travel west to Najida, where a stop was extremely likely, counting the presence of nand' Bren—of which we are relatively sure they are also aware. The Master of Jorida—one does not style him lord; he is not—has long traded and dealt with the Shadow Guild and likely has their agents close to him, whether or not he realizes it, so that information he has is likely shared in every detail with his new guests. Given all these things, we are uncertain who actually rules on Jorida Isle. Considering your great-grandmother's condition, that proximity under these circumstances is a serious situation, and we are anxiously observing.

It was nothing more than he knew or suspected, but that did not make it any less scary.

Our hope is that the Shadow Guild will not yet be organized enough on Jorida to launch an operation, and that your great-grandmother will recover sufficiently to resume her journey to Shejidan, perhaps even by tomorrow or the next day, so her stay will be too brief for the Shadow Guild to prepare a major attack. We hope they will have the sense not to move at all—the Guild force with her is formidable—but she is rarely this vulnerable, and their desperation now is extreme. I cannot overstate our concern, concern that reaches far beyond our personal connection.

You must be aware, son of mine, should the worst happen, her demise could immediately negate the unfiled agreements with Lord Topari, Lord Bregani, and Lord Machigi, while the war is still unsettled and some resistance continues in the Dojisigin. Her agreements in the Midlands, as yet unfulfilled, could also come undone. We would do all we could to maintain those agreements, but she is the binder and her Eastern resources and trade are key elements in those agreements. Malguri has no heir, and only she can appoint one. You see the significance.

Her . . . demise. He knew it was possible. Knew someday she would be gone, but it made him a little sick to have it put so bluntly. He had never thought about who would live in Malguri once she was gone. Malguri *was* mani.

The relations between Great-uncle Tatiseigi and the whole of the Padi Valley are equally fragile. With two major clans lordless, the entire region looks to him for stability, but that man'chi is unpredictable at best, in both directions. His control of the region is bolstered by his association with her and could come undone, requiring new agreements throughout the region . . . all critical arrangements that potentially involve the jealousy and competition of neighbors, not even mentioning that the Kadagidi estate has not so much as a potential lord, leaving that clan in suspension—and that Ajuri's last qualified heir as well as Brenpaidhi is in proximity to your great-grandmother and in equal jeopardy. It is imperative that we get all three back in Shejidan as soon as she is well enough to make that trip safely.

On the space station, Lord Geigi's situation is becoming more difficult because of the delay already caused by your great-grandmother's southern adventure. He diverted his attention from his own difficulties to provide secure communication during the operation in Senjin and the Dojisigin, and without it, we would be far more exposed to mischief than we are. But as a consequence of that delay, Geigi is under increasing pressure and the human authorities on the station are growing desperate in the deteriorating supply situation. You see the interrelationship of these situations, and their seriousness.

He did, extremely well, and from first hand. He had been on the station. He had heard of the conditions of the refugees, lodged in a once-abandoned section of the station. He knew how desperate things had gotten—he knew that better than his father did.

Things could not be more perilous. Man'chi will bind Atageini to us because your sister is heir, and if Great-uncle remains there, his influence might hold the rest of the Padi Valley, but it is foreseeable we could see extreme unrest arise in the East, if Malguri's lordship falls vacant. In the loss of his promised railroad and his steel ships, Lord Machigi's ambition could drive him to fill the power vacuum the fall of the Dojisigin will create in the Marid, and that would be a problem possibly threatening Senjin. The remnants of the Shadow Guild in the north would undoubtedly take advantage of chaos in the Marid in that case, possibly to sow fear throughout the continent regarding the human refugees about to land. We have attempted to keep publicity on that event to a minimum.

And far beyond the politics, I am personally concerned for Grandmother, and I know your attachment to her is no less than mine. I am sending a medical team from Cobo to Najida: they are preparing as I write this. For obvious reasons we do not want news of her ill health to get out, but there were whispers of her condition as far back as Koperna, and this morning I received an inquiry from the Presidenta on Mospheira. We do not know how he became aware, since to our knowledge there has been no communication of that rumor and we have held it close, but clearly the rumor has now broken in places where humans have connections, and the mere speculation on her fragility will embolden resistance in the Marid, raise questions there, and do other damage we do not yet reckon of. As for Mospheira, it may well have gotten there from the human side of the space station where communication is less regulated—by its nature, rumor always has a way of getting where we would least want it—but we do not know.

I need not tell my son that Grandmother's health has been of concern before. We have certain protocols in place in event of your great-grandmother's demise, but we are not prepared to lose the paidhi-aiji at the same time, and at the moment, both are within reach of a desperate and angry enemy. I have sent a message to Lord Tatiseigi, who has expressed his intention to come to the capital to meet the Red Train. I have requested him to stay in Tirnamardi, as a stabilizing influence in the Padi Valley; but I have not yet informed him of this latest news. It is vital that he remain focused on all those who depend upon him. His presence in the Padi Valley will help that, at what may become a very critical time. It is why, son of mine who will one day take my place, the aiji must remain in Shejidan in times of crisis despite one's most fervent wish to have a personal hand in the matter. It is a hard reality, but one we must accept. Our people depend upon it.

Cenedi can reach me directly, and he says they are adequately supplied and that her physician has all he needs. For now we must trust his word on this, but word has now come from Lord Geigi that Bren-paidhi has not been given a secure com as we ordered. This explains his silence, but also raises questions as to why he was not given it. Cenedi will follow her orders and if those orders are to keep us ignorant, there is very little we can do about it. Hopefully these are baseless concerns and we will know more about your great-grandmother's condition in the morning. Then I will reevaluate what Lord Tatiseigi needs to know, since he is a person directly concerned in all aspects of this situation.

Meanwhile all things we discussed earlier are still valid, but with greater need for security and with even more urgency. Please keep this letter as a statement of my intent, should that ever come in question, and safeguard it. Should any event place responsibility on you, this letter will prove my concerns and my will in this matter. I regret that you are now managing with new staff and I wish that it were otherwise, but they have at least passed rigorous security checks, and I hope they may serve you well. Keep yourself safe. I am recalling your senior bodyguard for your protection as I am recalling some of mine.

There followed two pages of very legal-sounding words, pages he simply folded in with the rest without even trying to read.

How bad is it? His brain continued to spin on that question. What is wrong with her? Is it her heart?

He read it through again, hoping he had missed something . . .

It was a very long letter, filled with a great deal to think about, but he *still* did not know . . . Was he so stupid he simply could not read as an adult what he was being told? Father was saying, was he not, that mani was very possibly dying, and that Uncle Tatiseigi had to stay where he was to hold the midlands secure. Against what? Some untoward move out of the Shadow Guild?

But was an attack expected in the north, with all the confusion going on in the Marid? Except . . . Father had not spoken of attack. Father had been speaking about man'chi. About two clans without anchors who depended on Great-uncle. And *one* of the candidates, Nomari, was in Najida, under whatever danger existed down there.

What was Father doing to help mani right now? A medical team from Cobo? When Cenedi insisted Siegi had all he needed? Was it precaution? Or did Father not trust Cenedi to tell the truth? Father had said Cenedi would tell him what mani told Cenedi to say. That made sense . . . and was scary, if mani was not herself because she was ill.

Even more scary—his stomach felt suddenly cold—was she even still alive? There were times when Father did not tell all the truth. He knew that above all things. But the letter did not feel like that. Father was worried about her and worried about what he was getting from Cenedi. If mani were . . . dead . . . what *would* Cenedi say, even on that new com? What final orders might mani have given him?

His mind would not go there. He had to believe mani was still alive. Maybe she was not able to give orders, but what was clear was that, sick or not, mani could *not* stay in Najida. She had to get back to Shejidan, where they had the best hospitals, where she would be *safe*. If she was alive and telling Cenedi to say things that would keep Father from interfering, as she would think it, then someone had to talk to her. Tell her to get strong enough to come home. He knew nand' Bren would try, knew nand' Bren would see everything he did, everything Father had said, but could nand' Bren move her, if she were determined?

Worse, could nand' Bren get past Cenedi even to see her?

He had to know . . . were they doing all they could to encourage her to get better, to come home, or was it beyond hope, and everybody was being political and following some plan for such things?

He sat a moment, staring at the wall, wishing he could order a train—even call the young lord of Dur and his yellow plane and ask him for transport—

Reijiri of Dur *could* get there. Reijiri's yellow plane could land on any flat road—the market road beside the train station would work. Any field. No airport needed, for Dur.

But that was exactly the kind of irresponsible thing his being heir to the aishidi'tat said he could not do.

. . . It is why, son of mine who will one day take my place, the aiji must remain in Shejidan in times of crisis . . .

Father was saying he could not go to her either, and Father had the power of the whole aishidi'tat at his disposal. Not just because it was not safe, not just because it would do no good and possibly complicate everything—if the Shadow Guild was about to move on Najida, how much more would they risk to assassinate the aiji-dowager *and* the aiji? But what Father was saying was that he had to stay here in Shejidan, remembering what had to be most important to the aiji: all the people of the aishidi'tat. Everything Father could do was too large, and involved the legislature, and clan rights, and all that.

He sat digging a heel into the historic carpet and wishing . . . and thinking . . . and thinking.

The door into his suite opened, and Jegari and Antaro came in, then Lucasi and Veijico, all looking somber.

"Jeri-ji," Jegari said. "Pardon. Your great-grandmother is reported ill."

His blood had near frozen just in the first half of that. But then "reported ill" was no worse than he had just heard.

"The news is out, then."

They all made a half circle in front of his chair, solemn and worried. Antaro asked: "It is being reported even in Hasjuran and Koperna, and over all the official stations. It is not yet on the television. But have *you* any news, nandi?"

"I would have told you," he said, chilled by the formality of the *nandi*, but then, all the rest of the situation stuck in his throat: Father's privately assigning him to handle the refugees, giving him real power; Father's putting him into the succession, without Mother as regent . . . that part only now hit him with full impact and set his heart pounding in dread. It would please Great-grandmother. It would upset Mother greatly. But no . . . Father had said Mother already knew, had long since accepted it.

And did his older aishid know *that* part already? His younger unit might not.

"Father told me she is staying at Najida," he said, "and he gave me nand' Bren's duty at the spaceport, because nand' Bren is down in Najida with Great-grandmother, and the Dojisigi are that close, and trouble could spill over there." He was not necessarily making sense. "Father is worried about the succession. I know Mother would make good decisions. But he has named *me*, now, if it had to be, if anything happened to him. I have no idea—he may have promised mani about that. And right now—he knows things directly from Cenedi. He has the new com system, with Lord Geigi. One has no idea whether Father is talking to Cenedi, or with Rieni, or Lord Geigi, or who has those things, or how things are going in the Marid and whether there is reason to worry there. I know Father would want to talk to nand' Bren, except for protocols, and security . . . And mani is very sick. They have stopped in Najida in reach of the Shadow Guild, and I do not know whether they will not *tell* me how she is or even if Cenedi will tell Father the truth, especially if mani orders otherwise. I am greatly upset, nadiin-ji. One regrets—I am upset, and I am not making sense."

"Nand' Bren would find a way," Antaro said. "Lord Geigi will know where the train is. Nand' Bren could get through to *him* from Najida if he felt he had to, if they were in danger. A little rest, a little calm . . . Your great-grandmother has been through a hard journey. They *all* must be exhausted."

"One hopes that is all," he said. "You *will* tell me if you hear things. *Anything*. I do not trust Machigi. Most of all, I do not trust Machigi."

"He was left in the Marid," Lucasi said.

"His lands run right up to Najida's and Kajiminda's market road. All that hunting range—is his."

"But he has war on his doorstep, in the Marid."

"And a piece of it has taken a ship over to Jorida, at his back door. The Shadow Guild is there—the *worst* of the Shadow Guild. Mani was not supposed to stay at Najida."

"Lord Geigi will be looking down from the heavens on all this," Jegari said, "with great suspicion. He will know where the Red Train is sitting, even if no one has told him. And he has a personal treaty with the Edi, who have their own eyes on Ashidama Bay. Now that nand' Bren is at Najida, Lord Geigi can phone nand' Bren and set a watch on everything that moves or breathes, from Najida southward. Lord Geigi's estate lies between Najida and Ashidama Bay. He will not let that come to harm. Neither will the Edi."

"And the Edi," Veijico said, "have been standing off the Masters of Jorida since the War of the Landing."

"This is not just the Master's people, it is Shadow Guild."

"True," Lucasi said. "But the Edi are alert, they are well-armed, they know the woods on the peninsula and they are between nand' Bren and Jorida, on both peninsulas. They even touch the shore of Ashidama Bay, right up to the edges of the Townships. The Guild itself *learns* from them, where it comes to woodland operations. The Edi will not hesitate to move if the Shadow Guild thinks to make Najida a target."

"The Edi also owe Lord Geigi," Veijico said, "for giving them the land and the use of the estate."

That was all common sense. Jegari made a sensible point of it. It did nothing to say mani would be fine, but it did say the Shadow Guild would have the Edi to contend with, as well as all the Guild she had with her on the Red Train.

"Besides, she has been on that train for days," Antaro said. "Surely a little rest will help. Morning may bring better news."

It was what he wanted to hear. He had seen crises every year of his life. And what his aishid said was comforting, and all reasonable, and just their presence and their voices brought sanity to the air. But he still had a heavy weight about his heart. Everything about the trip mani had organized had been rushed, and strange, and everything she had done had cut her off from Uncle and most of the people she ordinarily relied on. She had taken offence at Uncle and Mother settling on baby Seimei for Uncle's heir, and for putting Nomari forward, all without consulting her. She had been on her way to Shejidan to deal with that, and instead, she had gone immediately to Najida to await Lord Bren's return from Mospheira.

And to meet with Lord Machigi. That was disturbing. She was trusting people like Lord Machigi, making deals with Lord Machigi . . . whom Uncle regarded with extreme distrust. He agreed with Uncle's suspicion. And after meeting with Lord Machigi, she had made another sudden trip . . . on *behalf* of Lord Machigi, and without settling matters with Uncle first, or even consulting him . . . which had brought her to this dangerous situation, ill, alone, not listening to anyone who would argue her into sensible behavior. He wanted to be with her. He wanted to defend her. And he felt everything stretched thin to the point of breaking, because there was nothing he could do.

Not personally. But there was *one* thing he *could* do. It might be useless. It might be a bad idea, disturbing what Cenedi and Lord Bren were trying to do to protect Najida and Kajiminda. . . . But he *had* allies. There were people he had known from earliest memory, and whose sense he respected, and there was one most of all who *should* have been involved all along . . . and who *could* reach her, who could get past Cenedi, and who *could* be counted on to tell him . . . and Father . . . what was really going on.

"I am sending a message," he said, "to Atageini." That was Uncle. "And another to Dur. Eisi and Liedi can go. The new people can manage things here. They can learn how." And he added, fully aware how serious it all was for them: "We need not tell my father. We need not tell Eisi and Liedi the reason—just that there must be secrecy."

They looked perturbed. They were that honest about the idea. And they were right: Father was going to have more than a word with him. Possibly Father would reconsider his idea of writing him into direct succession in his own right. Father had decided not to tell Uncle Tatiseigi that mani was ailing, because he wanted Uncle to stay where he was, to keep the midlands calm, and it was terribly serious. He understood all that, but so would mani returning to Shejidan keep the midlands *and* Uncle calm. Not telling Uncle held back the best encouragement mani could have beside her, if she was sick. *Uncle* could talk to her. Uncle could urge her to sensible behavior in ways nand' Bren could not, Uncle being mani's closest and strongest ally. If he did not get that chance, Uncle would feel that wound forever, and more so if mani did not recover.

And *that* made sense politically. Father and the aishidi'tat could not afford to lose Uncle's man'chi, but he was not certain Father understood that by tricking Uncle into staying with lies and secrecy, he could lose that man'chi regardless of what happened with mani.

The problem was, Father did not know Uncle the way he had come to know him, in mani's company. Father needed to know what he knew, but he feared Father would not see what he saw . . . because, he suddenly realized, Father was *here*, in Shejidan, with all that responsibility to the whole of the aishidi'tat weighing on him. He *could* not see beyond that. He could not *afford* to act beyond that. That was what Father had been trying to tell him.

Father was not going to listen. One was fairly sure of that . . . for all Father might *wish* to do precisely what Cajeiri was planning to do.

"I am serious," he said. "Will you do as I ask, nadiin-ji?"

"Yes," Antaro said. And that was an unconditional yes that the elder aishid would never give him, which was why he could not send them, serious authority that they were—or even have them know what he was about.

And he was not sure how he was going to explain to the larger household where Eisi and Liedi had gone, if anyone asked.

He could be quite honest, and say that they were taking a message to Dur. He could claim it was asking that Dur would take his little yellow plane and come down to the spaceport when he called, to help him reassure the humans.

It was sort of true.

Almost true.

No, it was an outright lie. He might suffer Father's extreme displeasure. And he should not build too tall a structure of lies, or make it too complicated. Just a few little ones.

And he should not give anybody but his aishid more information than they needed to have—mani had taught him that. It not only protected that plan . . . it also protected them. From Father.

He penned two letters, carefully leaving out any mention of Great-grandmother. He signed them by hand, because he did not have a proper seal of his own. And he delivered them to Eisi and Liedi, with two little bronze and very old tokens the household had, each bearing a stamp and a number, that would charge their expenses to the household. The tokens were a privilege, items rarely permitted to leave the apartment, and the spare was only because one of them might be in use down in the market, or his staff might need them when he was traveling—but both were valid.

He handed one to Eisi and the other to Liedi.

"Whatever you need. Any comfort. And transport. The trains. The Cobo ferry to Dur, if it would be quicker than the train. The phones. Clothing. A personal memento. Just something you want. One hardly cares. You will deliver these messages and take whatever means you can find to come back as quickly as you can. Wear common clothes. Be as inconspicuous as possible about who you are and where you are going. Is it agreed, nadiin-ji? Because I can send my aishidi if you are not willing. I will tell you all of it when you get back. I swear to you, I *will* stand between you and my father, whatever happens. It is on *me*. Say no if you wish. I can send Veijico and Lucasi. But you will rouse less attention. You have to decide now, and be out of the Bujavid quickly in case my older aishid comes back."

"Yes," Eisi said. "Yes, nandi," Liedi said.

"Speak to no one, until you get to Dur and Uncle. Tell them and only them that I am very concerned about mani's health. That, combined with what is in those letters will tell them what they need to know. I shall bring Tariko and Dimaji in for the front room duty so long as you are gone and tell them that they are to learn the routine. I shall tell my elder aishid if they do come back that you are on leave while leave is possible, because you are overdue for it and I promised and things are uncertain, due to the refugees and the task my father has given me. That at least is true. Please. Go now. One has no idea when Rieni's unit may be back, so hurry."

"Yes, nandi."

"Do not carry evident baggage," he added. He had thought of these things while he was writing the letters. "If you need things, buy them. Go out by the great steps. Take the public bus to the city train station. Buy separate tickets, one of you to Cobo and up to Dur, the other to the Taiben stop. Use the phone at the city station and advise Uncle and Dur both that you are coming from me and that it is secret. Someone will surely come for you where you get off."

They understood. It was evening. There was a night train that ran to Cobo and intersected the northern line, and another that would stop at that lonely station in the Taiben forest, a fair drive from Tirnamardi. He knew these things, as he knew his maps, not only the pins in them for man'chi, but how they connected, and when and where they connected, in case it should ever matter how to reach his closest allies—all childish plans, now set in motion.

Father might disavow him. He was sneaking past Father's decisions in matters of the aishidi'tat, and man'chi, and he was breaking trust with Father; but not with mani. Never with mani. Mother had said outright she had lost him to Great-grandmother when they had gone up to the station, and feelings had never connected between him and Mother as they should. *Father* had trusted him. Mother had always expected the disconnection. Accepted it. Father—had not.

But it came down to the fact someone had to tell Uncle. Someone had to find out what was going on in Najida, someone with authority and the power to do things even nand' Bren could not.

Father might feel the same. Very likely he did. But Father would have to be sensible and put the aishidi'tat first.

He was not quite in Father's position. Not yet. If there was blame later, if things went wrong, he would have to stand up and take that on, too. Even if Father politically had to disown him and everything he had done.

8

A bath—so warm and comforting one could easily fall asleep in it—or possibly drown, but one held oneself awake with the promise of food.

And food there was. Abundant food, warm and simple, and ever so welcome. Bren ate two helpings of what was provided for himself and his aishid and his servants, the latter dividing their choices between the bath two halls over and the buffet in the sitting room of the suite—Bindanda himself glad to enjoy a meal he had not cooked.

After Senjin, after the affairs there, and the relentless racket and rocking of the train, this house was quiet, it was safe, and there was leisure to think—all too much leisure to think . . . with a brain highly deficient in information. One wanted news. Facts. Anything other than speculation. But no information came, and despite a body drooping with fatigue, with food, and strong tea, he began to be too awake, when he truly wished he were not.

He could call Ramaso, he thought, and get the local news from him. And should do that. But it would be local matters only: he was not yet up to giving Ramaso the complete explanation he had promised.

And all the while he would be thinking—he *knew* he would be thinking—of the broader situation, the Shadow Guild setting up on Jorida, the dowager ailing, and Tabini now in process of doing *something*, he was sure—but what Tabini might be doing, or how the fighting in the Marid was turning out . . .

There was just a stew of business unresolved, including with

Geigi. He had not asked Geigi details about Geigi's own crisis aboard the station. Should he call Geigi back now and ask?

And say . . . what? There was nothing he *could* say that he had not already said: I may not be available. I have no way to predict. All of which Geigi already knew, and Geigi would be madly working on some contingency plan. Another interruption would not help him.

None of it would improve by aimlessly circling about what he did not know tonight. But he knew he was going to do exactly that, as soon as his head hit the pillow.

He set his plate aside, poured himself a second glass of wine, thinking that might dull the muddled mess in his head.

Came a knock at the door.

Jeladi silently rose to answer it, and in that doorway was Casimi, of the dowager's aishid, with a message cylinder.

Bren set down the wineglass, his heart speeding. Casimi left. Jeladi brought the cylinder, one of the dowager's formal cylinders, and Bren extracted the note, which was in Cenedi's sketchy, heavy hand. Had Ilisidi taken a turn for the worse? Please God—

It said:

The aiji-dowager sends this, dictated.

Clean and wash the bus and make it ready for travel. Stock it with pickle and supplies for all for twenty-seven days. We will require a breakfast of eggs and sweet sauce, sausage and toast and plain cakes, with strong tea, in my room two hours before dawn. Invite the Grandmother of the Edi for first dawn, under the portico. We wish to speak with her.

Pack court dress, one instance, with a spare shirt. Your valets may accompany us. And your excellent cook. There is no need to suffer.

My son worries too much. Do not inform him.

No reply is necessary.

The first line encouraged him to hope. By the last, he felt chilled despite the warmth of the room. Pickle? And court dress?

Invite the Grandmother? He could beg. His relations with the Edi gave him no way to fulfill that request, but he could ask . . .

It made no sense. Disjointed demands lacking any connective tissue. The bus? Twenty-seven days? To go where?

He had to believe it truly was her dictation. *Cenedi* would certainly not have made up such a collection of insanities. One could imagine Cenedi painfully writing all this, then delivering it as ordered, *because* it was ordered. Comment on it? No. Cenedi would not admit his worry. Nothing against man'chi.

Cenedi would not disobey an order . . . unless or until it was patently injurious to the dowager.

But—

Damn.

Was she sliding downhill, mentally?

So why did he suddenly think, most vividly, of Malguri, a fireside, his first real meeting with Ilisidi, and a cup of tea?

She could have killed him. She had not been, at that time, all that glad that she had missed.

He had never detected a shred of regret for that event, never truly expected any. If anything, it had amused her, in that strange sense of things that—whatever the actual emotion was—pleased? Amused? Satisfied her, to have scored a point?

All those things wrapped in one atevi bundle, perhaps. There were moments humans were ashamed of themselves after the fact, and he was not sure it was in Ilisidi's makeup. Or Tabini's, for that matter.

It was a rare moment of complete translation failure; he was left in a desolation of landmarks.

To be sure, such moments were not unknown with Ilisidi: he often suspected her of deliberately confusing him for her own amusement. But again—what the hell?

At least he knew she was conscious.

Breakfast—two hours before dawn.

And the bus?

So . . . what would Ilisidi do if she were thirty again and situated where she was? The answer to that was simple, and it did not involve a northbound train.

What would Ilisidi do now . . . in her right mind, and possessed of all her faculties? He wished, he truly wished, he believed that answer would be different.

Damn.

Truly, *damn.*

Pickle? And where might they be going? Back to the train? And then to Cobo, and out of the danger, so far as that went? Not a chance. They would not need twenty-seven days of provisions for that.

Just a little jaunt to tour the Guild setup beside the train station?

Same answer.

Worst case—a venture south, toward Ashidama? To which, of the many possible destinations . . . and to what end?

Of course, it was also possible this middle-of-the-night order had been made in one of Ilisidi's moments of whimsy. It might have no other purpose than to thoroughly disrupt his sleep.

He was tempted to pen a note—*I shall include a supply of pickle, aiji-ma, and also my small firearm, for what service it can be. What do you intend us to do with the bus?*

Never mind Casimi had long since departed, not in the least waiting for a reply. All he could really do was follow her orders, and hope for some kind of explanation in the morning. The core of her message, the solid part, was a reasonable request for breakfast—an order for it, with no hint of actually inviting him to share it—with the bus to be fueled and ready and cleaned of the day's mud, but there was that final request not to tell Tabini. And he had just asked Geigi to do precisely that.

Well, *that* would have happened by now, for good or for ill.

And he had not mentioned *pickle.*

His aishid and his servants said nothing—did not ask what was in the message, but in his long silence, and twice reading the message, they had to know there was a problem. He was not ready to answer them, and not sure how to answer her.

Calming his temper was first.

He composed his face. And said to his aishid and his staff: "The message is indefinite. One has no idea what it means, except that the dowager wants the bus cleaned and inquires about breakfast. Tano, I *will* reply. And we need to inform Ramaso."

"Nandi," Tano said, and went to put on his jacket, to take the messages.

Bren sat down at his writing desk, extracted a formal note-paper and uncapped the inkwell. He wrote, simply, politely: *Aiji-ma, be advised I have already informed Lord Geigi of our situation as obliquely as possible, and such as I was privy to at the time. I regret any inconvenience I have created.* That information, if she were indeed in full possession of her senses, would not please her. But it was done. And he would be at a safe remove while she read it. *I will see to the things you wish, including the bus and the pickle.*

Then he slipped it into the dowager's own message cylinder—that the message had come in it *did* invite response, if only by returning it—and gave the message to Tano to carry.

Hoping. Hoping he had read her.

And desperately afraid that he and Cenedi might need to confer in the morning if he had not.

"The dowager wants the bus before dawn," he said to his aishid and his staff. "She is awake, but may be confused. Certain details were missing; one is uncertain of the intended destination. We do as we can. She wants to see the Grandmother tomorrow at dawn. It may be a difficult day." His aishid well knew the Grandmother did not favor coming to the house, rather demanding he come to her, on the rare occasion they had business. "She wants breakfast two hours before first light, and I do not imagine that it will be generally available. I am thus far not bidden to it, nor do I assume I shall be, so we will see to that as we must. I have to instruct Ramaso regarding the Grandmother, and see what I can do regarding the rest. Banichi. Jago."

He put on his coat, and, with only Jago and Banichi, went to find Ramaso, who, being Edi himself, well knew how to contact the Grandmother of the Edi.

The question was whether one dared use the dowager's illness as an argument to get the Grandmother to come to the house.

But he needed to speak to the Grandmother as well, to warn

her and be sure she understood the new danger to the south. Likely she would understand that threat very well, the Edi having existed in a state of war with Jorida, actively so, from time to time—as long as Edi had been on the mainland.

There were things Ramaso himself needed to know, and in all courtesy it required sitting down with a pot of tea to explain things in terms of Najida's safety and to expound on the situation in the Marid, while explaining why they had two Dojisigi Guild with them; and a host of other things that perhaps should not wait until morning.

"Rama-ji," he said when he had found Ramaso in the kitchen, having tea and doubtless an informational session with Bindanda. Both began to rise. "No, no, I shall join you. Bindanda, please stay. I have a great deal to tell Ramaso, and there are details you should know."

"A new pot," Bindanda said, and pushed his portly self away from the table to provide that.

It came welcome, and, setting the new pot on the table, Bindanda also set the sugar jar directly in front of him. That came welcome, too. Energy in a teaspoon. Or two. One needed it, for at least an hour.

9

"**B**ren-ji."

Came a nudge in the back, in bed, from Jago. A light was on.

Something was wrong. Out of the very depth of sleep, so deep, so soft, so dark, and so wanted—alarm asserted itself. Bren sat bolt upright, confused, with blurring vision.

The room was not moving.

He was not on the train.

He collapsed back into the pillows, eyes closed, enjoying, just for the moment, that blessed stillness. He was in his bedroom, safely in Najida. Narani and Jeladi were there, unsurprising in any morning, ready to lay out his clothes and see him properly queued and be-ribboned for the day.

Never mind it was god-awful early.

The lights were still low. Jago was gathering up her clothes.

"What hour is it?" he asked, pushing himself up and raking loose hair out of his face. There were things to do. There were things that should have been done. Narani and Jeladi were waiting, and room lights began coming up. "I am awake. I am awake." He slid one foot over the edge of the bed, and Narani and Jeladi closed in.

Orders. The dowager. The bus. The Grandmother.

"Will the Grandmother come? Have we heard?"

"Not yet," Algini said. Lights came up full, unwelcome. But necessary.

He hurried through his routine, to be dressed in what Narani provided him: a serviceable and comfortable combination in modest brown—fit for a country walk; or a bus, if that was truly Ilisidi's intention.

Where the bus was going, with its supplies and all, the message had not said, but the excursion and twenty-seven days of supplies did not sound like a trip back up to Najida's train station. A bus trip up to Cobo was what he had decided to hope for, sometime around midnight, to take a train for a comparatively painless trip to Shejidan, leaving the bulk of her guard to protect Najida and leaving the Red Train available for Najida in case of need.

Or, God help them, a drive back to Shejidan *entirely* by bus—which was not even to be contemplated, compared to the comforts and defenses of the Red Train . . . or any train, for that matter.

One remote possibility . . . the dowager *might* intend to send the bus west to fetch the lord of the Maschi at Targai, several days' drive back the way they had come, and with a perfectly good little train station of its own, where they *had* stopped briefly for services on the way, at midnight and without calling on the estate. Them going back there now did not make sense. Involving the Maschi somewhat did, more as a courtesy than a help.

That was still no reason for including supplies of the sort the dowager wanted, but calling in neighboring Maschi clan might account for her intent to speak to the Grandmother of the Edi at first light, and it might reasonably involve the protection of Kajiminda, Lord Geigi's estate, a Maschi estate, vacant now save for its Edi caretakers, which sat between Najida and the Townships of Ashidama Bay. Lord Geigi had left his entire estate to Edi management after the disaster of having his nephew in charge of it; and had moreover granted the Edi the entire end of Kajiminda peninsula, where the Edi were building their own version of an estate and seat of governance—borrowing Najida's truck and Bren's yacht for ferrying materials in the process. The essential part of the Edi great house might be well on toward completion—

And Kajiminda, though not active enough to pose a threat to the Shadow Guild, might seem an easy target—if the Shadow Guild wanted to stir up trouble. The Edi historically enjoyed abysmal relations with the Townships of Separti and Talidi and, notably, with Jorida Isle, shipwrecking having been the Edi's local industry from the earliest days, and Jorida's ships had been their primary target. The Edi had not done it regularly since he had taken responsibility as lord—more particularly since he had instituted Edi trade with Cobo by rail and promised to secure the two Tribal Peoples seats and voices in the legislature if they would forswear that activity—

They had gotten their seats. They had made certain promises and the Edi's active enmity toward Jorida might have died back somewhat, but not significantly.

Animosity from the other direction, however, was another story; and there could indeed be trouble ahead for the Edi, with the arrival of the Shadow Guild on Jorida. If the Shadow Guild wanted a pretext for starting trouble in the area—that was a potential problem.

Perhaps Ilisidi intended to visit Kajiminda to insert a Guild presence there—right on the backside of the townships of Separti and Talidi, and the northern shore of Ashidama Bay.

That would be a *good* move. And if the dowager had ordered it, if *that* was her plan today, it was an indication she was aware, awake, and things were in far better state than he had supposed when he had gone to bed. If it were her intention to set up defenses that protected Kajidama, he heartily approved: not the involvement of the Edi, who had no stake in this; but defense of Geigi's estate, yes, and setting up the Guild force she had with her to protect the Edi who lived right up against the Townships . . .

God, utterly reasonable, but he did not want them involved in any Guild action.

Guild presence at Kajiminda, however, would make a strong statement over in Ashidama Bay. It would annoy them extremely and give them a focus other than Najida.

If *that* was what was going on, yes, he was entirely for it. Explaining it to the Edi—made thorough sense. It would not be an easy explanation, but—

"Nandi," Narani said quietly, as Bren slid his arm into the

offered coat, his better coat, of those available this morning, and before he could protest that choice: "Excellent news, nandi. The dowager indeed expects you for breakfast."

So she was not only having breakfast in this predawn hour, she wanted his company. Granted it *might* be only to give him a dressing-down for phoning Geigi, but that was all right. At this point, he would take whatever he could get. He stood still while Narani adjusted his queue and ribbon. Jago was putting on her jacket. "Jago-ji, everyone should have breakfast. Please. This *is* Najida. I shall not need attendance for this." He hoped. "Have we heard regarding the Grandmother?"

"Due at dawn," Narani said. "We have assurance from Ramaso. Everything is arranged. There, nandi. You are fit."

Bren took a deep breath and straightened his shoulders, hopeful—but unsure what he might have to deal with at breakfast.

And hoping to God the dowager *remembered* sending for the Grandmother last night.

The guest quarters, always maintained ready should the dowager visit, were in immaculate order, with two of her aishid on guard at the door, all regulations and stiff propriety, country estate or no. Her aishid, who served her as household staff might, attended the door as it opened, standing by, all those points of polite formality and ceremony that would be the case in the capital . . . with only three modest rooms to do it in.

Bren entered alone, in the informality he cultivated at Najida, letting his aishid and his staff go about their own business, and immediately it was clear that breakfast was intended in the middle room, where, beyond the archway, there was a small table set, with chairs at opposite ends. A rolling cart with covered dishes had been brought in, and the dowager's maid Asimi stood waiting in stiff formality at that side of the room. No one else was there.

Bren walked in and stood by one chair, waiting, not knowing how long he might have to wait, or whether there would, in fact, be breakfast at all.

A long moment later the further door opened, and there was a muffled light thump. And another. Then a footstep and the same impact on resounding wood.

Familiar sound, familiar pace. Ilisidi's cane—like the beat of a reviving heart. She walked into view, black figure in black shot through with rubies, cane in hand, and walking quite well, thank you, no assistance needed, though Cenedi followed her somewhat more closely than normal. She came into the room and went to her chair, which Cenedi drew back, taking the cane, as she sat down with authority.

Quite well, to all observation.

Perfectly well.

"Aiji-ma," Bren said. What *could* one say? He gave a little bow and, with her bodyguard's assistance, sat down in the facing chair.

What one wanted to say was, *Damn it, aiji-ma.* But there was no smug sparkle of wickedness in her expression, rather a deadly serious and questioning look, as if to say, silently, *So what are you thinking now, paidhi? Did I fool you?*

Or:

Did you think I would not know what you did last night?

What he did say was, "Aiji-ma. Are you well?"

She waved a bejeweled hand. "We are secure in this room. Let us have a good breakfast. We cannot guarantee the next several days."

"Aiji-ma, . . ."

"Patience, paidhi. No slight is given to your excellent staff, be it understood. There is no time for courtesies and ceremony this morning, but we shall have our eggs and our toast in as great a security as we could manage in the Bujavid. Enjoy this excellent breakfast."

She gestured, and her personal maid immediately undertook to uncover and serve the dishes Ilisidi had asked for. He had arrived with a modest appetite, and a suspicion that the whole show of breakfast was to provide a sad illusion of normalcy for a failing woman. Now that it was all turned inside out, he was feeling a surge of temper that did not combine well with worry, and he had to conjure his own personal normalcy and quietly partake of as much as he could swallow of a massive breakfast in this strange hour before dawn.

Nothing was wrong with *her* appetite. No move faltered. A sizeable number of eggs in sauce, three pieces of toast, and two spicy sausages disappeared. He did well to manage one sausage, a piece of toast and three cups of strong sugared tea.

"You must have this sausage," she said, of the last in the dish.

"I could not, aiji-ma. I have had enough."

"Well," Ilisidi said, and the lone sausage did not go to waste. "So you are dressed somewhat extravagantly for travel."

Said the woman dressed in rubies.

"Are we?" That came out somewhat sharply. "Traveling today?"

"Do you doubt it, paidhi? You must have understood the bus would be in use."

"I am dressed for whatever you intend, aiji-ma. The *details* have remained somewhat unclear."

That drew an infuriating smile, and did one only imagine a little gentleness in it? "If only all my advisors were so accommodating, paidhi. Listen to me. Our movements are surely being followed. Our regular transmissions are being monitored—last evening an observer was on the hill facing the train station and another turned up on the far side of the road, both of which we let go, intentionally."

He had seen nothing. But his attention had been on her.

"Our arrival was too long forecast," she said, "and of far too much concern in the southern bay, not to take advantage. So we have fed our enemies' curiosity."

She gave a slight, sly smile. Fed? Did she mean her apparent illness? Was she truly well?

"I regret we do not know about the informational security of the Bujavid itself . . . always difficult, since fools are easily come by, but we assume the Guild is likewise aware. Certainly my grandson is convinced of my imminent departure from this world. He is sending a medical team from Cobo to attend my final days." Another smile. "They shall, I fear, be sorely disappointed."

"Surely not, aiji-ma."

A shrug. A sip of tea.

"Lord Geigi is advised of our status and intent as of this hour, and is assisting. Your message did alarm him, and he did contact my grandson. I have told Lord Geigi *not* to recontact my grandson except in emergency. We do not want a flurry of communications to attract notice in the Bujavid and I do not want to risk some careless servant in the household exposing the truth."

Flurry of communications? Tabini had one of those new com units. Nothing in them to attract notice. Did she really think Geigi would fail to tell Tabini? He doubted that was really an issue.

"I can only apologize, aiji-ma." Not that he was actually sorry. Tabini deserved to know the truth, and if he had had that com Geigi said he was supposed to have . . . control of just such a direct report likely explained why Ilisidi had kept it from him.

A dismissive wave of the knife. A steady gaze, deep, and—perhaps deceptively—warmer. "I did not take you in confidence, paidhi. I did not take anyone in confidence but Cenedi and his unit. We have tested my staff and, most particularly the leadership of the Guild we left deployed at the train station. If there are any elements there who would pass a message southward or eastward, we have means to know—and I rejoice to say, *my* force seems secure." She ladled three more eggs onto her plate. "Do try these."

He took one, perforce. Hardly knowing what to say. Was she suggesting *his* people were suspect? Before he could frame a reply to that revelation:

"We had deep concerns particularly of two of our company," Ilisidi said, "and they have passed, thus far. We did give them standard Guild equipment, including communications, and last night we restored their status. This morning . . . they are gone. We do not entirely trust them, but we shall see. They do appear to have useful knowledge of a variety of venues."

Momichi and Homura. The Dojisigi half-aishid whose partners were either dead or held hostage, and if alive, possibly held close to Lord Tiajo, now in Jorida.

"They surely would suspect they are on trial," Bren began, and Ilisidi said:

"Standard equipment they have lets them penetrate Shadow Guild communications—if they know the codes, as they may well. We have given them the current ones as we know them. And they know we know. And we know they know we know. It is all very symmetrical."

One began to have an uncomfortable premonition—about the bus. And about Momichi and Homura. "I am extremely anxious to have Najida protected, aiji-ma. Najida and Kajiminda. Please allow me to say so. The force with us is sufficient for that, if left in place. If we simply stripped the Red Train down to the Red Car and your own, you could reach Shejidan . . ."

"Yes, yes," Ilisidi said slowly, in such a tone as shot the idea fatally, and let it fall. "We might do that. But we have other possibilities before us, opportunities that may not come again so nicely."

His heart sank. He was not ready to dismiss the issues of her health and her safety, not that blithely. "Aiji-ma. Forgive me. Is your general health at *all* a consideration in this?"

A light wave of her left hand. "I startled even Cenedi with that little machimi at the station.—Did I not?" This with a glance to Cenedi, who stood at the side of the room.

"Entirely," Cenedi said.

"Though not in all particulars," Ilisidi said, "Cenedi and I have consulted."

Cenedi gave nothing away. Nothing.

"A little white pill," Ilisidi said. "I have slept so ill on this journey. I *may* have taken one too many, perhaps, that final day on the train. And, perhaps a relief of tension, they all finally worked."

"Aiji-ma," Cenedi said. Flatly. Formally.

"Was that all of it?" Bren asked, neither flatly nor formally. "A *mistake?*"

"I am suspected of so many things," Ilisidi said. "Cenedi has spoken with my grandson, and we are under strictest orders to return to the capital where my grandson can wrap me in wool and keep us all safe." A sip of tea. "He has enemies, but the greater danger is his Ragi advisors. He focuses too much on the Padi Valley and lately on this interesting young man, this intimate of Machigi . . ."

Nomari.

What in hell did Nomari have to do with anything afoot?

"Do you doubt him, aiji-ma? And what does he have to do with the sleeping pills?"

Ilisidi laughed in delight, and poured another cup of tea. "Do drink, paidhi. No, nothing to do with the sleeping pills, and everything. Everything is falling into my grandson's hands, a most opportune moment for him to firm up the south and stabilize the north—*use* the bloodlines connecting the Marid to the Padi Valley and appoint this young man—"

"Then you do favor Nomari." That was a surprise.

"Oh, a great deal will lean upon this young man and his associations, not simply his personal ties to the Marid, and to the cleverest and most ambitious rogue in the region—"

Meaning Machigi of the Taisigin Marid, for whom Nomari had been a spy as a very young and desperate lad . . .

"Before we approved him to be lord of Ajuri," Ilisidi said, "—we wished to know something of his character. He is both a romantic and practical at once. That is in his favor. But no marriage to any child of the Marid! We are adamant."

Regarding that undeniable attraction on the part of Bregani's daughter Husai. Nomari *was* an attractive and available young man. But Husai was not a prospect he dared pursue, not if he wanted to take . . . and keep . . . the Ajuri lordship.

"But the sleeping pills, aiji-ma."

"We are old. We are fragile. We are so very fragile." Ilisidi's expression denied it. "If we sigh, if we languish, rumors fly through the aishidi'tat, and our enemies lay plans. I am here, I am languishing—I cannot possibly obey my grandson's notion of leaving a token force and surrendering the greater part of it to *his* war in the Marid. He needs no such thing. He is over-cautious. Senjin *will* stand firm in alliance with us, since death is the alternative, and Machigi wants his railroad, which he cannot get without cooperation. I do not say that young warlord is virtuous, but he has seen the future *without* that railroad, and he sees another future clearly now. A future which can give him all he needs for his people and his region. I get no sense of ambition beyond that . . . at least for many years to come. As for our . . . local situation . . . we are certain he knows Tiajo has fled the den and opened a new threat on the backside of the most priceless of his assets. We are curious what he will do."

His hunting range. Tiajo's escape to Ashidama Bay was a guarantee of Machigi's interest, God, yes—guaranteeing a move of a Marid lord against the west coast, where Edi folk would take extreme exception to intrusion.

"My grandson has never appreciated the west coast," Ilisidi said. "The lords of Shejidan have never valued it, or the Marid for that matter. They think everything stops with the Southern Mountains. When they looked for a valueless shore on which to site the Edi, they chose Najida. When they named its caretaker lords, they still gave them no great status—until your appointment, of course."

"One is flattered, aiji-ma."

"What value it has in our grandson's eyes is solely as your province, we assure you—as long as it maintains the peace. That is always the Ragi attitude toward the south. Nothing that happens here matters to the lords in Shejidan. The aishidi'tat has reached into space. The aishidi'tat has spanned the continent. The south can do as it pleases as long as the south is quiet, especially if we gain quiet in the Marid. My grandson wants me to come back to the center of the universe and sit quietly. Therefore the sleeping pills. Therefore that little machimi on arrival."

Machimi. The classic drama of the aishidi'tat. The historical tales of revenge, ambition, and betrayal.

"For him," Bren said, with extreme misgivings. "For your grandson."

"Because he will not *see*. Because he will not *commit*. I wish him to *worry* about the lands below the Southern Mountains, and if he will not worry about that, he may worry about *me*. He has thrown overwhelming force into the Marid, because the Guild advises him this must happen. But the Guild has never understood the south. The Guild concentrates too much on *records* in Amarja. History! When what matters is *now*, even more than the future. The *problem* is the Ojiri on Jorida Isle. The *problem* is attitudinal independence that cares nothing for anything other than its own wealth. Without Jorida, the Shadow Guild would have been starved out of existence within months of its discovery. Stop them in Ashidama and prevent the Ojiri from ever again repeating the situation! *That* is what the Guild should be concentrating on. Stability depends on legitimate, reliable *associations*. Jorida has none left, its economy has relied much too heavily on the Dojisigin, and it is thus *the* point of instability for the entire southwest."

She paused, staring intently at him, having been uncharacteristically forthcoming. It made sense, given what he had learned from Narani's book. Given what he understood about man'chi, for the Ojiri to attempt to stand alone now, a tiny clan ruling a much larger population of Maschi folk, periodically in violent conflict with the Edi, quarreling with Machigi's clan, opposing humans on Mospheira, opposing the aishidi'tat—it was way too many oppositions to benefit anybody. And with Machigi, another long-time antagonist, gaining power over their chief trading district and joining the aishidi'tat—the Ojiri had a lot to be unhappy about, but their solution *could* not be to shelter the Shadow Guild.

Evidently satisfied with what she saw in his face, Ilisidi gave a quick nod and tapped her cane. "As for what my grandson can do about the situation down here, *Cenedi* cannot be ordered by him. *Midagi* can."

Commander of the Guild forces aboard the train. Midagi. Northern Guild. Tabini's man. Directly under Tabini's authority. And there it was, out in the open. Cenedi, though of greater rank than Midagi, considering who he protected—was not bound by Tabini; but Cenedi could not command the Guild force to leave off assignment to the dowager and go take on an enemy in Jorida. Not without Tabini's direct backing. Cenedi was an Easterner, never granted supreme rank, except *as* Ilisidi's chief bodyguard.

"So we are not wholly displeased," Ilisidi said lightly, "that you sent that message to my grandson. Now he is worried. Not about the right things, but Midagi will *not* receive an order to decamp, and your requested Guild force, Lord of Najida, will stay in place. Lord Geigi will also be grateful. As should the Grandmother of the Edi be."

God. He *had* exactly what he wanted, but *not* by the means he would have asked to have it. "So you will stay here a time, aiji-ma."

"Let me reiterate, paidhi. My grandson is too conservative. Too Ragi. My *great-grandson* will rule the continent some day."

He wondered if Cajeiri understood her plans for him in that light, although . . . perhaps it was less her plans, than her judgment of the boy's character. She and Tabini could politically stabilize the south, could eliminate the Shadow Guild, could create a lucrative and mutually beneficial, continent-wide economy, but ruling the rivalries within it required a wider scope—a visceral commitment to the well-being of *all* its components. She called Tabini *too Ragi,* implying that he did not see past the Southern Mountains, and not past the Continental Divide—to her own region. Was that assessment justified?

It was very possible that she saw things no Ragi did simply because she *was* an outsider. She had entered the marriage with man'chi solidly based in the East, had *used* the aishidi'tat to unify her own people. She came into Shejidan already looking beyond the borders of the aishidi'tat, already understanding the value . . . and the potential danger . . . of the south.

Even more than Ilisidi, Cajeiri had seen things, had expanded what it meant to *be* atevi. He had traveled between stars. Had personally bridged the gap between humans, atevi, and the enigmatic kyo. Ilisidi had had a part in that, but *Cajeiri* had initiated it. Cajeiri had done things no atevi of any age had done—had made human children his close associates—and taken their welfare as personal to him, seeming *driven* to investigate and push boundaries. If Cajeiri were human, he would say the boy had a talent for charming those around him—but that drive was, in an atevi sense, aggressive.

Was Ilisidi implying that his scope, his . . . leadership . . . could expand to include the entire continent? That it was, what? Aggressive enough, flexible enough, to get man'chi across all borders?

It was not an entirely comfortable thought. Cajeiri seemed winningly humanlike at times. But having at least a working comprehension of man'chi—one could feel a twinge of unease.

"He cannot do it alone," Bren said, against her immediate ambitions—a reckless reach for involvement in the current situation. "He will need *you* for years to come."

"We shall endeavor to oblige."

That had not gone exactly where he hoped it would have gone. *What* was she up to?

"The damned pills—excuse me, aiji-ma. But was that all an act, on the platform?"

"Are we not allowed a small mistake? We took too many pills. Oh, I am ill. I am here. I am resting. The spies the Master undoubtedly has in place—they are *always* in place when I visit the south, poor nervous fellow—will tell the Master of Jorida that the old wi'itikin is grown frail and doddering, utterly spent by her adventure. But considering what has sailed into his harbor, he may hear that news with sincere regret. I am a *far* better neighbor than those vermin that have accompanied the bloody Dojisigin witch. Mark you, in my regencies, both of them, I have been extraordinarily patient with the Townships, and patient with more than this current Master of Jorida. I have very generously, and twice, offered them a railroad."

Railroad. It always came back to that. Even now, with the southern war brought to the coast. One could doubt one's ears . . . or the dowager's mental balance . . . with that word . . . railroad.

Except: *Stability depends on associations.* And: *The problem is attitudinal independence that cares nothing for anything other than its own wealth.*

For three generations she had pushed for that railroad . . . to bring Ashidama into direct contact . . . and association with . . . the aishidi'tat.

"I have read about that," he offered quietly. "My major domo had a book."

"Ah, yes. *That* one. Little read and underappreciated, in the self-sufficient north. I should recommend it to my grandson."

"One would hope your grandson *has* read it, aiji-ma."

"Oh, one would doubt he has. If it involves the south, he is remarkably, stubbornly under-read."

One hardly knew what to say, diplomatically. He was reluctant to see peaceful Najida become a bulwark of the north. The Edi had the least possible interest in northern politics for practical as well as historic reasons. But he was even more reluctant to see it face a Shadow Guild threat without northern help.

"I will tell you, paidhi, since you have become moderately learned in the matter—the Master of Jorida is a selfish, region-bound idiot and I am far out of patience with him. But I *will not* countenance that treacherous baggage Tiajo simpering about Jorida, crediting her brilliance for her own survival and calling *herself* lord. I intend to renew my offer to the Townships down in Ashidama district, extract that Dojisigi baggage from Jorida Isle, and settle the matter of trade along the southern coast once and for all. Whether or not Hurshina of Jorida *wishes* to be rescued is no particular concern of ours. But we shall do it. Utilizing his native authority is the easiest, most stable course, but not our only option."

He heard all that. And swallowed a difficult sip of tea before looking up. "Does—your grandson believe that this *illness* of yours will justify Midagi's long-term presence at Najida, aiji-ma?"

Ilisidi gave a very slight, very predatory smile. "You mean to ask, does my grandson foresee what I am about here? Possibly, though particulars likely elude him: he has attacks of deafness when I mention Jorida. He knows me, he knows that creature has escaped to Jorida, he knows where I am, and we would not be surprised to learn he views my reported ill health as comforting news, if it sends me back to Shejidan to sit and sip tea among the other antiques. However, he *does* know me and one is quite certain he will not recall Midagi from Najida until I am aboard the Red Train and headed north. *Hurshina*, however, may hear slightly better than previously. He may even be asking himself whether I will regard him as an asset or simply count him among my enemies. He may even see new appeal in a rail connection."

The railway. She did *not* give up her designs easily. Fate had thrown this opportunity to her, had handed her a vastly weakened, vulnerable opponent, and she was not about to back down, or even give him time to reconsider. But it was not just the railway. It was everything the railway represented. The aishidi'tat itself had been founded around the first railroad.

"I am very sure I have Jorida's attention," she continued. "Tiajo will be delighted by reports of my ill health, but then, she is a fool, and she does not know me as well as Hurshina of Jorida knows me. *He* will be beside himself to learn my intentions, and in that little machimi I have not only pinned down the Guild force my grandson would otherwise reclaim and send back to the Marid—I have waved a strand of hope past the old man in charge of Jorida. *He* is not a fool. Tiajo *is*. So whether Hurshina of Jorida is the treacherous and intelligent creature I used to deal with or whether he has mellowed too much to resist his houseguests—I am sure he will have heard how I have offered Machigi the steel ships. How I have made Machigi the most powerful lord in the Marid. Well, he may think, *now* she will need a counter to Machigi. And he would be right. This little old man of Jorida, who could have been a lord of the aishidi'tat, may suddenly see a way out of his situation. Now that he is old, now that he has attracted a thoroughly useless young woman and the remnant of the Shadow Guild, with interests that will never advantage him— will he believe my machimi is as simple as it is? Perhaps he has even finally seen the future and secretly wants a railroad and just cannot bring himself to say so. *I* have no reluctance to make compliance attractive to him. But we will see." She paused, looking beyond him, then gave a dismissive wave of her hand. "I have just received a signal that the Grandmother is indeed about to arrive."

Cenedi handed the dowager her cane, and offered a hand.

Bren rose, thinking frantically—God, there is no stopping this. She is moving on Tiajo and Tabini cannot stop her.

Should I?

How?

She had ordered the bus. And her favorite local delicacy—twenty-seven days' supply of pickle.

He began to understand he was right to pack exactly as the dowager had said. Including court clothes.

And that book. That book, which he hoped Narani had packed in his baggage. He wanted time to read parts he had half-skimmed or skipped altogether, because the overriding question remained: what had happened, that the Townships, coastal and dependent on Jorida and on the Marid, had succeeded time after time in standing off Ilisidi's lifelong design?

Why had she permitted it?

Lack of time and opportunity?

Or a certain strange sense of possibilities, times that were not right, opposition that was still too strong.

Concessions she would never, ever agree to?

Ilisidi did not give up on ideas. He had known that as long as he had known her.

Tabini should be informed.

He could reach Tabini—through Geigi, if by no other means.

And what could he say? Your grandmother is set on a railroad. And this time she will not stop.

10

Ilisidi's appearance in the central hall brought quiet startlement among the house staff; and not only the house staff. Banichi and Jago, then Tano and Algini fell in with Bren as they passed on their way to the outside doors. They had had *no* word to inform them, none of the ordinary monitoring of conversations their principal was involved in—and Bren had nothing to give them at the moment except a glance and a worried hand sign, Guild-fashion: *Confusion. No conclusion* . . .

Explain what he had just begun to grasp?

No. There was no way. Not in a handful of words.

The great doors of the central hall opened onto the live-flame lanterns of the portico. Ilisidi and her aishid, eight in number, went out ahead of them, into the morning chill and the dark. The rain had stopped. A brisk wind was blowing. It fluttered the lights and cast erratic shadows on the columns of the far side. Three chairs with three little side tables stood waiting, poised in a triangle in the center of the light. The bus had been moved off a distance. Bren noted it down by the garage as he walked out into the dark, and berated himself that he had not worn a heavier coat to breakfast. He knew her. He should have known. Now he was freezing, in a wind straight off the bay.

And out of nowhere a whisper of cloth and a weight settled about his shoulders, enabling him to slip on the warmth of his greatcoat, fresh from the wardrobe crate: Jeladi was there, in the dark, taking care of him, comfort of presence, comfort of warm wool together with the care—thin human skin, he would say:

intolerant of chill; and his staff knew, and foresaw the need. He was massively grateful.

Ilisidi, who tolerated the chill perfectly well, reached the three chairs and stopped, waiting, as Bren joined her. And just beyond past the bus, faintly discernible in the light of the lanterns, a party afoot trudged up the road, slowly, slowly. The Grandmother arrived, not in a vehicle, and with an accompaniment of—as they came clearer—a number of grey-haired elders.

No, the Grandmother of the Edi would not agree to a conveyance. Such were modern things. Nor, indeed, would she enter into a Ragi house, especially one built on Edi land. Ragi were not the enemy lately; but *lately* as the Edi defined time involved a very long memory. The Edi's own great house, under construction over on Kajiminda Peninsula, so Bren had had described to him, was nothing like a Ragi construction, rather an aggregation of peak-roofed houses stacked in tiers, little residences gathered about a common space open to the sky. One of the little houses was to be the Grandmother's, but was reported—by Ramaso, who should know—indistinguishable from any other.

The Edi folk had begun finally to build in wood and stone, after they had been granted a seat in the legislature in Shejidan, and a voice in the aishidi'tat. Permanence was taking shape over there, on land Lord Geigi had freely given them. The Edi were putting down roots for the first time in their centuries on the mainland. That pleased him, though he wished they had felt able to do it on Najida, near the old village.

Now the Grandmother came to Najida's great house, courtesy to a supposedly ailing aiji-dowager, who was standing hale and well in front of her. Bren sorted through things he could possibly say to smooth rough waters if *that* question came up, and not damned much, was his conclusion. Exhaustion from the trip? Extreme thanks to the Grandmother . . . but what excuse was there to offer for Ilisidi's actions, besides an equally obdurate personality?

The Grandmother entered the shelter of the portico with her heads of clans, an apparition out of the night, a stout woman of no distinctive stature, using a walking stick festooned with cords and brass ornaments, shells and carved bone. She came in knee-high felted boots and a knee-length robe of many colors, the same as every woman with her—there were six. They had walked the whole long distance uphill from Najida village, to visit this foreign construction on their land, while the aiji-dowager sat, and her guard stood like a solid piece of night in the lamplight, only the chatoyance of atevi eyes relieving the shadow. There were the colors of the Edi, the stark black of the Guild and the dowager, and one too-pale human in a brown greatcoat, who felt the chill in the wind and hoped not, please God, to have an incident blossom forth before any peaceful and appropriate words could be exchanged. He was the interpreter, the translator, the lord of Najida, but he could not, of all people, interpret for the Edi. Ilisidi might not be Ragi. But she stood for the ancient enemy—who had forced the removal of the Edi from Mospheira to this coast.

For the sake of peace. For the sake of a place to isolate the humans. To stop a ruinous war.

The Grandmother arrived under the portico, at the third point of the circle. Her party ranged themselves behind her.

There were *three* chairs in the arrangement Ramaso had set. In Shejidan, in formal court, the paidhi's place was on the *steps* of the dais—once sitting; lately standing, by Tabini's decree. Here, he was in fact a third authority, lord of the province. And damned uncomfortable in that capacity. He stood; more to the point, Ilisidi rose and stood, an unexpected and gratifying model of courtesy, as the Grandmother reached her chair and her six escorts ranged themselves behind her. The Grandmother sat down, relying on her stick. Ilisidi sat, placed her cane across her lap, and Bren settled into the remaining chair, quietly, aware of his aishid and Ilisidi's as a black Ragi wall behind them, grim counter to the firelit colors of the Edi.

"Grandmother," Bren said, against the flutter of live flame from the lamps, "welcome. The aiji-dowager of Shejidan thanks you and appreciates your great courtesy to her in coming here. Please be welcome at this house. *Naikantshhi o'i mihi.*" Peace. Ramaso had taught him that courtesy. It fell unacknowledged in the Ragi presence, in the meeting of generational adversaries. And one Ragi-appointed human.

There was, silently, the service of tea, steaming in the chill air. Ramaso managed it simultaneously, with his staff. There was a little pause, and the Grandmother sipped hers once, deference to the Ragi custom; then went on to drink it all: it had been a long, chill walk, and there would be a great deal of sugar in it. The Grandmother, Ramaso had said once, liked sugar as much as Najida's human lord.

"Grandmother of the Edi," Ilisidi said, setting down her own cup. "We understand the inconvenience of our request at this hour, in this weather, without warning. As allies and a member state of the aishidi'tat—" One did not use the word *province* in Edi hearing. Bren gratefully heard that deft substitution. "—We have arrived from the Marid, where the aishidi'tat is removing outlaw Guild from the Dojisigin. Senjin has made new agreements with all the other states of the Marid, involving a railroad to the south in that district."

She did not directly mention Machigi, whose hunting range abutted Najida, Kajiminda, and Ashidama. Machigi's district, the Taisigin, was not a good word among the Edi: Machigi's rangers had clashed repeatedly with the Edi. But then—

"Let me be honest," Bren said, "Grandmother of the Edi. From this conflict in the Marid, much to the relief of her own neighbors, the lord of the Dojisigi took alarm and fled. She has arrived on Jorida Isle, along with the leader of the outlaw Guild."

"We know," the Grandmother said grimly; *that* statement was a mild surprise, but then, Ramaso might have broken that news. "Your Ragi war has come to this coast."

Ilisidi set her cane upright. "We deeply regret this. We do not know whether the Master of Jorida has welcomed these people, but if he has, he endangers all of us, especially the Edi. We expect that these outlaws will very quickly strike at Lord Geigi's estate and Lord Bren's in revenge—and we will not wait for that to happen. We ask the Edi people for *permission* to cross Edi lands to deal with this."

God, over that word *permission* bitter incidents had been fought.

"Will you fight these intruders?"

"We will remove them, Grandmother of the Edi."

"Grandmother of the Ragi, we know each other. I remember. You wanted a railroad south to the Townships. You did not get it."

"No," Ilisidi said, "I did not get it. Neither did I bring war against the Edi—which was the price the Master of Jorida asked for the consent of the Townships to the railroad. The Farai lord of Najida wanted that war, *and* that railroad. He got neither. And neither he nor his son remain on Najida."

The Grandmother made a spitting motion. "We remember. We gave his name to the sea. It took him."

Drowned, the word had been. One had heard. One had heard he had quarreled with the village. And his son and heir drowned likewise, and his brother perished, all before the Farai fell afoul of the new aiji in Shejidan—Tabini.

At which point the Farai folded operations on the west coast altogether, vacating Najida.

And Bren's current apartment.

Which meant—

—at the time Ilisidi meant, the Farai had occupied *his* apartment, on the Bujavid's third floor, sharing a wall with the apartment that was now Tabini's, on the third floor of the Bujavid. A Marid clan had had *that* kind of influence, during Ilisidi's regency.

But admitted there—by whom? He had always wondered.

Not Ilisidi, he would be willing to wager, now. Ilisidi's son Valasi might have done it. Her unlamented son. Tabini's father.

But more likely her then-deceased husband of the same name, back in the day.

God, the threads, the threads—

"We know each other," Ilisidi was saying to the Grandmother, "and I well remember it. I well know, Grandmother of the Edi, that you have no patience with fools and less with liars. I share that sentiment. And I am of the same mind today as yesterday. I did not break the agreements with the Edi then, and I will not, now. Lord Geigi is my ally, and I will protect his agreements."

The Grandmother sat still and silent a moment. Then she said, "*All* his agreements."

"Yes. Build your village on the middle peninsula in safety. I will guarantee Jorida's behavior and I will protect Edi shore rights on the Ashidama side of Kajiminda. I will have that promise recorded and remembered among the Ragi. Individuals from the Marid have now appeared in Jorida, who wish to conduct war against the aishidi'tat. We wish to remove them and to end the threat. Will you walk a space alone with me and discuss this in the wind and under the sky, Grandmother of the Edi? We two have things to say to each other."

Silence ensued. The words *remove them* and *the threat* hung in the air. Little doubt now *what* she intended. The how . . . remained problematic.

The Grandmother's staff thumped the ground. Twice. A third time. The Grandmother said something in the Edi language, then made to rise, and Edi nearest her moved to assist her to her feet. Ilisidi rose, leaning on her cane, and indicated the farther reaches of the gravel driveway, beyond which the sky was just beginning to glow.

The Grandmother joined her, and the two walked out into the edge of the light, walked with their backs turned, Cenedi and the rest of her aishid watching, but, Bren judged, not even in atevi earshot.

They lingered some time, silhouettes against the dawn, the loudest sound the fluttering of the lamp flames. Evidently there was discussion out there. Lengthy discussion. At one point Ilisidi lifted her cane and pointed briefly at the sky. Conversation followed, seeming now easier, by the postures involved.

Then they turned and walked back into the lamplight, Ilisidi resuming her place, standing next to Cenedi as the Grandmother joined her own escort. That whole company of Edi then turned without a word and went back across the cobbles, heading toward the road, nothing explained, no further courtesies.

Was that refusal? Bren wondered as they dissolved into the general dark.

Was it acquiescence? Had there been agreement?

Ilisidi seemed satisfied. Bren cast a bewildered look toward Ramaso, over by the door, and Ramaso inclined his head slightly. Yes.

Yes.

Permissions granted? Matters understood?

But what?

The Edi categorically did not trust Ragi, never assimilated, never changed their ways—a people and a culture existing on a thread after their loss of Mospheira, first set under a Farai lord they had hated, and then under a human lord—descendant of the intruders who had made their exile necessary.

Discountable, the Edi, most times, in the affairs of the aishi-di'tat. Stand-offish.

Not grateful for gifts . . . since gifts were nothing but something handed back to them, after taking everything.

And at the moment he felt . . .

He was not sure. He wished Ilisidi well, because that was his loyalty. He wished the Edi well for a late-adopted reason. He wanted Najida safe, and wanted the Edi not to be the target of the Shadow Guild aiming at him for purely personal reasons. Neither did he want to see them made pawns in some Shadow Guild scheme to sow chaos by reviving old animosities. And he was not sure in that presentation Ilisidi had just made, how all that was going to turn out.

One thing was clear. They were going to stop the Shadow Guild—they and the Guild with them, while the rest of the Guild was occupied over in the Marid. Was the dowager going to muster that force she had brought and launch them in an assault on the Townships, and on Jorida?

Start a war on *this* coast while they were engaged to the hilt in the northern Marid? Tabini would have an apoplexy.

"We will be boarding," Cenedi's deep voice rang out, and at the same time Banichi, at Bren's side, said, "We are advising Narani, Bren-ji. We are packed. We are already under orders."

They were moving. "Is Bindanda with us?" he asked Banichi. Bindanda habitually took quarters in the kitchen adjunct, separate from Narani and Jeladi in function as well as in schedule.

"He is," Banichi said. "We are taking the truck. He will ride with the driver."

"Where are we going? To Separti?" If they were entraining any of the Guild force, they would go slower. If not—

"Apparently—to Kajiminda estate."

So. Kajiminda.

Bren settled into his seat opposite the dowager, beside Jago and behind Banichi in the brightly-lit interior of the bus. Shadows moved, in the early dawn beyond the windows. The three lights around the door shone like suns, illumining Edi staff that moved about. The rumble of the engine obscured sound from outside as more of Ilisidi's personal guard boarded and passed down the aisle.

The doors shut. The bus began a slow roll down the driveway, while the market truck growled its way past, headed for the portico to take on baggage—no way would wardrobe cases go on the bus.

Kajiminda. It was the best outcome. The absolute best. They could pay a visit to Geigi's estate for very little trouble—the staff there was a caretaker staff, all Edi, and if the Grandmother had put her blessing on Ilisidi's mission, the Edi folk there would cooperate and *perhaps* not try to take on the Shadow Guild alone.

If Ilisidi meant to order a long-term deployment of Guild who were currently simply holding the train station secure, there remained a question of *where* they were best to be located, to guard *both* Kajiminda and Najida. Kajiminda, being nearer the source of the trouble, with one side of its land abutting the Ashidama Townships—was a logical place to declare a border. It had one long shoreline on Ashidama Bay, and lay only a scant hour's drive from Separti Township, on that shore, and beyond that, Talidi Township.

But the Townships were Jorida's, with daily traffic across the bay and up and down the coast.

Open to Shadow Guild infiltration. Easily so.

The full complexities of trying to establish a defense on the west coast began to dawn with a range of problems, all bidding to involve the Edi, who would not cooperate well with Ilisidi's Guild force, nor take orders from any strangers from Shejidan.

He *needed* to consult with Ilisidi regarding dealing with the Edi—though Narani's book suggested Ilisidi indeed had some knowledge of those problems, far, far more than she had ever let on: that conversation with the Grandmother was as much as he had ever gotten, and granted the Grandmother was accustomed to laying down pronouncements and expecting results—so was the dowager inclined, extremely so, to do the same. Yet they had talked at length, two old women looking down a long history of problems, and they had agreed—on something.

He needed to consult with Tabini—he felt it strongly. But there was no likelihood of that until he got back to Shejidan and there was little likelihood Ilisidi was going to regard any order from her grandson. Guild forces were heavily committed in the Marid. They could not utterly drain the north of Guild to supply a second active operation. Ilisidi's smaller force, adequate to hold Najida, might not be enough, if the Edi's generations-old conflict with the towns of Ashidama broke out into warfare on a third front. And restraining the Edi if attacked, trying to persuade them to patience . . .

They needed more Guild force than they had. And there was none to be gotten without moving units from other critical positions. Geigi was the region's chief asset—physically out of reach, but emotionally tied to his land, his associations. He had forsworn his clan attachments. He had given away half he owned . . . given up all of it to take his post in the heavens.

Geigi could *see* what was happening. He could not reach it with anything in time to stop damage, or loss of life. He could deal with a threat to the dowager, with all that entailed—but with far too *much* destruction.

Beyond the ramifications of using space-based weaponry, the lord of Kajiminda had used to engage in regular trade with Separti, a very convenient and profitable relationship in the early days of what would become Patinandi Aerospace—when Geigi's uncle had inherited the first-ever airplane and motor vehicle manufactory. Back in the day, Jorida's deepwater harbor and Separti's proximity had been useful to Patinandi. Geigi had become one of the wealthiest lords in the aishidi'tat, not so much from manufacturing planes, but from aluminum mining and smelting interests that supplied them, and trade of those products to Mospheira and the Marid. That fortune had expanded exponentially when the starship had reopened contact with the world, and Patinandi had become the *only* aerospace industry on the mainland. Geigi, who had actually detested the factory, rejoiced to see it and the resultant spaceport relocated up north of Cobo, where, with easy access to rail, it flourished.

Now the lord who most detested metal and machines on his land had left the world—literally—going up to manage atevi affairs in a world *made* of metal and machines.

He had tried leaving his nephew Baiji in charge. That had not worked out, so Geigi had become the great benefactor of the Edi, putting the estate in *their* hands . . . and giving half the entire peninsula to the Edi for their own use.

The dowager's going to Kajiminda now—was a splendid idea, if it was going to leave the Red Train stopped at Najida station.

If that was the statement Ilisidi intended to make—drawing a line to keep the Edi out of reach of the Shadow Guild . . .

He could not argue. Even if he wanted to, he could not reach past Ilisidi's authority. Ilisidi sick abed was one matter, but Ilisidi awake and set on a plan was not a force he could divert. Nor did he want to.

Things set in place had to stay in place. Nomari, clearly, was to stay at Najida—*his* concerns were all northern, and none here at all. Nomari's guard would see to that. And he was not in sight this morning.

Nomari, Machigi's spy in Koperna, had proved almost as skilled as Guild in evading observation. *He* had not been out of his room this morning—one hoped—but how long before he learned what was afoot? What would he think when he realized he alone had been left behind?

Two individuals of greater concern had not been visible this morning, not only Guild but one-time Shadow Guild; and both Dojisigi to boot. The dowager had set them free.

"I do not see Homura or his partner this morning," he remarked to Jago.

"Nor have we," Jago said.

"The dowager has restored their status. And apparently their equipment."

Jago was silent a moment. "She must spare watchers for them or put them down. They will be in no doubt of this. One suspects they are nowhere on Najida Peninsula, and traveling faster than the bus—if by land. North could set them toward Cobo. Cross Kajidama Bay and they can walk to Separti."

The second was a worry. And likeliest, in his estimation.

"Read them for me, Jago-ji. Did they lie to us?"

"Oh, more complex than that, Bren-ji. The question now is whether their partners are living or dead, or ever existed, and if they exist, how they plan to free them in the remote chance Suratho has them. And she might well. This team was never so important to the Shadow Guild as when they pledged man'chi to the dowager. It might increase the value of their partners as hostages."

"To draw their man'chi back to Suratho?"

"Possibly." Jago looked out the window. It reflected a flash of golden eyes. "Our view? The dowager has loosed *our* problem and sent it to Jorida to do whatever they intend to do. They attached their man'chi at Tirnamardi—so they say—before they became invisible; and now they are back—but they have reappeared only close to the Shadow Guild, whether at Koperna, or here."

A half unit. Units that suffered loss of a person or a team sometimes combined with other such. Sometimes not.

Whatever had happened to them to make them a half unit *would* constitute a strong motive of some kind. But what motive?

If Jago could not figure them better than that—one wondered whether the dowager could.

Two Guild, one enigma.

And another enigma resided on Jorida, whether the Master of Jorida welcomed his new houseguests or was himself in need of rescue.

"I am not sure about any of this," he said quietly to Jago. "We may be losing my ability to contact Lord Geigi. I am not sure phones still exist where we are going. I do not know what kind of maintenance Kajiminda will have had, with no likelihood Geigi will return."

"Geigi will know the condition of it," Jago said. "And he will know when we arrive there. Whatever he is doing, you have gotten his attention."

True. Geigi would know where they were, at least. Geigi could watch the bus even in the dark: his view was that good. And *Geigi* would know at least when they arrived at Kajiminda, and Geigi would surely report to Shejidan and Tabini.

Which the dowager might also expect. So might Cenedi.

Of course, if *he* had the secure com Tabini and Geigi expected him to have, Geigi would not have to spend resources tracking them and trying to guess their moves. As was—they were with Cenedi, who was thus equipped, and Geigi would have conveyed the problem to Tabini, who *could* talk securely to Cenedi. And he did not want that interface to blow up, which a challenge for his designated communicator would almost assuredly do. Of all things, they did not want that to happen, with things as they were.

The best option was to keep a lid on the situation, keep in touch with what information Cenedi would give them, keep in the dowager's good graces, and hope that Geigi's own residence *might* have at least phone service maintained—if not its own high-tech access to Geigi.

He was accustomed to Cenedi's tendencies not to share the dowager's intentions. He tried hard *not* to be resentful. But damn . . . there were times . . .

Jago had been listening to something, her finger against her earpiece. "The market truck will stop at the encampment and pick up some surveillance equipment and heavier armament we did not bring to Najida."

"One is grateful," he said.

Kajiminda—please God they were in *fact* going to visit Kajiminda—was a logical and somewhat defensible position from which to set up spies, to track, on the ground, what was going on in Ashidama. How long would they stay? Twenty-seven days as her request for supplies implied? One hesitated to equate that request to anything real: Kajiminda would be in no need of supplies, except as courtesy, except for the pickle she so craved.

Except . . . it was well beyond a simple visit to the neighbors.

He hoped the house was somewhat in use. Possibly they could expect regular meals and warm beds: he hoped so for the dowager's sake. Whatever her plans—and it was by no means assured they were reasonable—she was still fragile and she had admitted to being overtired. Kajiminda at least would be dry, not a field camp in cold and wet.

Trust the Edi for that. They would not let the place have gone to ruin.

11

Breakfast was . . . different. Cajeiri was not in good appetite, and he tried desperately to be, as he met a new day, pretending everything was normal in his apartment.

Word had come early from his father: well before dawn Cenedi had called in saying mani had spent a quiet night and managed a moderate breakfast.

That was the first report.

Then the camp commander reported that nand' Bren had taken the bus early that morning to Kajiminda, to warn the Edi there about the Shadow Guild in Jorida, a trip which neither Cenedi nor the camp commander would have supported if there were acute danger. So it ought to be good news. They were preparing to hold Kajiminda.

But there was no information about mani except that she had had breakfast, encouraging in itself, but he was still worried about her; and worried about Eisi and Liedi and Dur and all of it.

His younger bodyguard, who shared the table with him, caught his glum mood—not frowning, but maintaining that expressionless Guild manner they held in crisis, a propriety his older aishid had been encouraging since their arrival. Faces usually cheerful were set in lines that were *not* full of fun and humor, he could not cheer them up as *he* felt, and he was only thankful his elder aishid remained absent—Rieni's unit had been days absent for reasons undefined, which he was sure had directly to do with what was going on in the Marid—if they were even still in Shejidan. Rieni and the others, all retired instructors, all experienced in real situations, had been called to war status, was what he guessed, because with the Guild fighting in the Marid they needed their most experienced people doing the thinking. The Guild had sent south people it now had to replace in the north, because there was active fighting going on where mani had *been* a few days ago. So they were probably still in the city, probably at Guild Headquarters—just not here.

And thinking of all that only reminded him that the trouble in the Marid was spreading to the west coast.

He had tried every means he knew to get information. His younger aishid had. There had been no word out of the west coast this morning, except the news of the bus trip—no word beyond that, with the Guild camp settling in for a stay. The silence from inside Najida was Unusual, as Veijico put it, and Veijico knew something about the west coast, being from there. Veijico knew where to look—and found nothing.

"Is that ordinary?" he had asked her, and Veijico had said, "No. There is never much. But channels are simply shut down."

That was spooky, but not wholly unreasonable given *they* knew that mani was there; and that nobody was going to give out much information about the bus. Where the Red Train went, there were always holes in information, and there was more than usual reason now.

The one place he knew there would be information was two doors down the hall: Father's office; and that was not where he wanted to be until Lord Tatiseigi had gotten to Najida—assuming he was on his way to Najida. Dimaji and Tariko meanwhile were soft-footing it about trying to do duties they had never practiced before, including getting breakfast from Father's kitchen, and bringing it quietly in from the back hall stairs. Nothing was broken, nothing even spilled; and if the tea was the evening tea instead of the morning blend, it was not worth mentioning, since he desperately did not want to attract Father's or Mother's attention at the moment, and staff confusion could accidentally do that. His aishid was quiet, and grim, also walking soft-footed. It was as if every tiny detail could explode, and Tariko and Dimaji were surely well aware something improper was going on. If they grew alarmed and decided to report—it was all up.

At breakfast with his aishid, the forbidden topic hovered all around the table. Attempted conversation died.

What Tariko and Dimaji must not do today was appeal to anyone outside the household for information, and he had, with a little truth, forestalled that.

"My great-grandmother is ill," he said. "If there is any message from anywhere, of any sort, bring it to me, even if it comes from house staff. I want to know. If anything seems wrong, I want to know."

"Yes, nandi," had been the answer.

It was enough reason to give them, and truthful. They served very quietly and competently: they had clearly listened to what instruction Eisi and Liedi had given them; and now they tried to be invisible amid all the anxiety at the table, and the general lack of appetites.

"Thank you," he said to the domestics, in sum. It was what Father would say, no matter the tea. He frowned, even thinking of Father, and as quickly stopped frowning. "Thank you, nadiin."

"Nandi." They had remembered to bring Boji's eggs and they had kept him quiet through breakfast. The apartment had not fallen apart in Eisi's and Liedi's absence. They had done everything right.

Now they began to gather up the dishes.

And froze in shock as the door to the main room opened without ceremony. Cajeiri's own heart jumped, and his aishid was out of their chairs on the instant.

But it was just Eisi, wild and windblown, with one hand full of packages, who pushed the door open, and Dimaji left the breakfast dishes and headed for the door, where he also was posted. He reached it in time to assist Eisi with the packages and hold the door for Liedi, whose arms held two very large sacks.

Cajeiri rose, heart thumping, and hoped it was success and good news that brought them so laden with purchases on the Bujavid tokens; and that Father's staff, who kept the front door to the whole section were not going to bring word to Father that Eisi and Liedi were somehow doing something questionable.

Eisi surrendered his packages to Dimaji and gave a deep, self-pleased bow. "I reported our mission to staff management as shopping, and we did not lie—all these from the station premises, this morning. And Lord Tatiseigi, nandi, is now in the air! Liedi will tell you."

Liedi was utterly a sight. His queue ribbon was a sad one-sided affair and his face looked burned, excepting lighter circles about the eyes, which gave him a wild and astonished look.

"Go, nadiin." Cajeiri waved a dismissal at Dimaji and Tariko, who gathered up dishes as they went, not without alarmed glances. And to Eisi and Liedi: "How did it go?"

"Lord Tatiseigi is indeed on his way, nandi," Liedi had set down his packages, and made a broad gesture. "All, all done. I changed trains in Cobo. When I got to Dur the young lord was immediately on the phone and we were aloft within the hour. We had to land twice to fill up the plane, but Lord Dur had called ahead and there was no delay at all when we got to these places. People were waiting in the middle of the night for us, and on we went. And Tirnamardi was just as ready. We landed on the lawn, right inside the great hedge, the flat part, you know, so the lord was driven down from the house, but he could not take his baggage. The young lord only stood on the wing to help Lord Tatiseigi up, and then they were off. The young lord was sure they could make Cobo with just one refueling stop. By what he said, he is surely there by now."

"And Lord Tatiseigi instantly agreed when I arrived at Tirnamardi and told him," Eisi said. "He is extremely concerned about your great-grandmother. He said he has never flown, let alone in an open plane, but he swore he had no fear at all, as old as he is. He also said to say he is forever in your debt, nandi, and he called you his favorite nephew."

His grand-nephew, and the only nephew Uncle Tatiseigi had ever had, but that was indeed the very sort of thing Great-uncle would say.

"Also—he said he would call from Najida," Eisi said. "I did not know what to say, nandi. I did not know how to say no to him. I only said, Please think of my lord and be careful. And he said, *Let him forbid me!* And I do not think he meant you, nandi. I have to apologize."

The two of them had hurried. They were still out of breath, and doubtless exhausted.

Dishes rattled. A misstep. Dimaji had returned for the remainder of the dishes, in full hearing of the last sentences. Cajeiri looked askance at him and decided, then and there, because everything they were doing *would* be known, that it was better to offer trust, flat on the table, do or do not.

"Call Tariko," he said. "You are household. Come. We shall wait for you."

Dimaji set down his burden of dishes, went back into the bedrooms and called Tariko, who came out looking confused and worried, looking from him to his aishid, to the uncommon appearance of Eisi and Liedi.

Dimaji and Tariko were adults. That was the fact that set them apart. They were also sober and sensible and loyal to the house, or Father would not have had them in his household.

But that was the one troubling fact. Father *had* had them in his household.

"This is the day," Cajeiri said, "that you choose, nadiin, whether your man'chi belongs to me—or to my father. If your man'chi is to me, he will blame me, never you, and I will tell him so. Never will I do anything against my father *or* my mother, but I will do things, things I believe right and necessary, and I will make mistakes. Just—which side of the door do you wish to be on, and where does your man'chi rest, nadiin? Tell me and I will not send you away or complain of you at all. I only ask—which side of the door do you wish to be on when we are discussing the things I do?"

There was stark silence a space. Then they held each other's hand and one gave a little nod and the other did. "Yours, nandi," Dimaji said, and: "This side," Tariko said. "This is your house, nandi. These rooms. We wish to be here."

That was the first time they had ever said—his house. So they decided, the way his aishid had, the way Eisi and Liedi had, and put up with his stupid ideas, and Boji's mischief, and all of it. They were different than his older aishid, who might never truly be his, though they served him.

"Eisi-ji," he said, "Liedi-ji, how did it go? Every detail."

Eisi looked at Liedi.

Liedi said, "Eisi took the train to Taiben, nandi. I went to Cobo, and caught the next train up to the coast."

"I had the easier trip," Eisi said, "by far. We reached the train station. And I used the phone to call the major d' of Tirnamardi. And when I arrived in Taiben, in the woods, expecting to wait, Lord Tatiseigi's car was waiting. And when I got to Tirnamardi I talked to Lord Tatiseigi himself, and gave him your letter and told him everything. He was very concerned about the dowager, honor to her name. And he immediately waked up all his staff, and began packing and choosing a coat. Liedi was arriving at Cobo about then."

"With just barely enough time to catch the north spur train," Liedi said, "because the Cobo train had to wait for the transcontinental. I was afraid I would miss it, but when we got there, I ran, nandi, and I used the Bujavid token at the ticket office to hold the train, I regret, nandi, but I would have missed the train and there is not another until the morning."

"Well done!" Cajeiri said, though he was sure that using the token to hold a train might draw attention in Accounts. So might the train tickets, much more than the parcels, and he might hear from Father a little sooner than he feared; but if Liedi had done all the rest it was too late for that—and he wanted the rest of the story. "So you came to Cobo."

"After mid of the night, indeed, nandi. Anyway, I took the train to the north, I got off at Dur Astandi, and tried to call Dur, but their phone was out—it appears a storm had come through earlier and knocked down lines—so I walked to the great house and their gate was open, so that part was easy. I just walked up the hill to the door and knocked and knocked, until the night staff asked my business. Then I showed the token to the night watch, told him I came from you, and I had to speak to the young lord. The night staff sent someone to wake the young lord, and he came down in his nightshirt, in a great hurry. I told him everything you said and gave him the letter. He read it quickly, and he asked no questions at all: he waked staff and sent people running out to the field to wake the mechanic and make his plane ready. He said—shall I shorten this, nandi?"

"No, no, I want to hear it. All of it. Was he upset?"

"Not at all, nandi. He was—he was as good as you could ask. He called a servant to serve *me* tea, nandi! And dressed right in the hall, and called for his flight jacket and his helmet, and ordered someone to find the fault in the phone lines all in one string of orders. And then in all that commotion, he asked me how I was getting back to the Bujavid, because I had told him, you know, there were two of us, and that Eisi had gone to Tirnamardi, and that Lord Tatiseigi would be wanting to go before—" Liedi stopped, with a shift of the eyes toward Father's apartment, as if Father could hear right through the walls. "Wanting to go as soon as he could. So he, the young lord, Lord Reijiri, he set his aishid to making phone calls to arrange things along the way, as soon as the lines were back up. And he said to me, 'You had as well be gone from here or spend all day answering my father's questions. Staff can drive you to the train station. But I can get you to Tirnamardi, if you want to take the passenger seat, as fast as I get there myself, and you can meet your partner.' And I thought—I thought it would be better to get back as fast as I could, so I agreed, and I rode in the plane, nandi. In the open air, with no windows!"

Cajeiri knew that plane, knew it very well—from the ground— and oh, he would have accepted such a ride in a moment. He wanted to hear every detail of it. But he said, to get to Uncle, and the essentials—"So you flew to Tirnamardi with him."

"I did, nandi. And at Tirnamardi they had lights set all over the lawn in front, which is a long hill, but a flat space near the gates. And we landed there. We were hardly on the ground and stopped when Lord Tatiseigi came down in his motorcar, with his aishid. And baggage, but Lord Reijiri said they could not take it, it would have to go by train, and we, Eisi and I, we would take it to Taiben and have the conductor tag it for Najida, so it will get there—"

"We took it in the motorcar," Eisi said. "But Lord Tatiseigi's aishid came with us and took care of it, as they were heading for Najida to join Lord Tatiseigi."

"And I gave Lord Tatiseigi the goggles," Liedi said. "Nobody had brought a ladder, and they were going to go get one, but Lord Dur said to move the motorcar up to the wing, and Lord Tatiseigi got up onto the car and up he went with Lord Dur's help onto the wing, and climbed into the seat I had had. Like a young man, nandi. You would have been amazed!"

The image of it was amazing, no question.

"And Lord Dur got in and they took off, and they just barely cleared the hedge. Lord Dur said they were going to refuel at Cobo." Liedi drew a deep breath. "They should be there by now."

"And we rode in the motorcar with the luggage right from there," Eisi said, "because we could just make the night train if we hurried; and staff said they would call the railroad in Shejidan to have them hold at Taiben Station, because we were coming. But we made it, anyway, without them even waiting."

It was not exactly an expedition innocent of traces left along the way. Now the railroad office *and* the Bujavid offices knew that *his* servants had been to Tirnamardi and back. And Cobo would know Lord Tatiseigi's luggage had to go to Najida, along with Uncle's aishid.

Father was going to know, if enough questions met each other, and it was very likely something would get his attention.

But Uncle was well on his way by now, and even if Father was probably going to be upset, it had all worked, and he had done what he needed to do for mani. And for Uncle. If she was terribly, terribly ill—if she was that ill, she would want to see Lord Tatiseigi above all her associates, maybe even above him. Lord Tatiseigi had been worried and very, very put out when she had taken off on the trip to Hasjuran with Lord Machigi, whom *nobody* trusted, and then—

Then everything had blown up down in the Marid, and all sorts of things started shifting and changing, like objects on a shelf that just started to fail, a cascade of things that never had happened suddenly sliding and changing other things . . .

Lord Tatiseigi, just like Father, just like him, had been supposed to sit up here in the north and hear the reports of Great-grandmother being sick and do nothing. But Uncle would encourage her. Uncle could talk to her. Mani was entirely unreasonable when she was not feeling well, and particularly when things were not going well. Cenedi could argue with her up to a point, but then he would do whatever mani wanted, while nand' Bren had no way to argue with mani *or* Cenedi if it came to that.

But Lord Tatiseigi could. Lord Tatiseigi could even tell mani she was wrong, when nobody else could.

So he had put it all together and he had done everything he could reach to do. He ought to feel better about that.

But it had been a lot noisier than he would have wished, and involved far more people, and left way too many traces. It had not been what mani would call a neat operation.

Even in his own premises he had now involved Dimaji and Tariko, and his younger aishid. And his two senior servants most of all.

The whole household stood assembled; and he was not happy, but he found himself at least not that unhappy with what he had done. It was a semicircle of grim faces, and several worried ones. Only his older aishid was missing from their midst. One could imagine them—frowning. Darkly.

"Nadiin," he said to them then, "my father may be extremely unhappy with me when he finds out all I have done; and what part you do not know, you do not need to know." The faces were so uniformly grim a little lightness seemed in order. "So do not be afraid of consequences. I will *not* ask you go with me if he sends me to live in Hasjuran."

"Nandi," Eisi said quietly, appalled.

"One doubts it would be Hasjuran," he said. "But we should *not* discuss what I have done anywhere in the house. The more that hear of it, the worse it will be if it goes wrong—as it could. My father and I will discuss what I have done, when he finds out, which I am fairly sure will be this morning, but I had rather it be as late as possible. I shall not blame any of you if you wish to leave my service. I shall not blame you. Truthfully, I had thought I would do better this year. But at times it seems reasonable to do things of which my father may not approve—and you who are very new should know that." He tried to think of what else to say and nothing else occurred to him. "You may go now. All of you."

"Nandi," Tariko said, and Dimaji echoed her. Tariko gave a prolonged—a very prolonged bow; so did Dimaji; and straightened up and gave a solemn little bow to Eisi and Liedi, respecting the order of the household.

Were they satisfied? Were they vowing to apply to Services as soon as the matter broke, and find another household?

Either was possible.

Of Eisi and Liedi he had no doubt. Nor any of his younger aishid—at all, or ever. They would not leave him. And for them— honestly—he was scared.

But not repentant.

He only dreaded what his elder aishid would say when they found out.

"Go rest," he said to Eisi and Liedi. "Go to bed. My aishid and I will deal with everything as it happens. Take the rest of the day, and sleep. With my thanks, nadiin-ji."

There were apt to be messages soon, from Father. They could manage. *He* could manage. His aishid had had nothing to do with it. He had been careful on that score, too. It was his plan, and he would say that when Father asked. He could say it with absolute truthfulness.

His older aishid was not here, and his younger one could hardly be held accountable for orders he gave to his two senior servants, in private. He had protected everybody, and mani herself could not have managed better in that part. He had learned her ways, knew how to keep his face perfectly calm; and he knew through what channels orders and information flowed, what moved where, when the trains ran, carrying what—all those dreary, dull lessons about all the commerce and transportation of the aishidi'tat.

She might be proud of him.

His father probably—well, possibly Father would explain to him in specific why he was wrong, but he was relatively sure his staff were in the clear, even Eisi and Liedi.

And if Father did not find out about it until enough time had elapsed for Uncle to get to Najida—

Then he had to gather up his courage, tell Father what he had done and let Father decide what to do about it, because it was needful that Father know Uncle had left Tirnamardi, and that Uncle, mani, *and* nand' Bren were down in Najida definitely needing protection from the Shadow Guild.

There *was* that considerable Guild force sitting there, with the Red Train. They had the equipment. They were prepared, if someone gave the order. And if mani could not give it, Father certainly could.

As for the young lord of Dur being at fault—at no time had Liedi informed him that Lord Tatiseigi had been told *not* to come to Najida—since he had not given Liedi that information. He had been very careful.

Technically—well, Dur, who was an ally he valued personally, and would rely on in any crisis—Dur would certainly be justified in being upset with him, and that was deeply upsetting.

But he had made his choice and now he had only to give Uncle enough time to get to Najida. At least time enough for Lord Dur's yellow plane to take on fuel at Cobo and get back into the air.

Then maybe—

A terrible, terrible thought dawned on him—maybe someone should urgently tell Father to tell the Guild at Najida that that bright yellow plane was going to need to land, and that they should not shoot at it.

How long did it take to refuel?

What if they delayed there—for breakfast—or just to rest, for Uncle's sake? How long did it take to fly between Cobo and Najida?

A motorized Guild escort fell in with the bus at the intersection of the train station road and the market road—two of the fast-moving light vehicles, offloaded from the train. Bren turned in his seat as one blazed by in a spray of mud, taking the lead, and the other fell out of sight, likely still with them.

Those were on Cenedi's orders, one was sure; part of the initial force Ilisidi had brought with them to Hasjuran.

And the deployment had erected rows of tents beside the market road, pale canvas ghosts in the foggy morning light. That was comforting to see—Guild poised to move, if movement became the order—but stationed there in the meantime for the protection of Najida and Najida village. It was both ominous, that martial intrusion into a peaceful meadow, and immensely reassuring, because of what else might be moving up and down that road. One was hopeful their orders would still be to protect Najida, and that they were not moving.

The threat they themselves might run into?

There was that to think about.

The dowager only glanced out the window at the encampment. She might have been passing some ceremonial review. It was that kind of expression.

Cenedi, however, had gotten up and moved down the aisle, perhaps to have a view of the tents from the rear windows, perhaps in the process of delivering orders to the Guild officer in charge of the train and the encampment, who, one believed, did have one or more of Lord Geigi's special communications units.

Possibly *his*. If that were the case, he could think of no better use for it at this time, if it meant safety for Najida. Still . . . it would have been nice to have been *asked*. It would have been nicer to have *one* of the two they had had at Koperna.

The vehicle in front of them ran along the grassy margin. The bus and presumably the truck that would be following them were on the one-lane market road, a track worn in sandstone intermittent with sand, that ran from the station as far as Ashidama before the sandstone gave out and the road became—whatever lack of maintenance let it become. Every neighbor to a road was *supposed* to maintain his own stretch of roadway; but Ashidama only maintained the market roads in certain seasons—and since Lord Geigi had gone away to space and Kajidama maintenance devolved entirely on Najida, which did have heavy equipment, it was fine near the rail station—but what lay ahead and whether it would hold up all the way to Kajiminda's share of the road, which the Edi did not use, was a question.

Jago cast a look out the window as far back as she conveniently could and faced forward again.

"Is the second vehicle still behind us?" Bren asked.

"Yes," Jago said.

Tano stood up and came as far as Banichi's seat, foremost. Tano sat down. Those two talked, silhouetted against the grey dawn. One recalled without overmuch happiness that mines, explosives, demolitions, and ambushes were Tano's particular field of expertise, and one had to wonder what the discussion was.

Himself—he decided that sleep was available for the next small stretch of road and murky morning, and he settled down against Jago's shoulder, shutting his eyes and sinking into the steady noise of the bus. The dowager had had days to sleep. The dowager was intent now on moving with dispatch, to what precise purpose he was not sure, but thus far an encampment of Guild and a reassurance that the dowager *had* a plan and a purpose was enough, compared to last night, to let him let go of higher thought and concentrate instead on what he might do—

He slept. Let go entirely.

It was time. By the clock, by his maps, by everything Cajeiri had been able to figure from what Liedi knew and remembered from his late-night flight, it was time enough for the plane to have reached Cobo airport and to refuel to fly to Najida—it was not a long operation.

Now it was time to send a message to Father.

Honored Father, I have received reliable information—

That was a proper formal beginning. A lot of official dispatches started that way.

Reliable information. That was true.

I have received very reliable information that Uncle Tatiseigi has joined the young lord of Dur—

No, that was not at all good. That made it sound as if Dur had done everything, and that would have Father mad at Dur, who by no means deserved it.

Lord Tatiseigi has taken a trip south with Lord Reijiri . . .

No. That sounded like a country outing of two fools.

Great-uncle has become concerned about Great-grandmother and he is flying out of Cobo—

Better. A little better.

Great-uncle has become very concerned because of news about Great-grandmother—

Rumors did get out. And that was how Great-uncle would react. Absolutely.

He is in the air right now, flying south with young Dur—

Well, it dodged explaining how Dur had gotten involved, but it did not blame Dur, either.

And then to the really serious problem, the problem that had his stomach upset the last three hours:

And since the Guild has taken a position at the train station, which is near the road, which is the only flat place to land, one is very concerned that the Guild might mistake them for Shadow Guild.

That was good.

Please inform the Guild sitting at Najida that this plane is Dur and Atageini. Please do it very quickly. I believe the plane has now left Cobo, heading for Najida, so there is not much time.

This is very—

No. Not enough.

This is extremely urgent.

He almost added: *I am very sorry.* But that was what he was going to have to say when Father called him in, and there was only weakness in repeating himself.

I forgot to tell him about the Guild camp.

That was the sorry truth. And his guilt, his fault if anything happened. He really, truly felt sick at his stomach, and had the last three hours.

He called in his whole younger aishid to carry the message—they were technically never, ever all supposed to leave him at once, considering that his older aishid was still absent, but technically, too, he was inside the protection of Father's aishid, and Mother's, so it was not quite like violating the rules. They were still inside the apartment, on the sacrosanct third floor of the Bujavid, and he wanted Father to have no possible doubt that the message was urgent.

"Do whatever you have to," he said, "to get this to Father. Say it is life and death. But if you cannot reach him personally to put this in his hand, come and get me, and I will go talk to him myself."

And if he could not penetrate Father's working security in the next few minutes, he had already determined, he would go to Mother—who, he realized with a little shock, probably really *should* be told, Great-uncle being *her* uncle, and Atageini being the inheritance of his baby sister. The protocols of that situation had not even crossed his mind in the thought of the yellow plane and the Guild encampment bristling with guns.

He went back to his desk and penned another note.

Honored Mother, Great-uncle is flying into Najida from Cobo, in Dur's plane. He does not know about the Guild camped down there. I have sent a warning to Father. Please be sure he is warning the Guild not to shoot at them. It is extremely urgent.

He was out of people to send. He went and found Dimaji in the new hall, behind his bedroom, and handed him the rolled note, with: "Maji-ji, *run* and give this to my mother immediately and say it is urgent. Tell her she must read it now. Immediately."

His heart was beating very fast as Dimaji left. He was alone in his apartment now, except for Tariko, who looked confused as Dimaji hurried past her with no explanation.

Tariko looked after Dimaji, then at him, and what could he say?

"I have to talk to my father. My good coat, nadi-ji. My best day coat."

Tariko asked no questions, just hurried ahead of him to the bedroom and the wardrobe, and hesitated between two coats . . . "That one," he said. It was not her job, and she was not Liedi, but she took it from the hanger and held it for him for a quick change.

Then he hurried out the door and down the hall with no

attendance. Father was in his office—the presence of Father's guard indicated that, and he went to that door and knocked at it himself, with no regard to the Guild who ordinarily would have had advisement from *his* guard he was coming. He gave one rap and opened it himself.

Father, at his desk, gave one sharp look up and signed to the guard who were on either side of him, taken by surprise.

The note was in Father's hand. His younger aishid were still in Father's office. And the look on Father's face was apprehension and question at once.

One hasty bow. "Honored Father."

"What *is* this?" Father asked.

With his message in hand.

So Father knew the essentials. The only thing left was to bow respectfully. The only thing left to say was: "Please tell the Guild to protect the plane."

"You arranged this."

"Yes, honored Father."

There was a moment of intense silence, Father looking at him, him looking back with as composed a face as he could manage.

"You may go," Father said to his younger aishid, who—force of habit—looked first to him. Cajeiri dipped his chin and they silently eased themselves out the door and shut it.

It was very quiet for a moment. It was a very long quiet.

"Do you *know* the consequences, son of mine, should we lose Tatiseigi and Dur to this adventure?"

"I know we would lose Uncle's man'chi if mani died, and he could not go."

"That is a judgment call."

"Yes, honored Father." He brought his chin up and almost looked Father straight in the eye. "It was." He had thought that was all he would have time to say, and that maybe the last was a little too pert for safety. But Father let the silence hang. So he added: "Uncle would not forgive us, honored Father. And he *is* Atageini."

There was a long, long silence. Father's angry stare scared

people. He had never been the recipient of it. Now he was. And he resolved, if he was ever aiji, he had to develop a stare of his own. He set his jaw, met Father's eyes and stared back, and for a long, long time there was quiet.

"One is informed," Father said, "that your two senior staff traveled to Tirnamardi to set this in motion."

"One, actually," he said. "The other went to Dur and flew down with the plane." There was a chance to do justice. "My message did not tell Dur that Uncle was under any orders. It is not Dur's fault."

Lengthy silence attended that, too.

"Do we detect *pride* in this achievement, son of mine?"

"Yes, honored Father. In duty to my mother. To my *sister*, who stands to inherit Tirnamardi." He took it one dangerous step further. "To Uncle. Who trusts Shejidan. One saw a way. Which should be safe, if only you will advise the Guild not to shoot at them."

"Rest assured I have just done that," Father said. *"Gods less fortunate, son of mine!* Kindly *suggest* your innovative solutions to me beforehand, in the future! You have put the entire succession of the Padi Valley *and* the lord of the northeast coast in jeopardy, right along with the paidhi-aiji and your great-grandmother! If our enemies were hesitant to make an attack now, you will have decided their course beyond any doubt. We are engaged to the hilt in the Dojisigin Marid, we have no units to spare for a second front, and you may have just opened one."

"Mani has a Guild force."

"Who have to hold the whole of the southwest—half the continent—including some who *claim* to be allies. *Lord Machigi* holds the entire southern hunting range, clear to the Ashidama market road!"

"Lord Machigi has concerns at home just now. And off his coast."

"Does he not? But his opportunity for mischief in the south has now become extravagant—if only something befalls Grandmother. Has that thought not crossed your imagination? Or do you suppose he is trustworthy?"

"Honored Father, I agree. But if mani dies, or goes away north and never does anything to secure the west coast, then Machigi will be there in the middle of it all. His forces were never able to stop the Shadow Guild. If he chooses to go after Jorida by sea or land, it will be just the same. Harder, because Jorida is said to be . . . impregnable." He had learned that word just that morning from his books. "Best do it while we have a Guild force there. And *we* direct things."

Father gazed at him a moment, then rested chin on fist and continued to stare. "We are aware. You are *confident* of the thoroughness of your studies, son of mine?"

That was a question. It was full of traps. But it was also a challenge.

"I am nearly to my tenth year, the unluckiest two and the moderately fortunate five, yes, and I know bad decisions look fair. I did think, honored Father. I know why *you* cannot take certain decisions. But I also know when *you* cannot do certain things because of policy, you rely on mani to do them. And now mani is ill. So who is to do those things? I know Uncle, I know him and I am that sure of Uncle's man'chi. I know Lord Geigi, and I am very sure that Lord Geigi will move to protect Kajiminda and Najida, which involves his land, does it not? So mani's Guild force will not have to worry about *that.* If you call Lord Geigi and tell him the whole situation, I think that will set him free to do what he can do from where he is."

"He *has* no more landers! The one he sent down is on the edge of a bog in the Marid. Mobile it may be, but it cannot hike across the entire southern plateau!"

"Things can be done from up there."

"Limited things."

"I have been there, honored Father. I have seen the world from there. And Lord Geigi can see everything. He will protect what has to be protected."

"Kajiminda sits within easy reach of Separti, just a walk through the woods. And Separti is little more than an hour from Jorida itself by the slowest barge afloat. In your knowledge of Lord Geigi's power to do something, does it occur to you that it is one thing for him to *see* a situation on Earth, and as long as five hours for him to send even the fastest response down from his high perch—ample time for the situation on the ground to change. Your great-uncle and your great-grandmother together, not to mention the paidhi-aiji, are an irresistible target for those whose response can be instant in comparison."

"Then our enemies may make a mistake."

"You sound just like Grandmother."

He was inwardly pleased by Father saying that. But certainly Father was not pleased when he said it.

"You *could* move the Guild force, honored Father, in a much shorter time. You could order them to circle Najida."

"So can she," Father said. "And since she has had her way, with a Guild force at her disposal, one might trust she will defend herself and Lord Bren. Not to mention, now, the lord of Atageini and the younger lord of Dur. Fortunate gods, son of mine! We have a war in the Marid, alliance with *two* unstable warlords in the heart of that action, not to mention little Hasjuran passionately sworn to defend us, gods save us—all signatures so new the ink has hardly dried on their promises—and with all this at our backs, she forces us to take on a problem that has resisted solution for three hundred years. Upon which, my son suggests I toss in the force that is protecting the gateway to Cobo, which is where, in no few days, we will begin to receive an unprecedented number of humans! We can by no means risk the Shadow Guild getting near them!"

It was a problem, but: "All the more reason to have Uncle in a position to make mani see reason. If she is being devious, if she is *not* ill and plans to take on the Shadow Guild directly, *Uncle* can make her remain at Najida, rather than trying to be in the middle of it."

"Let me inform you, son of mine, she is *not* at Najida."

It took a moment for his ears to hear that.

"Not at Najida?"

"She has risen from her bed, boarded the estate bus, and decamped with nand' Bren to Kajiminda in the dark—politely leaving the Guild force where I put them—while Cenedi, our only means of communication, was assuring me she was *sleeping*. Sedated!"

There was no proper response to that. None.

"So?" Father asked.

The only thing that came clear was a question. "How sick is she?"

Father gave a short, wordless, unhappy sound. "We are not sure. We have to communicate through Cenedi, who *for some reason* is not responding to us."

Now his heart had begun to beat somewhat rapidly. "Under her orders."

"We *assume* that. The only reason we know where she is gone is because the presumptive heir of Ajuri—who was evidently left behind, and who, you may recall, was once Machigi's agent—sent one of his aishid to Guild commander Midagi to ask what *he* knew about the expedition. *Nomari* had been told, by Cenedi, that Lord Bren was taking the bus, with an armed escort, to Kajiminda—personally to inform the caretakers of the situation. *Nomari's man* informed Midagi that his were the only Guild left inside Najida. We therefore assume she boarded the bus. We *assume* the paidhi is with her. We have no idea about the two presumably reformed Shadow Guild agents they had with them—Nomari's man did not mention them. Lord Geigi avows he has the entire area under observation, and he believes that the destination is indeed Kajiminda. He himself cannot attest as to who is aboard the bus and he has no information on their intentions. But he has no precise observation of detail because of the weather down there. Be informed: this, son of mine, is your great-grandmother. *This* is what it is to sit in Shejidan and have an array of possibilities *she* has set in motion, not knowing whether she has the strength, the force, the health, *or* the good fortune to carry them out. Nor does *she* know these things, though she will avow she does. We *assume* she is in charge, and we presume she is *actively* in charge, in some capacity. We assume the paidhi is with her, but he can only contact us indirectly, *despite* the fact we specifically ordered he be given one of the communicators. *Cenedi* decided otherwise. Most likely at *her* orders, but not necessarily so, if he deems the paidhi having access to *me* constitutes a danger . . . or even simply an inconvenience . . . to *her*. Do you see what it is to sit on the other end of such a transaction?"

He did. His confidence was shaken.

"I cannot have *two* such operations afoot," Father continued. "I cannot contact Najida over the phone system as it is, and I cannot reach Cenedi on the secure system—one assumes that silence is not due to some problem in the system, but because he is simply not answering. Which argues that Grandmother *is* aboard and that he is under orders not to respond."

"But you *were* able to contact the Guild commander." Cajeiri blurted that out without forethought, and Father lifted an eyebrow. "Regarding the plane, I mean."

"That I was. One *rejoices* that was the case. They will attempt to send Lord Tatiseigi safely back to Atageini, removing the Red Train at least temporarily from your great-grandmother's options as we convey Lord Tatiseigi. We hope that will not become a problem."

"I do not think he will go," Cajeiri said, and Father frowned.

"I do not think he will, either," Father said. "Granted he survives the flight. He is an old man, son of mine. Gods less fortunate, consider what you ask of him."

That was a thought. It was not a thought he had understood until he had seen Liedi's face windburned as it was.

"One regrets that, honored Father. I know now that it was. Was he seen at Cobo? *Have* they refueled?"

"The young lord of Dur has indeed refueled. He may have had a passenger. The young lord of Dur often refuels at Cobo. Asking further could only attract attention and inspire questions in a port city, where rumors are salable. At least we have assured his safe landing, which should be soon."

"Yes, Father."

"'Yes, Father.' *Continue* to think about the possibilities, son of mine. You have obedience from your staff. That is faultless. Secrecy from your own side, however, can be fatal to your people. Have you any *other* plan you wish to confide in me? Any feature of this one you now regret? Any small increase in understanding?"

There were. Several. Heat flooded his face. "I did not think about the Guild and the plane. That was stupid. I did not see how the Guild camp was protecting Cobo as well as Najida. I will remember that. I worried about Kajiminda."

"Justifiably."

"But the Edi are there. And they are fierce fighters."

"One hopes someone has warned *them* not to shoot."

That, he had not thought of.

Father stared at him, saying nothing. Then: "Go back to your staff. You have no *other* agents out and about, do you?"

"No, honored Father." It was a dismissal. He gave a bow deeper than usual. Father's stare was unremitting.

"Do you acknowledge anything I have said?" Father asked.

"I do, honored Father. I do. All of it."

"Can I trust you?"

That was a question. He drew a deep breath, held it, and let fly. "I trust mani, honored Father. And I want to know when you order the Guild. I want to know when you plan things."

He expected to be sent out of Father's office in the next breath. And maybe to be restricted for the next whole year.

"I have a serious question for you," Father said. "If I ask you absolutely *not* to share certain knowledge beyond the two of us, can I rely on that?"

He had not expected that. He could not *answer* it. Not for a moment, at least.

Then he said: "Not yet, honored Father. I could not lie to mani. She would know. And then things would be worse."

"Absolutely correct," Father said. "Well that you think about that. And while on the topic of *trust*, well that you come to me on your more extravagant ideas . . . those regarding life and death, for instance. Those would be advisable."

"Honored Father." He made a step toward the door. The room seemed dissolved about him, as if nothing in it were familiar. "I will think. I will think about it."

"You are given assets," Father said, "some of whom have been absent. That is my fault. That will be remedied."

He had expected anger. Rage, even. Nothing so simple. Nothing so effective. His older aishid was being recalled.

The world lurched.

And righted itself.

Bren sat upright, and the bus struggled. Edi maintenance of the road had given out.

Mud slowed them. Considerably. At times they lurched over potholes, and occasionally lumbered off the road to avoid some worse problem.

It was the clay of the mainland end of Kajiminda Bay, veins of which went to oiled slickness when water gathered in low spots after a rain—if there were Marid spies about, one uncharitably wished them baths in it. But the way became easier if lumpier, as the land rose on the left, and there were again stretches of bumpy sandstone ridges matched in places by eroded sandstone cliffs.

Machigi's land, the uplands, the plateau that slanted away east, toward the Marid—often disputed, never actively claimed, since the Maschi clan that held the piedmont in the north stayed out of Marid politics as much as possible. It was a grassy high-lands on which the whole west coast poached and trespassed from time to time. Modestly. Minor thefts which the lords of the Taisigin Marid were generally too busy to pursue.

Which meant an easy route for problems that might be up there, but as the sky brightened outside the steamed windows, as the noon sun began to poke feebly through the clouds, the view was mostly weeds and brush, some of it in the roadway, by the sound of what scraped the underside.

Sandwiches happened, and tea in covered mugs. Bren ate with a fair appetite, visited the facility at the back of the bus, then settled against Jago's shoulder and shut his eyes, hoping for a return to dark nowhere.

He wondered if Kajiminda had been warned of their coming, which brought up the issue of whether or not Kajiminda still had phone service.

It was a question.

Surely Lord Geigi, director of half the space station, had not let his estate fall utterly out of the modern age.

But then—Edi were in charge of it now. And phones were not necessarily on their list of priorities, though the lines visible from the window appeared intact, even in this neglected stretch of road.

Damn. He had found the thought that interfered with his sleep. It could have been any of a number of thoughts. But this one had lurked in ambush.

"Do you suppose Kajiminda has a telephone?" he asked Jago.

"One supposes it does," Jago said; and then, after an instant's thought: "But we have no assurance of it."

Which could mean Ilisidi had not even tried to call Kajiminda to warn of their coming . . . or if she had, *his* aishid had not been informed of the matter. Damn, this whole communication business had him second guessing *everything*. It was not as if he had not been out of the loop before. He would know what was necessary for him to know when it became necessary for him to know it. In the meantime, observe, recall what he did know . . . and prepare for that moment of enlightenment.

He had not personally traveled this way since—God, since the start of the space program. In his memory, there was a security gate to mark the entrance to Kajiminda and there was a huge building that he knew would no longer be there. In his mind, this rutted road had been well-maintained, graveled, leveled—a condition that had once held all the way to Cobo.

He in no wise recognized where they were, but they were headed more or less south, and past Banichi's shoulder, the panorama across the windshield had become on the one side sloping gold sandstone, and on the other, an increasingly weedy scrubland barely admitting the road's existence.

And trees, part of the scrub, but sapling trees. Grey-green and darker foliage began to close off the horizon.

The market road had used to continue all the way to Ashidama Bay. And Kajidama had had a road direct to Separti that was somewhat seasonal, but well-kept. Was it completely overgrown? He was asking himself that as the road they were on met an obstacle they could not drive over: an infelicitous pair of saplings standing right in the roadway—trees years old, saying, indeed, maintenance had utterly given up. The wild had won, the road, such as it was, having devolved to a pair of ruts around the obstacle. There was, briefly, a distant view of water on the right— Kajiminda Bay. But more scrub trees soon cut off the view, and soon there was that stage of growth on both sides of the road. Still the dual ruts persisted—so there remained some traffic, perhaps seasonal, with the harvests.

It began to rain again, a fitful spatter that did little to clear the splashes of mud on the side windows.

An hour and more later, they made a right-hand turn toward an equally abandoned-looking track of eroded ruts, over weeds and scrub that scraped the underside of the bus.

Was it indeed the Kajiminda access road?

If road it was. It appeared with weedy brush on the left, and a wide expanse of silvery grass past Banichi's shoulder. A trio of grazers wandered off from their approach, tails switching in annoyance. Idyllic view, wildlife unconcerned by the rain, in a silver meadow much like the hunting range now at their backs.

A meadow, where sprawling and blocky modern buildings had lately stood. Lord Geigi had ordered the demolition of the structures of what had become Patinandi Aerospace, source of much of Geigi's considerable wealth—and once crews had carried out the order, indeed, there remained not so much as a concrete slab in view, if one was right about the location, and he was fairly sure of it. He had heard of the demolition—had not had the occasion to come down this road in years, but he had heard it was thorough, when Patinandi had gone beyond its manufactory of the air age—and, as he saw around him, leaving behind it not so much as a straight line in the landscape. The space program had needed a broad, flat area, an airport, a spaceport—

And Geigi had simply folded up operations here and moved the whole of Patinandi Aerospace to the north coast, for its good approach over the sea, its far wider expanse of flat land—its access to rail, and in the day, the great dish at Mogari-nai, which still had its uses. Geigi had, the Edi had told him, removed even the concrete basements. The historic building that had built the commercial air fleet and the very first elements of the shuttle fleet was now an extensive breakwater on Kajidama Peninsula.

While Lord Geigi had planted, yes, another orchard. The silver meadow gave way to orderly young trees on either hand, leafless in this season.

They were on the road to the estate that had sat behind the industrial complex—or at least the roadway, such as it was: it smoothed out somewhat, though potholes still abounded, and the young orchard gave way on the left to another broad expanse of meadow, by the look of it. More grazers wandered here, alarmed at the bus, disappearing into the general fog on the windows.

Tended, this orchard, this meadow. There had once been concrete buildings here, a veritable maze, obscuring the great house itself. And now—

Now this orchard, and well-established meadow. Beyond it, according finally with memory, if only of old photos, was Kajiminda itself: older than sprawling, relatively modern wood-and-stone Najida, but heavily reconstructed, as one recalled the history. He had been inside it—from Patinandi's halls. Memory painted formal halls, polished marble, live-flame lamps and opulence on a scale of the Bujavid itself. What appeared from the outside was shockingly modern—with ground-floor windows, windows on every level. It had the foundations of the old building—but larger.

And the windows—considering it sat in a region fought over and fought upon for centuries—were a challenge in every direction.

Arrogance?

Deliberate, provocative fragility?

He had not seen them when he had been inside Patinandi. This was not quite modern—the core of the structure looked old. But the outside—no great house on Earth dared expose so fragile a face to the world.

Kajiminda had been the greatest power in the south, once upon a time, when Maschi clan had stood off both the Townships of Ashidama Bay and the ambitions of the more distant Marid. They had been a great deal on show, those lords, in their day. They had maintained a hired force of their own, absent the northern Guild, and shared that vast hunting range with the Taisigin, too powerful, for a time, for the Taisigin to push them out.

Then Geigi's predecessors had built a factory for small engines, and Patinandi had grown from that.

Geigi preferred orchards, and moved all the machines and the employees and the smoke all up past Cobo.

Geigi, who loved trees, now refused to come down from the space station, whether taken by the sights of the cosmos—or the power and the freedom he had in his office.

Freedom and endless possibilities . . . until humans turned out to have lied, and turned up with five thousand refugees the station could not support.

God, he *had* to talk to Geigi on that issue . . . had commitments to keep. He had just never anticipated having to do it from Geigi's own house, with a Shadow Guild problem intruding onto what was now Edi land. Pardon us, esteemed neighbor—we have a war likely to produce another front, here. Regarding that promise I made, I could be late. . . .

He had not, in years, visited his neighbor's establishment on Earth—though he knew well Geigi's home aloft. He had known, of course, that Patinandi had gone—but not so completely. He had known there were modifications, but to this hour he had envisioned Kajiminda as a stronghold—a place of safety. The windows were not extravagant—for an upper floor. In Shejidan.

He wondered if Ilisidi was having second thoughts of Kajiminda as a secure base for whatever she meant to do.

And then he asked himself, knowing Geigi, whether Geigi would leave the Edi such a fragile place to defend.

There was an uneasiness about Kajiminda—if one came looking at it as an attacker. Senses would say—this is an invitation . . .

Knowing Geigi . . . one began to think, indeed . . . a statement to the neighbors. Do not take my absence as an invitation.

I look easy, Kajiminda said. Do you really think I am?

12

A meadow, and then another graceful sweep of orchard plant-ings, where once a factory and offices and small residences had stood.

And a house of many windows.

Even while Geigi was serving the aishidi'tat in orbit, he had continued the demolition of the factories—one had heard of that. Trucks had moved the moveables up past Cobo. Trucks had deliv-ered the slabs of concrete to the breakwater, that slowed erosion of the peninsula under fierce winter gales.

Even while his scoundrel nephew was styling himself Lord of Kajiminda and disposing of prize elements of Geigi's collections to pay for his extravagances—machines had been at work, dig-ging up the old foundations of Patinandi Aerospace, under Geigi's orders.

He had not let his nephew profit from Patinandi; had, in fact, *spent* a fortune destroying it. Not that he had left that nephew destitute, but certainly none the richer.

So his disgruntled nephew had laid hands on the priceless por-celain collections—illegally—and vengefully sold them, likely, one could surmise in retrospect, utilizing the established mar-kets of the Master of Jorida.

It had all been a great mess. And a scandal. The nephew was banished—well, contract-married to an Eastern lady of Ilisidi's choosing, and now out of a lordship. He certainly was not coming back here. Geigi had that understanding with the previous lord of Maschi clan—no model of virtue either; but Geigi had made the point. Geigi had put the estate under Edi management, installing his former gardener as de facto lord of the manor.

Betan, the name was. Ramaso respected him. Bren had written to him, offering Najida estate's help if needed; Betan had answered politely, through Ramaso, and asked for none.

And what had Betan done, thus handed a lord's authority, if not a lordly title, along with all this wealth?

Being Edi, and Lord Geigi's loyal retainer, he had planted trees. And not just trees—orchards. Disciplined, orderly orchards, equally spaced, neat and well-tended, adding to Kajiminda's wealth. They were driving through the newest of them. These were a few years older, perhaps beginning to bear—

Visible from orbit, such orderly patterns. A letter written on the earth, Bren thought, all around the house. A message to Geigi, who could look down on the estate and read the state of affairs.

One could appreciate this man, Betan, whose Edi culture might have said—let wild forest take all.

But orchards were Geigi's delight. Geigi had no need of the income, where he was, but then, Bren reflected, neither had he: he had given away his own fishing rights, let all of it accrue to the Edi, for their use, their own purposes, which included building on land Geigi had ceded to them . . . and here was a situation he had never seen in operation—permanent building, establishment of trade—

In a culture that had never cared for either, previously.

Was it a good change? One was a little disquieted: the Edi had fought hard to maintain their character.

And then he thought, well, it was an Edi change. It was developing in peace. That was something.

Except an area that had been objecting to the Edi arrival for two hundred years might now find the Shadow Guild settling next door.

The Shadow Guild could not destroy the sea: the fisheries were not all that vulnerable.

But these orchards were. Fragile as Geigi's precious porcelains. Fragile as the windows. All the orderly rows of work . . . laid out around a house apparently much more vulnerable than Najida,

sharing the peninsula with the Townships, who were themselves
threatened. And not threatened by the Edi, for all the Townships
might not yet realize it.

The great house stood clear and sharp now, low-lying windows, ornate doors inset with glass.

Not designed for defense, no. In sowing his relays across the
continent, those self-defending mobile towers, Geigi might have
spared one for his own estate, and solved so much. Tabini would
not have objected.

But such a tower would have agitated his neighbors. And Geigi
had traded with the Townships and the Edi alike, shipping to the
Marid as well as to Cobo, all places alike to him. He had never
threatened anyone—until he had found the need, seeing Tabini
overthrown, to set that matter right.

Geigi had built the mobile relays and sent them down from the
heavens, prepared, Bren was almost certain, to make himself
aiji if he had to—until Tabini had gathered force enough to
re-establish lawful government. Geigi had then settled back and
declined to rule the aishidi'tat, quite content, as he avowed.

The last rows of new orchard passed. The doors and windows
of Kajiminda reflected light, confident in their safety from enemies.

The door flashed open and a group of children ran out, by no
means as restrained as Ragi youngsters. Adults appeared in
the doorway—several, and came out onto the broad porch.

The driver Casimi, one of the dowager's own aishid—drove
close and turned the bus about to present the door to the house.
Beyond the windshield, the two Guild escort vehicles could
be seen headed back the way they came, returning, one assumed,
to the Najida encampment.

Bren leaned forward and looked around Cenedi, to find the
dowager peacefully napping, catching up on her early morning.
She lifted her head, looked toward the house, and Cenedi carefully got up and offered a hand.

No one else would rise until the dowager had. Bren held his
place as the bus shut down, and Ilisidi, with Cenedi, passed his
row and Banichi's. The back rows were by then stirring, preparing

to disembark, and visible in the window, Ilisidi descended to a welcome by the staff—that older man coming forward would be Betan, Bren was sure, though they had never met; and the young man beside him likely his son, of whom he had heard, but also never met.

Children danced about the bus, excited and noisy, darting in and out and about. Had Ramaso made a phone call? They certainly seemed not to occasion a surprise or an alarm: the presence of the children said that.

Banichi had risen meanwhile, gathering up his personal baggage before heading toward the door. Bren moved out with Jago, and Tano and Algini held back traffic in the aisle while Bren and Jago descended the steps to the bottom. Banichi's steadying hand was there, a good thing, on the uneven ground—it was all meadow grass, clear to the porch. Ahead of them, Ilisidi walked with her left hand in Cenedi's arm, and the formidable cane in good use.

The one who would seem to be Betan, the manager, bowed as they reached the steps. "Welcome, Grandmother of the Ragi."

Grandmother of the Ragi she was not, not technically. Grandmother of *one* Ragi, yes. But Ilisidi passed smoothly over that detail. She gave a little nod, deep courtesy in northern terms. "Grandson of Tepesht, we offer this."

Ilisidi held out her hand to Betan and Betan, unhesitating, came and received some small item from her, then tucking that hand against his chest.

What that object was, Bren had no idea. It was small—something expected, perhaps, or recognized—something, one could guess, that *had* to have passed this morning, a token from the Grandmother, whose personal name he realized he might just have heard for the first time. When had Ilisidi learned that?

Betan held up the object, then, a silver disc that reflected the murky daylight.

Authority, that seemed clear. An object of reverence. Adults made soft whistles, and stood still. The children, group by group, stopped scampering and dodging about, the older ones collecting the younger to solemn quiet.

"The Grandmothers of two nations," Ilisidi said in a voice

clear, though thin, "agree on action. Strangers are landing on Jorida. Whether or not Jorida consents, whether or not the Townships consent, Kajiminda and Najida do *not* consent to their presence. What you are building on the land—is not for them to take. Lord Geigi will not permit it. Lord Bren will not permit it. The aishidi'tat will not permit it. We will take no land. We will not permit these strangers in Ashidama to take it, either. That is our word."

"*Geta!*" Betan said, and others did. There was no exact translation of that in Mosphei' or Ragi. It was a sort of cheer. A sort of invocation. A sort of oath. "*Geta!*" Hands clapped. In unison. Even the children clapped, in childish enthusiasm, and cheered in high-pitched voices.

"Welcome!" Betan said, and stood back to usher them in. "*Geta!*" the children shouted, bringing up the rear, until someone directed the small-scale mob to a side hall, and their echoes faded, shushed.

The main hall opened on a room as grand and as Ragi as the Bujavid itself could offer, gilt and ivory all about, floral designs— and in the walls, in scores of lighted niches—porcelains, Geigi's world-famous collection—which was far more extensive than the twenty or so displayed; but unhappily less than what Geigi had lost, thanks to his disgraced nephew. They had recovered half of the missing items. If Machigi's suspicions held out, if the Master of Jorida *was* somehow the broker of those sales, it was possible records existed, somewhere on the island. Possibly the collection might yet be restored. Some might well have gone to the Marid. He knew Geigi had had a handful of porcelains that had survived the Great Wave, priceless objects produced using colors and glazes modern science was still unraveling.

Priceless. Except in the hands of a scoundrel. Baiji's tenure had been brief once Geigi found it out.

And for a time the leadership of Maschi clan itself, over in Targai, had been in similarly self-interested hands—Bren had found that out, personally and painfully—but Geigi's leadership from this outlier of Maschi glory had redeemed Maschi clan, no question; and Geigi had then settled the matter of

Kajiminda by putting it under Edi management, to the dismay of other lords.

But it shone now, testament to that decision. It was immaculate, as if there had never been a factory, never been a thieving nephew, and awaited its proper lord at any given moment.

One was glad to see it. One was glad to make the acquaintance of such neighbors. While Betan personally showed the dowager and her escort upstairs to their rooms, Betan's son came, offering to escort him and his in the other direction.

He complied, at least as far as a very luxurious suite in the same style, itself graced by a few of the collection.

"Najida's market truck will arrive," Bren said to the escort, "with luggage. Quite a bit of it."

"Oh, one remembers Lord Geigi's cases," was the cheerful answer, in very good Ragi. "We can manage it, nandi."

One thought they could, indeed.

"Thank you," Bren said. "Thank you very much."

"We have a dinner cooking," the man said. "And the great table laid. We are aware of the special food requirements of our honored neighbor, Lord of Najida, and have adjusted the meal to accommodate." And with a slight bow: "In Lord Geigi's house, by his grace, welcome to his guests."

All honors. He could not decline the supper in the dowager's name and he was, he was well sure, no proper judge of her state of being—not since breakfast with her.

There was no turning aside Edi hospitality, so graciously given, either. "Thank you. Thank you and thank Lord Geigi, nadi."

For the rest—after Betan's son had departed, with meticulous and fluent courtesies:

"One supposes we are to unpack," Bren said to his own household, "once the cases arrive—but I would not gamble on it." Narani and Jeladi were standing with nothing to do but test the water in the samovar and inspect the tea caddy, while his aishid was surveying the premises and doing a meticulous security check.

Banichi stood looking out the unsecured window, having run a small instrument up the woodwork, thinking, surely, about the grounds, and security, if there were installations not in their hands. Complete dependence on other security systems was not a situation his aishid approved, generally—but that system was Geigi's. And then one had to think—if there were devices installed, it had not been Geigi personally who had installed them, but the Edi. The Edi, who were, on the surface, against technology.

But Ramaso, among others, was proof that it was not an insurmountable objection.

There were so many things he wanted to know about the limits of that local system, but whatever the security was, whether local or orbital, even overcast as the heavens were: Geigi, he was sure, was monitoring them by various means, or had staff doing it. They were not alone here.

"The windows are more secure than they look," Algini said. "Should one wonder."

Some very perilous things had come from human tech, loosed from the Archive during the War of the Landing—tech that was, for the most part, later outlawed, but not all. And if any place on the face of the earth might have devices it should not have—they were standing in it. The risk to Geigi's home had been greater than most, long before the Shadow Guild had come into the picture.

"How is it?" he asked quietly. "Within the treaties?"

"By appearance," Algini said quietly. "However it could link to a much more sophisticated system. Sound and visual surveillance. Staff of Geigi's on the station have come and gone here, at various times—hosted here, likely doing work. One doubts all this was in place before Baiji's tenure, or there were areas he knew to avoid. But one doubts this is aimed at the staff. One expects it extends outside the house, probably with a monitoring station."

"Is the system active?"

"Yes," Algini said. "One suspects it cannot all be deactivated *except* from the station: that would be a defensive measure. Its extent is not apparent, but seems lawful . . . marginally . . . so far as is apparent in this suite. We know what we are looking at. I am not sure others would, who have not spent time on the starship."

That was news to him. One wondered what *else* his aishid had picked up on that trip between stars, but one also knew better than to ask.

"One doubts much that moves outdoors go unnoticed, either. There may be lethals. But there will be some master control governing those. I would expect it to be local as well as aloft."

That was chilling. Mospheira would definitely not approve. Historically, after the War of the Landing, humans had been extremely careful about letting high tech loose. One door opened led to others, with highly unpredictable ramifications within the atevi culture. Atevi patience with tech in general had been minimal until recently, and by treaty, Mospheira kept their own tech at a level comparable to what the atevi would accept. Television had been welcomed on the mainland in Wilson's time; personal communications—still were extremely restricted.

When the starship, centuries absent, had come back, shoved the space station back into reach of the Earth—the resources to build ascent vehicles being all on atevi soil—they had bartered half the station for those vehicles (hence Geigi's reign over that half), while simultaneously propelling the entire world into the interstellar age, (hence Geigi's access to things even Mospheira, long divorced from starship tech, scarcely dreamed existed.)

Had Geigi imported forbidden things to defend Kajiminda? Algini said . . . maybe. Were the systems connected to the station? Almost undoubtedly.

All he knew was, what protected this place . . . was best left protecting it. Geigi was Geigi, unique in power, unique in choices made for the world's benefit.

So far . . . that arrangement had worked pretty damned well. And one no longer questioned the windows.

"Fair enough," he said. "We should sleep better for it. If you—"

Algini had turned his back—faced the window, looking up into the darkening sky, disregarding him and what he was about to say—

That was not ordinary. An alarming thought? Something forgotten?

Then his own ears picked up a hum. It was no sound of nature, nor the market truck, nor ordinary machinery.

A motor. A machine. Not in the direction he sensed the road to be, but from the north.

Tano and Jago appeared from the next room. Then Banichi.

"A plane," he said. God knew, he had spent his time in airports in the early part of his tenure. He knew that sound.

Not a jet. A small plane. His heart sped.

"They must not shoot!" he said, and headed for the door, calling out, "Advise Betan, they must not shoot!"

He was running when he reached the great room. Two of the Guild shouted something indistinct about a plane. Startled Edi did not get to the door in time. Bren shoved hard at the latch himself, opened it. The glass door beyond obstructed him. Banichi shoved that wide. Bren caught his balance and was down off the broad porch in three strides, running.

There was the clear space around the manor house—there were the rows of young fruit trees ahead of them, and above that, above the heads of the few Edi, armed, who guarded the front, soared a bright yellow plane.

"Do not fire!" Bren shouted in his best try at the Edi language. "Do not fire! Do not fire!"

A few shots went off beyond the orchard, and Bren ran, ill-dressed for running, in dress boots, frock coat, and lace, but he gave it all he had—still passed by Algini and Banichi, with Tano and Jago beside him. He ran through the tall grass the bus had flattened, otherwise knee high to him; and he ran shouting, "Do not fire!" at whatever Edi were ahead of them to hear. Banichi shouted the same, and "Stand down!"

—Which might have had some effect. The plane went out of sight, off above the older, taller trees, the native trees, and disappeared, at which Bren had the worst thought—

But the sound of the engine persisted, then changed, and, as they came to the wide meadow, where three of the household had taken position, rifles lifted uncertainly.

Another shout of "Hold fire!" made itself understood, and rifles lowered.

Bren reeled to a stop, braced hands on knees and gasped for

breath, trying to get a look at the sky. The sound changed pitch, and came close, passing right overhead as the yellow plane rushed across the lowering clouds and went past, tilting wildly as it went.

Two aboard; both seats occupied. The plane described a wide high loop as Edi from the household overtook them, some with rifles, others with pistols, one with, God save them, a hunting bow. And belatedly, on the track he had taken, other Guild appeared: Ilisidi's, armed with rifles, but not threatening the plane—trying to wave the Edi back.

There was a clear space, at least. Bren gulped down breaths, pressed a hand to the ache in his side and tried to assume some dignity as he stood watching the plane come over in another pass. He lifted a hand and waved, sure in his mind who the pilot was and reckoning the passenger in the forward seat perhaps as young Dur's long-suffering chief of bodyguard. The helmet and goggles gave no identity, but the brave yellow of the aircraft did. It was, without doubt and of all people on Earth, Reijiri of Dur, who waved back, and made other signals trying to indicate, Bren suddenly realized, the direction he wanted to come in . . . an area rapidly filling with curious onlookers.

Of course. Take off into the wind. Land into the wind. Perfect sense. And the wind was—

The plane roared off skyward for another pass, and Bren signaled to Banichi and the rest to clear a west-east path. "He will land toward the house, Nichi-ji! People should go over to the south, over there—" He was still out of breath. Hands against his knees, hardly a lordly pose, thinking, in rapid fire: *God! Is there trouble in the north?* and, *Surely Tabini would have told Cenedi!* And, *Surely Cenedi would have told us . . . would he not?*

On that terrifying twist, he sought out Ilisidi's men, found them doing nothing more threatening than holding the Edi back . . . and banished that notion, at least.

The plane finished its run and looped around again, losing altitude, the engine sounding weak, a little less certain. It sputtered. It sounded unhealthy. Bren forced himself upright and watched it anxiously as it waggled and wobbled its way lower, flaps engaged, the engine not making a confident sound.

It brushed the tops of the grass, its wind flattened them and its tires touched and found ground. It slewed a little, movable bits on wings and tail working, as the Edi cried out in dismay, but it had found the ground, and rolled to a stop, engine coughing, and the propeller slowed to a rest.

Bren headed for it—not running, doing his best to exude dignity, entirely conscious of armed Edi, fraught nerves, armed Guild, and the need not to have any misunderstandings. He waved. The second seat—young Dur, waved back, and began to clamber out onto the lower wing, to assist his passenger, who was moving, but not vigorously—just a limp wave of the hand to those approaching.

One could not see; one could hardly clamber up there. But the passenger seemed in some distress. Injured? Bren wondered, as Reijiri attempted to assist him out.

Bren came as far as the wing, everything out of reach, nothing in view except Reijiri himself, who appeared to be having some difficulty getting the passenger free.

Banichi and Jago came up close beside him. Jago took a boost from Banichi and gained her footing on the wing, to assist Reijiri with the passenger—

Cajeiri? Bren thought wildly. The boy had the damnedest knack for being where he was not supposed to be, and he had associations with Dur.

But no, it was a tall man, a thin man, an old man, by the grey hair escaping under his helmet and the edges of the obscuring goggles—and half a heartbeat later, one recognized the green and white queue ribbons and the aggregate of gold finger rings.

Lord Tatiseigi.

"God," Bren muttered, and started forward, as close to the wing as let him see and, helplessly, offer a hand to the situation. Lord Tatiseigi made it out of the seat, onto the wing with Reijiri's support and Jago's, and, amid a gathering semicircle of Edi, made a careful descent to the edge.

"Banichi," Bren said, and need not have. Banichi, Tano, and Algini offered assistance below and Jago and Reijiri above, lowering Tatiseigi safely from the wing to the ground—standing. The old man was too proud to do otherwise. He pushed back the goggles. His face was burned, his eternally neat queue was half undone, the helmet, as he slipped it off, completed the wreck of his grey hair, and he had a shocked look as he gazed about.

"Nandi," Bren said with a deep bow. "Nandi, you are at Kajiminda."

"Well, I should hope to be!" Tatiseigi said in a voice far gone in hoarseness. Then: "Nandi, I have come to see the dowager."

"That I am sure you will," Bren said. "Banichi, carry him."

"No such thing!" Tatiseigi declared, though Jago and Reijiri both were supporting him. "I shall walk. How is she?"

"Well, *well,* nandi. Be assured. She is quite well. We will walk there very slowly."

It had to be slowly. They reached the track the bus had made, which was easier going through the grass, and the crowd of onlookers and confused Guild melted back to let them pass.

"I must secure the plane," Reijiri said. "I have left things in a state."

"Go," Bren said taking his place at Tatiseigi's side, and: "Tano, Algini, help him."

Reijiri himself looked to be in a state of exhaustion, but he was in no difficulty. Tatiseigi, however, was spent, and would not ordinarily accept as much help as he was getting, Bren on one arm, Jago on the other. "Nandi," Banichi said, and substituted himself for Bren's assistance, at a greater advantage of height and strength.

And now there was a tide of children, some running, and the older carrying the younger, all to see the wonder that had arrived in the meadow. Adults came, trying not to stare at Tatiseigi as they passed. Cenedi and a small number of Guild waited on the porch.

"We must have a guard on the plane," Bren said, walking beside Banichi, still out of breath. "Or they will be pushing buttons."

"Day and night," Banichi said, and in a tone not entirely approving: *"Cenedi* is giving orders now. *He* had word of the plane from Midagi."

And had not passed that information on to his second-in-command. He suspected words would be passed at some point, and was glad, very glad he had not told Banichi about the com they were *supposed* to have.

But it was a situation which could not continue. Banichi had not been told. Bren had not been told, and consequently the Edi, armed and everywhere, had not been told. The possible ramifications were terrifying.

"We," Tatiseigi managed to say, "were very short of fuel. One does not think it can take off. We reached Najida. And they said you had gone to Kajiminda. And offered to take us in the truck. But the plane is faster. Much faster."

"That it would be, nandi." Trudging back at Tatiseigi's pace was far, far longer than it had taken to reach the meadow. The house was very far away. But now the older Edi were coming out, and Casimi, one of Ilisidi's aishid, came running toward them.

"Lord Tatiseigi!" Casimi exclaimed. "They are bringing a truck."

And in short order such a vehicle did appear, making slow passage through the stream of spectators. It pulled up, and an Edi stepped down from the doorless cab and offered them the single other seat in the cab.

"I am doing quite well," Tatiseigi protested.

"The dowager is waiting," Bren said, and motioned toward the offered seat. "Nandi."

The lord was still not pleased with the truck, but Banichi and Jago bundled him into the passenger seat, and Bren and Casimi climbed up into the bed, both hard-breathing. Banichi and Jago followed.

The truck turned and picked up its pace.

"How has *Dur* gotten involved?" Banichi asked. And: "Why not a train?"

They sent the truck back for Reijiri before heading into the house. The old lord was afire to see Ilisidi, no question, but two necessities intervened once inside—first a visit to the accommodation, and then an attempt at restoring his appearance. Bren availed himself of the same while Narani assisted Lord Tatiseigi, re-braiding his queue and straightening his collar. Bren's own body informed him he had not run that distance that fast in over a decade. His throat threatened to be sore. He had shouted that loud. His hands still shook—he tested that steadiness determinedly, attempted to slow his heartbeat, as Tatiseigi declared himself ready and headed out the door, understandably bent on seeing Ilisidi immediately.

That had been clear, and there was no arguing with him.

Leaving Narani and the others, Bren followed Tatiseigi down the stairs. Banichi and Jago waited for them in the hall, and escorted them to a sitting room adjacent to the great hall, where Tano and Algini joined them, back from the plane, where two of Ilisidi's guard had replaced them.

They had secured the plane firmly with ties driven into the ground, while Reijiri, they said, was busy giving the older Edi children, well supervised, a chance to sit a moment in the plane. But he would be in in time for dinner.

Beyond that, everything was in Edi hands, the door-keeping, the watch in the halls, the food they were to eat. Which circumstance made his aishid uneasy, no question; but it was an allied house, and the staff, while not his staff, moved about with efficiency, as if guests were quite an ordinary thing and twenty-odd people for an unplanned dinner did not daunt them.

Two young Edi, in brown leather, hair in multiple braids, waited by a table with a tea service—blue porcelain, on white linen. Betan was not there, but everything in the reception and the surrounds was immaculate. The dowager, not a hair out of place, sat with her sole female servant poised beside her and with Cenedi and Nawari standing behind—the picture of Ragi authority. But her first glance at Tatiseigi as he entered, with Tano at his elbow, shattered the appearance of serenity.

"Tati-ji." It was a tone of alarm.

"Aiji-ma," the old man said, with a shaky bow.

"Sit. Sit down!" She invited that with a gesture. "A chair, a chair, nadiin. Assist!"

The two Edi moved hesitantly, likely uncertain how to properly rearrange the seating. Nawari seized the nearest chair from the orderly arrangement and planted it in front of Ilisidi, and Ilisidi's servant gently adjusted its proper angle. Tatiseigi sat down, stiffly proper, with Tano at the ready beside him.

Ilisidi asked, more calmly, then, "Tea? Or would you rather brandy, nandi?"

"Brandy," Tatiseigi said instantly. "My throat. The wind."

Brandy was procured from the side table, offered in a delicate glass, and Tatiseigi took a very small sip, accompanied by a grimace of honest pain.

"The news," Ilisidi said. "The news, Tati-ji. What brought on this desperate venture?"

"*The news?*" Tatiseigi's voice cracked. "Woman, the news is that you are dying! The assumption in Shejidan is that you are lying abed and helpless in Najida surrounded by Shadow Guild enemies!"

Ilisidi's face took on a strange expression—one might even venture to say—chagrin.

"An indisposition," she said with a flick of her hand. "A little machimi for the local folk. And to ensure my grandson would *not* be reappropriating the Guild force I borrowed. Has he hung the banners and declared an official mourning in the capital? Or did you grow worried on your own?"

"Of course I have been worried. I wanted to come to Shejidan for better contact with events, even before I heard any of this—I planned to meet you on your return. But your grandson ordered me very specifically to stay in Tirnamardi, for whatever reasons of the hour, I suppose—as if the storm in the Marid could touch the midlands! But I have worried with you down here—that perhaps the situation in the Marid was more than was being released outside the Bujavid—and I own that my concern was excess . . . excess . . ." He coughed, stilled the cough with brandy. "*Excessive.* Forgive me. But my information to the contrary came in the night. With a phone call. And an airplane. Your great-grandson. My grand-nephew. Forgive me." The cough was threatening again.

"Cajeiri. *He* is in Tirnamardi?"

"He is still in Shejidan. In Shejidan, safe, absolutely." A third spate of coughing, and a sip of brandy. Tano seized the glass to refill it, and Tatiseigi took down the whole glass with a long grimace of pain. "Your great-grandson sent his servants, one to Dur, one to me, saying, by way of our ally and neighbor Dur, that you—" A third time Tano filled the glass, and the sip this time was more modest. "That you were gravely ill. I did not question *why* it was the young gentleman's message and not your grandson's. I attributed it to policy, and security, and your grandson's concerns. Reasonable concerns, I thought. But I had to be here, if you were ill. Your great-grandson's servant arrived at the train station in the middle of the night—on a freight train—to give me this news in a letter, and to tell me Dur would take me to Najida. And indeed, just before dawn, the plane landed on the grounds, and Dur and I flew to Cobo, refueled and flew to Najida. We feared being shot, when we saw some sort of gathering at the train station, so we veered over—quite a *steep* turn—and landed far from the house, on the lower shore, while young Dur—" Another modest sip. "Lord Reijiri is quite remarkable. He speaks a language which he says is nearly Edi, and the villagers told us you were not at the house, that you had taken the estate bus to Kajiminda. So I hoped you were better than I had feared. But we took off again, and went up over the woods and across the bay before we dared follow the road. We were not sure of being able to see our landing if we were much later and we were looking for the house, having no idea where it was. And not as near the market road as we thought. One believes we are now out of gas. It sounded very unhealthy coming down."

"One would agree with that," Bren said, standing, hands folded behind him. "One is very glad you landed when you did."

"Well, well," Ilisidi said. "Sit, paidhi. Sit. Will you take a brandy?"

"Tea, aiji-ma. Water, if possible. And we might send someone to the plane to save Lord Reijiri from his new enthusiasts. It appears the Edi children are determined to become pilots."

A wave of the dowager's hand. "Yes. Do. Wari-ji, see to it."

Nawari moved toward the door.

"Also, aiji-ma," Bren said. "The plane will not use the same fuel as the truck. It comes from Cobo airport. And it will need—whatever it takes."

"Details, details," the dowager said, and made another wave of her hand. "Wari-ji, a fuel truck, the train, whatever enables it."

"Yes," Nawari said and slipped out the door.

"Dur has made a great effort for us," Ilisidi continued. "Lord Reijiri should certainly have the means to take his plane home, whatever happens here, at whatever inconvenience. And in that consideration," Ilisidi added, purpose crackling in her tone, "trusting that the bus has fuel, you have your own choice, Tati-ji. Take nand' Bren's bus back to Najida tonight or wait for the plane to refuel tomorrow, and go with Dur as far as Najida. In either case the train Cobo sends down with the fuel will be there to carry you back to the main line. You can do us a favor by gathering up the prospective lord of Ajuri and taking him back to the midlands with you. I am done with him. I have formed my impression. He is sitting idle in Najida and he can tell you all he has been through, satisfying all your curiosity. *I* am busy."

"I shall not budge from this place without you," Tatiseigi said.

"You will do what benefits us all, nandi," Ilisidi said, "and take your valuable self back where you can provide the center of the aishidi'tat with the stability it is in danger of losing, with you and Dur cavorting about the skies and landing with nothing in the tank."

"You are ill!"

"I am *not* ill! We started the rumors of my declining health purely for our enemies' delight. *And* to stave off my grandson's insistent demands on us to come home and leave matters to him. *You* have elected to come flying in here in a mode far less stealthy than the paidhi's bus—certainly within view of any observers from the cliffs above the market road—and for all I know, within view of Separti, so now we may have extremely unwelcome visitors on our doorstep. How far south *did* you fly in the process of landing?"

"We went *no* further south. We found the house. As we intended. And by no choice of mine, the direst possible rumor of your failing health is now current at Tirnamardi and among all my staff. And in Dur. Possibly on the rail system, which my aishid *and* Dur's will be using to join us in Najida, not to mention farms where Dur refueled on his way to Tirnamardi, not to mention Cobo airport, where we again refueled, and, by now, very likely the rumor is on the streets of Shejidan, multiplied and elaborated. *Discretion* is not possible in this, 'Sidi-ji, whatever you wish were true, and if you truly *are* ill—Cenedi, paidhi, betray her at least to those few most concerned for her, for her own sake. *Is* she lying to me?"

Bren made an involuntary glance toward Cenedi, who had, for a fleeting moment, a worried frown.

"Nandi,—" Cenedi began, and Ilisidi brought the ferrule of her cane down on the tiles.

"I am perfectly well, nandi!"

"The travel," Cenedi interposed quietly in the shocked hush, "has been wearing even aboard the Red Train. She is exhausted. And there have been too many sleeping pills to too little effect until yesterday. Aiji-ma," he said, as Ilisidi gave him an angry glance, "I am obliged to say it to the paidhi-aiji and to the lord of Atageini, who will surely observe discretion; and the others are all Lord Geigi's. She does not sleep, nandiin. She does not sleep."

Ilisidi made an impatient gesture. "A waste of time, with our enemies digging themselves into Jorida. Give me compliance with my orders and provide me information. When I know how to lay hands on that fool Hurshina and bring him to reason, then we *all* may find a peaceful night's sleep."

Hurshina. The Master of Jorida. The same who had resisted Ilisidi's offers for decades.

"Can we possibly do that?" Bren asked, anxious to bend the argument in some productive direction. "Lay hands on him?"

"It is uncertain whether he is still alive," Cenedi said, "unless he has been cooperative with the Shadow Guild or fast in some bolt-hole. He does not have—has never had—a defense remotely equaling the Guild. He has trusted the sea and Jorida's cliff for isolation."

"The first objective is his whereabouts," Ilisidi said. "And to know whether the Shadow Guild has yet extended its reach toward

Separti . . . whether they will challenge Lord Geigi, who is potent even in absence, or whether these intruders will pretend they are not in the area. My guess, since we are dealing with Suratho, who is such a person—she will move. By all reports she has never been a patient sort—which can be a weakness. They will likely try to set Tiajo in Hurshina's place—if they have not pitched her overboard on the voyage."

"Betan may know something," Bren said. "One believes he has sources."

Several glances turned on him.

"Sources he can discreetly access, do you think?" Ilisidi asked. "Not that our arrival has been quiet, but we would hope our information-gathering might be a bit more subtle."

"One would hope the Edi who come and go are still safe," Bren said. "Trade has always persisted—fruits and timber from Kajiminda, shipped to the Marid, trucked to Najida, shipped north by train to the rest of the aishidi'tat. There are many shippers, companies of some antiquity, and while they are not easy with the Edi, the Ashidama shore has always traded with Kajiminda, even after Lord Geigi's departure. None of them will be happy to have that trade disrupted by outsiders claiming Jorida, and I suspect Betan will know accesses."

"Ask him," Ilisidi said. "Pursue what you can. Boats, among other matters."

That foreboded a move on Jorida itself.

"I will ask," Bren said.

Ilisidi drew a deep breath, let it go, and shut her eyes.

They stayed shut.

Is she all right? Bren asked himself.

It went a moment longer. Everyone was silent, unmoving.

Eyes flashed open. "I believe I *am* disposed to sleep," she said. "Tonight, without the racket of the train or the prospect of the bus, or imminent threat from Ashidama, I may well sleep. Hand us no more difficulties for a few hours." She extended a hand toward Cenedi, and with his hand and the cane, rose. They all did, including Tatiseigi, who had no staff to assist him. Tano quietly moved to offer a hand, and Tatiseigi accepted, troubled, at the limits of his own strength, and now dismissed, as Ilisidi left with Cenedi.

"Gods less fortunate." Lord Tatiseigi sank back into his chair. "I know this act of hers!"

"Then I ask," Bren said, "respectfully. Nandi. You have seen her briefly. How is she?"

"She is exhausted, she is too tired to make wise decisions, she will not leave matters even to Cenedi, she has not yet made up her mind what to do, and she is determined not to surrender one infinitesimally small piece of power over the situation. *That* is how she is. That is how she always is."

From Tatiseigi, more loyal to her, one suspected, than to anyone living, it was astonishing frankness—especially when directed to a human once the focus of Tatiseigi's extreme displeasure.

And did the old man look to regret saying it? His breathing was rapid, his dark face thunderous, but not, it seemed, toward him.

"Your influence," Bren said as honestly, "may be extremely beneficial here, nandi."

"She knows. She *knows* all the reasons, nandi, and she acts when she has decided to act. What *is* her plan? Or has she expounded upon it?"

Nandi. Not paidhi. The entitled lordship, not the civil office assigned by humans. From Tatiseigi, on any day, it was extraordinary. And failed in any way to blame him for the situation . . . when he assigned that blame to himself. It was beyond charitable.

"At this stage, nandi," Bren said, "she has the Edi and the forest on her side, and the Edi *in* the forest are formidable. She will want information from the Townships on this shore of Ashidama Bay. Separti, with whom the Edi do their trading, and Talidi, smaller, a little more remote, and not as receptive to the Edi. That is the situation. The Master of Jorida is possibly on Jorida, possibly negotiating with the Shadow Guild, possibly in hiding anywhere along the shores of the very large bay. His whereabouts, I think, she will want to know on priority."

"And she will deal with him?"

"One assumes."

Tatiseigi frowned at him, speculatively. "You know his offense."

"Offense, nandi?"

Tatiseigi drew in a lengthy breath. "The Master of Jorida proposed *marriage* to her, to the regent of the aishidi'tat, and she has never forgiven him."

God. Bren dropped into his own chair, facing Tatiseigi. "Clearly that is not *all* the reason the Master has been at odds with the aishidi'tat."

"Oh, it is far, far more than that, paidhi. Before any of us were born, the War of the Landing settled the Edi on this shore, over Ojiri protests, over Maschi objections, and not to the liking of the Edi, either. Kajiminda was established to gratify Maschi, and to snatch the middle peninsula out of the reach of the Master of that day. Najida—one assumes you know—was created to gratify the Maschi's ally, Farai clan, *and* to manage the Edi's conflict with the Master, the wrecking, precisely. And now, quite in the face of all this historical maneuvering, Lord Geigi grants half of Kajiminda to the Edi and gives *them* management of the estate—directly trading with Separti in his own name. One watched in disbelief, paidhi, but one cannot say this place is ill-managed—especially after that scoundrel nephew. The splendid collection in the great hall—maintained and handled—even rescued, one understands, by Edi, no less!"

Tact was not in Tatiseigi's repertoire. While his attitudes had changed immensely in recent years, particularly where at least a handful of humans were concerned, sometimes the old disdain came through.

"Rescued, indeed. Staff *hid* the important pieces," Bren said, "until justice caught up with Geigi's nephew. They are still searching for some—one understands, one was recovered just lately, efforts aided by records the Edi staff kept."

"Extraordinary," Tatiseigi said. "One cannot in the least fault them. Excellent care for the dowager." For a moment, on that thought, the old man seemed on the edge of emotion. "Excellent. Excellent care for her comfort. But she *must* take herself out of this place. There is cover for every sort of mischief. Forest. Unmanaged forest on every hand. The windows—"

"It is not unprotected. There are the Edi," Bren said, "who are not amused by intruders bent on mischief. And, so my aishid believe, electronic protections placed by Geigi. I do not believe these windows are as naive as they seem. Break a single one, and I would fear the result.—Still, if you can persuade her, nandi, do. I cannot. I also cannot leave this situation. There is a crisis on the station; but I cannot leave her and I cannot leave these people— but there is the bus, nandi, which could bring you safely—"

"No such thing!"

"Nor will she, I fear."

"I will argue with her," Tatiseigi said then. "As I argue with you, nand' paidhi. At least go back to Najida. This house is not safe, this close to the enemy, even with the best will of these people! They are armed—quite evidently!—but they are not Guild. And even her aishid could be overwhelmed by numbers . . ."

"There is little chance it will be a frontal assault. The Shadow Guild has increasingly relied on subterfuge, on kidnappings and threats—one suspects their numbers are greatly limited—and they have only just arrived. The Master of Jorida and the people of the Townships are their likeliest targets."

"If they can find him. Hostages will do little good for them: that old skinflint has neither heir nor family—last of his line, with nothing he values as much as his balance books and a price on everything. He will know every hiding place in Ashidama, while *we* lie in plain sight—he will *hope* the Dojisigi concentrate on us!"

"Well, they will not get in here easily." That was a younger voice, from the doorway. Bren turned in his chair to a welcome sight, a slightly-built young man, better-composed than Tatiseigi had been, but still windburned and weary.

"Nand' Reijiri!" Bren rose to receive the cheerful half-bow of the young lord of Dur, in the doorway. "Welcome! You have survived the onslaught!"

"Barely, but yes.—One understands the dowager is up and about," Reijiri said. "I hope this is true."

"She is," Bren said. "Though she is resting at the moment." He gestured toward Ilisidi's newly vacated chair, and: "—Nadi," he addressed the Edi lad left standing by the service table, "water, and brandy. Or tea, should you wish, nandi . . ."

"Water, yes. And tea." Reijiri settled into the chair with an audible sigh. "And you are all right, nandi?" The latter, toward Tatiseigi. "It was bravely done, *bravely* done. I am greatly impressed.—He boarded at Tirnamardi, understand, nand' paidhi. All this way, and not a word of complaint."

"Nothing to the course Dur has run!" Tatiseigi said. "Understand, paidhi! This young man left Dur just after midnight, flew to Tirnamardi, then to Cobo, and Najida. And here. With no sleep at all. When we refueled—we had several times to refuel—he was out of the plane, into it, springing about on the wing, asking after *my* comfort—and when they said you were not at Najida it was no complaint, none, and on we went, where he had never landed, nor anyone, ever before, one is sure! Gallantry. Gallantry, nandi, all the way. My remotest neighbor—now and forevermore welcome to land on my lawn whenever he wishes. And we shall keep his special fuel available in case of need."

Reijiri, receiving a glass of water from one direction, managed a seated bow in the other. "We are neighbors forever, nandi, despite the clans between. Bravely done, I say." A sip. "And one was *very* glad to see the meadow. The road was quite unexpectedly narrow through the orchard . . . and the wind coming from the northwest. That was becoming a worry."

"Fuel will be here," Bren said, "by train from Cobo, perhaps tomorrow—the dowager's order."

"Then I must thank her," Reijiri said, and exchanged the empty glass for the offered teacup. "Is she receiving today, at all?"

"Perhaps at dinner. There will be dinner, shortly. You will certainly stay the night . . . well, fuel and all. There will be a room. For you, too, of course, Lord Tatiseigi."

"I have brought nothing," Tatiseigi said. "Nor has Dur. They would not let me bring a single case aboard—the fuel. The fuel weight, one understands. But here we sit, Dur and I, without so much as a change of linen."

"Staff will manage," Bren said. "Our wardrobes will be here soon, I think—they are coming from Najida—a little delayed: but they will make it. My clothes are entirely too small, but between our aishidi and house staff, we may put something together while staff restores your own. You both should have a choice by morning."

"Most appreciated," Reijiri said. "Most gratefully appreciated."

"The bath, as well. Any need. Lord Geigi's staff is very, very good—he loves his comforts. Anything you need in a well-appointed house, staff is likely to find."

"Nand' Bren," Tatiseigi said—had he ever named him so familiarly? One thought not. "Excellently done. Excellently." The old lord made an attempt to rise. A failure. Bren moved, fearing a fall, but Tano was there, taller, and stronger, with help less socially charged. Bren simply stood there, sympathetic. Reijiri likewise had stood up. Tatiseigi, his hand in Tano's younger, stronger one, stayed standing in place, with the Edi staffer to the other side, ready to assist.

"The legs," Tatiseigi said ruefully. "A mecheita is an easier seat, Lord Dur, I do maintain it. You should deepen the padding, I say, a good deal thicker cushion would do very nicely. But then, if we likely could not board so much as sandwiches, could we deal with pillows?"

"Lord," Reijiri said, also on his feet, "if I take you up again, I promise better cushions."

"Then we might have run out of fuel before we reached the meadow, might we not? I renounce the cushions, young lord, I do earnestly renounce them. Tano. It is Tano, is it not? The bath would be welcome. Let us go, if you please. I had to leave my aishid. They were not pleased. They will be on their way to Najida. But slower than we. Much slower."

Bren stood and watched the departure. Reijiri offered Tatiseigi his arm for support, and Algini followed, in case of need. Two lords of the aishidi'tat had come without their bodyguards, and if Tatiseigi's was on their way, very likely another aishid was coming down from Dur, all considerably distressed. That would be eight more Guild in their company fairly soon, granted they got past the encampment at Najida, not at all a bad thing, in his opinion.

Banichi and Jago remained, over against the wall. He and his were now sole possessors of the sitting room, with tea and brandy set out. "We are informal here," Bren said to Banichi and Jago. "As at home. This is where we will stay a few days. At very least."

"One hardly needs mention," Banichi said, "the risk here. Ourselves. Only four. And the dowager's eight. With limited communication. Najida is under an order of silence. We are. We have Lord Geigi's installations, which the Edi staff may know far more about than we have yet found. We will apparently have two units inbound. But this place has far too many windows, far too much cover approaching it, and unless the trees are wired—which is a distinct possibility—we will be reliant on Lord Geigi and the Edi command of the systems for security on the approaches. Most of all, we do not know what orders may come."

"Tabini-aiji will not be pleased with this entire situation," Bren said. "We could not stop her. I could not stop her, if Cenedi would not. I do not, at present, see a way to be useful, but we cannot leave until she will."

"We could," Banichi said, "once the plane is refueled, send you—"

"No."

"Alternatively, one of us could go as far as Shejidan and report the situation in detail. Dur would be willing to fly there."

"So could the Guild commander send a such a message," Jago said, arriving with two cups of tea, one for Banichi. "On his secure com. At gunpoint. After a reasonable explanation fails."

"Midagi would not bypass Cenedi's orders on our word," Banichi said to Bren. "Not while the dowager is in the field. You *would* have to shoot him. But a flight to Shejidan remains a serious option—and a shorter distance, by air. You could go, Bren-ji. Or one of us could. If only as far as Cobo. You would be out of her field of operations."

The dowager would never forgive him. Pushing the communicator issue with the encampment risked an obdurate commander arresting one of his aishid—and ultimately it challenged the dowager. Flying to Shejidan and questioning the dowager's actions in Tabini's office was an option, but it risked his relationship with Ilisidi while doing nothing to solve the problem in Ashidama, since the dowager would still be in the field—outranked only by Tabini, who would still be hamstrung by lack of current information, because at the moment *he* had none. Ultimately, Ilisidi was, however reckless her *methods*, not moving precipitately. The dust had not settled yet from their arrival . . . let alone Dur's, they were in an excellent position to gather intelligence, and the dowager had *ordered* nothing reckless. Yet. That one knew of.

One could not but think of the cliffs to the east of the market road, the escarpment that ended the great southern plateau and furnished such a grand viewing platform over the market road and the bag end of Ashidama Bay. Kajiminda, as the border between Ashidama and the aishidi'tat, was a prime location for spies. And snipers. One could not but wonder whether the Guild commander, on Ilisidi's orders, had made the spies and snipers up there theirs instead of Machigi's rangers, or one of the entities of Ashidama—now including the Shadow Guild. And if those spies had been replaced, *who* might take exception and how fast?

There were so many possibilities.

If Ilisidi's actions *did* change from surveillance to open aggression, if at some point the necessity of getting word to Tabini did take absolute precedence . . . having Reijiri here with his plane offered options he otherwise might not have. But leaving that option open meant keeping yet one more northern lord in the danger zone.

Make a second phone call to Geigi? By what they had discovered here, Betan obviously had some means of doing so, and might even allow him to use it. But what could he could say other than the bus, obviously, is here. The sky had cleared, the storm moved on. The red bus *and* the yellow plane were likely identifiable from orbit—Lord Geigi had no few eyes in low orbit, providing weather reports. And those other, more terrestrial conveniences Algini had noted in the house, were undoubtedly providing constant reports. No matter how busy Geigi was up there, knowing there was trouble in the area, Geigi would, at the very least, have a subordinate sitting at a dedicated console watching, non-stop, what might be happening on this coast.

The dowager had pushed forward as hard and as long as she was able. One fact was undeniable: she had not retired out of boredom this evening. Ordinarily she would be in the middle of everything. She would be down here right now, planning. But even after Tatiseigi's arrival, and obviously with a tale waiting to be told, a tale which ordinarily would have her full interest and lively curiosity—she had gone, not even waiting for Dur's arrival.

Unusual, but understandable. *He* was tired. They all were tired. But none of them carried the weight of the world as she did, along with the weight of sheer age. Movement upon movement had gotten them here, brought them as close to the enemy as a day's walk through the woods . . . and without any clear plan, if Tatiseigi's assessment was accurate. Thus far the plan was simply to *be* close to the enemy—whose stage of preparedness and whose local contacts—entirely possible through years and decades of trade relations—they did not know.

It was lunacy to be this close, the paidhi-aiji could think. But then—he was not Guild. Nor was he the aiji-dowager, who had been playing this chess game for three generations.

Banichi might be able to tell him how, in atevi terms, it made sense. He could ask questions. He *had* asked them. But then—asking questions on proposed operations injected *his* thinking into theirs, and interfering with a Guild assessment of possibilities was not the best thing to do at the moment.

It all just made him damned nervous.

He got up and refilled his own teacup. Doing small things for himself all but required stealth, with staff about, trying to do their duty.

But the Edi lad had left the room—reasonably so, though uncommon in atevi households.

As he debated on a third teaspoon of sugar, there came a disturbance in the hall—not a quiet conversation, but hushed, and urgent . . . and approaching them.

Edi. His ears made out that much before he looked toward the door.

Betan. With company. An older woman arrived in the sitting room—and among Edi, that could mean authority that they had *not* seen. Authority higher than Betan's and apart from Kajiminda estate.

"This is Seiatchet," Betan said first-off.

"Seiatchet-mala," Bren echoed with a little bow, used his limited command of Edi courtesies, and the woman gave a short, stiff nod, Edi-style.

"Daughter of the Grandmother," Betan said, and if Betan was doing the talking in this lady's presence, this lady either could not or did not choose to speak Ragi. Meanwhile Seiatchet's frown betokened nothing pleasant.

"Welcome," Bren said in the Edi language. "We shall sit happily." Verbs in the Edi language were complex and problematic—jussive was to be avoided, above all, with this lady. And his vocabulary was sadly inadequate for problems.

Seiatchet moved her head. Negative. Refusal. Not happy at all.

"What can I do?" Bren asked.

"Gan," Seiatchet said sharply. Just that. Gan. The name of the *other* Tribal People, up near Dur . . . enemies of the Edi on Mospheira, both transported to the mainland during the War of the Landing, but sited at opposite ends of the west coast because of their history. One-handed, angry, she mimed the plane.

Two and two made a clear problem in this place, outside Najida's forgiving atmosphere. "Reijiri of Dur came. He is Ragi. An ally."

Betan launched into a sentence in which Geigi figured, Dur, and the Grandmother, and the token the Grandmother had given. Seiatchet's harshness gave way a little at that, and she turned a sidelong look on Bren—looking down somewhat. "Bren of Najida."

"Yes."

She made an irreverent sound as if unconvinced.

"Betan-nadi, please, in the interests of the Edi and Lord Geigi, explain to her that the young man with the plane is Ragi, yes, the lord of Dur, neighbors to the Gan. He heard the Grandmother of the Ragi was in danger. He came from the far north, bringing her valued advisor. He tried to speak to you in your language—" That was the imagination he had of the situation—"wishing to be understood and pay you courtesy. He has come a long way to offer his help."

Betan rendered that, or something similar, along with *unlock the door*, which if literal—locks being a foreign invention to the Edi, built on a Ragi word and no reasonable part of a discussion of nand' Reijiri suggested that an intervention might be in order. There followed a rapid exchange involving the words *Ragi, Geigi,* and *Grandmother* on one side, then *table, food,* and *Gan* on the other, but resulting finally, apparently, in frowning assent.

"There will be dinner soon," Betan said then, earnestly. "The lord of Dur will be welcome."

"He has a room, surely, nadi-ji." One was uneasy, regarding doors and locks.

"Soon," Betan said, covering the matter with a polite bow. "He will be at dinner."

At a certain point, not wishing to dig the pit wider, it was best to leave it to Betan.

He stood there, asking himself what that had been about. And turned, looking at Banichi and Jago.

"I have signaled Tano and Algini," Banichi said. "Do we have a problem?"

"I believe Lord Reijiri may have gotten into difficulty. But it seems to be settled. He will be at dinner—one trusts, uninjured."

"It is close to the hour," Jago said. "Bindanda and the market truck are finally on the grounds. With the wardrobes. There was a security hold at the camp, now settled. And a flat tire on the way. But there will be a change of clothes before dinner, should you wish it."

That . . . was a very pleasant option.

13

Two of their number were to take supper in their rooms—or in one room: Tatiseigi, otherwise alone, was receiving his with the dowager, and Bren wished he were attending—but with Cenedi and six other of the dowager's aishid looming in the background, there would be little relaxation for the paidhi-aiji, who might *not* be made privy to needful information. But then—she might not tell Tatiseigi her intentions either.

Algini, however, currently meeting with Nawari on Guild matters, might manage to find some answers. Or at least hints of them.

He would have, for official dinner company, Reijiri, in all the opulence of the grand dining room—just the two of them.

"Are you all right?" he asked Reijiri on their meeting in the transverse hall, Banichi, Jago, and Tano in attendance. The Lord of Dur arrived down the hall starkly alone, but bearing no marks of violence. "One feared there might have been a problem, nandi."

Ilisidi should have provided Reijiri at least one bodyguard. She would have at any other time in his experience; but it seemed likely to fall to him to do so, when he had fairly acute need for his entire team to be with him, dealing with the Edi staff. It was yet one more disturbing failure of basic courtesies.

"There seems to have been some sort of misunderstanding," Reijiri said, quite good naturedly. "First I am offered a rather dank basement with a locked door and then a fairly glorious suite with satin sheets, a sitting room, and a flower arrangement. One was most bemused by the flower arrangement. It seemed to wish me a happy birthing."

One was appalled. But Reijiri's spirit, at least, was undampened.

"But you *are* all right. Betan assured me you were being properly attended."

"I am perfectly all right, nandi. There may have been a missed communication. Staff did apologize."

"A basement."

"Not at least a pit. We were not communicating well."

"I regret to say it is the Gan accent," Bren said. "I hope it is sufficiently cleared up. The alarm, that is."

Reijiri laughed, then turned serious as they started down the hall, with Bren's partial bodyguard behind. "The Edi," Reijiri said, "have been at war and on guard in this place, in one way or another, for decades. The Gan have not, in the north. They interact little with outsiders, but they are not nearly so wary. Not so long in necessary contact with Ragi folk. Nor at war with the neighbors."

"This place built planes once, and much of the first shuttle. Edi workers *and* Ragi. But there were only temporary Edi camps on Kajiminda, none otherwise in residence, excepting the household and orchard staff—until Lord Geigi began to move all the industry up to Cobo. The Edi kept the grounds, the orchards—which Najida's rocky soil scarcely grows. They fish, but they are very good at gardening—given peace. Which I hope they will have plenty of in our lifetime. I doubt Lord Geigi will come down to earth again and I cannot see a successor for myself, unless Tabini-aiji appoints one. The land will all come to them, if I have my way. That is granted we can settle this, truly settle this business this round."

"We have been fortunate in the north. Our colder water favors fish, and gods be thanked, not politics and not territorial feuds. The Gan are good neighbors. They fit well with us."

"Down here—one hopes at some point Ashidama and the northern Marid alike will admit they cannot rebuild the lost Empire and simply trade and move goods. The Edi here actually *have* a just complaint against their neighbors, but they had rather plant trees.—The oldest orchard trees have names, do you know? They are spoken to. Informed of important things."

"Truly?"

"I learned it from my major d', in Najida. It is *not* a naive custom. It connects generations. I tell you, Geigi's nephew, who was indiscriminately logging the forest and hacking down parts of the orchard, is very fortunate to be set at siring an heir for Calrunaidi. Lord Geigi would have Filed on him."

"He will not come back."

"Oh, Baiji will not leave the East. The dowager has given orders. His conniving is at an end."

"Well done, that, nandi."

"Bren is enough, if you will. We have so many causes in common."

"Honored. Honored. Jiri, likewise. Causes in common, indeed. I by no means regret joining you in whatever it is we are engaged in down here—with the dowager involved, it cannot be a small matter."

"It is not. Your presence, and Lord Tatiseigi's—are very welcome. And a very hard trip, without guard and without baggage— I would offer wardrobe, but it would hardly fit—nor will Lord Geigi's. And how we shall outfit Lord Tatiseigi is another matter . . ."

"*I* am not a concern. My aishid will be here, with my baggage, I have no doubt, by tomorrow or the day after. I was to fly down and back, and when I do not contact them from Cobo, I do not doubt they will be on their way, *without* the detour to Atageini. I only hope they can get past Najida station to reach your major d'."

"I shall advise Cenedi. He is the one who can get a message to the encampment *and* to Najida." They had paused in the hall. But now a young man appeared at an intersection of the hall, waiting for them by an open door, and there was indeed a faint spice in the air. "I think supper will be—"

—*just ourselves,* had been on his tongue.

But a door slammed somewhere unseen and running steps sounded behind them—another young man rushing from the great room, as they both turned, and Banichi and Jago instantly blocked the hall with Tano to the fore.

"Guild, nandiin!" the Edi exclaimed, skidding to a prudent halt. And still from that distance: "Guild! Four! On the shore!"

Four Guild was somebody's aishid. A unit lacking someone. It *might* be Reijiri's.

Except the timing.

"Which shore?" Banichi asked. "North or south?"

"North!" the young man exclaimed.

"Someone is using com," Jago advised him. Which was not a good thing.

"Tano," Banichi said. "Notify Cenedi."

Tano ran back the way they had come, breakneck for the stairs.

"They could possibly be mine," Reijiri said. "Or Lord Tatiseigi's."

"Banichi," Bren said.

"One hears," Banichi said. "We are understaffed here. Nadi! Who has seen them? Have they engaged?"

The young Edi, very out of breath, and wearing a heavy vest, outdoor wear, looked entirely confused. Reijiri uttered a string of words and they seemed to make sense. The lad, almost certainly having come in from outside, answered.

"The house has patrols out," Reijiri said. "They found two boats. Four Guild, briefly spotted."

"*Two* boats," Bren objected, "and four Guild."

"Did they *see* the Guild?" Banichi asked of the Edi, who looked both alarmed and offered a shrug.

"Did they see?" Bren repeated in the Edi language.

Violent gesture, affirmative. "We all saw. Then they disappeared. They told me run to the house." There was more, something about following.

Jago's head turned, her focus directed to the hall, and everything moved at once—a hand grabbed Bren's arm and slung him behind a half-column, so hard that stars exploded and for a moment the whole view was wall. Guns were out, safeties clicked, and Bren turned against the wall, bruised and doing his best to stay behind that thin half-column. Guns were out. Safeties off. No shots had been fired. Reijiri was flat against the other wall, and as much as he could see past the column, the Edi messenger was on the floor over against Reijiri's wall; and Banichi, Jago, and Tano were covering a single plainclothes figure far down the hallway, hands empty and held open in plain view.

Nomari.

"Stand still!" Banichi said, as Nomari started to move.

"Bren-nandi!" Nomari called out. "I am not armed!"

"That will be proved," Banichi said. "Stand still. Nandiin, stay back!"

Behind the decorative half-pillars, that was. Bren stayed as much within the shelter as he could, risked a little more exposure to watch as Banichi none too politely advanced on Nomari.

No courtesy from Banichi in meeting, either, except to holster the pistol and seize Nomari's arm, then shove him against the corridor wall and search him for weapons.

At that point it seemed safe enough to leave cover. Tano and Jago, pistols in hand, had not lowered them. Reijiri stood out from the wall, the unfortunate Edi lad gathered himself up from the floor, and they waited until Banichi abruptly turned the prospective lord of Ajuri about and brought him to face them.

Nomari stood there hard-breathing, no bow, not even a nod of courtesy.

"Two boats on the shore," Banichi said. "One is yours, nadi?"

"One, yes," Nomari said.

"No other boat with you."

"No," Nomari said.

"When?"

"Sundown. I came alone."

"There *was* a second boat," Banichi said. "How did you leave your bodyguard?"

Two blinks. No other movement. "I simply walked away."

"Indeed. If your bodyguard has followed you, and it is certain they will, their lives are in danger, nandi. And so are Edi, by mistake." Banichi rarely showed anger. He clearly did, now. "And if that boat means enemies, they are ashore and hunting all of us."

A moment of silence. A scarcely controlled: "They can protect themselves."

To Banichi, he dared say that. Bren sucked in a breath and strode into the midpoint of the hall.

"You have touched off the dowager's security, nadi. An alarm at Najida will have touched off the encampment, and your bodyguard will have followed you. We, Najida, *and* the Guild camp are under a communications blackout for a reason. Need one explain the risk to local people *and* your bodyguard?"

Nomari stood there glaring down at him, necessarily down, from his height, locked in his own sense of righteousness.

"And *you*, nand' paidhi," Nomari said, "should *not* have left me behind."

Regrets? An apology? Recognition of the situation?

Damned right Nomari understood, and his reaction was damned well *not* remorse. Anger. Resentment. Distress. He radiated all that and more.

Bren took a deep breath, seeking to calm the adrenaline rush. Anger was the antithesis of the paidhi's job. He was the peacemaker. The negotiator. The translator. Others could be angry. He could not stand between sides, if he began to be. And he had just broken his own cardinal rule.

So, also, had the prospective lord of Ajuri, whose expression was unreadable. Violent. And distraught.

Steps thundered down the stairs at mid-hall, behind him. Multiple. With, one did not need to look to know, weapons in hand.

Nomari did not even glance that direction.

"What is this?" Cenedi's voice.

"Nomari-nadi crossed the bay from Najida alone," Banichi said as Cenedi and Nawari joined them, with Algini. "His aishid is possibly in the woods northward. They *may* have observed current orders. They *may* have sent a runner to the encampment. I do not know the unit. This person's talent we already know."

"Nadiin," Nomari said, "I laid false trail, toward the upper road, for other searchers. *They* are better than that. *Very* much better. Let me go back. They are looking to find *me*. I can find them."

Cenedi turned a deadly cold look on Nomari.

"I ask," Nomari said to Banichi. The anger melted, his voice broke. "If they came—they expect to find *me*. They will respect the blackout. They will not use coms."

Cenedi was not, technically, in charge—but he might assert that, anyway. Less so, technically, was Banichi.

"Let him go," Bren said. "If they are *not* his—he is slippery enough. He still stands a chance."

Two senior Guild looked reluctant. But Banichi nodded and gestured dismissal. "Go. The paidhi's word on it. Go."

Nomari hesitated a heartbeat, looked straight at Bren, then turned and ran.

"Someone should follow him," Cenedi said grimly.

"Tano," Banichi said. "Algini."

They went, at a more deliberate pace. Nomari was already well down the hall.

Bren drew in a long breath, not looking at Banichi or Cenedi. Fool, to bet on the man? Neither had objected, and it was not protocol that stayed them: the paidhi's authority, even as a court official, was marginal, if Guild objected.

Nomari turned a corner. A door slammed open and, several moments later, clicked shut.

Reijiri moved closer, doubt in his expression at the moment, but he said nothing.

One might just have done something both foolish and dangerous—with the dowager, Atageini, and Dur all at risk.

Not to mention Ajuri, who was, if those were *not* his guards, at the greatest risk of all.

I should not have called that, Bren thought, heart pounding, and a bruised shoulder making itself felt. I should not have made that call.

"That was," Reijiri said calmly, "dare one guess . . . the lord of Ajuri?"

The lad who had brought the message still lingered.

"Well done, nadi," Bren said. "Very well done. Go advise Betan-nadi of all of it. We know the man. It is all right. But we regret another room must be made ready for another guest, when they return."

The young man bowed and departed. Another, older Edi

appeared at the door, half in, half out, and looking uncertain. "Dinner is ready to be served," he said in passable Ragi. "If you wish."

It took a moment of thought. Of sanity.

He managed to say to Reijiri, without irony, "If you still wish to join me, informally, there is dinner. If there is no other event. Or upstairs, if you wish."

"Indeed," Reijiri said. "With pleasure."

"I will go up," Cenedi said. "Banichi. I trust you have matters in hand."

"As much as possible," Banichi said. "We have not breached silence . . . unless Nomari's guard has."

Cenedi said nothing, just exchanged a direct look with Banichi, and things were surely understood.

Your principal took charge, that was to say. Deal with it.

Cenedi and Nawari headed for the stairs. Banichi and Jago stayed. Reijiri stood among them.

What was there to say, Reijiri being present? What he would have said is, Am I a fool?

Appetite had fled. His shoulder hurt. Tano would regret the shoulder if he knew.

Tano and Algini were in potential danger out there, in the cover of the woods. While inside they were trying to stay discreet and quiet, despite all. The plane. Two boats.

God.

A bottle disappeared in the first course. The food was elegant, extremely so. But sparse, given the massive seasonal arrangement. The wine deserved more studied attention, and did not get it.

One had to thank the cook, however, a modest woman, young, very young for the post. "Please go upstairs," Bren said, "inquire at my rooms, and say to Bindanda, who is the heart of my own kitchen, that you and he and my staff should enjoy two bottles of this wine tonight, in appreciation of this beautiful dinner. Will you do that?"

The very young woman put hands to her face—embarrassment,

and bowed twice. "One is honored, nand' paidhi." It was not the best Ragi, but it far exceeded his own ability to say it in Edi—a sin one vowed to remedy.

"Indeed," Reijiri said, and said it in Edi. Or Gan, the two being that close. The young woman looked abashed, and happy, and exhausted, and she probably would not say exactly what he had said. But the wine would get upstairs. And Bindanda and this talented young cook should meet.

Himself, he wanted to bow his head in his hands and not think for a space, after, but he cast a sidelong look at Reijiri and flexed his shoulders back.

Reijiri looked as undone—lack of sleep. The wine. Being slammed into the other wall.

"There is a second room in my suite, if you would prefer it over the birthing day bouquet," Bren said. "And I have staff to lend, if not a wardrobe that fits. If you will, nandi."

"Jiri," Reijiri reminded him. "And I would be grateful. Extremely. A bed. A bath. In either order."

"Both. Take precedence in the bath. I have a problem afoot."

Reijiri hesitated a moment. "Is he . . . much like that?"

Referring to the prospective lord of Ajuri. One hesitated in turn—how much to say. But a great deal had been laid bare out in the hallway. "One could surmise—he finds himself close to the agency that killed his family and is restricted from joining us. He was a child at the time. He was there. You know the event."

"Yes."

"He escaped—at an age when children are still guided by their parents. He survived—he has never said how. He moved from place to place—one suspects, on the railroad, alone, with no fare. He became very adept at vanishing, at very least. He was a switchman for the railroad. He moved with the trains. He ended up in the Marid, with what purpose is uncertain, but he employed his skills for Lord Machigi, ultimately, when Tiajo took over the Dojisigin, and the Shadow Guild began to make its moves—aided by—originated by—an Ajuri in Shejidan, an officer of the Guild, one Shishogi. Discovery of Shishogi's work—to compress a great deal—illumined a great many things that had gone on in Ajuri."

"Dur paid sharp attention to that," Reijiri said. "And it did explain certain things. But not all. That the trouble moved to the Marid seemed to us to be a good thing, at the time."

"Nomari was involved as Lord Machigi's agent, mostly in Senjin, to my understanding, mostly reporting on Dojisigin operatives in Koperna—and the traffic that crossed over to the Dojisigin. He still has a relationship with Lord Machigi, now that he has made his identity apparent, now that he is standing for the lordship of Ajuri. The potential politics of that are uncertain. But, yes, between us and many others, that relationship is a concern."

"A far distance between Ajuri and the Taisigin."

"Indeed. But Kadagidi clan—Lord Tatiseigi's neighbor—and Ajuri's—had a penchant for trade relationships. And marriages with Dojisigi women."

"Until the overthrow. Dur held as far apart as possible in that year. There was little we could do *except* hold apart."

"One appreciates the difficulty.—By this time, I think Nomarinadi was in the Marid. The Kadagidi went down. So did, ultimately, Ajuri, and Shishogi, in the Guild. But in all the turmoil in the north, the Dojisigi remained untouched in the South. And the Shadow Guild had surfaced, taking down Machigi's father, and trying to take down Machigi. But Machigi formed a very efficient network working against the Dojisigin, *and* the Shadow Guild. And *that* is the time in which Nomari supplied Machigi with information, which he got as a common railway worker, moving from place to place, wherever trains run. *That* is Nomari. He lacks certain graces. Lacks fear, to my observation, which ordinary caution would suggest. He has qualities that recommend him *as* a successor in Ajuri. He is suspicious. Quick. And has the skills of the Guild, not officially acquired. He is accustomed to operate without associates. To think without associates. But his clan accepts him. Fervently. More to the point, as this human understands it—he attaches to *them*."

"Down to that one point, one could fear this neighbor," Reijiri said. "He has that man'chi. You are sure."

"It is hard for me to judge. My attachments are—as my aishid informs me—occasionally hazardous. But I understand passion.

And that seems to exist in him. Deeply. One believes he feels compelled to be part of whatever is going to happen here."

"And resents being left behind and ignorant," Reijiri said quietly. "One caught that as well."

"The question is—with the Shadow Guild, who killed his family and ruined his clan, involved—*what* drives him now. Is it revenge for his own losses? Or his responsibility to his clan? But he has gone back after his guards . . . with, I think, concern."

Reijiri drew a long, deep breath and let it go. "It is said humans cannot comprehend man'chi. You disprove this assumption." And before Bren could respond: "Your assessment agrees with what I sense. He is one thing. And he is the other. He is broken. Looking for his pieces."

"Looking for his bodyguards, for a beginning," Bren said with a chill thought of the woods, and too many people on edge tonight. "And I hope he turns up with them, but he is not incapable of taking out in the other direction, to Separti, and a boat. To take on the Shadow Guild in his own way—which is not ineffective. I should also say—from our party, we have more than one unit at loose ends out there: two Guild that left us at Najida, that have no association with him or us. They are looking for their own missing pieces."

"Guild? *Two?*"

"Guild or Shadow Guild. Which they are—still remains a question. They insist their duty was forced, not given. They believe their partners could be held now in Jorida."

"An unhappy situation."

"To say the least."

Staff was waiting to clear away the dinner and the arrangement. Banichi and Jago were in conference at a table beyond the official tables, and they could have no word from Tano and Algini, who were out there trying to assure nothing worse arrived.

Reijiri, obviously exhausted, excused himself to the promised bath.

14

Reijiri did not make it past the bath, where he fell asleep on the dressing bench in his borrowed bathrobe, so the Edi reported; and Bren looked in to find staff had kept the furnace up, and simply reported the matter. Bren closed the garment bag to protect the clothes—Guild- and Edi-lent—then delivered Reijiri's own clothing to staff, to launder and have ready in the morning. "Keep the heat going," he told staff, and went upstairs to advise Narani their intended guest was camped elsewhere, and to change his dinner coat for a hardier one.

"If he comes here," he told Narani, "give him whatever hospitality he needs."

"Yes," Narani said. And did not even ask whether he was going to bed now. He had arrived alone, a spooky feeling after all these years, going about in a strange house, with no one attending: Banichi and Jago were separately maintaining a watch on the north entry, Reijiri, likewise unattended, was lying on a bench in the bath, and there was yet no word from Tano and Algini, who were out there not to interfere in Nomari's search for his bodyguard, but to keep a line on the situation, as the saying went.

And Banichi and Jago *trusted* that he was safely situated in the sitting room, with no outside windows, waiting for Reijiri, with Betan's day staff winding down their shift—so he was morally obliged to be there until they came for him. Likely there *was* no regular night staff in the house except the watch, but laundry was being done and dishes were being washed. Cenedi was closeted with Nawari and several of the dowager's aishid in a smaller room nearby with maps and charts. His own aishid was fully occupied. And he wished he knew where and how far Tano and Algini were tracking. There were patrols out, Edi folk, armed and vigilant, and not necessarily well-informed. One hoped they understood. Betan was no novice at managing the estate grounds.

He had left a packet there, that Betan had gathered for him, a collection of maps, hand-marked by previous users, showing the position of Kajiminda on the peninsula—showing, in erasable marker, the area of the peninsula ceded to the Edi—it might be Geigi's own hand that had made that line. There was a mark for, he was sure, the building site where Edi folk were building a permanent structure—the first since they had worked to build Najida itself, under Ragi direction, and probably—he hated to think so—under armed guard.

But this one, this new place out on the end of the peninsula, was Edi, foundation to roof. It was not yet finished: the yacht—his yacht, moored at Najida, shallow enough of draft to navigate the Kajiminda northern shore, routinely moved supplies brought down by rail and truck. The Edi, though not seafarers like the Gan, were still very adept sailors—the yacht fared very well in their hands. And got use. And maintenance.

That was the extreme end of the peninsula. In the massive bay to the south, Jorida Isle was marked, with the outline of the old town, and an inset for the detail of its streets. The map was hand-drawn in ink; by whom and when was not indicated, but any number of things might have changed since it was made.

Damn, he wished he would hear from Tano and Algini—which was not to be, under the general blackout. He wished they were back—he wished they were back with Nomari *and* his bodyguards—simply guards, as Nomari had apparently chosen to regard them, though one would have hoped he and they had formed a different perspective, since Koperna and the last time he had slipped away.

It was possible Nomari was not out searching for them at all. Possible he had used his skills simply to go the other way, taking

that semi-permanent road marked on this map from the outbuildings of Kajiminda estate, straight down to Separti Township. If
he reached there he could lose himself, shifting accents—a lin-
guist noted that ability, conscious or unconscious, that let him fit
in Koperna or in the Ragi midlands: quickly native, and unre-
markable, perhaps even in another language. It was a gift. Where
he had traveled, how he had traveled, it had been survival.

Now it could become damned inconvenient.

He was sure that, not far away, Cenedi and his people were
making similar calculations, weighing options. Preparing against
attack. And he could not forget Kajiminda's low, ground-level
windows, open invitation . . . deception, maybe. But—

He had no desire to see the result. Image of windows gave way
to image of Geigi, in his nest of consoles that could contact all
sorts of functions on the space station, and might well do the
same down here.

He wanted to call Geigi on a number of matters, the current
situation in Ashidama Bay tonight being one of the chief ones.
But the phone was forbidden: Cenedi had specifically widened the
prohibition. There *might* be other means that Betan had, means
somewhat less vulnerable, possibly as secure as the new coms,
but he did not know and was not quite certain how to ask without trading hospitality for a little information. It was very possible Geigi had instructed Betan years ago to keep Kajiminda's
abilities secret. Geigi might even monitor voices in the house.
How that fitted with the general blackout Cenedi had imposed on
Kajiminda and whether it posed any risk of interception, Bren had
no remote idea, but he doubted Betan would admit it, let alone
give him access, if such communication did exist, Betan having
helped keep that secret for too many years. Things ran, in Kajiminda, in eerie combinations of century-old function with constant information to—whatever communicated with Lord Geigi's
metal and plastics office.

What should he say to Cenedi? What *could* he say that would
not involve Algini's suspicions? *The opening of the upstairs
rooms has probably broken our silence!* And if there were listen-
ers that finely tuned, what could the Shadow Guild do with that

information that the presence of a large red and black bus and a yellow airplane could not tell a watcher on the cliffs, out on the market road?

Ask whether a watcher on the cliffs would be safe to radio Jorida—well, no. But it would be very likely that if said watcher existed, said watcher's continued life was simply problematic to take. For now. What they knew, what the Shadow Guild knew, how much they knew and were set up to detect—others knew, and he did not.

God, he wanted to know what was going on out there. He *lived* with communications. Having everything cut off was maddening.

The map and what he had seen before sundown at least gave his imagination detail—the ragged brown ink line of a coast flashed to imagination of saltwater chop washing rocks. The indication of trees was older orchard giving way to—it was indicated on the map—the ancient forest, trees that the Edi would have named, and a seasonally maintained road, that double line that went to what was, by what he knew—a walled town, which itself was something unique to Ashidama district. Separti and Talidi had had to keep the Edi out. Jorida had its height above the waves, and all the bay to defend it. But both the Townships had built walls, each had one approach by land, and of course a wide-open and ample approach from the bay.

One gate. One presumably closeable gate to each town on the land of the peninsula, and an open face to the sea. Nothing built a hundred years ago—or even last year—was going to stand against Guild determination to get through, as *they* were equipped.

But blowing up the gate was not the quiet way to get at their enemies, if that was what Cenedi was dealing with on the other side of that wall. The Guild preferred quieter operations. One could even be underway—without his knowing it. Less likely—without Banichi knowing it. And Banichi would let him know. So no, they had not moved yet. But it would not be long.

Was the dowager getting a restful sleep—finally? One hoped so. Perhaps, if she were rested and clear-headed tomorrow morning, she would realize that keeping everyone else ignorant and out of discussions was a damned poor use of resources.

If all else failed, perhaps Tatiseigi would have more information for them in the morning . . . meaning yet another night of endless circular thinking for him.

The whole house was trying to be quiet in cooperation, right down to the council of war and the search for intruders, and the Edi staff was trying to manage necessary operations like laundry and kitchen without any racket in the corridors or stairwells.

It was, in fact, now getting ghostly quiet.

And a distant opening door *did* make itself heard.

He froze, not sure he had heard it, and then decided he had. Quiet continued in the house. If there was danger in the halls it was damned stealthy, and he did have—quietly protected—his own small pistol; and the bulletproof vest. He had wanted to shed it, in the house. No, Banichi had said. So *no* it was.

He had released the fastening on his left side. He drew a deep, deep breath.

In all that quiet—another door opened. North door.

He pressed the closures shut again, rising from his chair, trying to be quiet about it.

The map . . . should not be left. He rolled it. He shoved it into a convenient shelf unit, silently put the chair back as if no one had been there. He soft-footed it out into the hall, saw Jago in the far distance, and Banichi—his height and size relative to hers— then Nomari, his blue coat; then Guild black. Several.

Bren started walking, rapidly. Tano and Algini were there. That was enough. *His* bodyguard was back. And safe. And nobody had weapons in hand. That was all he truly needed to know.

He stopped at the intersection with the main hall—not helpful to go involve himself with that sort-out of Nomari and his aishid, which Banichi would certainly manage. He waited as they escorted Nomari and his four to the foot of the upward stairs.

And he was, himself, over-tired. Glad. Ineffably glad to be done with the day. His own were there. Everything was all right.

He watched as Banichi gave orders sending everybody upstairs, Nomari and his four; and Tano and Algini, to escort and interface with house staff—there were numerous rooms upstairs, all of which were secure territory: one suite cleared for his use, one for the dowager, one for Tatiseigi. *Somebody* was going to camp in the hall all night, he was absolutely sure, making sure that none of those rooms was disturbed by Nomari taking a second stealthy leave of his bodyguard. At least he was getting a bed—not being locked in a—

Reijiri—God, Reijiri was still asleep in the bath. Staff needed to put him somewhere, if *he* waked and looked for a proper bed. But sleep was sleep tonight, and if one had it, best take it where it was. He wanted his own bed—he would have it. He wanted his aishid safe—he had that. And he wanted their uninvited guest *and* his aishid settled, four men who had started out elite Guild assigned as part of Ilisidi's contingent—proper Guild, proper clearances, proper, respectable men, who might, on official assignment by the dowager to a prospective lord of the aishidi'tat, have believed they *might* achieve a long-term assignment—

That situation was *not* going to settle without a deep, difficult discussion that had to involve *their* rightful expectations and Nomari's lifelong purpose . . . which might be fulfilled in the next number of days.

Leaving Nomari with—what? A clan that wanted him—without knowing him. An aishid he had wounded—to whatever degree.

Nomari facing him and his aishid down in the hallway had been one sort . . . and the first real hint of a potentially healthy, lordly arrogance Bren had seen from him—his normal affect was quiet, self-effacing, and slightly overwhelmed. And his actions betrayed a dangerous degree of self-focus for a lord. A self-focused lord placed more than his own life in danger: too many people depended on him to stay alive and keep his head. What Tatiseigi had done . . . coming down into a potential war zone in Reijiri's plane without his aishid . . . that was a once in a lifetime judgment call, and not a decision Tatiseigi had made at all lightly. In that sense, one might think Tatiseigi's man'chi had a serious vulnerability where Ilisidi was involved.

One might think that, but knowing Tatiseigi, one would not lay money on it. That was a wise and battle-tested leader doing what supported his strongest ally.

On the other hand, the Nomari who begged leave to go *find* the men risking themselves to track him down—implied a dawning of necessary concern for those dependent on him. Balanced against all the fuss and concern Nomari's stunt had caused . . . well, one hoped Nomari could learn to make those instincts work for him—if he had them. If he had a purpose beyond his objective: that was the key. At the moment, one had no idea which one would prevail in him if all the issues of his lost family were done and he simply had to live his life and serve his people.

"What happened out there?" he asked Banichi.

"They found him," Banichi said. "Or rather he tried to be found, beginning at their boat and moving inland from there. Tano and Algini observed at distance. To their credit, his aishid became aware of us, and made proper contact, after which we pointed the way to him and advised them to come in as soon as they had him, which they agreed they would do. There *will* be a discussion in that aishid tonight, before anybody sleeps. One is sure of that. Meanwhile we have two fishing boats, valuable property to their owners, that we cannot notify without more noise than we would like, and a very anxious search stirred up at Najida."

"We will notify them," Bren said. "Whatever compensation Ramaso promises regarding the boats, we will do. We should ask Cenedi to notify the camp commander."

"*Cenedi* is unavailable." Banichi's growing irritation with the situation was evident. "*Cenedi* is meeting with his units. Planning. I think. One does not know what."

"At this point, Nichi-ji, they will do what the dowager determines to do. But he *will* listen to you if it is unworkable. He has thus far. Come upstairs."

Banichi cast a doubtful look down the hall, then: "Yes," he said, definitive answer.

Yes. Banichi was . . . decidedly . . . not happy.

* * *

"We have *no* further information from the Guild camp," Father said. It was a meeting with Father *and* Mother—breakfast, which was the first time Father had taken any meal outside his office in days, so right away, things seemed a little better.

But Father's opening dashed that hope. Cajeiri poked a coddled egg with, suddenly, less appetite. No word, no news forthcoming, nothing but breakfast. And maybe with words about to come from Mother, who had not yet given him her opinion on what he had done.

"I have, however, heard from Cenedi this morning," Father said, scooping three eggs onto his plate. "He has *finally* deigned to answer com. They *are* there. They *are* safe. They have had a quiet night."

No question who "they" referred to. The yellow plane had made it to Kajiminda. Uncle and Lord Reijiri were safe. Yet somehow appetite did not return. Cajeiri swallowed a lump in his throat that felt as if it were a whole egg. Shell and all. It was good news. He had no idea why his heart was beating that hard and felt as if it could explode.

"Good," he got out, finally, past the egg.

"You might say more than that," Mother said.

He had a fork in hand. The lump was not going away and he did not want to pretend he felt nothing: that was not the thing to do.

"I *am* sorry," he said.

"You were more confident *before* we reported them safe at Kajiminda," Father observed.

He could not talk at the moment. And both his parents were looking at him, everything at a standstill.

The lump finally went down. He drew a breath. And another. He felt as if he was going to have hiccups. He fought them off. "I do *not* think I made a mistake," he said. "I am just glad they are safe." Father had been in touch with Cenedi. So Father knew things. Things Father had *promised* to share. "Is Great-grandmother all right?"

"Grandmother is on her feet, and in possession of Lord Geigi's armament, inconveniently fixed in place as it is and utterly useless in doing anything about the situation on Jorida. Grandmother, through Cenedi, has imposed a dome of silence over the entire west coast, everything south of Cobo. I could countermand that order, but that could expose her operation, whatever it is, and risk all of them. And despite the fact I have *again* ordered Cenedi to give one of the communicators to Bren-paidhi, somehow I suspect this has not happened. Who could order Cenedi with more force at close range than I can, from Shejidan?"

There was a prolonged silence at table.

"Great-grandmother," Cajeiri said, there being absolutely no other answer.

"And she has now shut down *all* communication. Do you form a picture, son of mine?"

"Let us have breakfast," Mother said, delivering a small fish to her plate. "Bini-ji. I ask."

She was trying to keep breakfast calm. Maybe to protect him. But somehow he could not let the matter drop. There was more information. He *needed* to know. *Needed* to understand.

"I *do* see," Cajeiri said, and forced the hands in his lap to relax. "But I do not know why she has held this from nand' Bren."

"I will tell you frankly that I do *not* think it is for fear of his talking to *me*. I think it is fear of his talking to Lord Geigi, who controls unguessed aspects of that house. She knows what is happening on the station is reaching crisis and does not want Bren-paidhi's man'chi to the humans to pull him from her."

That was not what he expected. At all. But:

"Humans do not have man'chi, Father."

"One is aware. So is Grandmother. Yet that is how she thinks of human connections, still, and she cannot risk his man'chi to humans being greater than his man'chi to her. She needs him, for some reason only she knows. She is certainly not seeking his advice, by what he said on the phone to Lord Geigi."

"And cannot Lord Geigi's staff, in his house, reach nand' Bren at any time? He does not really *need* that communicator, does he?"

"One does not hazard even a guess at what abilities Lord Geigi has. That does not mean the staff will share that means with Bren-paidhi, if Lord Geigi has told them to conceal it. And how much *can* they explain—when your great-grandmother has taken over the house and overawed them with her protection? You know full well how all bow to her wishes, once she enters. Nand' Bren will follow her blindly . . . up to a point. He has no other real option. But in reality, what are his options? He cannot countermand her, where it comes to the Guild. Certainly he cannot use the Red Train without her releasing it. He must stay where he is and deal with the situation she creates. He will be trying to judge her competency, which generally has been unquestionable, but without knowing her intentions. Are they wise? Are they even rational? Are they in *any* sense coordinated with Geigi—who has little time to coordinate anything? We do not know, son of mine. *We do not know.* We do not know what she has told the Edi, what she has *asked* of them, or by what means. The Edi will not know whether her actions are authorized . . . and will not truly care, if she has made the request in the right way. She is gifted with the ability to manipulate. Lord Geigi could counter that request, but if I throw this into his lap, with the station crisis as it is, what can he do but restrain the Edi from cooperation? He could do that . . . which might expose her—and Lord Bren, your great-uncle, and Lord Reijiri—to failure, thus damaging the aishidi'tat and empowering these renegades to do wider harm. Or to worse. *Because we do not know what she is doing.* We have three lords of the aishidi'tat backing her blindly. And their lives at risk. Nand' Bren cannot restrain her. It is very remotely possible that Lord Tatiseigi might succeed where others could not, but we do not know, and cannot learn, the state of Lord Tatiseigi's health. We could move the Guild to Kajiminda—but that violates agreements with the Edi, which can lead to no good things. More, *Geigi* is out of time, pressed by emergencies aloft, which could bring the space station itself into danger, and if, in order to save the lives of *five* lords of the aishidi'tat, he was forced to take what action he could from where he is, *his* kind of action would create a precedent I do *not* want to set. We *can* deal with scoundrels on an island in Ashidama, complicated as it may be with the Edi. I do not want a disaster in the heavens, on whatever scale.—But it would be far easier to accomplish if your great-grandmother would simply *deign* to confer!"

His head was spinning with all the pieces spinning out of control. The station crisis could *not* wait. He could imagine the section in which the refugees from Reunion were housed—a place so bad, so unruly the great gates in the station ring had had to be shut, people penned up inside, clamoring to be out. There was no way to *let* them out, except for them to come down to Earth. *That* had to proceed, and nand' Bren was himself involved with mani, and trying to keep *mani* alive.

He thought far and wide what could be done. Desperately, for everybody involved down there. Things to stop the Shadow Guild. He thought of chess, with mani.

"There is one Navy ship left in the Strait," he said.

Father looked at him long and hard.

Perhaps, he thought, he had been brilliant.

Perhaps he was just stupid, and had already made everything worse.

"I have already moved it," Father said.

Mother was looking at them, fork in hand.

"There is a complication, however. That ship, which your great-grandmother graciously did *not* move to the Marid . . . is our tracking station for the shuttle landing at the spaceport. It will enter the bay under cover of darkness and will attempt to intervene at Jorida. We will use Mospheira's tracking, with its attendant communication difficulties, if the shuttle's return precedes its return to the Strait. The shuttle, unhappily, does not have a second-pass option. We are greatly invested in accurate communication the first time, you surely understand."

"Do not lay too much on him." Mother had not eaten the fish, though she had poured sauce on it. "For how much can he be responsible? The weather? The action of our enemies? *Her* choices?"

I am responsible, Cajeiri was about to say, but:

"I have already given instruction," Father said, "that in the future our son can reach me, day or night, whether or not I am in a meeting. I have *promised* our son to keep him informed . . . of *all* things. I *trust* he will use that privilege appropriately.—Will you, son of ours?"

"Yes," he said. "*Yes,* honored Father."

There was so much to know, so many things in so many places. He wanted to be with mani. And could not be. He wanted to be in the midst of things and know everything, and he would do nothing good by being there.

So, too, had Father felt. For years and years and years. And now they had the com that would let mani keep them informed . . . and Cenedi told them, at best, half-truths.

Lord Bren would tell them honestly, if he could.

"I think the fish is a loss," Mother said. "The winter fruit will not be. And there are the little cakes."

Mother changed the topic, and passed the little cakes. They ate this way for what Father called informational breakfasts, at the little table, Mother's idea, with no servants. Mother had started them. Father had ordered this one. He had come in hoping for news.

And gotten far more . . . and not enough. But he was getting what Father knew . . . which had only upset his stomach again. If this was mani's normal method of taking action, he could well understand Father's sometime frustration.

The cakes at least looked good. He took one, then just stared at it.

Father had moved things, done things, supported mani— because he had to. Father would never desert her, any more than he would. It came to him that there had been a time *Father* had been his age, and trying to work with mani, maybe without being told things . . . mani was not what Father called forthcoming. There had been times *Father* would have tried things, done things, that might have had problems.

Because he had had to act on limited knowledge.

One began to suspect why mani had said, all that long time ago, about him trusting he knew more than he did being part of who he was . . . and telling him to ask his father about it.

Things were changing. Informational breakfasts would never

be quite the same. He was going to be told what was going on, and he knew, now, that Father was not going to be careful about how he said these things.

And Mother had defended him. He never remembered Mother doing that so strongly. He had been with mani for all his early years, and Mother never trusted him. Mother had had his sister Seimei, and he had thought that was good: now Mother had a baby who would listen to *her*, and that might make her happier. Mother was under no fair obligation to take care of *him*.

And yet Mother tried to make peace now and again. She really tried. And this morning she defended him.

He remained surprised by that, and wondered why, or what her reason was, whether she and Father had argued, or whether it was to get the better of mani in something. And now he wondered if maybe it was not something else. She and Father argued, sometimes heatedly. He understood now that her ability to argue with him that way was one of the things that held them together. But she *knew* how he argued and maybe she stepped in now with comments about fish and cakes, to moderate his father's temper.

She had said once, that she regretted losing him. He regretted losing her, in fact. There were times it would be easy to think that moved her. But Mother, who was Ajuri and then Atageini, was complicated; and she was upset by mani taking Nomari away with her, with her assumption that Mother and Uncle could not make a sound assessment of their own *on* one of their own. Mother had motives. Mother was very smart.

He *had* felt something just now, when she defended him. And he thought now he should be careful of that, because mixed feelings were what he already had with mani taking Nomari, and with Nomari himself and his connection to Lord Machigi; and with mani taking nand' Bren, and keeping him silent when Father and Lord Geigi needed him—and now *he* was going to have to go to the spaceport and be nand' Bren. He was not ready to be. And because mani would not give nand' Bren his communicator, he had no means to confer with nand' Bren about the plans he had been making.

Plans he could not concentrate on when the Shadow Guild was taking every opportunity to make everything go wrong, just to hurt all those who had run them out of the Dojisigin.

No, that was crooked thinking. Mani would tell him that. The Shadow Guild was not after revenge. They were after winning.

15

Dawn, after an otherwise quiet remainder of the night—at least there had been no alarms—but Reijiri had not come upstairs.

"You have had no word about him," Bren asked of Narani and Jeladi, as he was dressing, and no, they had not.

But: "Staff has taken him in hand," Banichi said, when they were leaving the suite.

"One hopes he did not spend the night on that bench."

"One thinks he did not," Banichi said. "Likely he awakened and staff found him and put him to bed." Then, with a finger pressed to his earpiece: "A message from Cenedi. The dowager asks you to breakfast. Immediately."

"God." That, in Mosphei,' but Banichi understood it.

"We are, by the wording, excluded," Banichi added, in a very carefully modulated tone.

Temper rose up along with the intent to refuse the order or refuse the invitation, but his aishid would then have Cenedi to deal with, after the resultant argument, none of *their* fault. He had a bad feeling about it all. A foreboding. And not just for his own sake.

"Breakfast at leisure," he said. "Extravagantly. At leisure. Go downstairs and send trays up." For Narani, Jeladi, and Bindanda, that was. "Anything you want."

"Bren-ji," Banichi said levelly. Just that. *Calm*. In a meeting into which none of them could go. "We *can* take station."

Bujavid discipline. Ceremony and show.

"No." One careful breath. "I shall do nothing to provoke a

problem." He included all of them in a glance, all concerned. "And I will join you downstairs when I am done. I may be in want of something stronger than tea."

"Cenedi has been unreachable," Banichi said, "and evasive. He was *not* pleased last night, but has said nothing further about it. One suspects, he is *not* in favor of this expedition, or at least not pleased with certain aspects of it. He may be in agreement with you, Bren-ji."

"That would be a novelty."

"Nevertheless. That is the sense I have, and Algini agrees."

"Agreement with me at present . . . is a divided landscape. I had rather have us all back in Najida.—I will come down when I am done, granted I have no *contrary* instruction."

Ilisidi's rooms were Geigi's own suite, the end of the hall. There was no guard outside: ceremony seemed not as valuable to her today, either, which in itself said that she was resting more than herself, letting her aishid rest, anticipating—whatever she had in mind.

He rapped once, and the door opened—Casimi let him in and showed him through the foyer and the sitting room to a breakfast nook that, with shockingly expansive windows, looked out over orchard and forest as far as the eye could see.

Sunlight came through the clouds. There was blue sky beyond.

Geigi, whose rooms these were when he had been in residence, could look down from the heavens and *see* Kajiminda today. Kajiminda, and Ashidama, so close to each other from heavenly perspective. A bay one could span with a fingertip . . . from there.

And the clouds had moved. The horizon was clear. And in front of that window, a table, the dowager, already seated; and a vacant chair. Cenedi was alone, on duty, standing by her chair.

Of course he was.

Bren walked to the vacant seat, bowed, and let Ilisidi's sole female servant wrestle the heavy thing back on resistant carpet.

He sat down, drawing the chair close himself.

"Aiji-ma."

Ilisidi gestured to the teapot. The servant poured, first Ilisidi's cup, then his. And uncovered the dishes. Including, yes, the requested pickle.

"We are informal," Ilisidi said. "Did you sleep, paidhi? We are informed the lord of Dur was rescued from the bath and taken to bed. Lord Tatiseigi is sleeping in this morning, as he should. And we acquired Nomari-nadi last night, with four good men, who may be more useful."

"It was a busy night," Bren said dryly, "aiji-ma."

Ilisidi quirked a brow.

It was not blowing a cold gale from some open window—her usual ploy to discomfit a human. It was a sunny view of forest where anything might be going on. He sipped tea—with a certain memory—he took two eggs and a piece of toast, thinking perhaps he should take a third—but his stomach could not deal with the idea, and in the end he could not finish even what he had put on his plate.

He laid his fork down. He took a sip of tea. She also finished, and let the servant take away the plates.

Tea remained. The servant poured, one and the other.

"Have you talked to Lord Geigi?" Ilisidi asked.

"No, aiji-ma."

"Well. We suppose he is watching, still. Tell me, paidhi. Apply your military sense. What should we do about Jorida?"

"My military sense, aiji-ma, says that I should consult the Guild and let them act."

"Indeed. And what, first, do you think the Guild would suggest?"

"To put indispensable assets out of reach of the enemy."

Ilisidi nodded slowly. "Return to Shejidan and be safe, is it?"

"At least to Najida. Delay this until Lord Geigi can free himself of one problem and assist with this. Set a guard to protect his house, and move back within reach of the Guild. Allow me to return to Shejidan long enough to get the refugee operation in motion, so that I can return and offer you my fullest attention."

"*Have* you spoken to Lord Geigi?"

Perhaps Betan *had* resisted the Guild getting into house systems.

"No, aiji-ma. I have not! At Najida, I did what, minimally, I had to do, under my roof. For my guest."

There was a lengthy silence. A very lengthy silence. And Ilisidi took something from her lap, under the table, and laid it beside her plate.

One of the new coms.

"You may have it. You *were* to have it. That you do, removes it from the Guild we will leave at Kajiminda, unless you stay."

Stay here. Implying there was *only* this one available, when the same words could mean there might be dozens. God, the woman could manipulate. Nonetheless, thoughts, obligations, *needs* tumbled one over the other, Najida, Geigi, the station, Jorida, Tabini. And his bus.

She had laid the communicator within his reach. *Dared* him to leave with it. To return to Shejidan and the problems of the station. He took it. Firmly. He slid it into his coat pocket.

"Jorida," she said, "is an old, old business of mine. Unfinished business with a stubborn old man who may or may not be alive. I hope he is alive. I want to see him acknowledge his situation."

"Hurshina." It was no wide guess.

"Hurshina. Whose network reaches all the way across that great hunting range to the east. Who has contacts, both high and lowest of the low, up in all the ports of the Marid. He has radio. Indeed—radio. With no one to call for help—but having the same knowledge we have—of those two ships that fled the Dojisigin."

"*Two* ships." So . . . confirmation: Geigi had meant the plural.

"One in the lead, one following. Two."

A larger number of Shadow Guild, then. Perhaps more than they even suspected were left.

"Will Hurshina have defended the island?" Ilisidi asked—clearly a rhetorical question. "There is artillery. Cannon and powder. We have not let him have the advantages of the Guild: the price of his infernal independence. Jorida has the sea for a defense, and that is all—the cannon fire on holidays, and occasions. But those ships may bring heavier weapons, modern rifles. Likely even more deadly things. You may know—Ashidama has had bitter relations with the Edi, and the aishidi'tat has limited both, and threatened fire and thunder if they even attempt to acquire modern armament."

There had been skirmishes with the Edi, fought with pistols and rifles, sometimes bows . . . never with heavier armament, generally at Talidi Township, to the west, on the end of the peninsula. Talidi, desirous of timber, had had particularly strong objection to Lord Geigi's gift of the land to the Edi—it had come to a few shots fired last year, and a severe warning to both sides.

Lord Geigi's mere word had settled it. Geigi had, since his gift, that kind of power with the Edi. Himself, he had done what he could, and preserved the peace on Najida.

"If the Edi are involved again," he said, "it will be harder to stop."

"Indeed," Ilisidi said, "and we had rather not. We rely on you for that. And on Lord Geigi. Who surely can communicate with Betan."

"I will do everything I can."

"You will succeed," Ilisidi said. It *was* the jussive form. An order.

"Yes, aiji-ma." God, they were *going* to move. To *attack* . . .

"Doubtless you will immediately contact Lord Geigi. Extend our greetings."

"I will."

"The Master's communication will have been shut down. The Townships may receive information of what has happened when those ships docked, but they are otherwise helpless against Guild-level operations. And it is very likely that Hurshina himself will not have waited to welcome his visitors. To go to Talidi would strand him on the extreme end of the peninsula, nearest the Edi construction of their great house, not in the most welcoming area of the peninsula. He would have more hope of Separti, larger, and within reach of Kajiminda, where he might at least meet Edi who would consult before shooting him. We have somewhat expected him to come here. But—perhaps the Shadow Guild is on his trail, if they do not have him already. Our next hope is to infiltrate, inform the populace, and create a resistant environment for the

Shadow Guild in Separti—unfortunate for the populace, but to their good, also. That is the plan."

It was a good plan. Certainly more conservative than the outright assault on Jorida he had feared. It risked Guild lives. More, it risked a good many townfolk. It was not going to be quick, and if the spread of rumor was too slow, it would degenerate into an unpleasant, messy situation. It put the Edi at risk. It put *everything* at risk.

"You do not approve."

That was extreme irony.

"I am concerned for the Edi," Bren said. "My province. My neighbors. But with stopping the Shadow Guild before they kidnap and threaten their way into a new stronghold—I do not argue with that. Only—"

"You know Lord Geigi's resources. *Are* there means to defeat our enemy in his arsenal? Or can he obtain them from the shipfolk?"

Now it was clear why Ilisidi had briefed him—finally—and to a far greater extent than ordinary. *After* handing him the com. She either did *not* know what options Geigi might have, or had indeed been thwarted in her attempt to get him to use them to stop the ship while still en route. It was even possible she had brought them here to Kajiminda to force Geigi's hand. And now she wanted *him* to use that com to convince Geigi.

Well, he was not about to. It was a question far scarier than reliance on Guild resources, and one to which he did not really know the full answer, only that what he did know was enough to send a chill down his spine. The whole resource of the station aloft—not to mention the starship *Phoenix*—might well have a variety of ways to dislodge a hundred or so Guild from an island, but with what damage? And with what consequence to the world? The principle of slow change would be violated in an instant, with whatever they could bring down.

And yet, there was no denying time was their enemy. The station was in crisis—its own functions on the edge with riot and aged equipment. Finesse was not apt to be the answer. Stalling the whole situation off until the refugee population had gotten off the station and let it recover—would take the better part of a year, during which the difficulty on Jorida would spread, to the disadvantage of the Edi, and of Ashidama itself . . . not to mention the aishidi'tat.

"I will think on it," he said. "And I will ask Geigi."

"Good," she said. And laid her napkin on the table. Cenedi drew back her chair.

Bren shoved hard at his own, against heavy furniture and a deep carpet. It gave. He stood and gave the requisite little bow, watching Ilisidi depart into the inner rooms of the suite.

Nawari gestured, an offer to see him out.

He had been handed a question. And there *were* answers. There had to be answers without invoking *Phoenix* tech and seeding another leap into advanced tech for a world that found too many ways to use it.

Lights in the sky?

Pyrotechnics from heaven?

The Guild did not frighten. The Guild would demand to know the secrets of such power. And God knew what additional knowledge it would bring down.

There had to be another way. The dowager's plan revolved around rumor, about revealing the presence and threat of the Shadow Guild to all the public, all at once. Communicate with the entire Ashidama populace at once. Set them against the Shadow Guild. Suddenly, unexpectedly . . .

Out of a plethora of tech that atevi did not use in their disputes—

There was one sitting in the meadow.

There *was* an answer rooted in human history, deep, deep in the era of little planes . . .

"Paper," he asked his aishid. "How much paper do we have?" And a questioning look passed around the assembled group: his aishid, Lord Reijiri, Lord Tatiseigi, and Betan-nadi—the latter somewhat uneasy at sharing the table with three lords of the aishidi'tat and a Guild unit.

Betan sent staff to find out. The lad brought back a box of

vellum and a writing-set. It was—perhaps a hundred, two hundred little sheets such as one used in messaging.

"There is more at Najida," Bren said. He had no idea how much: staff doled it out in tasteful little containers. "There will be more with the train and the Guild camp."

"We have paper in the kitchen, nandi," Betan said, "that we use for wrapping. It is in rolls."

"It can be cut," Bren said, heartened entirely. "Tell me, Betan, is there a printer?" It was a human word, massaged into Ragi, one of those unlicensed imports. "A machine that writes."

"The messenger machine," Betan said. "It writes. And it has paper."

The whole company—Tatiseigi walking more slowly, with a cane—migrated down the hall to a room they had not seen. Massive tables, likely as old as Kajiminda itself, supported a bank of electronics that would send shivers into the regulators of such things on Mospheira . . . things of far more potential, one feared, than Geigi's communicators—equivalent, it might be, to the lander that had thundered down from the heavens at the edge of the Dojisigin, a massive thing that had set itself up to create a network the Shadow Guild could not penetrate.

They had *had* this—all the while.

His heartbeat had doubled. The possibilities in this place—the potential, the contravention of laws and treaties—including the possibility that, in some minuscule nook of what he saw here, some piece of electronics too small to notice—the entire human *archive* might be here. Geigi should not have done this. Geigi *had* to have shipped it down in pieces, instructed Edi staff how to connect it—

When?

Not recently. Not *that* recently. But there was more than Cobo spaceport in terms of getting things from orbit. The way the lander had come down. And as a last resort, the petal sails.

Could such equipment survive the landing? Likely. People had.

And there had been a time . . . a critical time . . . when, during the absence of the dowager, the heir—and himself—Tabini had

been overthrown, Murini of Kadagidi clan had assumed the aijinate and tried to rule.

And Geigi, from orbit, watching the whole aishidi'tat and all
the agreements with humans about to go up in flames—had contemplated seizing the aijinate himself, ruling from the heavens,
by whatever force was necessary to put Murini down. Geigi had
had no inclination to do that. Geigi had no desire to deal with
war, or government, or any such thing: he had the knowledge of
the universe at his fingertips, he had human engineering laid out
for him in its highest development, he was an artistic man, a
scholar, and *curious* about everything, while wanting to skip on
to the next thing and the next and the next. Dealing with the
day-to-day governance of the aishidi'tat was far from the life he
wanted. But he had been preparing to take the aijinate and wield
it, with whatever force it required, as long as it required.

And was *this* the nerve center of the effort it would have
taken—manned by Edi folk, protected by God-knew-what? Those
with him, those who had never stood on the space station—
looked about them in unconcealed awe. Even Tatiseigi allowed
himself that.

"Is it safe to use these things, nadi?" he asked Betan.

"Lord Geigi manages this room," Betan said. "We use this
machine." Betan indicated the keyboard in the section at the end.
"We push this button." He indicated it. "We speak to him. We
wait—sometimes a long wait—and he answers. Sometimes *this*
machine—" He indicated the printer—Mospheiran in origin. The
station rarely used paper. "—answers. Sometimes with drawings.
Sometimes with words."

Few of the Edi on Najida read or wrote. Ramaso did, with ease
and competency. Najida's cook did. The rest—he had offered the
village schooling, but what he offered had necessarily been Ragi,
and they had not wanted that, no.

"In your language?" As far as he knew, in what was ever found
on Mospheira, there *was* no written Edi language and no indication one ever existed.

"Human symbols," Betan said, opened a drawer and drew out
a printed message.

Human letters for Edi words. Simple, phonetic symbols, not the history-laden complexity of Ragi.

Forbidden technology, printers. The human alphabet opened the language, the computer language opened everything to do with human tech, every window, every gateway. Mospheira's once-absolute seal on the knowledge of the archive, preventing anything reaching the continent by accident . . . was breached.

A wealth of prohibited tech was in this room, and wherever else the Edi had found it useful. Reijiri was at his shoulder, looking at the note, at script that was, to the continent, known somewhat now, but never proliferated, rejected, as not kabiu. Not harmonious, not desirable.

"Geigi's name," Bren said, indicating the string of letters, for Reijiri's benefit—who would not need that many clues for what he saw. And Reijiri took that in before letting his gaze shift, taking in the wonders around him, his eyes alight with interest.

Reijiri was no stranger to computers or their printing. The Messengers' Guild had fought it, then fought to manage the whole computer field, which the Engineers and the 'counters argued was properly theirs. Then the Merchants had gotten into the fray. It was still in litigation.

Here—all that was entirely moot.

"Lord Geigi's paper," Betan said, and opened a cabinet.

Which made all other sources irrelevant.

"What we need to do," Bren said, "is get rumor started. Warn the Ashidama residents of what has invaded their midst." He took a deep breath and launched into the explanation which, even to himself, seemed more than a little crazy. "Granted that this machine can print anything shown to it, we can print all this paper with that warning, in Ragi, and then . . . what has to be done, Jiri-ji, is to distribute it. We need to fly over the townships and over Jorida itself—none of them safe from rifle fire—and let them go, where the wind will carry them—with our message, for anyone to pick up in the streets."

Reijiri looked at him—understanding, clearly, thoughts flickering through his eyes, all the way to enthusiasm. "I can do it."

"Can you do it safely?"

"I need an accurate map."

Maps of the north were abundant. Of the south, and the Marid—far less so. And not assured to fill that requirement.

Except—

"Geigi," Bren said. "Lord Geigi will have that. This printer can render it. What more?"

"A map. Weather, if he can say. The weight of the paper— perhaps not *all* that is here will be necessary. The weight of the fuel. Ideally—someone to deal with the paper. That person's weight. Whether to do it in one flight or several. It all has to be figured."

"How much weight of fuel?"

"That depends on the map."

"I am," Bren said, "the lightest person besides the children."

"Nand' Bren," Banichi said from behind his shoulder. "No."

Formal no.

"I weigh far less," Bren said.

"I also," Lord Tatiseigi said. "Is our mission to rain an account of the Shadow Guild onto these places? And to alert all this region? It seems worth it."

The old man was walking with a cane, not his usual habit, was wind-burned, and it had been a serious question whether he had to be carried from the plane on arrival.

But would he do it? One had absolutely no doubt Tatiseigi would do it.

"No, nandi," Bren said. "*I* am replaceable. The keystone of the Padi Valley is not, especially with nand' Reijiri already and nec-essarily at risk. If it has to be done—and we have yet to make the calculation—I will go."

His aishid was not happy. Not in the least. He could not say he was particularly thrilled with that reality . . . but there was not a one of them who weighed less.

"We do not know the numbers yet," Reijiri said. Which usu-ally meant felicity or infelicity, in the language of the 'counters, but for Reijiri it meant distances and weight and fuel.

It fairly well still meant that, Bren thought, but did not say. There was still, unsuperstitious as present company was, that sensitivity that employed the 'counters in complicated situations. One was glad not to have to deal with that here.

But one did not live years on the mainland without beginning to add and divide things into fortunate and unfortunate.

He truly was not in command of the numbers on this one. The calculation was Reijiri's.

He had to explain it to Geigi.

And to Tabini.

After he had gotten Ilisidi's agreement.

"Aiji-ma," Bren said. "I have a plan. A means."

Ilisidi listened, chin on fist. Cenedi, Nawari, and Casimi ranged themselves behind her.

She listened. And in the silence after the explanation, she frowned.

"And you propose to fly with him."

"Because of my weight, aiji-ma. The plane can only carry so much. And I am the lightest."

"Well," she said. "You *are* to take care. You and the lord of Dur. Let us not have a disaster. You will not fall out of the plane."

"I will not. I will observe all caution."

The frown deepened. "Prudence. *Prudence,* nand' paidhi. Have you explained this to my grandson? Or consulted Lord Geigi?"

"I have that yet to do, aiji-ma."

"Pish. Do not worry my grandson. It will work or it will not. Geigi is a necessity."

"Aiji-ma. I *have* to call your grandson."

"You do not."

"And yet your great-grandson, uninformed, has already found his way into this."

Yet a deeper frown. Ilisidi waved her hand, cutting off that line of argument.

"Telling," she said dryly. "Let us not have that. Argue with my grandson. I yield you the pleasure."

"Aiji-ma." He rose. Bowed. Made his retreat to the hall, where Tano and Algini waited. Banichi and Jago were out in the meadow with Reijiri, taking a survey of the plane.

"She agrees," he said. "She does not think us insane. People used to do this. Humans. In planes of that design."

His aishid was not pleased with the arrangement, but there was no arguing with the math of it all.

"Now we get the materials from Lord Geigi," he said, "hoping that the station has not entered utter crisis. And that he can give us what we need."

His own suite afforded most privacy, and Narani and Jeladi stationed themselves at the door while Tano and Algini went with Bindanda into the remote recesses of the suite to talk . . . Bindanda himself being plainclothes Guild, in addition to his notable skills in the kitchen.

Bren drew the new com unit from his pocket and settled into a well-stuffed chair—oversized: his feet did not reach the floor, but his back reached the cushions, and one elbow found rest on a small pillow.

He activated the unit—its buttons were typical of the atevi system, and the black button was the on switch. Functions presented no great puzzle when the small screen lit with a set of familiar codes and a cursor.

He moved the white toggle to his choice, clicked the red, and connected to, he hoped, the atevi version of Central.

He waited. And waited. Then a mechanical voice said, in Ragi, from the space station: *"This is the Director's office. If you wish to leave a message . . ."*

No. No. *No.*

He sat upright. "This is Bren, paidhi-aiji. Notify Lord Geigi. Bren. Urgently!"

There were a series of clicks. Then:

"Please wait."

Long breath. *Geigi* had been the right word. The idiot robot had gotten that much. But it was taking too long, and he found himself on his feet, pacing.

Then, at last, a rattle, and: *"Bren-paidhi?"*

He exhaled. Dropped back into the chair. "Nand' Geigi."

"So they have finally given you the com unit. I have called

three times unanswered. Even by Cenedi. Are you truly in my house!"

"Yes." The mind sorted through *finally* and *unanswered* and *truly* and drew conclusions . . . unhappy conclusions involving arguments surrounding him, at high levels. "Perhaps an hour ago, the dowager gave a com to me. I do not know whether it is Cenedi's, or—"

"It is yours. It was always supposed to be yours, in Senjin."

"My aishid had it while we were there. Cenedi took it back before we left. One understood they were limited in number and we assumed they were needed for Guild coms."

"So we perceived. I spoke to Tabini-aiji following yesterday's call. I gave him your message. His expectation was that you had the secure unit, yet his calls were not reaching you. Your silence was most disturbing."

Damn it.—*Damn it!*

"Tabini-aiji again ordered its return to you after your call to me. So he said. Yesterday, when I realized you did not have it."

Geigi, even-tempered Geigi, had not been pleased.

He was not pleased. Ilisidi had prevented him reporting for days aboard the train and had played devilishly fast and loose with his relationship with Tabini-aiji. God, he *hoped* Tabini understood. He was not unreasonable. Had Cenedi needed those units for Guild coordination with the camp, he would not have objected. Had the aiji-dowager felt the need to keep certain information from her grandson for a time . . . just tell him that! At least tell Tabini the silence was not *his* choice.

But nothing could be gained by dwelling on the matter now.

"The situation," he said, "seems to have been resolved, now that we are here, where she wants us to be."

A small silence. He could imagine Geigi sitting in his office, with the weight of the entire station crisis on his shoulders and now the frustrations regarding the vital communication he had tried to give the on-world operation. Geigi was ordinarily the most forgiving and easy-going of atevi, but clearly he was struggling with his temper.

"Where she wants you," Geigi echoed him. *"In Kajiminda.*

With Lord Reijiri's plane in my meadow, the Red Train at Najida, and with Lord Reijiri and Lord Tatiseigi, not to mention the proposed lord of Ajuri, all installed in my house, within reach of honorless enemies. Does she in the least *acknowledge how vulnerable you all are?"*

"One believes she expects you to defend us."

"My answer remains unchanged. She entirely misjudges my willingness to intervene, and you may feel free to tell her that. See if that gets her to withdraw."

Unchanged. Confirmation: she *had* asked. Bren drew a deep breath. "One doubts it will. However, one also believes we have a plan that could tip the scales entirely to our favor, with minimal risk on our part."

"Should I have the details?"

"You have enough on your shoulders, nandi-ji, but if you can send us a high resolution image of Ashidama Bay and a weather forecast for the next few days, we would be most appreciative. Rest assured we will *not* see the Edi harmed or damage to this house—not a hostile foot set on its land. Leave this to us and simply assign staff to monitor any intrusion out of Separti. Given warning—we can deal with it." One was not that entirely confident. He might owe Geigi a personal apology. But Geigi had the entire space operation on his shoulders and could not afford a crisis under his feet, so to speak.

"You are sure."

"Yes." It was worth a lie, in the dowager's name. At least he could claim he was doing all he could do to handle the problem. If Geigi believed he was better off knowing, he would press.

The pause became extended, then: *"The household has means to monitor intrusions. The same as what we can do from here. I shall send instructions for staff to keep watch. Only you need know where that is coming from."*

Meaning, he did not want Ilisidi knowing the extent of his operations. He thought of his own aishid, and Reijiri and Tatiseigi in that hub, and hoped to God he could warn the others before Cenedi got his hands on those terminals. Cenedi might demand things from Geigi. It was also foreseeable, however, that Geigi, from his place in the heavens, could affect every system in the house, enforcing his own demands—Geigi had a temper, good-natured though he was.

"I shall have it clear—they need my cooperation. I assure you, Geigi-ji, it will have boundaries."

Then, and to his relief, with an audible sigh on the far end, Geigi let the subject drop.

"Staff informs me the dowager is now fully recovered and in charge. I have assigned her my own suite. I hope your own comfort is adequate."

"Excellent. And your staff has answered every need. Apologies, nandi-ji, profound apologies for the lack of a call this morning, as soon as I received the communicator."

"Do not be so formal. I might have contacted you through staff, Bren-ji, were the case dire. I had reports from them stacked up in my queue, while you were relatively busy last night. How are the lord of Dur and Lord Tatiseigi? How is Dur's little plane, for that matter?"

"Well. All well, though the flight was hard on Lord Tatiseigi, and the plane was coughing as it came in. One assumes merely a matter of fuel."

"One trusts he will rest until his aishid arrives, then take the train back to Tirnamardi.—Late last night you acquired Nomarinadi. I assume this was unplanned."

"Indeed. His motives were understandable: the aiji-dowager had left him behind with virtually no information. I believe he did as his man'chi demanded. One believes he and his aishid have come to terms with this."

"Indeed. Indeed." Geigi sounded distracted. Perhaps another message was coming in. But then Geigi said: *"I have sent the image you requested to the household system. This morning the two Dojisigin ships continue in port at Jorida—we followed their progress despite the weather, which has cleared now to very clear detail, and bids fair to continue the next few days. A few small powered boats have come and gone to Separti. A medium-sized vessel is on its way from Talidi to Jorida, typical of local trade. Fishermen are out at Talidi. We have observed no overt*

movement of force in any location. A train has left Cobo on the southern route, with two passenger cars and a single flatcar carrying two tanker trucks. It should reach Najida station in a few hours."

Two? He did not ask. Frayed nerves surely fueled that high-speed string of observations, saying, clearly, *We are watching, we are aware, this is what I know, and I have a great deal else on my mind. I need to get to other things.*

But it summarized very useful information.

"Geigi-ji, we welcome all observations. We will endeavor to find at least a temporary settlement here as quickly as possible. I am still *hoping* to get to Cobo.—What is your own situation? Do we have a schedule?"

Which was to say he had not resigned his other obligations.

"The Mospheiran shuttle, still under maintenance, is not available. Rising Star, *fueling at Cobo, passenger module installed. They have stacked critical supplies in the module.* Felicity *in station dock. Repairs complete, fueling, prepping for flight. Do not distract yourself with our problems, Bren-ji. The situation is covered. The heir will meet the first humans on landing, to interpret."*

Cajeiri?

Somewhere in Geigi's vicinity, now, a mechanical voice demanded attention. It sounded like an alert.

"I have to go, Bren-ji," Geigi said.

"Geigi-ji,—take care. I will call only at need."

There was no answer. Another atevi voice said, over com: *"Nandi. We are informed you wish to print?"*

Insanity. Utter insanity. He drew a breath.

"Yes. Yes, I shall wish to print."

An hour, perhaps two, of writing and rewriting, with input from everyone from Tatiseigi to Betan. A final draft to Ilisidi . . . approved . . . and they were ready for a test run.

The printer spat out a copy.

Two copies a page, he had decided, to be cut apart. Large enough for notice, small enough to maximize the number of flyers—weight *and* volume being an issue. Margins to a minimum. Brief enough to encourage a thorough reading.

Space sacrificed to one line of bold.

Invaders, it said. ***The Master Threatened. Beware the Foreign Ships.***

And below that:

Citizens of the Townships, the Guild war in the Marid has driven Lord Tiajo from the Dojisigin. She has deserted her supporters and brought her remaining force of outlaw Guild leadership to usurp control of Ashidama. She intends to overthrow the Master, rule in his place, and use Jorida and the Township as a fortress against the aishidi'tat. Once in power, she will suspend local law, execute opponents, kidnap the children of those who resist to force cooperation, and confiscate your property at will.

This is her record in the Dojisigin.

Senjin has joined the aishidi'tat. The Dojisigin will follow. The rest of the Marid, allied with the Taisigin, backs Senjin and the aishidi'tat in pursuit of the outlaw Guild and the lord of the Dojisigin.

These fugitives are now among you. They arrived on the two ships that have docked at Jorida, where the outlaw Guild intends to create a new base of operations against the aishidi'tat. Know that these intruders have no legitimate backing in the Marid nor anywhere else. This threat is moving among you now. Block your streets, defend your neighborhoods and your harbors. Do not let this threat to peace take control of your lives. They are far fewer than you at this point and they do not know your streets, your exits, and your entrances. Most of all they do not expect you to resist. Be clever. Use your advantages. Take them down if you can. You are not alone in this fight. Your neighbors are with you and will not give refuge to these intruders when you drive them out.

A finger-wide space, and the same message repeated.

"Is that all right, nandi?" Geigi's staffer asked.

"Perfect," Bren said, and the machine began spitting out copies.

16

The tanker arrived as the sun was beginning to set. The two truck drivers' day had started in Cobo yesterday, when the dowager's order had sent Guild to call the airport and launched a sequence which involved the airport general office, the refueler, a transport company, the regulatory office, the airport authority, the Transportation Guild, and the railway office to commandeer one engine, one flatcar, and a tanker with the proper fuel . . .

Only to discover there was no need.

The train that had arrived at Najida station, despite a Guild hold on all trains moving south of the Southern Mountains, had delivered a flat car on which sat *two* small fuel tankers, not only the one ordered by the dowager, but also one arranged earlier, along with a passenger car, by a bright young elite Guild unit from Dur. That order had been stalled by the hold on southbound traffic. The dowager's fuel order was attached to Dur's—no one was going to cancel *hers*—so both were sent, and that young aishid had courteously provided seats aboard for a second, grey-haired Guild unit from Tirnamardi, who had arrived in Cobo desperate for whatever transport they could find for Najida.

And attached to it all was a specialized medical car ordered by Tabini.

The camp commander, Midagi, receiving all of it, had off-loaded the tankers and sent one on south, *with* two runabouts and drivers to deliver both Reijiri's aishid and Tatiseigi's to Kajiminda. The second, he kept at Najida so the first would not have to return to refuel the yellow plane following the upcoming flyer drop, if circumstances had them landing at Najida.

Tabini's medical relief was currently sipping tea in Najida, awaiting further instructions.

It had not exactly been a silent transaction.

Bren had discovered the whole complexity of it when he found his new communications unit held a list of Cenedi's communications, the whole proliferation of confusion and conflicting orders.

What mattered was, they had fuel. Never mind how it had gotten here. The truckers, Transportation Guild, moved the truck through knee-high grass toward the plane in the meadow, while Reijiri greeted his aishid, climbing out of the first-arrived runabout that had accompanied the trucks. Tatiseigi's aishid, with a nod to Banichi, headed toward the front steps, where their own principal, Tatiseigi, stood waiting to welcome them at the top.

Eight more Guild. And four more last night. Reijiri had, along with the fuel, a sudden abundance of help with the plane, a high-spirited exchange of information, and, as the fuel truck began to maneuver out to the plane, a discussion involving broad gestures toward the nearby trees. Reijiri nodded, and to Bren's astonishment, Reijiri and his aishid simply grabbed handles on the wings and tail and . . . lifted the tail to pivot the plane about on its front wheels.

It appeared disconcertingly light.

The drivers returned to the truck, one to the cab, one to the back bumper, moving it into position, with encouragement and opinions from the drivers of the second truck, as Reijiri, clearly with the agility of practice, took a boost from one of his aishid, and clambered up to stand atop the engine. The driver handed the fuel nozzle to Reijiri's man, who handed it up to Reijiri, who guided it into the upper wing as the second trucker powered up and began the fueling process.

Bren watched with curiosity and unease, as his mind began calculating the liquid weight going into that high wing versus the apparent weight of a plane lifted and turned completely about by three men . . . he had no idea what a measure of it weighed, but even a rough calculation said it was like a third man—an ateva—sitting up there atop it all, diminishing during the flight, that and themselves making the whole quite top-heavy.

But it could not be a problem. Surely. Reijiri had been flying this little plane for years, had gotten Tatiseigi down here safely . . . Reijiri had calculated their weight, the weight of the fuel, the weight of the bags of paper going on—they had gotten a scale to weigh the bags and themselves; and besides that they had two small bottles of water and his own pistol—he had had that in his pocket and they had had their coats when they weighed themselves. It mattered, Reijiri gave him to understand. He was willing to believe it.

The daylight was going fast as they worked, the sun plunging to a pink and golden death beyond the great house, its outbuildings, and the substantial woods on either hand. Details were already less sharp to human eyes as Reijiri's young Guild senior came over to where Bren watched from a respectful distance, Banichi and the others beside him.

"Lord Reijiri will join you as soon as he has thanked the drivers."

"You had the truck already requested in Cobo. Did he anticipate—?"

The young man's lips twitched ever so slightly as he watched Reijiri. "It is not the first time. Weather. A mechanical issue. One is accustomed."

Amusedly. Lightly said, in line with Reijiri's own easy sense of humor. One only wished the young man had not said *mechanical issue.*

Frequent? he wanted to ask, but decided he did not want the answer.

The tanker pump went silent, and a different motor began to reel in the fuel line. Reijiri slid nimbly down from the engine cowling, talking amiably with the truckers until the operation was complete and the truck ready to move back. Reijiri lifted a hand to the drivers, then strode over to join them, wiping his hands on a cloth and fastening his worn leather jacket, the same he had arrived in, before pulling on heavy gloves.

"A good night," Reijiri declared, looking up at the clear sky. Several early stars and a planet shone above the meadow. He arched his back, stretched, and spun about with arms spread. "A clear night, a wind from the southeast! We should do it!"

And his eyes were alight with excitement.

"Now?" Surely he meant in the morning.

"Safer from rifle fire," Reijiri said cheerfully. "Are you ready for this, Bren-ji?"

Ready, no. He was not. But he would be no better in the morning.

The printing was done. The bags of paper were in the house. The plane was fueled and ready. They were dressed for it, down to the gun in his pocket. The matter of rifle fire was a serious argument.

He looked at his aishid, who simply looked grim. For the first time, they had no way remotely possible to protect him, and they were not happy about that part. Not in the least.

But—the matter of rifle fire *was* a potent argument.

"Have you done such a thing?" Banichi asked Reijiri. "Dropping things from the sky?"

It seemed a reasonable question—one they possibly should have asked from the start.

"When I was younger," Reijiri said, "I put more than a few things into the kitchen courtyard, which is not a large target. And I dropped emergency provisions to firefighters, once. As for night flying, I have many times flown at night . . . most recently, nandi-ji, to Atageini and Cobo."

Of course he had.

And one had to recall that, when they all were younger, Reijiri, desirous of using the larger airports, and notoriously resentful of the new concept of air traffic control, had flown many places he was not supposed to have flown, violated air boundaries around the Bujavid, and disputed right of way with jets at Shejidan Airport.

He had at least lived to tell the tales.

"Safer from rifles," Bren echoed, in a voice a little strained, and gathered his courage. "The messages are bagged and ready, nadiin-ji. We can take a little supper with us . . ."

"No, no," Reijiri said, and flashed a grin. "No food, no drink. One will *absolutely* regret it."

He did not ask Reijiri to explain. The grin said enough.

And if they were going, it was time. No waiting to worry about it. His aishid was not happy. *He* was not happy. But all the effort this afternoon was toward one purpose, and the sooner it was done, the sooner they would finish. "We need the bags of papers where I sit," he said.

"You will need a warmer coat," Reijiri, already in his well-worn leathers, said, giving him a critical look. "A *much* warmer coat."

"That, I do have," he said. "We packed for Hasjuran. Can we stand the extra weight?"

"We have the leeway."

He looked at the plane, the two pits, one between the wings, one somewhat behind, where Reijiri had sat. There were no doors: one climbed in over the side.

Tatiseigi had survived *hours* of it.

He swallowed. Hard.

Surely . . . *surely* there was a seat belt.

Getting up to the wing—Reijiri had a knack. Bren had a heavier and encumbering coat, but he had help—Banichi's boost from behind, Reijiri lifting from above. From there it was up the slant, using a variety of handholds, to the forward pit, and a not-at-all practiced move to get up and over, onto the seat and down into the footwell, behind an entirely inadequate-looking windscreen and a panel with no controls, only three instruments. Reijiri, moving with perfect confidence, and some urgency, took up the bags of paper, three of different sizes, and handed them to him, which helped fill the space left in the seat, one after the other, until he was packed in.

There *was* a seat belt. He fastened it, yanked it tight . . . *too* tight. That was a first. He worked it free, pulled it out and tried again, tugging gently, testing as he went to make certain he could still twist to release the flyers. Then he set about securing the sacks of paper around him—hitching their pull strings to what seemed to be an intended handhold at the side: losing one en route was not in the plan.

The plane bounced violently. He grabbed the handhold for dear life . . . until he realized it was just the plane reacting to Reijiri dropping into the seat behind him. He took several slow, deep breaths, and ordered his heart to behave as he pried his gloved fingers free of the handhold.

Small bumps and thumps vibrated about the plane. Flaps . . . no . . . *ailerons* . . . moved: Reijiri testing his controls, one imagined. Sounds from the rear that were likely the . . . vertical stabilizer . . . no, the rudder *on* the vertical stabilizer. Or possibly it was the . . . elevators.

God . . . he had spent far too much time studying the anatomy of aircraft while they were waiting for the trucks.

There were more small bumps from somewhere. His heart rate picked up again. Damn it. He was being stupid. He had climbed mountains, back on Mospheira, and skied down them, statistically far more dangerous than flying. He had gone to space. Ridden the shuttle before it was all that proven. He had flown in jetliners with far more problematic glide ratios than Reijiri's lightweight craft . . . or so he had heard. Somewhere. Once. He had been unable to find a reference on that one. He could ask Reijiri. Pride kept him silent.

But a plane that reacted to every slight movement was so small, and light, its functions, while apparent and basic, seemed so delicate—and imagination of the ground coming up far too suddenly as it went down had become increasingly vivid.

He was, frankly, terrified.

He tested the seat belt. Again. He pulled on the leather helmet Lord Tatiseigi had worn and adjusted the chin strap—they had had to pad it: it was too big in all dimensions, and the goggles that protected his eyes were, even with the strap taken up as far as it could be, a little too wide across the nose. Not the best view, but then there was not that much view to be had—and not that much that he would need. The plane was tilted up, having a very little, very ineffectual-looking rear wheel that sat the tail right down on the ground—and all he had, past the very small windscreen, was a view of the clear and increasingly dusky sky, the treetops, and the propeller. At least they had padded the seat for him, a thick cushion screwed down with straps to make it secure: a good thing, as without that added height, he would never be able to reach over the side to release the flyers.

The panel in front of him was not what he had imagined. He had, for control of the situation, absolutely nothing, for which he was exceedingly grateful: there would be no inadvertent maneuvers on his part. There was only a trio of instruments the function of which he had absolutely no idea, and what Reijiri had called a speaking tube, which was a sort of funnel and hose through which, theoretically, they could yell at each other over the noise of wind and engine. Fortunately, in lieu of that rather chancy system, there was a modern headset and microphone that came with the helmet, and covered the ears, to help block, according to Tatiseigi, the rude volume of the engine. He settled it in place and the sounds of the outside world indeed diminished, though not perhaps as thoroughly as they would without the padding.

It was not a pleasant feeling: his ears felt as if he had a violent head cold. He pressed the com's power button, and the sound of Reijiri's steady breathing, the clicks and sighs of his movements relieved the disturbing dead zone. He could talk to Reijiri as well, he supposed, but he had no desire to distract his pilot from his preparations back there. Reijiri, so he had explained some time that afternoon, had a different, less isolating headset, as he needed to *hear* the wind across the wings.

Bren could pass on that experience. Gladly.

He leaned to look over the side—there was wing above and below, and a little view of the crowd . . . but not the people he wanted to see. Damn it.

Their plans had adjusted for this night run. Landing in this field at night, so Reijiri said, would be unnecessarily dangerous. Following the old market road up to the wide flat near the well-lighted Guild camp made far more sense. Cenedi had contacted Midagi, the Guild commander, and the camp would be looking for them. They could refuel there with the second truck then return to Kajiminda in the morning.

It had been years since he had been separated from his aishid for so long, and then only to go back to Mospheira. Being separated from them on the mainland was . . . beyond unsettling; and he had the feeling it upset them no less.

Over the com came a long, slow breath, a rustle of leather and a final wiggling of the flaps.

"Are you set up there?" A perfectly cheerful question, also over the com. They were to be careful about names and titles. They had agreed to that. *"Do you have any problems?"*

"No problems." He tried not to sound terrified.

"Nothing loose."

He had been to space and back. "Absolutely nothing loose."

"Excellent!"

The propeller moved, turned—the plane jolted. That was not the engine. Someone was out there turning it, full around—he could feel the contact, if not see it. Was *that* how it started?

"Oil," Reijiri said. *"It settles. Stand by."*

The engine coughed, barely audible, but he could feel it through the plane itself. Could feel that engine make several tries. And fail.

A chuckle from the com and: *"We did come in on the final fumes! Do not worry! The next try should do it."*

It actually took two more attempts before the propeller continued to turn, an irregular beat that swiftly became a blur, through which one saw a darkening sky, and winter treetops, as the engine roared, then settled to what sounded like a clicking purr from inside the protective headset. With a little jerk of released brakes, the plane began to roll.

They were committed. There was no stopping at this point.

Bren cast a desperate look left, through the misfit goggles, caught a glimpse of black uniforms amid the colors of the crowd and raised a gloved hand, hoping the black belonged to *his* people. Children ran along with the plane, quickly left behind.

The engine roared and rattled, and the bumps came faster and faster and faster, a slight slew as the tail lifted from the grass . . .

Then the tail did a waggle, corrected, and his heartbeat

accelerated right with the plane as bumps ceased and everything smoothed and grew heavier at once.

Heavier, as the engine sang. Heavier still, as they lifted up and up, until there was no view but one early star. There was absolutely no view but sky in front of him.

"Can you see?" he asked. It seemed—a reasonable question.

"Not as much as you can," Reijiri answered. Then: *"My angle is no better than yours, nandi-ji."*

God.

Logic. But—

Weight said they were climbing. The sound of the engine—with its crown of cylinders—up around the propeller—was a steady powerful rumble on the far side of his headset, through the walls, through the seat.

His heart raced. The wind whipped his face. A flash of the downhill run on Mount Adams. Sincerely not caring if he broke his neck. Highlight of his youth. At once the captive and master of gravity. Broad, sweeping turns, a sudden weightlessness as he caught air. This was the reverse, a defiance of gravity, a climb into the wind itself, to the high, steady sound of the engine. His hands ached with a death grip, not on poles but on the bags and their straps, which did him, when he traced that pain to its source, not a damned bit of good.

The plane tipped, *banked* was the right word, and the star swung out of view, and *down* became, visually, between the two starboard-side wings, treetops grown miniature, still glowing with the last rays of the run. His body and mind argued as gravity pressed him one way and the acceleration of the turn pressed another.

Oh, the g-force going askew he *had* felt. In the station, with the rotational artificial gravity.

On the slopes with unexpected dips and fast turns, moments of force, moments of weightlessness.

But never quite like this. Not even airliners or shuttles. He tried to ignore the sensation, sought landmarks he knew. There was the great house. The meadow, the people, a scatter of lights, then the orchard, and sky, and then it all disappeared as the plane leveled off abruptly, and they were climbing again.

He closed his eyes then, letting his body rule his sense of direction . . . and his heartbeat went wild. He was *in* the wind. A part of it. There was a texture, a solidity to it, little bumps and sways, eddies and flows that a jet never reacted to. And down settled finally in a normal direction, with sky in front of him.

"Are you all right?" the question came, sharp and metallic in his ear. Worried. And he realized he was breathing heavily.

He had not felt the like in years. Still felt it, breathing into the wind, sucking up air that tingled in his nose.

"Yes," he said. "Absolutely." And it was true. He was—not afraid, though it felt like fear. Not panicked, for all the world was coming too fast. His heart was speeding. He *wanted* to control what was going on and knew absolutely that was disaster. He was out of place up here. But he was always out of place. Thinking too slow.

But as fast as he could.

Far from where he was comfortable.

And entirely alive.

Something hit the windshield. He jumped. A splat of grease, was all, and not the first, from the streaks. Reijiri had warned him it did that. The tanker that had brought the fuel had brought a supply of that, too. The propeller had called it up.

One reason for the windshield, Reijiri had said.

It was. It did its job. The plane was level and they were up. And the engine was steady.

Mount Adams had been the adversary, back in his skiing days. He could lose, he could draw . . . but he could not win against the mountain. And the *end* had not truly mattered then. The *doing* had been the rush. The difference was . . . he had had no allies to call on, then.

Now he did have. The best. And he was not used to getting out in front of them. He wanted them with him. He wanted to be back there, at that speed. In one piece.

The plane tilted over again. The last color was leaving the sky, leaving only a residual glow and highlighted clouds. The moon not yet risen. The plane banked slowly, side to side. The irregular darkness of trees was below them, and then what might be water, featureless dark, darker than the sky. It made him uneasy. Or maybe that was just the sway of the plane.

"*Getting my bearings,*" Reijiri said. "*We will move quickly now. I have calculated a heading for Separti, but we shall cross to Ashidama Bay first and approach from the east, along the water—to be certain, and to avoid notice as long as possible. But I would like to get a look at Jorida before we lose all the light—to see how it lies.*"

"And see what is in port," Bren agreed. "That, too, would be useful."

"*The moon is rising. That will help in the actual drops.*"

The clouds to the east had indeed begun to show the moon's arrival.

The plane dipped the left wing, took a slightly new heading, the nose dipped, and the engine roared. The wind came harder, colder, but the winter coat was enough. There was little to see in any direction, and for a time, flying, from exhilarating, became a lot like suspension in a dark grey room, just the wind and the engine sound to say they were moving at all.

Over the left side, there was nothing.

There was what seemed a long, long time of nothing in any direction. The darkness grew, purer, blacker. Stars appeared, two at first.

Then on the right—there were brighter lights. Kajiminda? Not unless they had flown in a circle. They were over water, and the faraway lights were on the right, in the north if he had his bearings right.

"Separti over there?" Bren suggested.

"*Yes. I think it is. We are quite losing our twilight. But we are nearly there.*" The plane banked slightly to the left, and indeed there were a few scattered lights on what might be the Ashidama Peninsula shoreline.

A little motion of the plane and brighter lights definitely

appeared ahead, a line of them, and a slanted scatter further on. A sharp-edged silhouette stood above the water.

Jorida Isle, and its citadel.

"*Well,*" Reijiri said briskly. "*I have seen their height, I think. It is what I have heard of it. I am satisfied. And if they have heard our arrival, they have none the less left the lights on. Let us meander up and see what Talidi looks like. They are smaller, yes?*"

"Half the size of Separti. With wharves, however. We think maybe seven thousand population. If that."

"*We shall practice on them, shall we?*"

The plane suddenly banked left.

Alarmingly so. Bren swallowed hard, *very* glad not to have had that supper.

"*Those would be the Dojisigi ships down there,*" Reijiri said.

Two masted ships, spottily lit by the shore lights of Jorida, rode moored near one another.

There were other, smaller boats. The two Dojisigin ships loomed among them, a threat to the whole coast.

If only they had something to throw besides paper, Bren thought.

But they had what they had, and that was far more than paper, if those sheets fell into enough willing hands.

The plane leveled out to the northwest, with the stars above and to the front, nothing but black below, and it was as if they were hung in space. Frozen.

For a long, long time.

"*Lights can trick one at night,*" Reijiri commented. "*One can see a string of them and think them a horizon—when they are not—and that can be disaster. Or one can see a light ahead and think one has no air speed. In my first flight at night—I strongly felt the plane had stopped in mid-air, that the instruments were lying, and did very silly things trying to prove I was moving. It is a strange feeling. One could fly right into a lake, looking at lights on the shore.*"

"Or into a very large bay," Bren said.

"*That is indeed quite a lot of water down there. But the ocean* is wider still. I thought about flying to Mospheira when I was young. I thought I would fly over there and have a look. I had better sense by the time I acquired the plane."

"Who taught you to fly?" He had always wondered. Small-craft aviation had existed from early days on Mospheira, but small aircraft on the mainland, despite the huge distances, were an extreme rarity. "Where did you get the plane?"

"Oh, the plane is Patinandi, one of the earliest. Back from early days, when they were figuring it all out. They were clearing their warehouse. But there was no one precisely to teach me to fly. I had the engineers' notes and their checklist. The plane and I learned together. I have had to replace a few pieces over the years. Some expensive. But nothing too serious. The engine is unhappily right in line if I run into anything, and it is precious."

"A very different looking engine."

"A radial engine." The term was Mosphei'. "Nine cylinders, the most fortunate of numbers. Nine cylinders acting as one, with some very clever machinery in the middle—nothing like it in all the world. Very hardy. Very agile. It lands and takes off in, as you saw, fairly restricted situations. And has considerable power."

It conjured images. Arguing with a Mospheiran jet at Shejidan Airport, was one . . . when Reijiri had been, one calculated, still in his teens—and he himself had been new to the continent.

The big jets had been a world-changing gift in Wilson's time as paidhi, a frighteningly fast course, from little planes to commercial jets, that had given humans and atevi the ability to reach each other frighteningly fast, as well. And within his own time as paidhi, with intervention from the returning starship—they had the shuttles, putting Mospheirans and atevi in space.

God, that was a lot of change.

And none of the changes had made it down to this bay, where the only sound was the sound of their own engine and the rush of cold wind over them. The plane had running lights, but there being no other aircraft in the sky—they were not using them. The only light was starlight on their wings. No lights even from the two instruments on his own panel, though one trusted Reijiri could see his. Or perhaps the starlight was all his atevi eyes needed.

No other plane. No airports. No radar to spot them as they flew, and not even scattered villages along the coast, no spark of firelight or electricity to guide them. Their distinction of earth and sky was the black pit that was the water below and the galactic belt in the heavens above, gloriously clear—

He was glad of the stars, for his own peace of mind. And he hoped—God, he hoped—Reijiri's panel gave him more information than he had—or they could fly right out to sea. It was so black down there, utterly featureless. It was all, he was sure, water down there: and they had left Jorida at a northwesterly angle, over the bay.

Everything seemed stopped. The view did not change. It was illusion. He had been warned.

"We are coming up on Talidi," Reijiri said, startling burst of sound.

He saw nothing. Yet. But Reijiri thought so. Perhaps it was hidden from him by the lower wing.

And he suddenly had a job to do. A reason for occupying this seat.

He selected the sack that was for Talidi, the smallest one. He hauled it out of the footwell and onto his lap, having to remove his gloves to unwind its ties. He shoved the gloves into his coat pocket, and tucked one hand under his leg for warmth, holding the bag in his lap with the other. Then he continued to watch the unmoving stars. The lower half of his face was feeling the chill, extremely.

"I have advice," Reijiri said.

"I will more than gladly hear it."

"I shall go over the town low and fast, which will startle folk out of their houses. Then we shall come back more slowly, banking to the left, over the residences. This will give you the best opportunity to scatter the messages. I shall do this more than once, so they need not all go at one pass. Release fistfuls of notes as rapidly as you can. At the last, we may empty the sack, but

only on the turns. Turns will be steep. Under no circumstances release your seat belt."

Steep? "One hears. I will not *touch* the seat belt."

"If there is gunfire, I will take us out of range. I can do nothing else to protect us. We are quite thin-skinned. Should they hit the tank, I will try to bring us down near shore. The rest is forest, on the map."

"It is. Kajiminda forest. Quite thick in this area."

"Can you swim, Bren-ji?"

"Adequately," he said. Daunting question. "But let us try not to be hit."

"That would be my choice as well," Reijiri said.

And moments later, with a faint glow on the starboard even his human eyes could see: *"Talidi,"* Reijiri said. *"Drink shops near the harbor, most fishermen ashore at this hour. Betan said the harbor is too shallow draft for the Dojisigi ships. It is all fishermen and foresters and some local industry. Several distilleries. We will go over at speed and come back, the first pass fast, to see what we have, then as many slow passes as you need."*

"I hear," Bren said. He opened the smaller sack, double-checked the line that secured it to the plane, with visions of it flying loose and hitting Reijiri, or their tail. It was a matter of waiting, then.

Talidi came clearer and clearer. The harborside lights showed fishing boats at their moorings, one visible wall that went clear to the waters of the bay, and houses piled beyond it, wooden houses, wooden roofs, a jumble of roofs and lower windows showing dim light, a scattered few streetlamps. It all passed below at speed.

Well beyond the town, Reijiri banked, so sharply Bren was staring at the trees between the wings, banked and turned about, bringing them back toward the town at a leisurely amble, slower, scarily slow, as rooftops and streets passed under them.

"Now," Reijiri said, and tipped them far over.

Bren had already pulled out a thick fistful of papers, and let them go. The wind caught them. He grabbed another and another, releasing them as fast as he could, trying to ignore the scarily close rooftops. There were small explosions, faint and far, that might be gunfire. But nothing reached them and the plane's fortunate engine kept a steady pulse.

They cleared the town. Reijiri brought the plane about on another right-hand pass, and now lights everywhere were on, doors were wide open. People were out in the street, and bits of paper were visibly blowing about. Bren flung out more and more, clear across the town, northerly.

They swung all the way about where lights gave out, and made another slow pass. Bren threw a final fistful, then brought the sack up and upended it.

"The bag is empty!" he said to Reijiri, and leaned to look over the side of the plane. People were staring up at them and pointing. Some waved and might be shouting at them, but the only noise was the engine.

Reijiri righted the plane and gunned it, rising. Acceleration—surprisingly strong—pressed Bren back in the seat, and the view ahead was a scatter of brighter stars, his eyes still dazed by the town lights.

He breathed hard, stuffed the empty bag under his right knee, and fished up the second one, the largest one.

"That was a bit of gunfire back there," Reijiri said. *"Betan said the Talidi folk were a thankless lot!"*

"They seemed to be waving as we left," Bren said. "I do not think in good cheer. I hope we have no holes."

"I think we are in one piece," Reijiri said, and in the dark that enveloped them, ailerons worked and the plane wobbled and wove. *"We all work."*

"Separti?" he asked.

"Coming up. There will be turns to the left, and soon. We are no longer floating along. Can you manage?"

"Yes!" They *were* going markedly faster. Wind blasted at them. Bren conjured Geigi's map as he recalled it, took his mental bearings, began to undo the binding on the second bag. His heart was still beating hard, and his fingers were chilled, fumbling on the ties. He pulled the gloves back on and tucked one hand under his leg, trying to guess the thoughts of the Talidi.

They had been shot at, but they had not been hit. And the

second run had drawn no fire, that he had heard. He was . . . cautiously optimistic.

And Talidi Township, notorious among Edi, had its warning, granted they wanted to take it and take action. Fishermen and lumber workers, long at war with the Edi, had now more outsiders to worry about: outsiders that would affect Jorida, which was their market. Outsiders that might seem far more dangerous to their lives than the Edi. One doubted they would rush to embrace a new set of overlords from outside their small world. They had been ungracious enough toward the entire aishidi'tat, and not that compliant even toward the Master.

The warning was duly given, granted enough of them read. But it only took a few readers: gossip inevitably outraced legitimate news in the streets.

Still, Talidi's reaction was unpredictable. Najida had had its own set-tos with Talidi by proxy, exchanges of gunfire and charges of theft, poaching, and wanton destruction—markedly accelerated since Geigi had vacated Kajiminda and given half Kajidama Peninsula to the Edi, who had been enforcing boundaries with Talidi and Separti for as long as Kajiminda had stood. By that grant, Geigi had officially empowered the Edi with ownership, preventing Talidi from making the move they otherwise would surely have made when he left Kajiminda vacant.

Having just been shot at by the folk of Talidi—he felt fairly partisan himself at the moment. But if they *did* understand the message, they were very welcome to defend their town.

"*It looked fairly good back there,*" Reijiri said. "*What landed on the roofs was blowing into the streets. But we may move faster on the next pass. Likely Separti will be forewarned. Betan says there is no phone service at Talidi, but there certainly is radio.*"

"I will do it as fast as I can."

"*Just empty the bag. It looks to distribute quite well with that technique.*"

"But do you not have to go slow?"

"*You will have plenty of time. The wind has shifted, coming from the south-southeast, so begin dumping as soon as we reach the lights. We shall know if it succeeds as we cross the town. If it does not, we have the last bag. It should suffice to start rumors."*

They were speeding now, quite fast—Bren shifted to prepare the third bag as well as the second, holding it between his knees and clamped by his right leg, sheltering behind the small windscreen and now with the notion Separti should be coming up, obscured by the nose of the plane, not that far. Surely not that far, as they were traveling now.

He waited. He waited, everything prepared.

"We are nearly there," Reijiri said. "Are you ready, Bren-ji?"

"I am ready, yes." And this time, he could leave the gloves on.

"I am swinging inland. We will pass over the wall, north to south, banking left. When we turn, then is your chance. Hold onto the bag. Hold hard. We will be moving, and passing straight on to Jorida if this succeeds."

"I understand. Yes."

A moment later: *"We are there, Bren-ji!"*

And the plane banked, an appalling lurch, low—God!—over a wooden wall, and over rooftops and scattered lights. Bren heaved the open bag into the wind, held onto it as a pale fluttering stream of notes emptied into the winds. It almost went out of his hands and he fought to get it back, still clamping the remaining bag with his knee, trying to see, at a horrific incline, where the stream of paper was going, how it was spreading.

"You have got it!" Reijiri said, and the town rolled out of view as Bren seized the third bag in his hands and swallowed hard against the shift of pressure, his back against the cushion, the damned goggles slipping. He opted to hold onto the bag until the pressure eased, then risked a quick move to shove the goggles into place.

"Were they shooting?"

"There were people already in the street—I did not hear gunfire."

All he had heard was the engine. Fortunate nine cylinders, hauling them back into the sky and away.

"The papers—did they distribute?"

"Right down the street—the whole stream. Well done, well done!"

He rested against the seat back, adjusted the goggles a second time, and clung to the third sack with the other hand, breathing, not letting go his grip.

He had ridden the shuttle to space. He had traveled to far stars and back. He had felt acceleration. This little plane—this early experiment in the atevi ascent to the heavens—had pulled g's back there—Ragi was not supposed to borrow human words, but Ragi who flew had borrowed those. Those nine fortunate cylinders were doing their best, and paper was flying down the streets of Separti—

Block your streets, defend your neighborhoods and your harbors, unite with each other, and do not let this threat take root here . . .

You are not alone in this fight.

Would they listen?

If there was one thing that would rouse the atevi across clan lines, it was the notion of invasion. The people of Ashidama might not be Ragi, nor care about the aishidi'tat, but the atevi world had become very sensitive to the topic of invasion . . . humans on the world, Ragi on the south, the Marid on the Ragi, and the East on everybody else . . .

The Marid folk and their kin, these remnants of the Southern Isle, did not fly. But they knew the Ragi did. They would be surprised, but not terrorized. They would know it was a Ragi message, and ordinarily, in their view, a lie.

Betan, who knew Ashidama, thought it was a good message, that might rouse the Townships.

It certainly would not make the Shadow Guild happy.

But would they understand the Marid Shadow Guild, and not the Ragi, as the threat? One could only hope.

"There is Jorida left," Reijiri said. *"And there are Shadow Guild, and they will be forewarned. Are you game for another throw, nandi? How are you feeling the odds?"*

"I can do it. How are *you*, nandi-ji?" The answer came out of him without half-thought, and at the moment—at the moment he was eighteen, poised at the height of Mount Adams, looking down the slope. Like a lunatic. He was not that boy. He could not afford to be.

"*Willing!*" Reijiri said, and the nine-cylindered engine surged forward into the dark, with absolute black below, and the wind rushing past.

Like then. On the mountain. When gravity had been his ally, not his enemy. Pushing luck. But, damn it, the threat was just two ships and a scattered will to stop them; and if the Shadow Guild were warned about them, the population of Jorida were aware, too, that the Shadow Guild was not in control of everything. One close pass, one sound out of the night to let Jorida know they were not alone down here, and, granted he could shed the notes, give them encouragement that did not have to come by radio, information in their own hands.

That was the first thought. The second was saner.

"I think we should make this a fast one," he said. "Give me just enough time. I will be quick."

"*Agreed,*" Reijiri said.

And a few moments later, with lights showing on the island, fixed and broad, Jorida being just across the bay from Separti: "*Lights,*" Reijiri said. "*Do the fools hope to spot us?*"

"Surely," Bren said, with misgivings. There were five, six points of light across the bay. And more of them.

And more.

And more, as they approached the island.

"The lower town," Bren said, on a wild thought. "The lights are in the lower town. They are lighting up. They have heard from the other towns."

"*Then they will hear from us!*" Reijiri said, and began to climb, and climb up above the bay, high, high into the dark and the cold.

"*You will have one moment,*" Reijiri said as they still rose, pressure pushing against the cushions. "*One moment, Bren-ji! You will know the moment! If they want to shoot at us, let them try it! We will be moving!*"

The plane rolled, lights streaking below them as they went,

weightless for the moment, then screamed down like a thunderbolt.

One moment. One moment. Bren held the bag, heart hammering, no view, no chance, wondering had they been hit, had something snapped, had Reijiri any control at all.

Then they leveled out, and gut and lungs felt apt to trade places, simultaneous with an atevi scream, as lunatic a yell as human ears had ever heard.

They were level, out over the water, nine cylinders doing their jobs without a fault.

Bren sucked in a breath, remembering the bag he held—had held. It was gone. Along with his gloves. He felt frantically for the cord that held it, knotted to a stanchion.

There was only the frayed end left.

"Did you do it?" Reijiri asked him. *"Did it empty?"*

"The bag is gone," Bren said, and with relief, his stomach strained, his ears aching and moisture running from his nose. "But it was open when it left us."

"A success!" Reijiri cried.

17

It was amazingly quiet flying after—or his ears were affected, Bren thought. They had popped several times during that last. maneuver. And there was a bubble he could not quite shake. He had a pocket handkerchief, not standard for an atevi gentleman, but an item that had been useful now and again. It was useful now, to stop the nosebleed—one was not sure about the lace cuffs and collar, all the same, but he thought he had saved the coat. Insane thought that it was.

The engine was going along quite steadily. There was a little flutter on the right wing he had thought due to his ears, but Reijiri, with atevi night-sight, said it was definitely a bullet hole, likely from the height of Jorida.

"We have used up rather more fuel than I had planned for, particularly at the last," Reijiri remarked, the first he had said in a while. *"We may have to set down on the market road."*

"We are not going to make the Guild camp, then." Bren asked.

"We should *make it. We are taking advantage of the wind. And we do not have to push as we did coming over."*

Should. And using the wind did not inspire total confidence. But, he reminded himself, Reijiri had survived teaching himself to fly.

"We will *need to get down,"* Reijiri said after only a few more minutes of flying. *"Fuel is not extending as far as I hoped. I am contacting Kajiminda to advise them."*

There was a radio. They had that. It was not a secure contact. But trouble was considerably behind them . . . one hoped.

They flew on. The sound of the engine was a steady pulse. So far.

They banked.

A moment of silence. Then: *"There is supposed to be road. I cannot see it."*

"We are over trees," Bren said, looking over the side. "Not to complain, to be sure."

They continued a moment more. Then banked left, more steeply.

"We are changing course," Reijiri said. *"We are heading toward Kajiminda by the shortest route. The market road there, as we came in, did not look well-maintained."*

"It is not."

"Then the meadow where we started has become our best option. I have experienced it once, and we have enough . . . for that. I have advised them."

Was that a sputter of the com or a hesitation?

"How much fuel?"

"We will make it. I am confident of a second pass, if we need it. I am asking them to turn on the tanker's lights midway, at the side of our run."

The fuel tanker sitting near their landing path was not a happy thought. But its light was what they had. Contingency had become necessity if the flat up by the Guild camp was not in reach.

"I would suggest, when we land, Bren-ji, to duck down below the windscreen."

"One hears. One hopes you will. One hopes we will land brilliantly."

"We shall certainly try to do that, nandi-ji."

Slow breaths, then. Forest was doubtless still under them. There was silence, broken only by the wind, the noise of the engine, and the flutter of whatever was loose on the wing.

Then the plane wobbled in the air, its nose dropped and raised again.

Light shone in the dark. Far more lights than when they left. He saw Kajiminda itself illuminated as the plane veered off, and came about again.

There was miraculously, he could see as they turned, a landing field beyond, defined, *rimmed* in lights of various intensity and whiteness.

"Gods most fortunate," Reijiri said at the same moment. And: *"They have mown the ground for us!"*

They completed their turn, began to descend, the nose slowly rising in front of him. Bren put his crossed hands on the panel in front, intending to duck and protect his head—and realized, suddenly, he could barely hear the engine.

"Jiri-ji!" he said. "Is everything all right? The engine—"

"All is as it should be, Bren-ji!" The infectiously cheerful tone had returned at last, and the landing when it came moments later, was feather-light, a near imperceptible drop to a gentle touch of all three wheels in perfect unison, a slightly bumpy roll and a final settling of the engine, the nine faithful cylinders, to an easy, peaceful rhythm. They came to a safe, smooth stop.

Reijiri cut the engine, and the lights around the field broke formation and began to cascade toward them, Guild and Edi alike carrying every manner of light, flashlights, lanterns, candles in glass chimneys—burning steady white or fluttering with the wind.

Bren loosed his seat belt and put an arm over the side, levering himself up to set a shaking knee on the seat. Banichi and Jago, Tano and Algini, all four were there. Banichi waited for no one— seized a handhold and climbed up onto the wing, first to offer a hand to Reijiri, and then up the wing to him, to assist him out.

Legs were not quite as steady as one would wish. He was chilled through. But Banichi would not let him fall. He had every confidence.

"So all delivered," Ilisidi said cheerfully.

"The last rather in a mass," Bren said. He was moderately hoarse, and somewhat, he was sure, resembled Lord Tatiseigi in his initial appearance, with blood, to boot; and the coat had not escaped, thanks to the wind, nor likely had the plane. But the nosebleed had stopped, and the dowager would not afford him the grace to clean up, neither him nor Reijiri. She and Lord Tatiseigi

266 / C. J. CHERRYH & JANE S. FANCHER

must hear everything immediately as they arrived in the grand foyer, and so must the rest of the gathering. Nomari was there, with his aishid behind him, everything seeming reconciled. And Bindanda had said, quietly, intercepting him as they entered the interior hall, "There will be dinner, nandi, in the room, when you will, but the dowager will have you both in the sitting room."

Dinner was not yet welcome news. Bren was still walking askew, if imperceptibly so, perhaps the ears. Or lack of supper. He felt hollow down to his boots, but he had no appetite for food at the moment.

For a double dose of brandy, yes, and a seat near a portable stove, twice yes. He was prepared to drink two glasses and fall into bed, except that the room itself hardly felt steady about him, and the memory of the valiant engine was still buzzing in his ears.

What he truly wanted was to be in his bed, magically having finished this interview, eaten supper, soaked in the tub for, oh, three hours, and slept for about a week.

That . . . was not going to happen.

"We shall be taking the bus tomorrow," the dowager said, shattering his fantasy.

And he: "Where shall we be taking it, aiji-ma?"

"To visit your handiwork, paidhi-ji."

Paidhi-*ji*, was it? Approbation, from the dowager. That was very fine. It might even be worth his frozen feet and fingers if "his handiwork" meant returning to Najida.

One hoped, but one sincerely doubted.

"We have received a call from Najida," Ilisidi said. And after a pause for effect. "From the Master, indirectly."

"At *Najida*?"

"A call from Separti to Najida, in the belief, perhaps, that the plane had come from there. Perhaps because it landed there earlier, who knows? There was a call, not half an hour ago, asking us to come to meet with him."

As a consequence—perhaps—of the messages?

Surely not a coincidence. Half an hour ago. It was a fairly

instant response to being bombarded with warnings about his houseguests.

"You . . . specifically?"

"He failed to qualify."

But the Master was in a precarious situation; there was no question. "On Jorida Isle? Surely he would not expect you to go there."

"He did not specify. A very poor arrangement for meetings, do you not agree? But then . . . there was an element of tension in the call. Perhaps it was the plane passing over him. Perhaps not. And was it even his voice? We have spoken in the past. We were both younger. I did not form a strong memory of it then. And there still are no modern phones in Ashidama—*just* shortwave. Ramaso, clever fellow, recorded the call in its entirety. You must reward him appropriately."

Recorded. Of course. Ramaso was careful about messages, however received. Meticulous about origin and caller, and requests, possible and not. Still, the brain was not, at the moment, up to the intricacies of this explanation.

An unspecified meeting, was it? The *hell.* He looked at Reijiri, the other side of the small stove, and at Tatiseigi, still with his cane, still bundled against the slightest draft, who alone of those present, vividly imagined what the two of them had just been through; and at Nomari, who had joined their party and was now sitting in council with the dowager, with his aishid properly, inscrutably, behind him.

There was the dowager's extended guard listening to this. His. With Nomari's aishid, Reijiri's, and Tatiseigi's. The entire gathering was ringed with black and weaponry, a small expeditionary force with a larger one backing it up at Najida. The gathering in this room alone was, potentially, a match for a small town, and very much to be feared . . .

If the principals of this gathering were as ruthless as the Shadow Guild.

But they were not. And the civilized restraint of the northern Guild had been the Shadow Guild's greatest advantage from the start. There were the people of Separti and there were the Edi to suffer the consequences of a Guild-against-Guild clash, if they did not themselves set limits on the engagement and keep the enemy inside them. Since the Shadow Guild had no regard for civilian lives—*they* had to set the limits. And the Shadow Guild, once embedded among civilians, was not going to come out to fight.

"We—" His voice was unexpectedly hoarse from the wind. It cracked. "We hope we have warned the citizens—we hope to have made their operation more difficult. But is there any chance that the Master is going to hold out?"

"We do not know his voice," Cenedi said. "Betan does not. There is no knowing who we are actually dealing with, and as for sending someone in to find out—no. Stirring resistance in the Townships may delay the threat to the region, but Jorida has no Guild, has declined Guild protection, has no force of its own. The town mayors can at least muster a small guard, but no more than that, and they will not stand once a single unit of Guild comes ashore. What we hope is that they *have* had an easy entry, perhaps spread themselves too thin, and the public turning on them may have some early effect—but only briefly. Our window to act is narrow."

"Hurshina of Jorida is a *stubborn* old fool," Ilisidi said, setting her cane on the floor with a gentle tap. "But he has knowledge, he has contacts, he is devoted to profit and he is determined to hold power. But in his place, snug in his tower, would he risk his precious neck, when he believes I *can* reach him? I do not believe he made that call, or if he did it was for his own purpose, be it only survival. I suspect, rather, it comes from Suratho, with visions of luring *me* into a trap. If he is alive—and they would be fools to kill him—he will be up to his own game, wanting to use *our* forces to take out *his* new problem."

"He is nothing," Cenedi said, "but an inconvenience. When has he not been?"

"He was an inconvenience before most of this company was born. He is an inconvenience, a stubborn and occasionally irrational inconvenience, but some antiques deserve a second evaluation, particularly if they are in a position to become useful.

Unlike most of his people, he pays attention to the outside world. He will understand exactly how he will be treated by these Dojisigi, and he will have no illusions how they will treat this region—how long they will hesitate to remove him and his entire class if he resists. He has no heirs, no lateral relatives or kinships by marriages, no bond of man'chi, and no one he wishes to protect—he is in that regard the worst sort of enemy for them to have . . . outside of myself, who have *my* succession in Shejidan firmly in power and well out of their reach. His is simply *dead*. So let us go turn up on his doorstep before the Shadow Guild has a firm grip, and see what we shall find."

"We were shot at in Talidi," Bren said quietly. "I believe there is a bullet hole in the plane, aiji-ma, and we picked that up on Jorida. One is fairly sure the one at Talidi was a local and did not reach us, though the second one might have been our enemies, and somewhat higher caliber."

"Ah, well, I did not say we should be popular. If the people in general truly understood, they would sink Tiajo in the sea and shoot the Shadow Guild on sight without our invitation, but, then, we cannot claim an outstanding record of Ragi behavior in this region, either, can we? But the Master *is* an influence they will listen to. Whether or not that was his message that has come to us, we shall see. Perhaps circumstances will make him more reasonable . . . this round."

Come to the office, the note from Father said, long, long after dark—well past the hour Cajeiri was usually abed. It had already been a disturbing evening. Cajeiri had had dinner with his younger aishid—but his elder one, who had returned that afternoon, had chosen dinner in their quarters, to discuss privately whatever they discussed . . . not that they had never done such a thing, but tonight, in Cajeiri's view they had needed, soberly, to discuss things together: himself, them, and his younger aishid.

He had felt set down hard when they had gone to the back hall. He had all but heard the lock click. So had his younger aishid.

And now the note from Father. Which had arrived well past the point when, even on the long days, Father had usually given up the office, had dinner, and gone to bed. It worried him extremely. It *might* have to do with his elder aishid.

Or the things he had done.

Or *their* report to Father.

His younger aishid began to go for jackets, to go with him. "No, nadiin-ji," he said. "I shall deal with it. It will be all right." That was a promise he well knew he could not make, especially if something else had gone wrong—and there were so many things that could be.

His younger aishid deserved none of Father's displeasure. Nor did his servants.

They looked concerned, all of them, including Eisi and Liedi, who assisted with his coat and his queue, and let him out the door.

They would still be worrying. There was every reason. If it was very bad news—at this hour—he wanted to absorb it first.

It was a short, terrible walk to Father's office. He knocked, then with only silence answering, went in. Not even Father's aishid was in evidence, inside or out.

Father had a paper in his hand. He laid it on the desk.

"Sit," Father said in an ordinary tone, which was a little relief. Cajeiri sat in the interviewee's chair, keeping careful posture. Father took a sip of tea, and picked up the paper again.

"I have a curious thing here," Father said, then asked: "What do you think of Machigi?"

What did he think of *Machigi*?

Had Machigi been assassinated?

Had he assassinated someone else?

Why was this scary late call about Machigi?

"I . . ." He could not find words to answer so general a question, and Father lifted a hand to stop him.

"Listen to this," Father said, and began to read.

"'*Machigi, Lord of Tanaja and aiji of the Taisigin Marid, its territories westward, and its allies, the Sungeni Isles and the Dausigin Marid* . . .' Aiji is lowercase, be it noted, but it *is* unqualifiedly brash, in address to me, do you not think? '. . . *To Tabini-aiji, Aiji of the aishidi'tat, and of possessions aloft* . . .' Also rather grander than we are generally addressed, after his own as-sumption of title. We may assume he is advancing a point of argument."

"One has no idea, honored Father."

"Understand that the documents your great-grandmother signed, the very critical documents of agreement with Machigi, Topari of Hasjuran, Bregani, Lord of Senjin, and her—are still in Hasjuran, as the train with their new transformer has only now discharged its load, now to take these agreements aboard and bring them down to be filed in Shejidan. Understand too, that with these very significant documents still unfiled and with war still being waged in the Marid, your great-grandmother has decided to put herself in a very precarious situation on the other coast. Knowing, *knowing*, that should she die before those documents are properly filed, they legally become null and void."

"One understands, honored Father." He swallowed the question he desperately wanted to ask, as his father turned back to the letter.

"So, apparently, does Machigi. Let us continue: '*As I strongly support the documents to which I am signatory along with the aiji-dowager, Bregani, Lord of the Senjin Marid, and Topari, Lord of Hasjuran, I write to state that should any untoward event negate those documents or should they physically be lost before they reach you, I will support the letter and intent of said documents and agree again to the same terms, provided that other parties, significantly the aishidi'tat, shall also act according to those terms as we signed at Hasjuran. This being true, I shall consider the terms of the agreement already binding on all sides, as of the date of original signing, and will plan and act accordingly.*' Do you follow that, son of mine?"

"He is saying if the documents should fail to get here, he would sign the same again? And he considers it is already binding." That was surprising. His opinion of Machigi tilted ever so slightly. "Hasjuran would probably not object. They have nothing to lose and much to gain. Maybe Senjin would agree, especially if we destroy the Shadow Guild."

"As things stand in the Marid, with the Guild slicing through

the Dojisigin, with one warship of ours in the Dojisigin's harbor
and another sitting in Senjin's port, Senjin would likely be very
glad of Machigi's keeping the agreement with us—and *they*
would have every motive to keep it from their side. If Machigi
will abide by it, ours is the likeliest objection, and if we keep
mani's side of the agreement regarding that railroad and Hasjuran's warehouse—they benefit financially. And our commitment
is what this letter seems to want.—Do you understand what that
means?"

He thought about it a moment, then asked: "What exactly did
mani promise in this document?"

"An excellent question, son of mine. In a word: steel."

Another consideration. "Meaning she made these agreements
as lord of Malguri."

"Indeed."

"How can the aishidi'tat guarantee fulfillment, should something happen to mani? Would that not be up to her heir?"

"She has yet to declare one."

"Then what commitment can he ask of you?"

"I suspect he would expect the aishidi'tat to supply the steel,
one way or another."

He chewed the inside of his lip, then asked, "Has—" He swallowed hard. "Has something happened to mani, honored Father?
Is that why you are awake at this hour?"

"I am still awake, son of mine, for the same reason you are;
however, to answer your question, to our knowledge, she is safe
in Kajiminda, or as safe as Kajiminda is, and Lord Geigi would
involve us immediately if it were not. So let us hope for yet one
more reason that she gets back here safely and takes care of her
own succession in Malguri before the matter becomes an issue."

"That . . . would be a very good thing," Cajeiri said, past a
lump.

"But there is more to this letter." Father adjusted it in his hand.
*"'We have received word that the aiji-dowager, with the paidhi-
aiji, is currently attempting to prevent fugitives from the Dojisigin from creating a base in Ashidama Bay, and is at the moment
resident in Kajiminda, with a Guild force moved from Senjin*

and now encamped at Najida station. We strongly support the dowager's move to protect this region and we oppose the Dojisigin incursion into Ashidama. We are accordingly, as of this noon, sending a ship to the region to support her operation.'"

"A ship?" That seemed good news. Machigi had fought the Shadow Guild in his own land for years. "How soon can it get there?"

His father looked at him. "Not soon enough. And it is not a warship, but a trader equipped with small-bore deck pieces—You asked me why I was up. I have received word, from both Bren-paidhi and the Guild commander that your great-grandmother is making a move. Imminently."

That brought him to the edge of his chair, hands clenched on the arms. "What has she done?"

"It appears your introduction of Lord Reijiri and his plane into her arsenal has given her unexpected options. Lord Reijiri and Bren-paidhi have just returned from flying over the Townships *and* Jorida Island, dumping printed messages down on the heads of the unsuspecting civilians, informing them of the Dojisigin invasion and the presence of aishidi'tat Guild who intend to rid them of the problem."

"Lord . . . Bren? In Reijiri's plane?"

"You need not sound so jealous, son of mine. It was a dangerous stunt, one which placed both of them in great danger. As for the particulars, you will have to get him to tell you the story when he returns. I know only enough to know I would have argued against the plan, had I been informed beforehand. It appears it was Bren-paidhi's idea, which is likely *why* he did not inform me until after it was accomplished, and he was safely back in Kajiminda." His father raised a brow. "It appears the paidhi-aiji is learning from you and your great-grandmother."

"One is *certain* he felt it necessary. And it has all happened very quickly. Perhaps there was no time to call and explain."

"You will learn, son of mine, that silence is rarely a matter of necessity—more often one of policy. There are always reasons. One must admit, however, their message appears to have been effective. It roused an immediate response purportedly from the

Master of Jorida requesting a meeting with Grandmother. We do not believe it. *She* will not believe it. But all the same, *she* is moving, a move that will involve the force camped at Najida as well as the aishidi of *five* lords, all of whom have arrived at Kaji-minda. *She*, at least, will stay at Kajiminda, along with Lord Ta-tiseigi, his aishid, and Lord Bren, Lord Reijiri, *and*, one assumes, your cousin Nomari. Lord Geigi assures me they will be quite safe behind the defenses Lord Geigi has there. However, she *is* making her move, and one doubts she means to wait for rein-forcements. Even our ship will not arrive until afternoon at the earliest . . . which brings me to the next part of Machigi's letter."

His father flicked the papers straight, and began to read again:

"'*More, as of the same hour,*' Noon, he means, '*I have autho-rized my rangers to move to the western limit of my hunting range to stand by should the enemies of the aishidi'tat attempt to enter Taisigin territory. They are closer to the dowager's area of operation and can move overland with much greater speed. I anticipate them to be at the western border of the range by mid-night tonight at the latest. That border, already defended by cliffs, will not be open to fugitives from her operation, and I am empowering active pursuit onto and across the market road, should such an attempt be made.*'"

The paper lowered. "You realize what it means for his people to cross the market road."

Cajeiri thought hard and fast. "It is the boundary between his hunting grounds and Ashidama. Would that count as an inva-sion?"

"A point to keep in mind. He finishes with: '*I am, tonight, communicating the latter to the dowager by phone, with no care whatever whether the Dojisigin intercept it. If the threat of my rangers is alone sufficient to turn them from my borders, I shall count it a success. I shall, in addition, stand ready to cross that border in support of the dowager and our agreement in Hasjuran, should she or her forces be threatened.*'"

Was that good? It sounded good. But . . . military aid from Machigi? He hardly knew what to say.

"Well?" Father asked.

"One hardly knows, honored Father. Is that just another excuse to occupy Ashidama?"

"One needs to ask the question. Have you other thoughts?"

"One has very limited personal experience with him, but mani does not trust him. Not entirely. But . . . she did sign those agreements, which means she must trust him to abide by them. And he wants that rail link, does he not? And he opposes the Shadow Guild. Has since before he became lord of the Taisigin. It makes sense for him to honor the agreements . . . and part of those agreements *is* mutual support."

"And is that sufficient to explain him gathering his forces within reach of the aiji-dowager and *her* forces? Is that sufficient reason to believe in or trust his support in a move to save the Master from the Shadow Guild? Might he have alternative motives for crossing the market road into Ashidama? And how might he benefit, personally, from a power vacuum in Jorida?"

A power vacuum in Jorida?

Father waited, as if he was supposed to find some piece of wisdom.

"Machigi is bottled up by his position," Cajeiri answered slowly. "Right now there is no commercial route into the Taisigin but the Marid Sea at Tanaja, and the large protected hunting range on the other, with no land routes of his own. He wants the rail to Koperna, which would give him direct access to the aishidi'tat. He wants mani's steel ships and that trade with the East. Shipping is important to the Marid. Traditional. But the steel for those ships *and* the railroad cannot get to him right now except by sea, after crossing the continent to Cobo on rail, and then traveling all the way south and back again. The Taisigin sends some ships up the Strait to Cobo, but mostly that trade is controlled by Jorida, and the Master has made it very hard for Taisigin ships coming into Cobo to do business."

He blinked, focused on his father's unreadable face. He was almost sure of his facts. They were his studies. His tutor gave him good marks.

"So . . . if the Shadow Guild replaces the Master with Lord Tiajo, or if the Master is killed in all this, that means Cobo might start dealing directly with Lord Machigi . . . for all the Marid, if the Dojisigin are down for a time. Do you think that is what he wants? To reach out and bypass Ashidama by rail *and* sea?"

"One must consider the possibility. And we cannot let that happen, son of mine. The aishidi'tat cannot endorse a forceful takeover or an ongoing trade war, regardless of the circumstances. Grandmother has spent her life trying to tempt Ashidama to join the aishidi'tat—to get a rail link to the Townships, and get Ashidama a proper lordship and a seat in the legislature. Which is exactly what she will ask in return for freeing Jorida of Tiajo and her forces."

"But if Lord Machigi's force gets there first, they might try to take control of the operation—which is right up against land they already own. Is that what you think?"

"It is what I fear."

"I do not think Lord Machigi will try that."

Father's eyes narrowed. "And why do you think that?"

"Because Lord Machigi would not want mani to turn against him, because she would if he tried. If he tried, he would not get the steel for his rail and his ships, which are better for Taisigin than controlling Jorida—which will be far less profitable once Machigi's rail is established."

"It will indeed."

"Once he has the railroad link, the steel can come that way, but even once he has the steel, what he will have is shipbuilding. Which will be important. But he has to maintain good relations with mani or the steel stops. If it stops, he cannot make railroad cars *or* ships."

"You have studied."

"I am right, am I not? Mani has the steel and the plants, on both sides of the divide. Mani has almost all the foundries."

Father nodded. "All but one, and that one deals with Mospheira. But Machigi's steel ships, if he gets them, will not only go to mani's East, into that dangerous ocean, they will also want to go up to Cobo, by a much easier route."

"Which is Ashidama's shipping route," he said. "It would hurt their business. Without agreements, those large steel ships could destroy it."

"It certainly could, without agreements. There *have* to be agreements. Perhaps you can see further than I do, son of mine. Where you have been—sometimes I wonder what you do see. But there is no weapon in the heavens that will solve this problem, and no way for everybody to get *all* that they want. What they have to have is enough of what they want."

Enough of what they want. He thought about that, trying to be clever, wondering what he could possibly see that his father could not.

"It will be years before he can build steel ships," he said. "The rail to deliver the steel comes first. Then he will have that rail link to trade with the aishidi'tat so he will not *need* to send ships to Cobo. So on the one hand mani can make him rich. And spending everything taking Jorida now and losing that railroad would be very . . ." He searched for an appropriate big word, and unable to find it, settled on simply: ". . . stupid."

His father's mouth twitched. "Do we think Machigi sees that?"

"I think what he wants could be enough to keep him busy right now. He is not an ally of the Dojisigin. He has not generally attacked Senjin. So he might get along with Senjin very well if the Dojisigin are no longer forcing trouble. I think he really does want that link to the railroad, and his steel ships."

"If ever they are built."

"But if they are. No one has ever sailed all the way to the great East. And if he has it . . ."

"That would be a lot of building and a lot of sailing."

"It would. But it would be something to do. And it would be all his to deal with. We would have no interest. We have the space station."

"Half of it."

"But also the starship."

"If that thing is ever built."

"It can be. It *will* be, if we can get rid of all the problems of refugees and the Shadow Guild. And there are places to go up there."

"More Machigis," Father said. "More Tiajos."

"More Brens."

Father looked at him, silent then. Finally: "Preserve the aishidi'tat. That is *your* task, son of mine."

"That first, honored Father. First of all things."

Father said nothing for a considerable space. Then he slipped the paper into a drawer. "I shall give Machigi a civil thank you. I shall say that we also consider the agreement binding, and will see it honored. And if he can stand between these scoundrels in Ashidama and their escape into his lands, good."

The plane was in process of refueling. Bren sat at a small desk in the sitting room and wrote, with several strikeouts, and a smudge of ink: *The Master of Jorida has officially appealed for assistance from the aishidi'tat against the Dojisigin outlaws who have arrived in Ashidama Bay.*

That was a bit of a stretch, particularly if that message had *not* come from Hurshina, but considering what the message *had* said, one was allowed to assume he felt his own resources inadequate to the situation—or that he was being held from having opinions by Suratho.

In response to that request, the aiji-dowager has sent her own Guild forces into Ashidama Bay to restore independence to Jorida and the Townships. Bear in mind that these forces are indistinguishable in uniform from these intruders. Do not mistakenly fire on forces sent to help you. Know for a certainty that the lawful Guild will never attack civilians or demand entry into your homes: defend yourselves vigorously if threatened. Once the Master has been restored to power, Guild forces will withdraw, making no territorial claims on Ashidama.

For the people of Separti: The dowager's Guild forces will soon be arriving overland by the Kajiminda gate. Let this force, assuredly your allies, pass through to the docks, and provide them assistance to reach the Jorida waterfront.

For the people of Jorida: Seek shelter and stay hidden. Forces of the aiji-dowager, in alliance with the Master of Jorida, are in your midst. Allow them to deal with these outlaws and do not attempt to engage the enemy. Every effort will be made by the legitimate Guild to safeguard your lives and property.

Once again, the aiji-dowager, as an ally of the Master, declares that the aishidi'tat will make no territorial claims over Ashidama resulting from this action.

Help is not just coming. It is now.

In the name of Ilisidi, aiji-dowager of the aishidi'tat.

He read it through three times, eyes blurring, then handed it to Betan to oversee the printing and packing.

And having accomplished that edited and re-edited bit of composition, he levered himself up from the little table and, in a state of numbness, not even taking the time to climb the stairs to his suite, wandered down the hall to Reijiri's previous resort . . . the bath, warm, even stiflingly warm, dimly lit, and out of the flow of Edi hurrying about in preparations. He lay face down on the slats of the wooden bench, distributed himself as comfortably as he could, and tried to go unconscious, if only for an hour or so.

Reijiri was in worse case regarding sleep, and, one hoped, had achieved some comfort in the staff lounge by now. *His* sleep being life and death for both of them, Reijiri got the padded chair in absolute quiet. They did not dare take to beds, where sleep would come fast and deep. They had a little under two hours before they needed to take off again, at their best calculation of the time it would take for them to accomplish their mission and for the Najida bus, already en route, to get back to the main market road and travel the fairly long distance across the back of the bay—on a route that was, Betan said, seasonally used by fuel trucks serving Ashidama agriculture on that peninsula, so it would be kept generally free of larger slides from the cliffs above: the most recent surveillance photos that regularly came from Lord Geigi showed that to be the case. And *that* route connected to the long agricultural road that ran the length of Ashidama Peninsula's inner shore, with Jorida's one access to land halfway along that route.

There was word from the camp commander, Midagi. They

were coming, at all the speed Najida's truck, carrying the bulk of the force, could manage.

By the time they took off, word should have likewise come from Cenedi regarding the progress of the Najida estate bus on that route . . . he had given his own precious com to Banichi, as it was of more use between Banichi and Cenedi headed into action at Jorida than residing in his pocket during their flight— risky to have another of the new coms out there during combat, yes: they did not want to risk one of the units coming into the hands of the Shadow Guild, short-term. Not for fear of them using it—Geigi could burn that individual unit in an instant— but because Shadow Guild ignorance of the very existence of the secure system was half its advantage.

The plan was for Cenedi's team to cross the back of the bay, reach the better-maintained agricultural road that ran beside the grainfields of the southernmost peninsula, take that as far as the causeway between Ashidama Peninsula and Jorida Isle, and arrive still with a little of the night left for cover, even from atevi eyes. Then as Midagi's Guild force from the encampment began to enter the picture at Separti, hopefully crossing the bay, Cenedi's team would cross the causeway and get into the citadel, which rose on a sharply angled jut of rock above the town.

From there, Cenedi and the dowager's entire aishid, Bren's, Reijiri's, and Nomari's—a force of twenty-one . . . the one being Nomari himself . . . who had insisted on going *with* his newly recovered aishid—would endeavor to locate the Master, while eliminating any Shadow Guild that tried to stop them. Ilisidi's force was all committed in that operation, the *only* Guild unit left in Kajiminda now being Tatiseigi's grey-haired aishid, protection that Cenedi had insisted they reserve to stay with the dowager, in the extremely remote case the enemy got into Kajiminda itself. None of them believed that remotely possible—not past Edi staff. Not past Geigi's defenses. But in case.

Nomari, on the other hand . . .

There had been a significant exchange, as Bren had been trying to think and to write.

"I am useless here," Nomari's words—passionately, to Cenedi, in their organizing the bus. "I am *not* a lord, and you are going where I have skills to use, where I have *reason* to be, for my house, for my family, for my *clan*, nadi! I am unapproved as a lord. I count for nothing in Shejidan until I am. But I know faces in the Marid, in *their* organization. I know operations. I can use the accent. I am useful at this, if nothing else in the world. In this, I am useful *now*, when it counts everything!"

"He demonstrably has skills." Tatiseigi: from the dowager's side.

Ilisidi herself, seated, with a tap of the dreaded cane on the tiles:

"Ajuri is overdue a lord who will not be a fool."

"I am not, aiji-ma," Nomari had said—for the first time in Bren's hearing, that *aiji-ma,* fervently given. "I *ask.*"

A silence, then: "You will not give orders, nadi. You will take them. You will, above all, not jeopardize my aishid, or *they* will shoot you. This is my order. Vengeance is not the objective. Success is. Be useful."

"Aiji-ma." A glance at Cenedi, who simply nodded toward the main hall, where preparation was going on.

So it was twenty-one. A felicitous number, on that bus. One hoped—a felicitous number.

On a two-hour drive across the back bay. That was the estimate of the time it would take the bus to navigate the market road—which would not be in good condition. The drive up the long agricultural road beside the grainfields would go much faster—they should get to the causeway by first light, as, one hoped, Midagi's force was crossing the bay and landing in Jorida's lower town, with a populace advised help was not only coming, it was imminent.

His job, the latter, Bren told himself. His and Reijiri's. His not to worry about Nomari's state of mind—which was, no one could doubt, emotional. But his oft-demonstrated talents gave the mission on the causeway a better chance—and the mission on the far side of the bay a better chance of reaching a situation with the Shadow Guild's coordination made more difficult. It was a put-together unit: Cenedi and Banichi had worked together; but

Reijiri's aishid? No. And Nomari had never worked with his own aishid, though by now he knew Cenedi's and Banichi's abilities.

And the dowager risked them all with less concern than she personally had for Cenedi. Cold. One could not say that. No. Quite passionate, one was certain. And counting even Cenedi worth the cost.

Damn. *He* could not.

But there his mind was again, against his will, thinking about the bus and his own aishid, envisioning where they would go, all the dangers they might encounter on that dark forested road, about which he could do *nothing*—

Except get to sleep and support them where they were going, damn it all. *Sleep.*

For which his most desperate fallback was, finally, multiplications. Two times two. Four. Four times four. Sixteen. Sixteen times sixteen. Two fifty-six times two fifty-six. Sixty-five fifty-three thirty-six. . . . That point where the mind hit the wall it usually hit, muddling up the numbers beyond sanity.

He had to sleep just to throw paper out of the plane. *Reijiri* was the one who had to sleep to avoid flying them into a wall or, Reijiri's own fear, some power line. They had been over the route, thought they had all likely routes for such lines figured, but they had barely missed one in Separti, a fact Reijiri had revealed as they pored over those satellite images from Geigi, planning their next run . . .

Coming from the north and west this time. Reijiri was sure they could do it all again, to tell the Townships that help was not only imminent, it was *now.* That last line was Reijiri's own.

And it was real.

The dowager's side of the operation was already in motion: the Guild force was now on the move from Najida, their transports and the noisy market truck coming down the main road, while a quick-strike force was afoot, taking the short diagonal route past the end of Kajiminda Bay. Some of which might be beyond Kajiminda's outbuildings and on toward Separti before the plane ever took off. They would position themselves, possibly within Separti, gate or no gate—and it would be no gate, if Separti looked apt to

oppose the vehicles headed toward them, just as Separti waterfront would cooperate with the force or not, but Guild *would* get
across the bay. Time mattered. They needed to be crossing the
bay by first light and they ideally needed control of the Jorida
waterfront. And ideally—there would be local cooperation.

Both were dependent on his job. His word choice.

God, it needed to work.

Two times two. Four. Four times four. Sixteen . . .

A touch on his shoulder—Bren twitched, shoved himself up on
one arm, recognized Narani's grey hair against the nightlight in
the bath. Jeladi's shadow was behind him.

"A warm coat," Jeladi said, "nandi-ji."

He pushed himself up, swung his feet to the floor, and, elbows
on his knees, he rubbed his eyes and swiped loose hair back from
his face. Amazingly, his eyes agreed to stay open. He levered himself from the bench, stood up, and balanced on uncertain legs. He
accepted the clean coat, took the items Narani offered him, which
was the flight helmet and goggles . . . or rather, *a* flight helmet.
This was a newly-stitched and oiled-leather helmet, with quilted
padding . . . and, he discovered, Edi beading on the brow.

He cast a glance at Narani who said, with a perfectly sober
face: "For luck. The Edi are most grateful, nandi."

"As I am for this," he said, and when he slipped it on, was
happy to discover it fitted snugly to his head. "Excellent. Please
extend my . . ." He yawned helplessly. Hard. Was embarrassed.
And wished he dared just one cup of black, bitter tea before the
flight.

"It is ten after the hour," Narani said. "Be safe, nandi. Be safe
in this."

"We will be back here for breakfast," he said.

He would be back for breakfast if his mission went well. And
Reijiri would be.

At the same hour, Midagi's force should be crossing the bay
and entering Jorida's lower streets.

And Banichi and the others would be fighting their way into
the citadel—and he would not be with them.

Truth was, he would have no appetite for breakfast while any part of that was going on, but it was a promise to cheer Narani and Jeladi, all the same. Those in Cenedi's force, he told himself, were, all but Reijiri's unit, predominantly elite Guild, entirely capable of what they had to do—and granted the units from Najida did not hit a snag at the Separti gate—which their paper rain was designed to prevent—Separti would not only let them through, they would have boats ready to get those units across the bay.

If everything came off as they intended, the Shadow Guild would go down, decapitated, if not in time for breakfast, at least before supper. With a minimum of casualties.

That was—if everybody moved as they had to, as fast as they had to, and granted there was a minimum of shooting from a maximum of people with guns.

He could worry himself sick, however, before he could possibly have word from Banichi that everything was done, and in that regard he was *glad* to have the flight to occupy his mind. Once they did get back, there would be many, many tense hours of no word, no information, and no certainty.

"Toast and eggs," he said flippantly, to Narani and Jeladi, his breakfast order. "About three hours after our takeoff."

Narani gave the ordinary nod of the head, as calm as he tried to be. "Toast and eggs. Three hours, nandi-ji."

It was one of Tatiseigi's elderly aishid that gave him a boost up to the wing—which instantly recalled it was not Banichi. Bren caught his balance with a hand on the fuselage and made his way a little stiffly among the struts, up to the forward seat. The plane rocked under him as Reijiri stepped up behind him, absolutely needing no assistance, and Bren cast a look back as he stepped into his own seat. Reijiri gave him a cheerful wave.

Bren dropped into his seat—it felt higher than before . . . and harder . . . but then his whole body ached from the last flight.

Seat belt first. He carefully settled the goggles in place. They were cleaned of oil spatter. Immaculate. Sized to the new helmet, giving him much more visibility, and snug enough not to move under stress, which had been a problem. Narani had taken care of him. Everything seemed in better order. One of the Edi, edging along the wing, handed him the bags of notes—only two bags this time, bags with solid straps ending in a large carabiner snap and a useful short strap on the end for a second handhold—his suggestion. The Edi wished them both good fortune, and left, rocking the plane. One of the Edi gave the propeller a spin.

Reijiri started the engine.

One knew, now, what to expect. Bren clipped the cords onto the metal handhold and settled the bags about him, Separti's on top, everything in order, which vividly recalled how they had lost the Jorida bag the last time. That dive—

He had two handkerchiefs tucked in the front of his coat this time. For the oil spatter.

They were rolling.

This time he *expected* to have no view. He *expected* the steep turn when they had gotten up.

But this time the turn persisted. And persisted. They were not going as far as the bay. He expected that. The feeling grew queasy. The view off the left side was, first, the house, at fairly close range, and then the outbuildings, dimly lit by the lights of the grounds—and in the distance, a string of lights that might well be the force on its way from Najida.

Then dark branches laced the light; and beyond that, deeper dark, while they continued to turn and climb.

Below them now was the old orchard, that went on and on, fair-sized trees neatly, artificially spaced.

Then the old forest, that grew by its own rules. Massive trees. Tall trees. But by now those trees would be in miniature, a collective darkness. They had passed beyond the lights of Kajiminda.

There was, on the maps, a road down there, somewhere. It might be visible in the daylight, but the overhead crescent moon provided not nearly enough light for his eyes. Reijiri saw more down there, but Reijiri would be navigating by his compass and the plots he had made on Lord Geigi's photos. He had a little penlight with a wrist loop, had the marked-up photos tucked in his inside pocket—Bren had nothing of the sort. His heart was beating hard. And he was deliberately not thinking ahead. No. No worry. They were up. He used the handkerchief to wipe one lens of the goggles. A stray few specks had gotten past the stub of a windscreen, a trick of the air. Some had hit his face.

Just find their way across the woods, along this spur of Kaji-minda's private market road that led to Separti's outer wall. It was a fair distance. The plane was not pushing speed. It would inten-tionally take them the better part of an hour to Separti—and the force from Najida, and the bus, would advance well along their separate courses by then. Their arrival at Separti should give the Township promise of Midagi's force as allies—and not enough time for the Shadow Guild to fortify the gate or disable the boats.

They leveled out, on course, he was sure, but now they had only a night sky for a view—nearly free of clouds, showing stars, many, many stars, serene and apart from all the chaos of the night. One of the stars—actually the planet Maudit—was a steady, bright beacon in the west.

They had time now to catch their breath. The beat of the en-gine was a constant, unstressed. Time assumed a heart-pounding tedium. All they had to do was one pass over Separti, one over Jorida. In planning, Reijiri had sworn he would make that second pass a little less rapidly, and, thinking it over, Bren had said— reluctantly—"Maybe speed on that Jorida pass would still be a good idea. Given they will know what we are on this run."

To which Reijiri had nodded, on further consideration. "One is moved to agree. Fuel should not be a problem. We will be moving fast once we get there, but our path is more direct across—Talidi is on its own, this time."

Bren did not look forward to that downward run at Jorida, and he distracted himself from that thought instead by recalling what detail he had seen of Separti on their approach from the gate—the paved dockside, the wooden piers, boats, from two-masted motor-sailers to an outrigger trawler, all frozen in one brief view that had not, at the time, been still-frame, but a panicked rush. Aston-ishing, that clarity he had. Not entirely trustable in planning. He could not rely on it, but precision in releasing the paper rain was not required; and boats might move, but that long street to the waterfront would not. The wind was out of the east and a little south. As Reijiri had laid it out in planning, they would bank left this time, come over the defensive wall, over the roofs, and down that same main street that led to the harbor. He thought he might delay the release just a little, not to have many of the papers blow back over the gate. Save it for the heart of town where authority was and the taverns of the dockside where the owners of the boats might be.

If luck was with them, if Separti had welcomed the first message, they would not be shot at, this time.

Well . . . unless the Shadow Guild already had operations here: a few operatives could have infiltrated the Township, even going back years—one would actually be surprised if not. The question was whether the newly-arrived Shadow Guild, the elite, would spend manpower trying to take firm control over Separti, especially since their last flight, or whether they might have other things on their mind. The Shadow Guild on those ships would make their moves on the fortified height of Jorida to try to link up with or capture the Master, his assets and information—any concentrated move to organize a defense of the lower town might well have come only when the papers started raining onto the streets. It was even possible, if the situation were unfavorable and the Master had managed to stand them off, that they might even decide to bolt and run—but if that were the case, escaping by ship was no help—they were out of ports; and scattering afoot into the wilds of the south offered them little benefit except time. Getting control of Jorida at whatever costs had the largest, longest future in it for them—but even if they had agents prepositioned inside the citadel, and could use its defenses, they were still down to threatening the inhabitants and trying to bargain, a short-term situation, if they were walled in there.

Having the dowager follow their transfer to Jorida and advance against them from two sides within hours of their arrival was surely not their most hoped-for situation. They would have wanted months to work. Years, if possible: theirs had been a long-range pattern of positioning assets. It was possible they knew or at least had heard rumors of problems on the station. Possible they envisioned the aishidi'tat occupied with other matters, other problems, for years to come, not the least of which was Ilisidi's newest agreements. With Kajiminda's lord absent for years and the Edi in charge of the middle peninsula, they might have thought they had a grand opportunity in Ashidama . . . much better for their style than holding off the regular Guild in a Marid no longer fearful of them.

But Kajiminda's lord was not as absent from the equation as they might think, and the folk of Separti were not all that tightly bound to Jorida. Their long persistence on Kajiminda's shore, through lord after lord of Kajiminda, their trade interspersed with periods of acquiescence to Jorida but never surrender—their persistence in dealing with Lord Geigi, their collusion with his scoundrel nephew, their quiet politicking to maintain trade with the Edi despite Talidi's state of intermittent warfare and Jorida's attempted intervention—all of it said Separti's politics was not Jorida's or Talidi's. Separti had the largest population in Ashidama Bay, never mind Jorida's control of the grainfields, the farmers, and the shipping.

The Shadow Guild at this stage of things was surely not enough to hold all three towns, when the Master of Jorida himself could scarcely do that. And Kajiminda's *Hold on. You are not alone . . .* was at least some hope the people of Separti would let the Guild blow right through them and deal with their problem before it blossomed.

Midagi must be past Kajiminda by now. Cenedi's group on the bus had surely reached the open road on Ashidama. The darkness of trees continued below them, to a glance over the side. The engine continued its steady, comforting sound.

"We are fortunate in the weather tonight," Reijiri commented. *"The wind will continue to blow fairly briskly from the west, which will be fine for a landing at Najida. How are you faring, Bren-ji? It is a little colder tonight—decidedly colder at altitude."*

"One could wish for gloves, but I do have pockets."

"The engine does not favor cold, or cold does not favor the engine. Still we are running smoothly, but if it does complain, do not take alarm. We have no lack of fuel."

"I thank you for the warning."

"We shall be over Separti fairly soon—we shall make a quick transit, trusting the wind to spread the papers, then gain altitude over the bay before we reach Jorida. We shall bank sharply above the citadel height, then descend, and bank to the right. That should give you ample time to loose the notes as we descend at speed, and put us in line with Kajiminda across the bay to the northeast."

"I promised my staff to be home for breakfast. You will be very welcome to join me."

"I shall be delighted.—We are coming up on lights. I believe we are in line for the gate."

There was an obliging roll of the plane to give him a view. Bren strained to make out the gate, to no avail.

"Your eyesight will always be keener than mine. I trust yours."

"I am fairly certain. I believe I see lights in the distance, too, which would be Jorida at this angle. We are exactly on schedule."

Bren had his watch. Seeing it in the dark, through the goggles, was fairly hopeless. He did not try. "Good luck to us, then."

"Good luck to us," Reijiri echoed him. *"I shall line up to follow the same track as before. We know there are no power lines on that route."*

One wished Reijiri had not said power lines. He began to envision them.

"We shall be moving faster over Separti this time, as well, and for the same reason," Reijiri said. *"Be prepared."*

"I shall be." Bren opened the first bag, testing the strap that should retain it. He gathered as large a quantity of papers as he could hold in one chilled hand, organized everything as best he could, and firmly clamped the second, equally critical bag, with his leg against the seat.

"We are there!" Reijiri exclaimed and the plane banked. The engine sound increased. Bren braced his feet against the pit, maintained a firm grip on the bag with one hand, his fistful of notes in the other.

"Give it a count of seventy, Bren-ji! Then release them!"

He could see the town lights distinctly. He thought he could see the wall. He would have given it half seventy, but Reijiri was undoubtedly reading the wind. He counted. He waited.

The plane banked very steeply. He saw housetops. He released the papers and grabbed new handfuls as fast as he could—he saw people in the lighted streets, people pointing up, reaching up as the papers flew, people waving—some on rooftops, some rising from newly-made little defensive forts of boxes and bags and such in the streets. People had read their message.

Papers flew, a white torrent in the lights from the town, caught by the wind and flying across the roofs and down the street, inhabitants chasing them into nooks and crannies and the edges of the street, paper flying down the side streets. He threw handful after handful and then upended the bag, all in one wild stream, onto the plaza near the docks.

The plane roared up over the masts of fishing-boats and kept rising, rising, as Bren worked to exchange bags, pinning the spent one beneath his knee, pulling the one for Jorida, the smaller one, into his lap. Chilled fingers did not help with the fastenings. He finally resorted to his pocketknife and cut it—dropped the knife, but got the cord undone and the package open while the plane climbed over the darkness of the bay. He gathered a fistful of papers, the same as the other, as many as his hand could possibly hold, sucked in breaths and anticipated that giddy bank and stall at the top of the rise as the climb tugged at the sack and his arms—waiting for the downward pitch.

It came, in darkened heights, and the plane banked extremely, diving toward fire and smoke in the lower town. In the harbor. A ship was burning. Vision blurred. He fought, battered by the wind, to get his papers over the side as fast as he could. There were faint pops, unsure whether it was the engine or gunfire— and fires, at least two, what might be resistance underway in the street. Barricades. Definitely barricades down there.

Fistful after fistful—he bashed his knuckles, releasing papers as he could, getting them back in his face and fearing they might be in Reijiri's. Pull up, he wished Reijiri, completely blind to where they were on the downward rush. Pull up, pull *up.*

Then the engine roared and the pressure dragged at him—with a straight-down memory of the ships and fire and dock off the right wing as they righted themselves and began to climb again. Away from the dark water, up into the light-blinded dark of the sky, and climbing. He thought, for a moment, there was a tiny spot of light on the floor between his feet, but he blinked, and it was gone. Illusion. Possibly it had been his eyes. The pressure might have caused it.

Temporary problem, that . . . he hoped.

He still had the sack, not quite empty. That was all right. They had dumped most of it. There was a fluttery sound off the left wing, but they had had that, from the prior damage.

They were still rising, but moderately. Sanely. Flying straight ahead into the dark.

"*Well done, Bren-ji.*"

"Very well done, Jiri-ji. We did it."

"*It was a good release.*"

"I kept the bag, this time."

"*Indeed.*"

There was silence for a time. Then they banked right: a fairly lengthy adjustment.

And leveled. Headed for Kajiminda, he thought, and on to Najida, and a safe landing. The sun would be rising soon, with chaos in their wake, chaos to occupy the heights and help Cenedi . . . and Banichi . . .

"*We have a problem,*" Reijiri said, disturbing the sense of triumph, "*and there is water under us.*"

"What sort of problem?"

"*Fuel,*" Reijiri said. "*We seem to be losing it fairly rapidly. I believe we have picked up a hole at Jorida—that, rather than a loose line, to judge by the rate it is dropping. Your seat cushion is a life-preserver, Bren-ji, that is usually beneath the seat. We are a coastal clan. I am trying to get us to shore, however.*"

"Which shore?"

"*Ashidama, unfortunately. At this rate, I fear we cannot make Najida; it is questionable we can even make shore in that direction, and there is only woodland there if we do. The grainfields and the roads on the Jorida side, granted we can get there, are the best choice for a landing."*

Ashidama. That turn. The glow he could just see to the right was not dawn. That was—he stretched to check—Jorida. That was far from good news, but it was better news than the dark, cold water under them. Bren drew one breath considering that possibility.

And all possibilities.

"The bus," he said, "will be coming up that road."

"It seems our best option for a landing," Reijiri said, and banked gently left. *"Let us get over land first, shall we, look for the bus, see how far our fuel will hold, and see whether the grainfields look inviting."*

18

"We have no great amount of information," was the report from Cajeiri's elder aishid, his grim, grey-haired caretakers, summoned to his little office as they had come in, before breakfast, before the sun was even up—but he had told Eisi he wanted to see them, at whatever hour.

There was discomfort in his dealings with the elder four. There was always reluctance when he tried to get specifics. They had probably come in from no further away than Guild Headquarters, in the heart of the city, but they might as well be on the space station for all the access he had had to them. They were probably tired. They had probably been up all hours of the night, doing things that might be important to the war in the Marid; and they seemed still to be answering to Guild orders, which was not the way he understood things should go—not for anybody in Father's household—except as Father ordered the Guild.

So he still could not order their comings and goings, though Father could. And maybe Father had sent them back to the Guild, to consult or whatever they did.

Maybe Father had thought he would be so safe inside the apartment he had no need of them, and maybe the Guild needed them. Father had changed his mind on that score, calling them back to watch him. And what this elder aishid thought of him, now, the way they generally looked at him and the youngers, all unreadable and with that shield up—that had never changed.

They likely saw him as a child, a problem that should stay safe in the Bujavid and let adults run the world as they pleased. They probably thought if they just kept him uninformed, that would keep him and his younger aishid safe and harmless. But there was nowhere in the world safe if the worst things happened. And they, more than most, had to know that, too. He had gotten out of bed to deal with them. He had dressed to deal with them, not to be standing there barefoot in his nightshirt and with his hair around his shoulders, trying to get things out of a Guild unit all in uniform. He put on his coat and went to his office, where he had asked Liedi to send them.

There were five chairs there, for exactly such a conference. Rieni, Janachi, Haniri, Onami—all were seated, when he came in, all frowning, anticipating a request for information which they would avow was impossible to share.

And all having the power to report, to places he could not regulate, things that they might suspect . . . or faults they saw whenever they were here.

It had become a standoff. He kept things from them. They kept things from him. At times he wanted things the way they had been, but he could not order them to leave his service. Only Father had that power, even if he were grown. And clearly they saw their assignment as to keep him safe—and to prevent him going on such missions as he had sent Lord Tatiseigi.

He had determined all on his own that he should not go to Dur himself, had he not, much as he would wish to have flown where Liedi had? He had done that.

And that letter of Father's, that said there would be no regency, while they were talking about possibly losing mani—*that* had come down while they were gone, had it not? Everything had changed. And they had not been here to know that.

Everything had changed. It meant it was not games he was playing. He began a fight literally for his life, his father's, his mother's, and his sister's lives; and mani's. If the succession did suddenly grow thin, in losing mani, and therefore the East, and himself with only a paper claim on the aijinate—these four Assassins would turn very, very important.

And they had to be his. Not the other way around. He had to use them. Or they were useless.

"I have talked to my father," he said, taking his seat, as they all sat down. He picked every word carefully. "I know I am young. But you should know, nadiin, and you may ask him about this: I have not spent the last several years playing with toys. I have not had time. I have only had Boji for games. And he is going away. Now Father says should anything happen, there will be *no regency*, no matter how old I am, or am not, and that I would take up the aijinate ahead of my great-grandmother. I do not want that day. But it could happen."

They were, perhaps, surprised by that statement. It was hard to read them. They said nothing. But he thought he read that much.

"So there are no toys, nadiin. I know my great-grandmother. I know Lord Tatiseigi better than my father does. I did all I did to send Lord Tatiseigi to her, and I am not sorry about it, except it was not as well planned as it might have been—even if I had consulted my own aishid. I tried to keep them clean of all of it, because I was worrying about you being upset with them and I cannot defend them from you. That is *not* how things should be. But it was. I apologize for not trusting you, if it was unjustified. But you were not here. I could not inform you."

Rieni, Guild senior, started to say something. Cajeiri lifted a hand, a *no*, and Rieni stayed, to his slight surprise, silent.

"That is one thing," he continued in that silence. "And when I realized I had not thought about the Guild encampment, I waited a certain time, went to my father, and the Guild at Najida was warned to let them land safely. It seems now that mani is faring better than we thought. But *all* of that is not the point. The point *is* that, in my opinion—and I have talked about it with Father—I did the right thing, to send Uncle down there. He is protected by the camp and in reach of the Red Train. As is mani. As is nand' Bren. So I am not stupid. *Stupid* would be for people to lie to me or to keep things from me. Because I *will* do things if I think they need to be done. Father agrees that I am to have the same information he does, as soon as he does. That has changed. His door will always open to me: *that* has changed. And you may ask him about that. But from now, you have to tell me things you know.

And you have to do what I ask you to do. If I cannot depend on that, or if anyone else's orders can prevent that, I need to know it. If you have orders from any other place, I need to know it. I have to have a way to contact you at all hours, and I need to know that you will deliver my messages only where I send them and go only where I send you. It is the reason of the eight, is it not, that *half* of an eight always be able to be sent?"

"It is."

"I have to trust you. And the more I trust you, the more I will tell you. But the Guild should never call you away from me. And from now on, that also includes my younger aishid. Given what Father said about the succession—if you are half of my eight, you should never be called away from me."

There was a long, uncomfortable silence.

"There are situations of great delicacy," Rieni said. "I do not say that we would have left here without consulting your father. We have not felt empowered to advise you."

"From now on, this cannot happen."

"Let us also point out, however, young gentleman, that part of the staff of this apartment may not be permanent. This is a security concern. We have hesitated to be too forthcoming in a household with new, perhaps impermanent staff and man'chi that may not yet be settled. As for your younger aishid, they are . . . younger. But they are very broadly informed, and not, as you say, stupid. You have not been badly served. We will not object to informing them."

That was possibly the most pleasing thing this aishid had ever said to him. But it was very, very hard to relax his guard with these four, which was what that compliment might hope.

"Tariko and Dimaji will be permanent," Cajeiri said in his most businesslike way. "So you have had time. You have seen what we are. I have told you all the truth. You would be of great value, and I do not expect man'chi, being as young as I am—I would not expect it. But we have made a place for you; and I think if you had been with us, and informed me, and perhaps used permissions you have, we could have gotten Uncle down to Najida a great deal easier."

"You intend to include us in such operations."

He set his jaw. "We certainly would."

There was a subtle shift of eyes, one to the other, unreadable. Then just a single line of Rieni's face changed.

"Nandi," Rieni said, "this current operation still being unresolved, what *else* do you want?"

"Information, nadi. As much information as you can get, about mani, about what she is doing, everything—without spilling anything. And fix our communications so you can get what we need to know, and what my father should know."

There was quiet a moment. Then Rieni said: "Do you want a report?"

"On the situation with my great-grandmother, yes."

"The aiji-dowager has ordered Midagi, in command of the camp, to advance his force to Kajiminda, leaving three units for protection of Najida, and go to Separti by way of Kajiminda's local road, cross the bay with local transport, and deploy on Jorida waterfront. Cenedi, departing Kajiminda estate by other transportation, has taken five units southward to Ashidama Peninsula, to take the causeway to Jorida heights, coordinating with Midagi as he does so. The aiji-dowager has sealed Kajiminda, and one of Lord Geigi's subordinates on the space station, in communication with the dowager, has now taken over all aspects of defense of the estate. Lord Geigi himself is dealing with an emergency on the space station."

Pieces tumbled into frightening agreement. His heart beat fast. Jorida was a fortress. The bay—he knew the size of the southern bays—having experienced one of them with no skill, no oars, and a very small boat. It was not posturing, this movement of forces. War had spread out of the Marid to where mani was, and everybody he most valued was in the middle of it. The only consolation was Kajiminda being under Lord Geigi's protection, and Lord Geigi or whoever sat at Lord Geigi's boards could deal with any enemy who tried to attack it—while Lord Geigi was busy trying to save the space station, and people up there were being fools.

"So where are they now? What is going on?"

"Midagi's Guild force has passed Kajiminda estate and is advancing on Separti. Cenedi, moving west on Ashidama, will take the causeway that connects Ashidama Peninsula to Jorida. Midagi will cross from Separti to take the Jorida waterfront. From both sides, units will deal with the enemy, whether in the town or in the citadel. Your great-grandmother, the paidhi-aiji, and, we assume, Lord Tatiseigi, Lord Reijiri, and the candidate for Ajuri, are all in Kajiminda, likely with Lord Tatiseigi's aishid. Likely the five units with Cenedi are his own double unit, and that of the paidhi-aiji, with Banichi; Lord Reijiri's aishid, and the guard assigned to the candidate for Ajuri."

All at risk.

"Do you know the geography of the Southwest Coast, young gentleman?"

"I know it extremely well," he said, which was true. His heart had beat with anger at the beginning of it all. Now it was acute anxiety. "Nand' Bren has stayed with mani?" Surely he would. Nand' Bren took chances. But Banichi would not have him involved.

"We have no specific word," Rieni said, "regarding civilians. We assume Lord Tatiseigi's aishid has remained at Kajiminda: they are all aged past field service. The other units would total the five we are informed Cenedi has."

Banichi would not want nand' Bren to go. Cenedi absolutely would not want him to go—Cenedi was all regulations when he was under mani's orders. That was so. And if they had that many units moving the way Rieni said, it was all calculated. There would be discussion. Units would coordinate. They would offer the Shadow Guild a chance to surrender. The Shadow Guild actually *might*, but they would be lying. And Cenedi and Banichi certainly knew that. Sensible people were in charge down there, though he knew nothing about Midagi. It might actually finish the Shadow Guild. And that was good news, amid a lot else that upset his stomach.

"Thank you," he said. Maybe, with as much detail as they had just told him, and the difference between what they guessed and what they knew—it *was* everything. He hoped so. He hoped with all else that was going on, and all the uncomfortable changes, that he and the elder aishid he had to live with were settling into a way that would work.

"Nandi," Rieni said, with a little nod. Not coldly, not sullenly.

Rieni *had* told him as much as they knew. Which was not enough. But at least it was not disaster down there.

The valiant engine kept on—a balance between Reijiri's getting them over land and into the path of the bus as soon as possible—and their fuel leak. They were not pushing the speed now, having achieved as much altitude as Reijiri deemed prudent, concerning the fuel consumption.

Reaching land to the south was the first priority; and once over land, they would go east as long as they could, along the shoreline road that the bus would use. It was all grainfields ahead, and roadway that might, theoretically, be a better emergency strip. But not having a clear view of that road was potentially disastrous, especially if at any point it was cut into a bank with little clearance for the wings.

Ultimately, they would take what they could get.

"We can glide," Reijiri said, *"even once we run out of fuel—we can glide so well I have generally found the petal sails not worth the weight. Do not be alarmed if the engine cuts out entirely, Bren-ji. We still have altitude."*

"One is very glad to know it," Bren said. Over the side, the view was still the ink-black of the bay. Which would be a very cold bath, assuming that Reijiri could coax the plane into a sort of gentle slide to a stop in the water and not tip them end over end.

And upon that came the darker thought, that maintaining personal awareness of direction if they did end up in the water would not be a given. Swimming, but swimming on the wrong heading in the dark . . .

He did not want to think about that. He concentrated instead on trying to detect any possible view of land under them—the forward direction being only a view of the engine—but getting a very good look over the side meant releasing the safety belt, and he did not want to do that, either. Besides, getting them a good landing was Reijiri's job, all of it. "You are clearly doing excellently well," he said. Encouragement might at least be some comfort. "Can you see anything?"

"The back of your head," Reijiri reminded him, a strained attempt at humor. *"But I have a clear view of our compass, and south is unmistakable. Unless we have crossed the whole of Ashidama Peninsula, which I assure you is not remotely possible, there will be land ahead of us."*

Anywhere else on the continent there might be *some* beacon to guide them. There was absolutely nothing but seasonally tended fields on Ashidama Peninsula, so far as he knew. As for seeing their way down after they did find land—the moon was up, but in its last quarter, and if it helped Reijiri, it did not help human eyes much at all.

The plane banked a little.

"I think that might be water's edge," Reijiri said. *"A faint, faint pale line. Do you see it?"*

Bren looked over the side, eyes straining against the dark. "There might be." He feared it was a lie.

The engine coughed. The plane leveled out and resumed its steady ninefold heartbeat. Reijiri applied no fuel-consuming rush, just held steady toward the hope of grainfields. A broad, unpopulated hump of a peninsula where they could hope to come down in some gentle fashion.

Any half-gentle fashion. Anything in which the safety belt held.

How would cultivated fields be? Give or take plowed ground, perhaps less smooth than the untilled meadow at Kajiminda.

But they had altitude. Reijiri had landed, he had said, in many a grainfield across the north.

Reijiri had regaled him with, in the course of the flight, other dicey moments, learning to fly in the northern grainfields. They had not all gone well. The left wing had undergone repair.

It was not necessarily information he wanted. But the conversation maintained a thread of connection in the dark.

Altitude, Reijiri had said. That was a good thing. Altitude gave Reijiri a lot more time to do things.

"How much fuel have we?" Bren asked, thinking of the bus, and the single strand of road that connected Jorida to everywhere else.

"*It is getting very low. We are into the reserve. But we are lighter for it.*"

"One appreciates your cheerfulness in our situation."

"*One appreciates your appreciation, nandi. You are an excellent companion.*"

He *liked* Reijiri. Humanly speaking. He had liked him before, and now found reasons upon reasons to appreciate him, whatever the appreciation Reijiri had for him. "I can think of no one I had rather have sitting behind me tonight, nandi. You will get us down. You will surely get us down."

"*Getting down is a given,*" Reijiri said. "*One deserves no credit in that. But I shall do my—There indeed is land below us, nandi-ji! We are about to cross the edge!*"

"Excellent! Excellently done, Jiri-ji!" He drew larger breaths, one after the other in the rushing wind, chilled through, and without feeling in his hands—but now with the assurance of solid ground, however they managed to meet it, and the added fact that their engine was still going. He kept quiet and listened to the beat of that engine, steady, promising safety ahead, possibly even a little chance of picking a landing spot, and even meeting the bus.

"*I have no precise idea where we are coming in,*" Reijiri said, "*but my estimation is we are closer to Jorida than to the back of the bay and that the bus would not have gotten this far yet. How good is that road, do you think?*"

"My guess is that it has had maintenance at harvest—but perhaps none at the end of it. Cenedi took that into account. One would expect they are well *onto* the coastal road, perhaps halfway to Jorida. Where are we?"

"*I would judge, about a quarter of the way from Jorida to the back of the bay.*" A pause. Then: "*What would be your choice, Bren-ji? To meet the bus if we can, or to try to set down now?*"

"My choice would be the bus," he said. He was cold, he was tired, sleep had been at a premium for days, and the prospect of joining his aishid in an action called for resources he was not sure he had . . . But a long struggle to hike back to Kajiminda from a problematic landing was unthinkable—a prospect made only more problematic if one of them were injured in the landing. He had no desire to be left with the plane while Reijiri hiked back to try to find the bus, and God help Reijiri if their positions were reversed.

And if *both* of them were incapacitated—

"Definitely the bus."

The plane banked gently east. *"I agree. We are now indeed over land, Bren-ji, and I have no trouble distinguishing the road!"*

"Excellent! This far from Jorida, the bus should be using its headlights. We should be able to spot them." He deeply regretted not having the communicator at the moment. With it, he could call Cenedi, he could call Geigi, for that matter, and ask whether Geigi's eyes could get them to the bus. But he could not so much as mention that communications system to Reijiri. "We might turn our own lights on when we see them. They will know who it is, with no doubt, and we might be some help to them at Jorida, if only to guard the bus."

"I would agree. We shall simply follow the road as long as the fuel holds out . . . and do not worry, Bren. The plane does not drop out of the sky when the engine stops. We shall get down in fairly good order, right beside the road if I can find a smooth stretch that is wide enough—not to obstruct the bus."

"Excellent," Bren said, and allowed himself a dozen quieter breaths. They would not have to swim. They had land under them. He was not happy with the thought of the engine giving out, but Reijiri swore it was no problem . . . and given the scattered availability of fueling opportunities and the vast extent of farmland in the north of the aishidi'tat, where Reijiri had learned to fly, it did seem Reijiri might have had experience with uncertain landings, and know something about his fuel use. An excellent pilot, he swore to himself, no matter he had once sworn Reijiri was the most irresponsible young man on the planet—

They flew on, neither gaining nor losing altitude—occasionally banking a little to get a view, and truing up their course a little.

There was no view of the bus yet. No headlights, however dim, in the distance. No sign, yet, of dawn. There might be a bank of cloud in the west. There was a scarcity of stars there, when he twisted about to look.

And one began to worry. It seemed like a very long time— though they were flying conservatively, not climbing, not accelerating, not doing anything sudden.

They might be losing altitude—he thought at one point, on one of their small reorientations to have a look below.

Then as if it had done all it could, and had no more to give, the faithful, fortunate engine gave a considerable cough. And a second.

"One regrets. I am going to climb just a little. I want to give us as much vertical distance as possible. That may give us more choices about landing."

"Yes," Bren said, an atevi-style yes of agreement. Consent. Absolute—there being no damn choice else. His heart rate picked up. He felt the slight acceleration.

Then there was another cough. And another. They had, he was sure, achieved a little more altitude, and then had to laugh at himself. How would he know? He could barely make out the difference between land and water, when he could see below them.

He began experiencing a ridiculous series of shivers, which might legitimately be the cold—he tucked his hands in his armpits and tried to ignore his stomach upset—and might as equally be the result of sheer terror. Reijiri said it was not a problem, and he sounded calm. Confident. Veteran of many, *dozens* of tight situations, if his stories were to be believed. Reijiri was doing what he knew to do, and considering other chances Reijiri had taken, one was inclined to believe Reijiri could get them down.

The bus should have been in view by now. He was sure they had gone far enough, difficult as it was to judge. Either way, they were going down, and the shivers eased, the last dregs of adrenaline ebbing out. Now, of all times, when he *had* to summon it up—he and Reijiri would have to hike a wooded road all the way back to Kajiminda if they had somehow overshot the bus—and given that the clear view was always over the side, in the dark, they could conceivably have missed it.

Cough. Again.

"If we have gotten beyond them, we can walk back," he said. "Tracks will tell us."

"*I am going to have to—*" Reijiri began, and then whipped steeply over on the right wing and gunned it. "Gods *less fortunate!*"

There was black on one side, starry sky on the other and no view but the valiant engine in front. The engine coughed as the plane leveled out.

"*Cliff,*" Reijiri said, as the engine continued to cough. Lights under the lower wings flared on, illuminating the underside of the plane, spreading a glow on the yellow wings and struts and otherwise blinding them to the night, except the tops of brush below. The engine continued to cough. "*We are about to lose the engine. I am sorry about that!*"

"That would be the road back there," Bren said, informationally. "The cliffs are the edge of the Taisigin!"

"*We shall turn,*" Reijiri said, and there was a forced calm in his voice as they began to do exactly that. "*Did you see anything of the ground?*"

More than I wanted, was the honest answer, but it was not useful information. He tried to restructure the image he had had in that one glance over the right wing. "Scattered brush. If that is the Taisigi reserve above, then it should be grainfields west and south, not that far. And an access road separating the fields."

"*Do you know if they plow east to west or north to south?*"

"I am sorry! I have no idea!"

"*No matter—we have no choice anyway.*" There was quiet now, the nine cylinders gone utterly silent, the heartbeat of the plane given way to the rush of air and the mechanical movement of moveable surfaces. The propeller rotated occasionally with nothing from the engine. "*If you have anything to put between yourself and the forward panel, Bren-ji, put it there to cushion your head!*"

He had the empty bags. He feverishly unclipped them, rolled them into a tight mass and shoved them against the forward panel. Then he tested his seat belt with one hand, took one useless look at the yellow struts around him and braced himself, hands crossed.

"Brace!" Reijiri shouted.

Then the wheels touched, Bren met the crushed bags, jolted back, met the upper and lower belts as the plane bounced and touched again, swerved and took hold, lurched, lost the ground and came down again in slow motion and a series of impacts as they continued to bounce, one, two, three times before they tilted sharply to the left in a violent skid and neck-jerking half-spin.

Motion stopped. There was silence, except the ping of cooling metal. They had settled at a decided tilt, left lower wingtip on the ground or close to it.

Was he hurt? He was not sure. The belt had held. His body assured him of that. Various parts of him were bruised. His neck had suffered. One hand, still involved in the roll of stiff canvas bags, might be bleeding on the back side, crushed against the panel. Shoulder and ribs were going to be sore. "Reijiri?" he asked, but the com was out, dead as the lights, and his voice sounded thin and lonely. He unbuckled. That click was audible in what was, overall, deathly stillness. *"Reijiri?"*

"Bren-ji," the answer came back—faintly, or the helmet was muffling the sound. Bren shoved the goggles up, unsnapped the chin strap to help his hearing.

"Reijiri, are you all right?"

"As landings go, we are upright. It is east to west, Bren-ji. This was a good thing."

East to . . . laughter, more than half hysterical, threatened.

The question about plowing. East to west. As they had landed. East to west as the wheels had tracked.

And they were somewhere in a grainfield, amid the stubble, tilted, but alive. In the dark, after what felt like a lifetime of the steady beat of the engine, an utter stillness had settled, save the ping of metal and the scrape and thump of their own movements.

"We are down," he agreed hoarsely. "Bravely done, Jiri-ji. Splendidly done. I do not think anything is broken. How are you?"

"Relatively whole. The plane—fairly so."

Bren found himself shaking as he reached a hand toward the rim of the cockpit. "We will get your plane out of here. We shall get it back safely, if it takes Shejidani force to do it, and, I swear, restore it to perfection."

"One would be most grateful for that." A moment of silence, then the sounds of movement behind. "We are overheated, and this is dry stubble. We risk a field fire. Can you get out, Bren-ji?"

"I think so." He wanted the water bottle he had taken aboard, but wherever it was, it was not in reach. He abandoned it and anything else he had brought, just began to haul himself upright in the tilted geometry, to get hold of a strut and get his legs over the rim. Reijiri was doing the same, and the whole plane quivered and rocked to their movements.

"Go forward," Reijiri said. "Mind, step near the fuselage and hold to the struts. I shall go behind you. It will be a drop to the ground, but not a far one."

Moving along the textured footpath and holding himself from a fall strained muscles he had not yet tested. He reached the edge of the wing, poised in a wave of heat from the engine, and there was nothing for it but to jump.

He meant to catch his balance, and his legs just did not support the effort—he made a full-length landing on the sharp grain stubble and uneven ground, and rolled to the side as he heard Reijiri on the wing above him. He struggled to his feet as Reijiri followed him, landing in a crouch. Reijiri then straightened slowly, regarding the plane with, surely, regret.

"At least we have no fuel to spill," Reijiri said, and shifted into place a crossbody bag he had managed to bring with him. "We should go, Bren-ji, if we hope to find the road and the bus. There was no sign of them below us. They must to be yet to come."

"If they have not met an obstacle they cannot pass." Plans would change radically if somehow they could not bring the bus through. The pincer plan would evaporate. They would have to rely entirely on the Guild force, at much greater risk in crossing the bay—and Cenedi's smaller force would get there a day late, giving the Shadow Guild time to scatter in this direction at whatever strength they had managed to get out of Jorida. Cenedi's group might still have a function.

They, however, were right where the Shadow Guild would pass on any attempt to escape by land, in a sniper's haven between the cliffs and the back bay forest.

Hostages for the taking.

"We should indeed get over to the road," Bren said. The safety belt had bruised, there was strain in neck and shoulders that was apt to seize up, given rest, and his voice was far from steady. "As quickly as we can manage. The bus—may just have been delayed. If so—"

"I have water. I have a compass. The maps. A pistol and a box of ammunition." Reijiri sat down unexpectedly. "I am sorry. I think I need to rest a moment."

"Deservedly." Bren stood with legs braced, thinking he might do the same, and managed a calculated, less abrupt descent to the stubble. He had the familiar weight of his pistol still in his coat pocket. He had not lost that, small defense that it was. "One hopes we have stirred up enough trouble in Jorida and Separti to make us a lesser priority, but I fear we are out of the action."

"If we cannot reach the bus, one hopes they will think we are safe in Kajiminda and just keep going, as the plan is. We can rescue ourselves."

"Indeed."

They each had a mouthful of water. The air around them had a petroleum taint—from the plane, and themselves. For a few moments they sat, time measured in the cooling of the metal and the ebb and rise of a gentle breeze. Finally, with a sigh, Reijiri got up, consulted his compass, then silently indicated direction. "Straight north to the farm roads," he said. "If they have gotten beyond us, we could never catch them. If they have not—then we follow the road toward Kajiminda and hope to find them stalled by some washout. I would recommend the latter. There is a hint of dawn."

Trust atevi eyes to pick that up first. It was murk, still, to human eyes. And muscles were definitely trying to stiffen. Bren struggled again to his feet, thankful for Reijiri's helping hand, but once he was upright, and because Reijiri's longer strides tended to outpace him and Reijiri was younger, with more stamina: "We do not limp at the same pace. Go on ahead of me, Jiri-ji. I will be behind you. I cannot lose you. It is a simple straight line. And you can warn me of any pitfalls."

"Yes," Reijiri said, and lost no time passing him and widening the lead. Stars were fading and the land definitely tilted downward, toward the north and the shore. To the west, scattered monumental rocks loomed, too large to move, breaking the sameness of the stubble; and more than that Bren could not see. He just knew that cliffs, the abrupt demarcation of Taisigi land, had shed those enormous stones, the same as he knew the gentle downhill underfoot would eventually lead them to the Ashidama shore.

One hoped the bus had run without lights and somehow gotten past them . . . and if that had happened, if the bus was already underway as planned, the attack on Jorida might still come off. If it came down to the Guild force alone, it would be messier, longer . . . if a confrontation happened at all. There was always the chance the Shadow Guild would opt not to engage, but would take to the sea and escape the moment they read those flyers. Much depended on how many had actually arrived with Tiajo, and whether a single ship could handle them. By what he had seen in that final dive, one of those larger ships had been burning, a large, out-of-control blaze, possibly sunk by now.

But one way and another, the force from Najida *would* get onto Jorida and sort out the Master's problem for him, if the Master was still alive. It was frustrating that things on this side of the bay seemed to be, at the very least, badly behind schedule—fault of God knew what—one of those massive boulders on the road, a succession of trees too large to take out in time—they *would* have explosives with them. But hopefully they had met nothing more than that.

He twice regretted handing that communicator to Banichi. With it, he could call and reassure Cenedi they were alive. It was possible, even, that the bus itself had seen the plane go down—and also possible that Geigi or someone Geigi had appointed was keeping an eye on the situation, might even be able to track two tiny warm bodies crossing the grain stubble and advise the bus. It was going to be a long, slow hike otherwise—but compared to things that might have gone wrong, the bus being stalled on the backside of the bay was a far greater calamity.

Damn . . . he *did not* want an already delayed mission diverting from Jorida to search for them. Stopping to pick them up was one thing. Diverting the whole mission . . . God, no. And his brain was running in circles. Now even *he* could see the first glow of morning, as he followed Reijiri. Matching strides with a younger, taller ateva was impossible, and common sense said if Reijiri just got to the road and waited, there was no need of him trying so hard, but he *wanted* to make that intercept, and despite his resignation to the possibility—he just could not resign some hope of having the bus turn up, even late. Reijiri was well ahead of him—far ahead of him, now. There was just the contrast of a dark figure against the pale grain stubble to keep him in view. But now, to the best his eyes could make out, the stubbled field had a dark rim that might be the bay itself, and at the edge of the bay, had to be the road. If his eyes were not lying, they had almost made it, and surely there would be tire tracks— or not—to tell them whether the bus was ahead of them or behind them.

He had no—

A line of darker brush or rock moved as Reijiri passed. Black against the stubble.

He immediately crouched down, going for the gun in his pocket. There was motion—a dozen shadows out of nowhere enveloped Reijiri. Eight, ten, much more than ten of them moving in the dark. He saw that and went flat on the ground. They were outnumbered, caught, and in an ambush, just short of the road. If he could stay clear and free, the bus was coming—that was his thought. Shooting was the last thing he wanted to do.

Until, possibly, he saw the bus. It was the only way he could possibly call for help.

He heard voices. At least one Marid accent in the one that rose above the others. He caught enough to know they were looking for him, but not enough to betray them as Shadow Guild. He could fire now, randomly, hoping the bus was near enough to hear and investigate, but that would more than likely provoke a fusillade in return.

Even if they took him, too, he could trust his aishid, when they had finally gotten control of the whole of Ashidama, to take measures to get them out.

As for heroics—Jago's sternest tones rang in memory, a certain hillside, and her view of his attempting to protect *her*.

He shouted out as loudly and authoritatively as he could, still flat amid the grain stubble: "Nadiin, I am Bren-paidhi, of the aishidi'tat. My companion is the lord of Dur. Harming us in any way will bring you a great deal of trouble."

"Bren-nandi!" The answer came back, a voice of recent memory. "Is the plane yours or theirs?"

God, it sounded like *Machigi*.

"Ours!" he shouted back. "Reijiri-nandi, are you all right?"

"I am here!" Reijiri's voice came back. "They claim to be Taisigi."

He found himself ridiculously shaking, getting to his knees, trying to gain his feet. "Of Lord Machigi?" he asked.

"In person," the answer came back, definitely Machigi's dry, sardonic tone. "Follow the peacemaker, to find the next war! You are indeed Bren-nandi?"

Rhetorical: his voice, human amid atevi, was fairly distinctive. "Nandi, with the lord of Dur. One would appreciate the guns redirected." He was aware of the clicks of safeties—and multiple splinters of stubble embedded in his hand as he thumbed the safety on his own pistol and pocketed it. He began the too-long and shaky hike toward the shadow that was Reijiri and a good number of Taisigi. "We came under fire at Jorida—we were losing fuel and had to come back over land, attempting to find our own force." His voice wanted to break as he walked, and he was determined to avoid the humiliation of having his legs fold under him or to put a foot in a hole. They had come within speaking range now, and even human eyes began to make out details in at least a dozen shadow-shapes against the lesser dark. "Might you have seen a bus, nandi?"

"We have." Machigi indicated the northwest. "The bus, the force from the camp. What have we? Shejidan asserting a claim on Ashidama?"

Sharp-pointed, that. And himself and Reijiri in Taisigi hands, with Taisigi trade and security at issue.

"I can say to my honest belief, nand' Machigi, that the dowager's move is absolutely intended to take down the renegade Guild—to which end she has urged Ashidama to rise. She has *specifically* denied any territorial claims, nandi." Damn it, he was physically shaking, cold through and through. He steadied his voice. "In the interest of which we have twice flown over Separti and Jorida, showering them with notes to that effect. The dowager is more than content to leave shipping interests to others. She is specifically concerned with rail, and she is very serious about connecting the Taisigin to the network . . . which will indeed force changes on Ashidama and its monopoly, but no, nandi, this is *not* a conquest. The aishidi'tat itself is not desirous of upsetting the dowager's arrangement with you. She is denying the renegades—and Tiajo—a foothold. Their *last* foothold. At which point Jorida should be anxious to welcome Taisigi ships . . . with what you do not choose to ship by rail."

It was a long speech, made into the dark, and without, he feared, the greatest coherency.

After a long, silent moment, Machigi asked: "Are you *cold*, paidhi?"

"I am *damned* cold, nandi. I am also telling you the truth."

"Luck is with you. Your bus should be making its way through fairly soon," Machigi said. "What is your plan with it? To assault Jorida?"

"Delicately," Bren said. "If you would help us, nandi, not so much the appearance of Taisigi in Jorida—which might have problems—but in reception of any Shadow Guild who attempt to flee by the causeway—"

"Nadiin," Machigi said to his companions. "What do you think?"

It seemed affirmative. Bren thought so. He walked the final few steps, generally toward Reijiri, dimly aware first that there was a distinct lightening of the horizon and then that he could actually distinguish Reijiri from the Taisigi. Both of them were free. The Taisigi around them seemed disposed to cooperate. *Machigi* seemed apt to involve himself, which was both a bonus and a problem.

Reijiri, seated on a rock, handed him a flask. Thinking it was water, he took a healthy mouthful . . . and spat it out. It was *not* water. But it was good, it was not alcoholic, and it held none of the taint he had learned the hard way to associate with the alkaloids that were deadly to humans and favored by the atevi. He took another, more cautious sip, then handed it back to Reijiri.

There was a sound other than the quiet movements of the Taisigi about them . . . Reijiri turned in that direction, and the Taisigi did.

They did not see the lights yet. But those came, two lights and a general glow, and the sound of the bus engine in the distance. Bren moved in that direction, toward the road, not even considering the Taisigi. Reijiri got to his feet and did the same.

Taisigi passed them, going in the same direction.

"Much too slow, nandiin," Machigi said close at hand, and ahead of them, two of the Taisigi moved at a much faster clip toward an intercept.

19

Machigi was right. They would not have made it, at Bren's pace. When they arrived, the bus had stopped, avoiding the first Taisigi, who was standing in its headlights, waving empty hands. It stopped, let off one of its company, and that person—Bren thought it might be Banichi—looked uphill in their direction.

Bren wanted to run, but while whatever he had drunk provided energy, it did not provide steadiness of stomach . . . or knees. His gait was entirely uncertain on the slight downhill, on the slick stubble, and Reijiri moved no faster. Nor, for that matter, did Machigi and the Taisigi, not apparently anxious to precede him into contact with the Guild.

Banichi, indeed, a silhouette against the headlights, did not move, watching, fearing, perhaps, that a sudden move on his part would trigger Taisigin reflexes. But the moment Bren walked into the light—perhaps looking a little ragged—Banichi came toward him, holding out a hand to steady him as they met. Bren clung there a few breaths, managed to gasp out: "We distributed the papers." He was out of breath for anything more, except: "Reijiri made a fairly good landing."

He was content to breathe for a moment, unsure his knees would hold up. The rest of his aishid had gotten off the bus. Jago. Tano. Algini.

Teimi, Reijiri's Guild senior, was right behind them. Machigi, his aishid and his rangers, were at the edge of the headlights—no one having been shot by mistake, thank God. Cenedi joined Banichi, with Casimi beside him.

"The papers are delivered, nadi," Bren said. "We had to land. Fuel leak. Lord Machigi found us. He is willing to join us."

Reading Cenedi's face in good daylight was not easy. In half-silhouette in the headlights it was impossible. But, grim-faced, Cenedi nodded, a strangely easy acceptance of Taisigi presence, to Bren's own thinking.

"We have a meeting to make," Cenedi said. "Nand' Machigi, there is room for some in the aisle; and you are welcome. There are baggage ties atop, recessed, a slim handhold, but it will be very rough. We have to make speed. We are losing the night and we have a rendezvous to make."

As Banichi began to move him toward the bus, Bren felt a body-warmed object press into his hand. The new com. His. That he had given to Banichi.

He felt the urge to laugh: it was a little late now.

He pressed it back into Banichi's hand. "Better you have it." His voice had gone thready. "If you need Geigi, or Tabini, Nichi-ji, independent of me or Cenedi, use it."

Banichi pocketed it, then threw an arm around him, supporting him toward the bus steps, which loomed dauntingly steep at the moment. Jago went up, Banichi outright lifted him into Jago's reach and Jago pulled him aboard, then steered him to his usual aisle seat with more haste than gentleness. Reijiri came aboard, his aishid following, then Cenedi, Casimi, Machigi, his personal guard and five or six Taisigi rangers as the bus rocked and re-sounded to the efforts of other Taisigi taking to the roof up a baggage access ladder. Bren leaned his head back against the seat and shut his eyes, resigning care of anything at the moment. Job done.

At least . . . his part and Reijiri's part was done: they might still be wiser to try to hike several hours back to Kajiminda. Finding the bus might have been their object in getting down, but they had not planned to be as shaken up as they were. Getting aboard the bus and inserting himself into a Guild operation might be one of the stupider things he had ever done, but Reijiri had not protested; and straggling back alone only hoping the road was clear of action aimed at Kajiminda did not seem that grand an idea either . . . more, their bodyguards would resist letting him and Reijiri make that hike alone, taking a major part of Cenedi's force out of the action or at very least distracting them. In truth, they had had no *good* solution, from the moment a bullet pierced the fuel tank. They were alive, they were momentarily safe. He suspected his thinking was not at its finest at the moment—but he had a seat. Reijiri did. And there might be something useful he and Reijiri *could* do at Jorida once the Guild sorted it all out. They were authority. Their presence, under threat, authorized their protectors to take certain actions, unrestricted. That could become useful.

If he had a brain left, which at the moment was a serious question.

The bus shook to the overhead sort-out, shut its door—Nawari was in the driver's seat, and that was good. The engine revved and the bus moved, leaning and lurching in a way that could not be easy on those holding on atop.

Banichi dropped into his accustomed seat in the first row. Jago slipped past Bren into her accustomed window seat, set a hand on his, and he let himself relax into her familiar warmth, let his head rest against her shoulder. God, he was exhausted.

"One feared you might have passed," he said. "What held you up?"

"Road improvement," Jago said. "How far did you have to walk?"

"Not all that far." A residual shiver, though the whole bus was a refuge of warmth and he was sweating. Shock, he thought, and tried to even out his breathing and relax taut muscles—which refused to let go. "It is cold up there. Colder than you would think."

A voice above him, in the aisle, asked: "What are the Taisigi doing here?"

Cenedi.

"They saw the plane come down. They were watching you."

"And Machigi? He was to be in the Marid."

"I have no idea, nadi."

In front of him, Banichi turned in his seat, an arm along the seat back. "Any sight of Midagi's company as you went?"

"Maybe." A convulsive shiver. Jago slipped an arm about him. "We expected them to be arriving on the grounds fairly well as we were taking off, an hour, hour and a half ago. There were lights . . . Motorized units should . . . should have reached Separti. No—no word from him, yet?"

"Not yet," Cenedi said. "He will initiate contact between us when he begins the bay crossing. Or if he meets opposition in Separti. When did you make the drop?"

When? He had no clear way to judge. Accuracy mattered, but he had no idea how long since they had turned back, how long they had stayed aloft, how long they had walked . . . He raked through visual memory, sifted fatigue-hazed impressions, *tried* to recall places, put things in sequence, Guild-fashion. "Everything was on schedule, Midagi was behind us, all good to Separti. Lights were on. People welcoming the notes. We crossed to Jorida, made our run—that went off. Citadel courtyard was lighted, no sight of people at all. Lower streets—a lot of people. One of the ships was burning. Haze. We pulled up, we got out over the bay before Lord Reijiri realized we had a fuel leak . . . not likely to make Kajidama shore. Decided to find you." He shut his eyes, trying to rouse the image. "Quayside. Fire definitely on the ships. Both still looked afloat."

Banichi said, from beyond Cenedi. "Help from the locals. A problem when Guild arrives."

"At what point," Cenedi asked, "*where* did you take gunfire?"

"Near the citadel. Maybe from it. I am not sure. Lord Reijiri might have a clearer idea."

Cenedi and Banichi moved on, with that. Mercifully. Bren shut his eyes, but could not shut down the memory, now evoked, of that passage down the slant of Jorida's streets. And the vast black under them, while they were leaking fuel. And the buildings, warehouses, dark warehouses, many of them, up around the citadel walls. Jorida was not a layout of streets. It was a stack of walls and roofs with no great number of streets . . . maybe just one street, winding back and forth.

But *someone* had set a fire in the harbor. Someone had shot at them. Two sorts of opinion, in that stacked pastry cake of a town.

There were the people. The Master. The Shadow Guild. And, very soon, Separti seeming of a disposition to help—there was going to be yet another force on harbor level.

The causeway—that, they had not seen. *He* had not seen. If it came in from the Ashidama side of Jorida, it might come in higher up than the harbor. He wished he had asked these questions. They had seemed not his problem, back when the Guild was planning how they would do this. *He* had been too busy writing the text for the flyer.

His mind tried to construct it in the same colors, black and lamplit stone, that memory held, but he could not do it. Beyond the windshield the world was acquiring light, too much light, for eyes that wanted sleep. He hurt. He moved his head, hoping not to have muscles freeze, and Jago drew him closer as the bus jolted and rocked. Grain stubble on the left, rocks and slope to the bay on the right, a solid if rutted road between. No more falling. A limit to tilting. The bus was warm, even over-warm, the air flavored with gun oil, leather, and a close press of atevi bodies. Woodsmoke and evergreen was the Taisigi contribution. His own was engine oil, fuel, grain stubble, and exhausted human, and the closeness added up to blissful safety for the moment. No way to do anything, no need to do anything complicated—all an exhausted, undersized civil servant had to do was rest his head, shut his eyes, and let his senses go sliding sideways into the dark.

Jolt. Rock. Sick sway.

Steep bank. A little turbulence.

Flashback.

A view of grain stalks in the landing lights.

No, secure *sleep* was not going to happen. At least the exhausting shivers had abated at last.

He caught voices; forced himself not to listen. Not his business, the conference going on in the middle of the bus. He refused to care. Banichi and Cenedi and multiple Guild units who assuredly knew what they were doing were back there collaborating with a canny, chancy lord of the Marid and his rangers, joined by—he detected another voice: the potential lord of Ajuri. *Nomari* had involved himself in it.

How not? *Machigi* might have brought him into it, with who-knew-what reasons. It was the south of the continent. It was the backside of Machigi's own hunting range. Nomari of Ajuri had been his agent, on the rails, but who was to say where Machigi's agent had ranged, in the years Nomari had been his agent.

Had *Nomari* been to Jorida? Or was his participation back there only Machigi's willingness to promote him into councils?

If Nomari knew the inside of Jorida—Nomari could have said something. Nomari could well have said something.

It would not have necessarily made him more trusted on this mission.

But then—Nomari's service to Machigi was less going places than hearing things. Hearing a lot of things, not necessarily accurately, but if the prospective lord of Ajuri was actually trying to help, beyond just trying to attach to his newly-constituted aishid—if he was *trying* to be useful, for his own part—

He could be forgiven.

Trust the young man? Or not?

They had acquired Machigi, for God's sake. What risk was an *Ajuri* trying to be useful?

More use than he was, at the moment. He, himself, crafted words—and words were not needed in what was coming. Would not be needed until the paidhi-aiji had to sit down at a desk and write the documents to end it—and write a report on the entire operation.

There were clauses he wanted to insert in those agreements . . . protections for the Edi—who, unbeknownst to their lord in Najida, had been making their own accommodations with the space age. He was intrigued by the things he had found. He wanted a number of long talks with Betan.

But then—he had not the leisure to be down here for that many more days. The north needed him. Tabini did. Geigi did. There was that.

God, he did not need Machigi involved. But the added force—the rescue, out there—he could not regret that. It was possible the plane coming down had provided Machigi an excuse to get involved. Machigi *had* been perched at the end of his territory—justified in defending his own, no question; but crossing the market road, involving himself in Ashidama, which sat plump on the end of his already expansive territory . . . that was far more problematic.

It was not a good pillow, that kind of thinking. Elements of the past all muddled about in a head trying to form the documents that would determine the future of this region. The dowager's railroad. Geigi's provisions for the Edi. The grain, the fisheries, the orchards—a situation neglected because the aishidi'tat flatly did not care what went on in the south, so long as trade kept coming . . . and Lord Geigi, who had, through two aijinates in Shejidan, held it all in check.

Now an indigestible lump of Reunioner humans was about to enter Mospheiran society, rescued from a space-based existence under alien threat. Only five thousand of them. A threatening cancer up on the space station; a distinct minority on Mospheira—but bound to be a noisy one.

It was all a lightning flash of an idea across a dark landscape void of facts. No clue how it all fitted together. Mospheira had to absorb and moderate its bitter dose, the Edi had their part to play with Ashidama, and Jorida and its Townships had to figure that a Tribal People strongly connected to the space station required an adjustment in their delusions of superiority.

Some elements were bound to be disappointed.

All had to be prepared for change.

It was all one problem. To a great extent—it was all the same problem. From a space-based perspective there *were* sane answers.

One document, to solve *this* part of the equation.

If Ashidama *and* the Marid could be convinced, for a start, to look up and consider opportunities . . . instead of sharpening their knives for each other. . . .

The sun was coming, relentlessly, to a landscape of ancient feuds, old ambitions. Details stood out—grainfields on one side, seemingly endless, the bay on the other—Kajiminda, the Edi, and the Townships all in that haze to the north—

The documents that ended this had to solve that.
The Guild stopped disputes.
The paidhi had to unwire them.

Eyes drifted shut, and opened again.

In the windshield, past Banichi's shoulder, there rose a hazy irregularity offshore: Jorida Isle, with its pre-Landing citadel. Bren shut his eyes again, desperate for a few minutes more of sleep, but the brain began reconstructing the profile of Jorida, its highest rise, the citadel, its skirt of town around the docks, the waterside shielded from view at this angle. One stubborn upthrust of resistant rock had made a natural fortress long before humans, long before the aishidi'tat: geologic violence and layers of stone that had refused to erode into the sea . . . as close to a relic of the Southern Isle civilization as remained continually occupied, if one could believe the Ojiri . . .

He shut his eyes deliberately. Did achieve another period of exhausted oblivion if not real sleep . . . and opened his eyes as the bus slowed and Cenedi again came to the front, conferred with Banichi and their driver, Nawari . . . possibly having conferred also with Midagi—wherever that second force was: possibly delaying their crossing. That was a reasonable thought. Possibly delayed in Separti. That was a less comfortable one.

Ahead, Jorida Isle stood much clearer—along with the connection the ancient Ojiri had built to the peninsula, a stone causeway footed on several lumps of that same resistant rock that composed the island; and beyond it, less distinct, a shore-side sprawl of grain storage, equipment storage, and fuel storage on the peninsula—one assumed some sort of habitation along with them. Trucks used that causeway to get grain to the docks. It was road enough for those. It should be road enough for the bus. The hope was to get their armored and mobile shelter into the town by that route—take out the gate reports said existed between citadel and the town, and *maybe* get the bus all the way through to the fortress courtyard—which their aerial view had confirmed was large enough to maneuver in, on the back side of the citadel.

Machigi's men would deploy on the peninsula side of the

causeway, ready to prevent Shadow Guild from escaping to the grainfields . . . and if the bus could *not* cross the causeway—as one understood it—then they were going to have to maintain a base—the bus, if possible—for Cenedi, and let those several teams get into Jorida citadel by whatever route they could manage . . .

Where, if they had not already escaped by sea or, less likely, into the grainfields, several teams of Shadow Guild would be equally bent on stopping them. The town below the citadel would be distracted by the landing of Midagi's force from Separti—and possibly—ideally—they might have the support of citizens of Separti and Jorida itself. That was a chancy hope, the folk of Ashidama having no history with the Guild. And even if they were inclined to help, they had no understanding of what civilians should and should not do in a Guild action, which was to get to cover and stay out of the way. A great many weapons in non-Guild hands with no leader in charge and no means of telling friend from foe was the likely situation, and that meant holding onto the bus, clearing a perimeter, and getting teams into action inside the citadel *before* a mob could gather around them either to help them or to attack them.

If they could *find* the Master alive and gain control of the fortress, there was one plan—deal with the Shadow Guild and put the Master back in charge. If they could not find the Master, and if they could not quickly get the upper hand in the citadel, they simply had to hold out until Midagi's larger force worked their way toward them from the lower town. At that point, having eliminated the Shadow Guild from the citadel, and the bus being in useable condition, they could use it to take out stragglers on the return path, and evacuate all units safely, avoiding civilian casualties in the process.

Holding Jorida was not the plan. If Jorida wanted to isolate itself from the rest of the continent, even its own Townships, they could do that. If Jorida wanted to embrace the Guild—which meant embracing and joining the aishidi'tat—let them do that remotely, *after* everything was cleared and Guild forces were out of Jorida. There being no treaty, no agreements, no provision for Guild operation here, they could not have Guild unilaterally sorting out civilian riot conditions. If they found the Master, and the Master said, Establish order, favoring this side, they could. If the Master said, Favor the other, they would. If the Master could not be found alive—they could remove the Shadow Guild, but beyond that, they could not commit Guild lives to sorting out civilian divisions.

To allow the Shadow Guild to stay in control of the citadel was *not* an option. The Shadow Guild could *not* be allowed a foothold anywhere. Even if the Shadow Guild had come ashore on Mospheira itself—the Guild would have gone after them, the Treaty of the Landing notwithstanding. That was how it was. The ins and outs of Guild function were complex, but that one, the pursuit of Guild self-policing, was not. There would be no sanctuary.

The paidhi-aiji's presence was, however, *not* anticipated in the regulations. The paidhi-aiji's job was, technically, peace-making. Technically peace-making, between the aiji and humans, but not exclusively. And the paidhi-aiji's mind was not at peace with the Shadow Guild ensconced in a town of whatever political state. The paidhi-aiji had been shot at, and had a gun in his pocket, and the dearest people in the world to him put at risk by the Shadow Guild's intentions to use civilians as a shield. He was not in a peaceful frame of mind. He was sore, he was hurting, if he sat still his muscles were going to freeze, and he was not inclined to sit on a bus parked wherever they parked it while the Shadow Guild might view it as a moving fortress if they could take it.

It might have been a mistake for him and Reijiri to try to meet the bus. *Machigi* might be an unlooked-for asset. But *they* were a complication, for their aishidi, and *he* was a complication for the entire effort, powerless until their job was done, but a resource that had to be a consideration in Banichi's mind, even in Cenedi's; and he was not liking the situation he was apt to be left in if they could not get the bus across the causeway . . . namely sitting out on this road, obvious as a mecheita at a dinner party.

Damn the mess. He would have sat just as helpless had they landed safely back at Najida, just as worried. But—here, he had a function and could not exercise it until everything was over.

Until whatever was going to happen had happened—a good plan, as far as it went.

But—*damn.*

His presence and Reijiri's had to take at least one unit out of action, likeliest Reijiri's, staying on the bus to protect them, with guns and gear that should be a resource for the mission. Had they decided to hike back to Kajiminda, with whatever minor risks were in that—they would still have cost the effort a unit, and distracted his own aishid. And they were committed now. Irrevocably.

Tano got up and talked briefly with Banichi, then paused at Bren's seat.

"Midagi is starting to cross, Bren-ji," Tano said.

"Good news, then."

Jago also had heard. She settled back, happier.

Bren ought to be. The citadel ahead was losing its haze, becoming real, assuming detail. The causeway, massive stone blocks on the stubs of tiny islets, was at a right angle to them, occasionally visible down to the two small gaps where the water still surged through.

Far in the distance beyond it, as the road they were on continued, the granaries, the equipment barns, the garages and appurtenances of agriculture occupied the edge of the peninsula for an unguessed distance, not within their concern, though there was talk among those around him about snipers, and an offer of Taisigi rangers to go search those within range of the causeway.

One assumed those might be set to pick off fleeing Shadow Guild, but one did not bother asking.

The causeway itself looked solid—dressed stone, massive blocks from roadway to waterline, tracing what might have been, in geologic time, a natural connection of Jorida Isle to the peninsula. Beyond, Bren got his first real look at Jorida citadel, a hulking central building, surrounded by a massive wall. A large cluster of disordered roofs and structures rose up against it— undermining any defensive value of that wall. The harbor was beyond it all, but out of sight from their angle. There by daylight was the height they had reached in the plane, the slant down which they had gone scattering their message, as scary a descent as one had imagined it to be.

Compared to that . . . the causeway in an armored bus was going to be a breeze.

And it seemed, in the bouncing of the bus and the scattering of light on the spattered windshield, that one of the massive stone blocks ending the causeway ashore . . . had changed shape.

"Jago-ji," he said, because that change was about man-sized.

"Banichi," she said, and having Banichi's attention, signed toward the view. Banichi looked, said something, and a moment later Cenedi came forward with a pair of binoculars.

"Well," Cenedi said, "he has seen us, and does not care."

Cenedi gave an order. Nawari slowed the bus a little, but they did not stop. Aboard, there was a slight clatter of units in preparation for—

Ambush? Bren wondered. An enemy would be crazy to take them on out here, with no support, and exposed like that.

A lure to target a few of them? Likewise foolish.

Hard to make out detail at that distance, with the jolting of the road and the dirt on the windshield. But the pose was not warlike. One man, sitting on the rock, one knee up, the other casually tucked.

Some oblivious farmer?

Or had the Guild force gotten all the way through without them? Bren wondered. It could not be, yet, and Midagi, having a secure com, surely did not need to send a man to perch on a rock.

Closer and more definite now: a dark figure, rifle in hand. A figure in what looked like Guild black.

The figure remained seated as the bus came to a rolling stop, then advanced another small distance before it stopped completely and Banichi stepped down into the stairwell. Jago got up, stepped roughly past Bren, rifle similarly inclined as the bus door opened, and Banichi stepped out, his rifle slung at a momentarily peaceful angle.

The man on the rock, rifle slung to his shoulder, slid down, showing empty hands—only a pistol at his hip. Jago stepped down from the bus, rifle at the ready, as Banichi advanced a few steps.

Bren got to his feet, not *in* the aisle, leaving that free for response behind him; but ready to move if he could be of any use.

Outside, words were exchanged—and the unknown struck an attitude that nudged recent memory. Algini, in the row behind Bren, said:

"Homura."

Cenedi rose out of his seat opposite, standing beside Nawari. Machigi came forward and exchanged a word with Cenedi. Throughout the bus there was a sound of guns made ready.

Cenedi said, into his com, "What does he want?" and Bren, close beside, heard Banichi's answer. *"He says that the causeway is a risk—that barricades will not let us to the citadel. He offers another route. He offers to guide us."*

"What other route?" Cenedi asked. And Banichi: *"He says there is a passage within the causeway underside that goes up into the citadel itself. He says. He says there is riot in the streets and Guild uniforms make us targets."*

So leave the bus, while *we* sit out here as a larger target? Bren asked himself. One much preferred closer quarters, not a plan that removed them that far from their active force, not one that had them sitting out here in the open, well away from Midagi's force when it came in.

And where the hell was Homura's partner Momichi? There might be a rifle somewhere in the rocks to the left of the road. Or wherever that passage started.

Cenedi was silent a moment, then said, "Midagi's force is approaching the docks to come across. The Shadow Guild will have eyes on them—possibly on us. *We* can distract them by becoming a greater threat."

"Where is Momichi?" Banichi's voice came through.

Homura's voice then, faintly: *"Inside the citadel. Searching."*

Believe in Homura, trust his declaration of man'chi? One was far from sure.

"The streets being blocked," Banichi said, *"was the instruction in the notes."*

Which was true. An impediment to invaders became an impediment to *them.*

"We cannot waste time," Cenedi said then. And to the bus as a whole: *"Disembark!"*

Guild stood up from their seats. Rangers in the aisle gathered up whatever they had let to the deck and started forward on the instant. Cenedi went down the steps, followed by Casimi. Nawari shut down the bus and left his seat, behind them. Tano and Algini took the aisle as Machigi headed for the door.

Everybody was going. Taisigi shadows plummeted down past the windows, leaving the roof.

Hell. Cenedi might still assign a unit to watch the bus—and contents. The paidhi, along with the baggage. Reijiri was already in the aisle *with* his aishid. Nomari was with his.

Bren stood up, buttoned two buttons of his very civilian coat and inserted himself into the flow ahead of Reijiri, down the steps to an unassisted jump down to the road—nearly sprawled in the dirt as his knees betrayed him, staggered and recovered his balance, aches be damned. Units were sorting out. He had a clear view of his, and moved past three of the rangers to reach Tano and Algini while Cenedi was talking to Banichi.

"Bren-ji," Algini said. "Cenedi will assign a guard for the bus. It should not be us."

Leave him with some unassigned unit, that was. "No," he said, "no, Gini-ji. I have no desire to sit on that bus waiting to be shot at. Nor any desire to endanger *you*. Protect Banichi and Jago. I swear I will not be a fool."

It was not the first time under fire with his aishid, and there had been worse situations. The whole mission was going under concealment—more than the bus would be. He saw Reijiri and his aishid nearby, and caught Reijiri's sleeve. "Stay with me. It will make both our aishidi happier."

Nomari's aishid, he saw, was already engaged with Nawari. Likely that was best. That unit had been, prior to their assignment to Nomari, under Cenedi's command.

They were wasting no time. Nawari made one side move to lock the bus, its lights flashed brief acceptance of commands, while the company had already begun to move, with Homura and Cenedi in the lead—not onto the causeway, but down the rocky slope beside it, and down past several massive boulders—not on any evident path, but headed toward the sheer wall of the causeway . . . in which, beyond the curtain of tumbled rock, was indeed a dark angled gap between stonework and a boulder larger than the rest. Within that, a corroded black door stood half ajar, and into that dark place Homura led the lot of them—with guns at his back, no question. It was a chill, ink-dark space within, smelling of sea and mold, and a very small light came on, Homura likely being the figure holding it. It traveled over mossy stone to indicate a passage beyond, into deep dark. And traveled, their guide beginning to move.

Banichi would be among the first following. Bren made an effort to keep with the light.

Someone in the ensuing sort-out took hold of his arm. "Do not get ahead of us, Bren-ji." It was Tano's voice.

"Watch Banichi," he said. "I am fine."

"We are watching him."

They were. His own eyes made out the faintest of glows ahead—enough, evidently, for their eyes, not his. He had become an encumbrance. Blind. Where atevi enemies were not.

Ears said—stairs—as there was a change of rhythm in the press of bodies. He still stumbled as he met the upward steps, unable to gauge the height, and someone had to save him, keep him on his feet—Tano, he thought, making the next step on his own—high, even on an atevi scale, and after the battering he had had in the landing, his body was not happy with the effort.

Up and up a steep pitch, on legs with little reserve left, and, God, up to a new level, stone, dusty stone that gritted underfoot, a press of bodies around him, but at least level passage—perhaps a corridor through the causeway itself. His breaths were loud enough to pierce the sounds of the whole company moving. He staggered. Someone took his arm—Tano, he thought; but it could be Algini, even Reijiri—and kept him moving at pace with the rest. Soft clatter of armament else. And his own breathing. No words exchanged. No orders given—just move. Go. Climb again— his guardian provided the cue, a tug on his arm as his foot met a step.

One more painful effort. And still utter darkness. Then . . .

His foot hit something soft and hard, and the hand on his arm steered him onto the other foot, aside, jostling the man next over.

Someone down, he thought in disquiet, then: dead man. Or unconscious. A faint gleam of light through some chink in the stonework gave him a brief glimpse of the passage. They were above ground, maybe on the island side of the causeway. It was not a wide space, ceiling high enough—atevi-built, how not?—but less than a normal hallway; dry, and not dressed stone: he felt that where his other hand met it. There was no discernable air movement—a closed passage, he thought with—surely—a door of some kind. Eventually. Muscles quivered, about at their end of function, and, dammit, he was not going to have someone have to carry him.

Another stairs. He struggled. But it was only three steps. Dry, gritty stone underfoot. Uneven.

And Homura in the lead of it all, inspiring less confidence . . . but Banichi and Cenedi had accepted him. Kept with him, one supposed. With atevi reading atevi intent. The human was not so confident.

But they were going in the right direction, there was that. Trustable or not, whether or not they were headed into an ambush, they *were* climbing, not descending. An escape route for the upper town made sense—civic disorder not being infrequent in atevi politics, the Masters being what they were.

It stayed level for a time, lightless, gritty, and by all evidence, ancient. He moved, taking his pace from the bodies around him, using that contact, and his ears, where sight was inadequate—his chest hurt: part of that was the seat belt; his shoulders hurt, but hurt assumed a level, not getting worse. His legs, however, recovered since the climbing—until they came to another slant, shallow steps, thank God, but a climb all the same. Someone had his arm, steering him, keeping him on his feet, and someone behind him shoving with great familiarity: it might be Algini.

A fourth climb, then a level. The pace increased. He fell out of rhythm with whoever had his arm, and struggled to keep up, but whoever it was would not let him stumble—nor would the man behind.

Fifth climb. God. It was not doable. He hesitated, and the one behind him grabbed him roughly, threw him over a shoulder, and took the stairs in a rush. Metal grated against metal ahead and above. Air stirred, a veritable wind, carrying a dank, woodsmoke smell different than the air before, and as they went, his right hand brushed a corroded metal rim, cold and rough.

A loud clank from ahead, echoing. His carrier dropped him abruptly back to his own feet on uneven stone as a line of day-light speared past heads and shoulders and bodies, widening as a door opened. He glanced back at his helper, expecting Tano or Algini . . . and met eyes shimmering gold—in Machigi's dark face.

The first of them out separated to left and right, giving space to those behind, rapid movement now, and Bren struggled to match the pace, keeping ahead of Machigi through that opening and into a stonework hall, into a rush of air cleaner than where they had been, and light enough, barely enough—one ancient, dirty bulb in a chamber about the size of the sitting room in Ka-jiminda. He saw Banichi and Jago, he saw Cenedi. He saw Tano and Algini. Nomari was with his aishid, Reijiri on his other side.

And Machigi, with his aishid and his rangers, all in a brown that human eyes could barely discern from black, were gathering in a group. Others, black-uniformed Guild, all that had been on the bus. Everyone accounted for. He bent over, hands on knees, catching his breath—

Then looked up as the company began to move, this time split-ting in two directions. He still had Tano and Algini . . . still was with Banichi and Jago, while Cenedi and his group had gone an-other direction.

Banichi's group included Machigi and the Taisigi . . . by Machi-gi's choice it might be. And where Banichi was going, Bren had to. Tano and Algini moved to support him.

"Stay with Banichi," he said, on what wind he could muster. "I am here. I shall keep up unless there are stairs. If there are stairs—I shall get there."

They did move—they all moved, but now with caution. *They* had to look for danger. All the small, aching human had to do was move his legs. He made his best effort, wondering where they were, not seeing Homura at all—possibly ahead of them, possibly with Cenedi's group. He simply put his effort into following, not turning his head any more than he had to.

Reijiri caught his arm and kept him on course, if nothing else, through another doorway, another hall with small figured rugs, and, God, another stairs. He flattened himself against the wall and waited until Machigi surged past with the others, all but Reijiri's guard—before he began hauling himself up. . . . only to find faithful Tano, at the top, coming back for him—damn it all.

"Owe you an apology," he said to Tano, with no wind left. "Owe everyone an apology" . . . as Tano physically hauled him up the last, oversized step.

Into daylight. Blazing white daylight. Glazed windows. Wooden floor and carpet, a long hall beyond, with numerous rooms, windows on the right, that looked out on the bay and a lower-lying haze of smoke. In quick succession, all down the hall, Guild opened every door. The pace was slower now, as they began to follow. Room after room produced nothing. No one.

A door ended that hall. That door half-opened on abundant sunlight, a desk, a large office.

A shot went off—their side; the door slammed outward, wood splintering, their front rank fired—at least three, and fired again, in concert.

There was quiet then, except far away, somewhere below—a minor explosion. Then silence, except the shifting of bodies. Bren stood still, one traitor leg twitching, divorced from conscious control. Reijiri was beside him. Their group began slowly, one or two at a time, moving into the room ahead, another area of bright sunlight. A broken window admitted a slight breeze that lifted a gauzy curtain. A table, rather than a desk, stood at an angle in the corner, interview chairs before it. Someone's office.

There were bookshelves. Hangings. A figured carpet.

A downed man, dead, indisputably—Guild, still. Queue ribbon

was red, not black, as proper Guild should be. Had always been. Before the corruption.

Banichi opened a further door. God. Another corridor?

No. A similar, larger room—for which this was the anteroom. Two Guild went into it, quick moves, reported it empty.

Eight large windows, with a view of blue sky, a graveled flat roof, above the angled roofs and wooden shingles of other buildings, a room above the world. This had to be the crest of the citadel. Bren stood there, the knot in his chest slowly unwinding, legs feeling frozen in place—locked, not giving; but not apt to move, either. Tano and Algini were where they belonged, now, with Banichi, having survived his idiocy in trying to keep up. Reijiri and his young aishid gathered by him. The broken window in the anteroom let in the smell of smoke—or it was coming from elsewhere in the citadel.

Shots went off somewhere below. A wall seemed safer, in general, than the middle of the room. Bren found the power to move, slowly, nearer his aishid. Banichi was using the new com, speaking quietly, eyes constantly moving over the next room, the accesses, everything in his field of vision. Jago was right with him, rifle aimed down, everything around them, give or take the dead man, safe and settling—finally—toward peace.

Had they won? Had they—at least gained the highest position, from which the Shadow Guild had no choice but retreat from the attack coming at their waterfront?

There was still a civilian population down there, at risk if the Shadow Guild did not attempt to head for the grainfields, deprived of their ships, deprived of their fortress, and with nothing left but flight toward Machigi's unwelcoming rangeland.

Once it got past the civilian blockade of the causeway.

"Midagi is ashore," Banichi said to everyone in the room, which was great news. "We have not located the Master and we have not found more than a handful of the Shadow Guild. Tiajo and Suratho are still at large. Cenedi's group is continuing to search the mid-levels. We shall wait for them to finish that floor before moving. Catch your breath."

Would Banichi have said that if there were not a human in the company? One was unsure of that. Fool, he kept thinking. His legs were shaking. He should have stayed in the damned bus. He tried to relate where they were to what he had seen of the geometry of Jorida, and the best he could figure, they had indeed come up to the crest, while the rest of the town—

The town itself wound down the height to sea level, where the ships were, where Midagi was. The causeway had gone across to midtown, with most of the population, most of the dwelling places, below it. Anyone who wanted to escape out of the citadel had to go down all the way to the water—or reach the causeway, to escape by land—where the bus was. An enemy might think they could take it. It was a good bet Banichi had triggered its defenses. Or Nawari had.

Gunfire, far away, echoed up to them. Dockside, Bren thought. Maybe at the ships. It was not in the building.

It was not neat, or fast, what they had to do now. The citadel was not a simple structure. It was high, it went down to that courtyard they had seen twice from the air. Their enemy could be anywhere inside or beyond; and they hoped not to have to sort them out of the town.

"We hold here," Banichi said to all with him. "The commander—" That was Cenedi. "—is searching the ground floor. We hold the top. On signal, we will move down. He will move up. The Najida Guild force is coming up from the harbor. When they enter, they will descend to the basement. A force will go out, surface level, on the causeway—to be sure nothing escapes."

Who *was* with him on this level? His own aishid. Reijiri's. Machigi, his aishid, and four of the Taisigi rangers. Cenedi was below with his eleven—so was Nomari and his four, and not with Machigi, which was a little remarkable, but might be Cenedi's doing. A number of the Taisigi were not here. They *might* be with Cenedi, in that sorting-out below, surely on Machigi's orders . . . and surely with good intent: one could not align Machigi in *any* way as allied with Jorida, the dispute over their common border being a long-smoldering issue. Relations with the Shadow Guild itself involved the assassination of Machigi's father . . . *that* was outright blood feud.

Human instincts were *not*, however, happy with where they were, and experience said instinct was not wired to read all of it. There was the issue of what-happened-next, to-whose-advantage, and where man'chi was directed after the sort-out: Nomari *and* Machigi, once connected, Nomari's new Ragi aishid now taking Nomari in another direction, after that incident in Kajiminda . . . *if* his protestations were honest . . . one wondered how Machigi was reading *that*.

Machigi had insisted, from the beginning, that Nomari's work for him never involved man'chi, just money, payment for services rendered, safe passage when he needed it; but there was something there . . . he would call it mutual respect, if he was dealing with humans, but that was not a place that was ever safe to go. Would Nomari ever undermine Machigi, with that history?

As lord of Ajuri, which had had a long and troubled history of espionage and conspiracy against Tabini—and connections in the Dojisigin—how would he be?

One was not sure.

Algini had taken station by a window, casting a look downward at whatever he could see from there, Tano and Jago were watching the room, with *its* former relationships, and he was watching everybody, a little sick at his stomach from the exertion and lack of food and sleep, not trusting the apparent calm in the assorted company. Atevi emotions were hard to predict where man'chi was under stress—things like self-interest could flare up. Ancestral feuds. Ambition. Way too much was at issue since Machigi had shown up, and he was without a roadmap.

But of one thing he had become aware . . . just not aware he had felt it, but it was true. *He* was reinforcing Banichi—just by being here. Banichi had not resisted his coming. *Banichi's* lord being present and Cenedi's not—*had* weight in the chain of command; and the lord of Najida having personal business here, in a west coast situation—added another potency. It was a learned thing, maybe, maybe not a thoroughly human thing, but he could *feel*

334 / C. J. CHERRYH & JANE S. FANCHER

the connection with his aishid. They had gotten him up the climb, even Machigi had gotten behind and pushed—literally; and his presence now empowered a force not the dowager's to share command with Cenedi, rank be damned. His relationship with his aishid was solid, he was more senior and more local than Reijiri; even more senior and more local than Machigi, when it came to it—who could have outright stabbed him in the back, and instead had carried him up the stairs. Machigi would do what was in his interest to do. But right now Machigi had a restraint: a set of documents. His agreements. His ambitions. His prospects for rule in the Marid.

Fortunately for all of the continent, and thanks to Ilisidi's maneuvering, he had more than enough on his plate in his own territory for the next several generations.

God. He was woolgathering, standing in the heart of an invasion of which he was, de facto, one of the leaders, developing a headache and feeling as if pieces were spinning around him, connections a human could not feel, decisions about reliability no human should be making. Trust Banichi, his gut and his mind agreed. Trust his aishid to do that calculation. Listen to them, but—

He had felt he *had* to be here. He had felt he could not, would not have said to Banichi, give us an escort back to Kajiminda, sane as it might have been. He had not said, at the causeway, We will stay on the bus. He had felt he had to go, that he would be less of a distraction to Banichi, even less of a burden to the mission by going . . . and possibly he would find a way to be of use.

Until the stairs, the dark, the passage, when he had realized he was a fool. But he was not sorry to be here now—however that miracle had been achieved—with his aishid, lending moral force to Banichi, whose tactics were not as reckless as Cenedi's, whose solutions were both more careful of his forces and more inclined to take sudden risks for an outcome. Cenedi outranked him; but a lord's presence tilted the scales. *Banichi* had been pushing a loyal resistance to Cenedi's support of the dowager ever since they had left the train. Certainly Cenedi had been largely occupied with Ilisidi's health, but increasingly, particularly in the move to Kajiminda, and dealing with the Edi, Banichi had assumed command, and Cenedi had actually backed off. And now, in this place, in this situation—asking himself what he was doing, he knew he was here because *his* presence in *his* region supported Banichi, Tabini's man, and Tabini's authority on this coast. What happened in this southern grain belt of the aishidi'tat had consequences, what happened to Kajiminda and the Edi had consequences.

God, what was he thinking? Lord by appointment. Human. And playing push and shove in atevi politics and policy? But he could not desert Banichi and his aishid, who *knew* what they were doing, against Cenedi, who was pushing hard for Ilisidi's outcome. He had never dreamed of opposing Ilisidi. He never intended to.

But the solution could not be imposed. There had been far too many imposed solutions on this coast. The Edi had their issues. So did Ashidama. Mostly—they just had to grow things and fish and sell, and avoid killing each other every decade or so. Whether the future lay in Machigi's railroad, or the Master's ships, the people down there in the town, the people of Separti, the Edi . . . they all had to have their livelihoods. And not be afraid.

The room hazed out. He saw the ornate back of a chair in front of him and leaned on that, everything blurred for the moment.

"Bren-ji." Tano's hand on his shoulder. "Do you need to sit down?"

"If I sit down, I cannot get up," he said. He blinked, clearing his eyes, aware of both Tano and Algini at his side, and realizing that both Banichi and Jago were missing and that he was alone with Tano and Algini, Reijiri, and a handful of Taisigi. "Let us find Banichi and Jago. I am all right. Do not let us divide—"

Gunfire. Remote in the citadel, from a lower floor. Contact with some element of the problem. His heart rate ticked up a little. He drew a deep breath and let go of the chair.

Suddenly there was gunfire on *their* level, from the next room, where he supposed Banichi and Jago to have gone. Instinct pulled him one heartbeat toward that doorway, common sense sent him crouching against the massive desk between it and him. Algini dived to the same spot, rifle in hand, got a vantage past the edge, and dived for the side of that doorway. In both directions, both open doorways, Guild had gone to defensive positions.

Bren adjusted his position, prepared to hold it.

Then a waft of cold air swept past, not the temperature of the lower depths—but wind from the outside.

There was activity on com. Bren could hear it, from Algini's position. He could not make it out. He reached into his pocket, extracted his own light pistol, absolutely useless against Guild body armor. Having it in hand negated his own sacrosanctity as non-Guild, on an instinctual level with any Guild he faced.

But becoming another Shadow Guild hostage was not his plan either.

Movement behind. Tano arrived next to him.

"Bren-ji. Do not try. Stay down."

With Tano's near presence he could hear other com traffic—but it was Guild code. That seemed to indicate Cenedi's group was aware—or also engaged. He heard Banichi's voice, calm and steady.

Reijiri and his aishid were guarding the other doorway, without cover from this direction. Machigi and his rangers were over beneath the row of windows.

Algini moved suddenly, dived into the adjacent room, firing; and Tano slid into Algini's position, letting off one burst.

Then there was quiet. A lengthy period of quiet. Algini's calm voice from across the room, in two code words.

Tano got to his feet, beside that doorway.

Banichi and Jago? Bren wondered, his heart pounding. Experience held him right where he was. Tano abruptly disappeared into the next room. Two of Machigi's aishid left their position and did the same.

It stayed quiet. Bren urged his stiffening knees and neck to get him back on his feet and, presumption on a fool's part, took Tano's place beside the door, pistol in hand.

He could see nothing but a row of windows, and chairs somewhat in disarray, one overturned.

There were shouts now from further away. Glass shattered,

and automatic fire ripped across the adjacent room and right through the door, past Bren. Heart constricted, he held position, waiting for a target.

A woman's voice, then, from beyond that other room, distant, high, and angry.

Glass shattered across the room. Bren swung a look behind him, saw Machigi having taken out a window with a rifle butt, taking aim to the left, outside—only to pull back, frustrated.

Banichi's voice: "Surrender!"

Bren, shoulders against the wall by the door, spun himself inside as glass broke in that room.

It was empty, but for his own aishid and the two Taisigi. Jago was at a large window, clearing broken glass still in place with the barrel of her rifle. Banichi shouldered past, rifle in one hand and, ignoring the glass, scrambled through, to the graveled flat outside, a dizzying prospect of the town roofs below.

Jago followed. Bren moved to see and caught sight of two others out there on the graveled terrace . . . in Banichi's sights. And Jago's.

One in Guild black. One in azure blue. Backed up against a low wall.

Algini knocked out a jagged edge of glass and climbed out with less haste, also taking up position.

"We will accept surrender," Banichi repeated, and the woman lurched forward—hauled back on the instant, a living shield, crying:

"I accept! *I accept!* Let me go! Let me go, damn—"

The screams cut off as the woman in Guild black, jerking the other back by one arm, clamped a hand over her mouth.

The young woman—there were photos of her—that was Tiajo. Coiffured in jewelry, necklace and rings and bracelets flashing diamond-white in the sun as she struck and clawed at the Guildswoman holding her, still screaming in muffled outrage. It was a fair guess that the older woman holding her one-handed, and withstanding her furious blows, was Suratho.

And her eyes, cold and keen, flicked toward the window where Bren was standing.

"Ah . . . the paidhi is with us. How remarkable." Her attention went back to Banichi. "That would make you Banichi, am I correct?"

Before he could respond, Suratho jerked a bleeding hand away from Tiajo's mouth, and with the same hand struck the Dojisigin lord a backhanded blow to her bejeweled head. Tiajo staggered and attacked with a blow that sailed past. Suratho spun with it and seized her elaborate braid, dragging her back and getting an arm around her. Tiajo screamed in fury and hit at her, backward, to no avail.

"It is over, you stupid fool," Suratho said calmly, and to Banichi: "Is it not?"

"It is over," Banichi said.

"Kill her!" Tiajo screamed. "I can pay you! I can pay you anything you ask! The boat in the harbor is—"

"—at the bottom of the bay," Suratho finished for her, and Tiajo screamed, "Liar!" and flailed wildly.

Bren rested hands on the sill, mustering advice he dared not give, daring not distract anyone. Tano seized his arm. "I shall not," Bren said. "I shall not move . . ."

"Surrender," Banichi said again, "and live. Help us to repair the harm you have done, nadi."

"And *what!* Pledge man'chi to an aiji who brings us more humans? To a regime that wants the whole world and gives provinces away to tribes and foreigners, kabiu be damned?"

"I will help you!" Tiajo screamed. "There are records! Everything! I can—"

"Oh, for—" Suratho shifted her weight, pulling Tiajo around . . . and slung her over the edge. Her scream went on for a heartbeat, abruptly ended.

Everyone froze, as Suratho stared over the edge.

"Useless woman," Suratho said finally, then turned back, a pistol from within her jacket leveled at Banichi. "You lost your chance, Banichi-nadi."

"Say, rather, one hopes you see common sense, now that your shield is gone."

"Common sense. In a world ruled by humans."

"They do not and will not rule."

She stared at Banichi for a long moment. "Would that I had your faith in that." Her eyes shifted toward Bren, but went beyond. "Well. Machigi. It seems everyone is here. It wants only the dowager herself."

A rifle barrel appeared at Bren's side, as Tano pulled him back from the window.

Machigi said nothing, but his look in profile rivaled Tabini's at his most deadly.

"As you see," Machigi said. "You are out of step with the world, Suratho. The world changes. There will be no revival of the empire."

"As long as Hurshina lives, you all should watch your backs."

"Hurshina," Banichi said. "Where is he?"

A derisive snort, and the pistol, momentarily diverted, leveled at Banichi. "I wish you luck finding him. We have had none."

"Surrender, Suratho," Banichi said. "You will have a hearing. You can state your grievances. Make your case in court. Claim that right."

"Not interested." She lifted her pistol to her head. No one moved.

"If that is your choice," Banichi said, "we will not—"

A sudden spin, and all in a moment, Bren saw that pistol aimed directly at *him*, even as four shots rang out at once: Banichi's, Jago's, Algini's . . . and Machigi's. Bren found himself on the carpet, with Tano a live weight atop him, that shifted off, offering him a hand to get up.

He took it, a warm, strong grip. Tano drew him to his feet and he looked out the window to see Suratho, lying in a heap at the roof's edge, unmoving.

Banichi calmly lifted the com and spoke, almost certainly, to Cenedi, reporting simply, "Tiajo is likely dead, Suratho likewise," while Bren leaned on the sill, his ears ringing from Machigi's shot. He found himself wondering how high that fall was off the edge, what lay at the bottom . . . other than the remnants of a very selfish, very immature woman, a patricide, a dictator, a figurehead held in office by a corruption of law enforcement. Still in her twenties. Still thinking she was in charge. By the downward steps of rooftops in this view, that he had personally experienced in the swoop of the yellow plane, by the duration of that scream,—one did not see survival likely.

Bren drew back from the window, feeling a little shiver in his frame, watching Banichi and Jago walk toward that fatal edge and look down.

They seemed satisfied—lingered a moment to check Suratho—then Banichi made another report by com and, with Jago, walked back toward Bren's window. He climbed back through the window, and looked straight at Machigi. "Only one was fatal."

Machigi shrugged. "She was finished talking."

"She certainly is now," Banichi said, and turned to Bren. "Are you hurt, Bren-ji?"

Bren shook his head wearily. "No, no, not in the least."

"You can rest now. We all can. Midagi's forces will continue the clean-out of the Shadow Guild in the town—there will not be that many that arrived by the ships. We are getting help from the citizens and the Separti boatmen, clearing building by building, with more accuracy than we could apply."

"We still need to find Hurshina," Bren said.

Machigi gestured, shifting his rifle to the other hand. "*I* suggest you ask Nomari."

20

"I intended to tell Cenedi, nand' paidhi," Nomari said quietly, in the small sitting room Banichi had found: Bren had had more than enough of broad vistas for the time being. It was just Nomari, Bren, and their respective bodyguards. "I would have told him. But he does not trust me. I was going to tell Banichi. But—I waited. And Lord Machigi knows I have had interests in this place. I did confess that."

Bren wondered if Nomari would ever run out of ways to surprise them.

"So was Machigi correct? Do you know where the Master is likely to be?"

"I have an idea, nandi. You know I was a spy. I was a spy for the Dojisigin at that time. And for Lord Machigi, after. Which I told him when I came to be his. But you can see Cenedi has very good reasons for doubting me."

One was moderately taken aback. But Nomari was being, at least, open about these things, and did not seem overconfident in revealing it.

"I am listening, nadi."

"I moved about on the railroad, and later *with* the railroad. But no place was that secure for me. I always wanted to have a next place, protected from searchers from the last one. So Jorida strongly interested me; and there was a time I was planning to come here. I gathered information from anyone willing to talk. I heard a story about a Dojisigi, a ship's carpenter on a winter layover, who had gotten lost in the levels of this place, and found a

room like a palace . . . of course it involves treasure." A shrug.
"But over time I got to the heart of the story, which is just a room
on the second tier with a hidden access. There is no distinction
to it. It may be on the same level as the wine cellar and the
kitchen stores. So goes the story. I even drew plans of this place,
with all its layers—as I had heard it. I was sixteen. But I never
acted on it. I fell afoul of a man in Amarja and I found Machigi a
much safer harbor. I did tell him, when a matter came up, regarding the resources the Master has."

"It is no great trouble to look," Bren said, looking at Banichi.

Nomari said quietly. "I am fairly good at moving about and
finding things."

"The Master may have defenses," Banichi said.

"I have expected that," Nomari said. And added: "I have
thought about this place for years."

Bren considered it doubtfully, glanced at Banichi, and Banichi
frowned and looked at Nomari.

"Do not go alone, nadi," Banichi said.

Nomari frowned for a moment. It was *not* how Nomari had
tended to operate. But the expression changed and he glanced at
his own guard, who stood to the side, waiting. "Nadiin," he said,
and gathered them with him when he left.

"We are meditating trusting him with a province," Bren said.
"This is a little less, is it not?"

It took an hour. Only that. There was a considerable commotion on the stairs that made itself heard, and continued across the
upper gallery, with its broken windows. The Master was not
pleased to be found; the Master was not pleased with the break-
age. The Master was not pleased to find his office and his desk to
be occupied by a relatively small human with a large Guild presence surrounding him.

The Master's pleasure was irrelevant. For once, the Master had
no choice in the matter.

It had taken some persuasion to get the Master up the
stairs—though not violence. Bren had ordered care, the Master
being, as word came from those who found him, a frail person. And

indeed not a person of great stature or presence, either, as Bren discovered when the Master arrived in the doorway of his own office. Surprising, to say the least, in someone whose stubborn, greed-driven arrogance had generated so much death and terror.

"Hurshina-nadi." *That* was deliberate, the plain, titleless salutation. Hurshina had had his chance, more than one, to be a lord of the aishidi'tat. "I am Bren, Lord of Najida."

As if it was not fairly obvious.

Hurshina said not a thing. He looked, in fact, unwell as well as fragile. Bren refused to acknowledge that appearance. Whatever his state of health, this man had enabled a terrorist regime to gain and retain power for years. All they actually needed from him at the moment was permission to allow the Guild to complete the task of routing out the Shadow Guild. That was not the only concession Bren intended to pry out of him.

"I am speaking to you first," Bren said, "not as an official of the aishidi'tat, but as neighbor to Lord Geigi of Kajiminda, and as your neighbor in Najida. I am speaking in this capacity so as *not* to engage the aishidi'tat *or* the Guild in this appeal to my neighbor, Ashidama, to formally reject the presence of outlaw Guild."

"I will speak to the aiji-dowager!"

"That you will not, nadi. You will not *want* the attention of the aiji-dowager considering your reception of enemies who have assassinated members of the aishidi'tat and attacked the aiji and his family in attempt to overthrow the lawful government."

"No such thing! We are utterly outside the aishidi'tat! We have done nothing of the kind!"

"You have sheltered and traded with the perpetrators, nadi, during all that period and as recently as this morning." He paused, for effect. "—Unless, of course, you wish to claim unlawful invasion, formally renounce that historical association and request the help of the legitimate Guild to complete the removal of the renegade Guild from all of Ashidama Bay. Before you respond, be advised, their leader, Suratho, and the fugitive lord of Dojisigi have already been eliminated from power."

Angry silence.

"*Machigi* of the Taisigin Marid, newly in association with

Ilisidi of Malguri and Bregani of Senjin, also complains of your trade practices, particularly as they apply to the ships he sends to Cobo. Be advised, the Taisigin Marid will soon link with Koperna by rail. At that point, rail will become the primary means of trade transport. For the rest, the greater part of the Marid will receive favorable treatment in sea trade directly with Cobo—" Another pause. "—unless the Marid can receive reasonable agreement with Jorida."

He let that sink in a moment. Then: "Speaking now as paidhi-aiji, this is the situation, which I neither propose nor affect. The aiji-dowager may be receptive to a request for benevolent intervention, even a connection by rail from Cobo to Ashidama—should the Townships desire it. Plans are currently underway to extend it down near Kajiminda and an additional extension, say to the back of Ashidama Bay, would put them, and you, on a more even footing with the Marid."

"Impossible!"

"Hardly. May I point out to you that not only have you allied yourself with the Dojisigi and their rogue Guild, you have alienated the Taisigin, who are now allied with Senjin. The aiji-dowager is *not* well-disposed toward you. If you wish to continue trading in Cobo, you must negotiate with the aishidi'tat. It is *my* office as paidhi-aiji to mediate a fair arrangement, acceptable to all sides and interests, you, your neighbors, Najida, Kajiminda, the Edi, the Marid, and the aishidi'tat, and I can approach Tabini-aiji to initiate that process. I would think very carefully about your answer, nadi, most respectfully. It will not greatly disadvantage you. Nor disturb your industry, if I can manage it. Would you care for a glass of wine?"

"Mine!"

"Indeed. We do not deny it. We have tried not to damage the premises, and to protect shops and houses. Your Dojisigin allies were not as considerate. But I urge you take the time to think this through. We have no wish to impoverish our neighbor. It drags down the whole south. Done properly, the entire south will flourish and the likelihood is there will be *more* trade, more ships, as well as rail."

Hurshina's eyes flickered, a little spark of interest.

"Let us first assume you choose to not disavow any connection to the former lord of Dojisigin and her rogue Guild," Bren said. "I can promise you that any trade that can be linked to those entities will be denied in Cobo. That avenue is lost to you. In addition, in the near future, the rail link with Taisigin will effectively replace the need for any sea trade at all. Without protective agreements, other than for Ashidama's locally grown products, Jorida's ships will have *no* cargo. Without agreements, Jorida could find itself effectively obsolesced."

He waited to allow that to sink in. Hurshina had spent a lifetime on the assumption that he held all the cards. The fact now was, his hands were empty.

"That is not a future *any* of us wish to see. Therefore, let us examine the alternative. If Ashidama were to join the aishidi'tat, there would be an increase of markets, not a decrease. One suspects the Townships and even the people of Jorida would prefer that option. As part of the aishidi'tat, there would be a lordship available for the region. That lordship could go to Jorida . . . or to Separti. How much of that increased trade would be handled by Ashidama ships would rest in the hands of those making the negotiations, which would be that lord. Think of it, nadi. As lord of Ashidama, you could negotiate with your neighbors and with the rest of the aishidi'tat for trade and fair pricing, and the aishidi'tat would be here to see those terms upheld."

"In writing."

"With ribbons, cards, and wax, nadi. Absolutely, registered here and in Shejidan. Agreements as well with the various states of the Marid. Perhaps also with the East. A railway connection *would* open up that possibility. One is certain you can perceive the possibilities."

Hurshina cleared his throat. "The wine," he said. "Neighbor."

"Indeed," Bren said, and rose to go to the sideboard, to pour it himself.

Outside the window, afternoon sun—a view of the bay, a little haze of smoke, still, but dissipating. There were masts visible at dockside. Many.

"There is," Banichi said, having moved to stand at Bren's shoulder, "a Navy ship entering the bay."

One could not see it yet. It was out by Talidi. There was no question at all it had come from the north, the third ship of the navy of the aishidi'tat, moved down from its eternal watch over Mospheira . . .

For the first time since the War of the Landing, there were *no* ships standing guard between Mospheira and the aishidi'tat.

He poured the wine, a dark red, two glasses, and personally offered it to the old man. He stayed standing to take a sip, leaning back against the desk edge. Hurshina took his own sip, and a second, being, perhaps, a little dry-mouthed.

"I should like, nadi," Bren said, "to be a good neighbor. As Lord Geigi has generally been. Things change. Situations change. The war the Shadow Guild was fighting has ceased to be relevant. There is far too much to gain for all of us, if we work together."

The old man stared grimly into his glass, then lifted it in a toast. "Together."

The bus had far fewer passengers toward the end of the bay—Machigi left them, with his rangers, to take their own way up to Taisigin territory, where their cross-country transport awaited.

"We shall see," Machigi said in parting, "how well the old scoundrel keeps his word."

"We will draft a very careful document," Bren said, bidding him and his rangers farewell on the bus steps. "Extremely careful. The man maneuvers fast. And he is no fool."

After that it was a jolting ride on road that had stalled the bus on the way out.

And with many fewer people, there was comfort on the bus. Cenedi's eight sat on the left. Midagi was in charge, now, of the Guild force doing the assessment and cleanup on Jorida, the tally of expenses needed, the issuance of damage certificates—the adjudication of complaints, all the residual untidiness of a Guild action. Cenedi had officially surrendered command to him.

Reijiri and his aishid, Nomari and his four, Bren and his—outnumbering Cenedi's—sat on the right, indulging in sleep, no few of them. Bren found it occasionally possible, no matter how the bus pitched and bounced.

Homura was missing. So was his partner Momichi. They had been seen on the lower levels of the citadel and then not seen at all. They were in no one's command, but word had come that hostages had been found alive.

How was he not surprised?

Word had, meanwhile, come through from Lord Tatiseigi's aishid, on the regular com, that everything was entirely satisfactory. He most carefully did not reference the dowager's presence, but that was understood. And Bren had likewise contacted Ramaso, saying much the same—cautiously, in case there were stray elements of the Shadow Guild still wandering about. Without a head, that entity was little likely to cause trouble— but the Guild action in the Marid was likely to scatter a few pieces into the world at large. One never took good things for granted.

Bren had the com back. And there was the satisfaction of a good and detailed report to Tabini.

"You are well?" Tabini asked. It was rare, the concern. *"I have had Midagi's report. It is well and truly finished, down there?"*

"At least in the west," Bren said. "I shall be grateful, aiji-ma, if we can direct a flatbed truck down to Ashidama to pick up Lord Dur's plane, from the grainfield nearest the cliffs and the market road—then bring it up to Cobo. It should be relatively safe to do that at this point."

"I shall send it. And you? Are you well?"

"Remarkably," he said, and rubbed his neck, where some stiffness remained. Landing on the floor under Tano's weight had had some beneficial effect, at least, besides the bruises. "We will arrive in Kajiminda within the hour. I do not know how we shall survive the welcome—the aishidi'tat owes a great deal to Betannadi, of Geigi's staff. And I hope we will have paid it, if we can get a treaty out of Jorida. Separti is rather pleased with the Edi at the moment—crediting them somewhat with the plane and the messages. And the Edi with Separti, for fighting off the enemy. I plan to start drafting the documents tomorrow. We will stay a couple of days, if I can prevail on the dowager . . . but I have to get to Cobo."

A pause.

"The shuttle is already in descent."

"With the refugees, aiji-ma?"

"There was no waiting. My son is already on his way to the spaceport—with his senior aishid as well as his younger. He assures us he can do this."

One was appalled. But—

Cajeiri could.

He was fluent. There was that. He was a child in size—if the humans involved had the perception to realize that.

"I shall be there when I can. As soon as I can. Tonight if I have to."

"Rest, paidhi. Rest. Best you have your wits about you. You have a document to write."

A message had reached the Cobo train—an official message with Father's red seal, gotten aboard just as the train was leaving the Bujavid station. Eisi received it at the door at the very last moment, the train starting to roll as Cajeiri took the message from him at his seat. It was not a cylinder—it had come in haste, without a message cylinder—but a flat four-folded sheet, wax-sealed with Father's imprint.

Heart pounding, Cajeiri unfolded it and read Father's handwriting.

Good news. Cenedi, the paidhi, the lord of Dur, and the prospective lord of Ajuri have left Jorida and are safely on their way back to Kajiminda without incident, having dropped off Lord Machigi on the edge of the Taisigin. News of Lord Tiajo's death has now reached the Dojisigin Marid, and celebration has broken out in the capital and into the countryside, which is causing some difficulty with forces attempting to locate Shadow Guild remnants. This is not unforeseen, but the information is now widespread in the Marid.

The Master of Jorida having issued an order to the Townships to cooperate with Guild forces, Jorida town streets as well as the citadel upper levels are in possession of the Guild under Midagi.

Suratho perished with Tiajo. Two others of that unit are also confirmed killed. One remains at large and is being sought. Bear this in mind, son of mine.

Your mother and I send wishes for your success. You will do well.

He read it twice . . . three times . . . and the knot in his stomach slowly relaxed.

He had stayed out of Father's office this morning. Much as he had wanted to be there, he had had to pack for the spaceport, to meet the incoming refugees. He had gotten no sleep last night, with the news that nand' Bren and Dur had not returned to Kajiminda—he had not had relief until Lord Geigi called to tell them that the plane had landed safely in the grainfields of Ashidama Peninsula, that there were two people walking toward the road, and that Cenedi would be looking for them.

But then Banichi had reported a short while later to say that nand' Bren and Lord Reijiri *and* Machigi and a band of Taisigi were all on the bus, all headed to take on the Shadow Guild at Jorida, on a tight time schedule . . .

Banichi *said* they were not hurt, and that they could have walked back to Kajiminda, but it would have been a very long walk, and Banichi would not allow it, even had they been willing to do that. They could just have camped by the plane and waited for everything to be over and until there was a truck free to go get them, but there had been a danger that Shadow Guild leaving Jorida could come on them if they stayed by the plane.

So they had gone with the bus.

After that . . . he had refused to go to bed. He could not imagine nand' Bren sitting on the bus, out there in the middle of grainfields, for any sort of trouble to come upon. Nand' Bren would not pull Banichi and his aishid out of the operation to guard them; nor would Reijiri likely withdraw his. So they were, he had known, absolutely going where the Guild went—safe enough in the heart of the operation, but not armored.

Elsewhere the Guild force was going to cross the bay from

Separti; Cenedi's would enter Jorida across the causeway, catching the Shadow Guild between them.

Machigi's rangers could be useful or a distraction. They were not Guild trained, but if they behaved themselves, if Machigi did not try to take over . . .

One had had to believe that extra fighters would be a good thing and Cenedi would assign them something—but one had hoped that *something* would be as far from nand' Bren as possible. Granted, Machigi did have personal reasons for being involved—Ashidama being on his border, with old, old issues about trade, and the Shadow Guild having killed his father.

So in this, at least, and in the outcome—he was sure Machigi was going to get as much out of it as he could get, and double-crossing Cenedi and mani would not have been the way to get anything. Certainly he would not have been on the side of Jorida, and definitely, emphatically, not on the side of Lord Tiajo.

The Guild force, made aware by the new coms that Cenedi was running late, had delayed en route to keep their coordination with Cenedi's group and not forewarn Jorida . . . but that had not gone entirely smoothly: a number of Separti citizens had joined themselves to the operation and complicated the transport issue, delaying *them*.

So that all had happened, which they had gotten from the Guild force commander, Midagi, not from Cenedi: for a long, upsetting time it had been clearer what was happening down on the Separti waterfront than in Cenedi's operation entering Jorida.

That had been the situation going on this morning . . . when Lord Geigi had called from the station apologizing for being out of touch, and said they had had to launch and they were sending far more people than they had planned. It would still take time to get here, but the numbers had all changed and things had to be done in much more rapid order than they had planned.

He had had to leave his father's office and rush to get ready. In the depths of the Bujavid, a special train was being arranged. And all during his getting things in order and getting to the train, Father had not shared very many messages.

As a result, Cajeiri had had his mind going in two directions, and he had worried until his stomach was in knots. He had not even gotten to say a goodbye to Father and Mother: Father's aishid had told them to hurry—trains were being held from Shejidan to Cobo to let their special train enter the system.

And they had made it, they had gotten aboard.

And very surely Bren and Cenedi and all were going back to Kajiminda, where they would surely be safe.

There was a printed note on the other side of the paper, so Father had not even looked for stationery or bothered with a cylinder, just dashed off a note to get it to the train in time.

He began to read it, and thought that Father might have chosen it for a reason. It said, after a Guild heading and some code numbers and addressing to Father:

Search is being conducted through the town for certain Doji-sigin residents, eight in number, and four Joridi believed to be complicit with the Shadow Guild.

There has been armed civilian involvement in transporting Guild force across the bay by request of the mission commander. Civilians likewise were of significant and heroic assistance in establishing a demarcation in the lower town. At present Guild is restoring order, issuing certificates of compensation to owners and crew of transport used, and will issue more for the return transport of Guild once the operation is concluded.

Outlawed Guild, in total, thirty-one killed; two captured, wounded; twenty estimated to be aboard the ships, one ship being partially burned and partially sunk at dockside, the other significantly damaged. Two allied small craft cooperating with command were sunk.

Of commanders and officials: none injured or lost.

Of Guild under Cenedi's command: killed, one; significantly wounded, seven; captured, none; missing, two.

Of Guild under Midagi's command: killed, two; significantly wounded, nine; captured, none; missing, six.

Of local civilians: killed, three; significantly wounded, thirty-one; captured, none; missing, not yet tallied. Detained for perimeter violation, approximately fifty-two. Detained for protection: not yet tallied. Civilian minor injuries, not yet tallied.

That was all.

That was *all*.

The train started to move.

It was full daylight now.

They were counting at Jorida, so it sounded as if it all was over. It had not taken long, as such things could go, and he had been through a few.

Tiajo was dead. Suratho was. He was not sorry about Tiajo. Not at all. And he *really* was not sorry about Suratho.

His aishid was waiting to hear. He gave them the paper to read, and they passed Father's message around, all the good news.

"The back side is the numbers," Cajeiri said, and Antaro turned the paper backside up, which she scanned and passed to Jegari, who passed it around again.

"It is overall very good," Lucasi said. "The shooting was short, the movement was fast, the numbers were on our side. The casualties were very, very few."

It sounded good, Cajeiri thought.

But it was still numbers.

And all the numbers had names.

The Dual Regencies of Ilisidi of Malguri

Her Acts and Proposals on the Southern Coasts

Ashidama Bay is the largest natural harbor of the Great Continent, southernmost of the three bays of the Southwest Coast.

Jorida, the substantial island in the middle of the Ashidama Bay, has held power over it, both political and financial, from primitive times . . .

In the center of it, but connected to Ashidama Peninsula by a causeway, Jorida Isle is a natural fortress with excellent visibility toward the greater bay, with a sheltered deepwater port and town below. The Masters of Jorida, who claim to have records predating the Great Wave, aver that Ashidama Bay was once a trading center for the Great Southern Isle, and say that it alone, of all Southern Isle settlements, survived the cataclysm intact. Attempts have been made to claim the causeway as Southern Isle workmanship, and point to the close fit of the blocks, but the few northern experts who have visited it claim it is post-apocalyptic.

Considering its protected position deep within the west-facing bay, there is perhaps an element of truth in the claim of antiquity for the settlement, but the language of Ashidama is in common with the rest of the continent and shares most unique words with the northern Marid, which argues that if there was a Southern Isle settlement there, it left no traces either in stone or in speech.

The sole aristocratic clan of Jorida Isle, the Ojiri, claims to be descended directly from survivors of the Great Wave whose ships were safe in Ashidama Bay when the disaster struck. This makes sense, since the bay faces west and the elevation of Ashidama Peninsula is sufficient to have protected the bay from the Wave and indeed all beyond it from its effects. And as far as its claim to be the only such survival, devastation in the Marid was certainly greater, as the entry to the Marid Sea directly faces the Great Southern Isle, and its inner isles received the full force of the Wave, as well as sharing in the motion of the Earth after the quake. When the Great Wave struck, the bays of the west coast, facing into the Mospheiran Strait, were little affected—indeed they had no word of the disaster at all until ships from the Strait sailed toward the Marid, although they felt the shaking.

It is possible that the Ojiri were once a seagoing clan of the Great Southern Isle itself, or that they had marriage ties to the Southern Isle. They did have ships capable of the voyage, and they authored one of the notable reports of the disaster.

From Jorida Isle, the Ojiri allegedly attempted to return to the Southern Isle—an attempt of two ships which met disaster, only one returning—and also sought to rule the wave-wracked Marid basin by establishing Amarja in the Dojisigin; but after a new series of strong quakes rocked the Marid, they relinquished that ambition and returned to Jorida, where they gained dominance over the three peninsulas, trading with the Marid, and generally exploiting the aboriginal tribal peoples of Mospheira.

Maschi clan, originating in the piedmont of the mountains that divide the Great Continent, had ties with the northern Marid, which touched their eastern border, and which, less damaged than the south, recovered more quickly. Maschi clan at that time claimed all of the south of the Great Continent, excepting Ashidama Peninsula, and supported the less damaged northern Marid, which traded with Ashidama. The Taisigin Marid had largely escaped the violence of the Wave, which broke on the Sungeni Isles. The Taisigin expanded to claim the entire south coast of the Marid for its hunting range, while the Maschi, occupied with their contention with the Ojiri, did not strongly contest it. Thus the modern divisions of the south evolved.

The Maschi, allied by marriage with both the Senjin Marid immediately to their east, and with the Ragi up in Cobo, were primarily occupied with defending their ally Senjin against its eastern and southern neighbors, while on the west coast the Ojiri, unchecked, claimed all three peninsulas, Ashidama, Kajidama, and Najidama.

The Maschi, having suffered reverses in conflict with the Tai-sigin Marid and with the Ojiri, subsequently remained concentrated in their holdings at Targai. That state of affairs remained even through the crisis of the Landing, when humans entered the world.

The world prospered through the early stages of the human intrusion onto Mospheira. The northern clans, especially the Ragi, newly united around Shejidan by the building of the first railroad, dealt peaceably with the initial settlement of humans on Mospheira, and gladly received technological knowledge that gave them an advantage over rival clans far and wide. With such technology, the Ragi rose rapidly to dominance and organized the aishidi'tat around them, spreading the power of the aiji in Shejidan.

Meanwhile Jorida, trading with the states of the Marid, and having rich fishing along the coasts, along with its grain fields and orchards, prospered: it expanded its sea trade up to the Ragi town of Cobo, and thus profited from both Shejidan and, briefly, the human settlements on Mospheira. Prosperity grew until the War of the Landing, at which point the Ojiri directed most of their trade to the Marid and avoided the conflict, which had spilled across the Strait to Najida Peninsula as well as to Cobo.

When the War ended in the confinement of humans on Mospheira, and the ceding of that isle to human control, the Tribal Peoples of Mospheira had to be relocated, and the fact that the two Tribal Peoples were historically at war with each other had to be taken into account. The Gan People were settled in the north, in the isles off the territory of Dur. The Edi were settled on the largely deforested Najida Peninsula.

The Ojiri were not pleased with the appropriation of Najida Peninsula for the Edi, whom they had used to raid. But the north, well-armed from the War of the Landing, and possessing technology the Ojiri could not match, had its way, and the Edi people were thus settled on the mainland. The Maschi during the conflict had established a holding on Kajidama Bay, and claimed Najida. In compensation for the loss of Najida, needed for a place to settle the Edi, Shejidan established a new lordship, Najida, and appointed a Farai clan lord, the Farai being a staunch ally of the Maschi. Thus the Maschi and the Farai were set in place to restrain the Ojiri from contact with the Edi and the Edi from exceeding their boundaries. The fact that on either side of the peninsula, Najidama Bay and Kajidama Bay are shallow and rocky makes them inconvenient for ships of deep draft, and therefore less attractive to Joridan vessels, so random sea attack was not feasible.

Humans became the aishidi'tat's overriding concern—both using their knowledge and preventing them from setting foot on the mainland. But the technological advances secured in the War as well as the clause of the Treaty of the Landing, which said that humans should turn over from their archive annually one such invention as would not violate atevi law, and refrain from creating those that did, meant that the Ragi and their allies would gain these things, and by them, gain dominance over the entire world, slowly enough to assure their adoption was kabiu and not destructive of the traditions.

Thus supplied, with power centralized in Shejidan, and with firm alliances all about, Shejidan offered alliances and membership in the legislature of the aishidi'tat to all the south; and in subsequent generations, offered it to the East as well.

The Maschi accepted, alone of those approached. Its vast lands, largely uninhabited, provided a means of regular contact with the Ojiri of Jorida. But the Marid as a whole refused, except the Farai, allied to the Maschi and with the lordship of Najida. The Maschi thus held three seats in their influence, that at Targai, that at Kajiminda, and that at Najida, giving them considerable power in Shejidan, but the Maschi, distracted by events in the Marid, and with the lordship of Targai fallen under a succession of lords more interested in the Marid than in the aishidi'tat, soon found their better-managed second seat, that at Kajiminda, rising to supremacy in that clan. The lords in Kajiminda became more powerful than those in the original holding at Targai, and, but for Targai's claim on the senior seat in the legislature, would have dominated the clan politically. In none of the lords of Kajiminda, however, was there an inclination to politics: Kajiminda simply became rich by reason of its trade with Jorida, its orchards, and ultimately, its foresight in gaining control of all sources of bauxite and all the industry associated with it . . . just before the release of aviation from the human Archive.

Ashidama Peninsula and its region were never inclined to appoint a lord or to ask for membership in the aishidi'tat. Their chief concern was the relationship with the lords of Kajiminda, with whom they dealt, and with Cobo, the northern port they used, and with the states of the northern Marid. During the War of the Landing they had greatly reduced their trade with Cobo, and traded primarily with the Marid. In general, they stood apart from the aishidi'tat and refused orders as it suited them, being, in their view, a people apart both from the aishidi'tat and the Marid, content to have those regions argue among themselves while they profited off both sides' need for product and changed ports as often as politics required.

In their view, however, the aishidi'tat has incorrectly disregarded Jorida as an adjunct of the Marid states . . . and has not accorded it the importance it deserves.

This offence particularly stems from the Treaty of the Landing and the assignment of the Edi People to Najidama. Jorida, for the first time in its existence, applied to join the aishidi'tat while this was under debate, and sent a representative to Shejidan strongly protesting the settlement of the Edi on Najidama, but that objection, coming from a non-member district who had not helped in the war, was ignored as a last-moment obstacle to a move that, if not taken, could renew the War of the Landing. The legislature refused to hear the Jorida objection, Jorida walked out and withdrew its request for membership—continuing its trade at Cobo, however, but mostly doing business with Kajiminda and with the Marid.

As a modern state, Ashidama Bay in its two Townships, with Jorida Isle, currently presents as a fairly stable structure of clans and loyalties, trading with, of course, the aishidi'tat, and with the northern Marid, notably Senjin and the Dojisigin and the Taisigin, though disputes with the Taisigin, mostly over seasonal access to the hunting range of the central plateau, are frequent.

Several of the Masters of Jorida have been offered membership in the aishidi'tat over the years, along with the technical conversion of the office of Master of Jorida to a lordship, but Jorida has steadfastly refused on the grounds of Edi incursions on their land (in which they include part of Kajidama) violating the agreement, and various other objections of the moment.

As for the politics of Ashidama itself, the Master of Jorida rules a small council of wealthy captains, the majority of whom are Ojiri. They in turn rule the two coastal authorities, one the Voice of the Council of Separti and the other the Chief of the Council of Talidi, both offices elected from the local shore-side population, which consists of twelve clans of vague and unacknowledged ancestral relation to Maschi clan. These shore-side officials have limited power, rarely remaining in office more than three years running, or less if they disagree with Jorida.

The Master of Jorida has sea-going vessels. The Townships of Separti and Talidi have met misfortunes one after the other in their attempts to maintain their own, none proven attributable to the Edi, the usual claim of responsibility.

Ojiri relations with the Maschi had been mostly a policy of tolerance interspersed with acts of neighborliness, but not so with the Edi people. Edi have periodically wrecked and looted Ashidama ships, a practice they had perfected during the War of the Landing on the shores of Mospheira. Jorida Isle consequently has several times attempted to drive the Edi into the sea.

In fear that this conflict might unsettle no less than the Treaty of the Landing, Shejidan has taken many measures to limit that interaction, establishing the lordship of Najida purely to keep the Edi and the folk of Ashidama from conflict.

It is commonly held that only the fact that both Kajidama and Najidama harbors are rocky and problematic for ships of large draft kept the Ojiri from launching war against the Edi from the sea. . . .